The

HAWALADAR

A Novel

Book One Of

The Money Trail Series

by

David A. Stearns

Text copyright © 2020 by David A. Stearns, and David A. Stearns Publishing. All rights reserved.

ISBN: 978-1-7345202-1-7 Paperback

DEDICATION

To Rebecca, who has shown a lifetime of patience, and is the love of my life.

To Mark, Jennifer, Erik, Nathan, Alicia, Mason, Ava, Lucas and Lily who will forever be my greatest legacy

To Jack, who always offered encouragement in this endeavor

PROLOGUE

ITS ALLEYWAYS teeming from dawn until dusk with locals and tourists alike, the sights, sounds, and scents of the Raja Bazaar of Rawalpindi, Pakistan are all intoxicating. The Raja has long been one of the more popular shopping destinations for individuals looking for a more historic change-of-pace to the immediately adjacent—and significantly more modern—capital city of Islamabad. The always vibrant market is well-known as the place to go in the *Old City* when one wants to experience the flavor of doing business in a manner traditional to south Asia. Hyper-vigilance should be the rule of the day for any visitor, however. Not all who frequent the Raja are of the most desirable character.

This atmosphere of foreboding explained in great part the rather audible sigh of relief emanating from the tall, distinguished-looking Pakistani businessman as he entered the large, double front doors of Nasir Jewelers, one of the more prominent of the many dealers in precious metals and high quality, handmade jewelry located in the Raja. Nasir Jewelers had an international reputation for the quality and design of their workmanship, but they were perhaps better known for being purveyors of certain other very special services.

"Ah, Yafai al-Kassem, my excellent friend," gushed Salim Wajihuddin. Almost obnoxiously solicitous of anyone he deemed important, Wajihuddin was the highly regarded

3

manager of the store considered by most to be the flagship location of the nation-wide Nasir jewelry and precious metals chain. "*Massah al-khair*—good afternoon," effused the shopkeeper as he embraced the rugged-looking al-Kassem with a relaxed familiarity reserved for only his most preferred of recurring clients. Respectfully kissing his customer lightly on both cheeks, Wajihuddin steered him toward a small table to the rear of the store. "Please, please be seated dear brother and partake of some tea with me."

"Uh, yes—*massah al-noor*—the same to you, Mr. Wajihuddin," replied the noticeably much relieved al-Kassem as he seated himself next to a small, round table covered with a nicely pressed white linen tablecloth. Considering the large amount of cash on his person, the ring of the bell affixed to Nasir Jewelers' large front door had been a welcoming sound to al-Kassem. "It is good to see you again as well, but unfortunately, as much as I thank you wholeheartedly for your usual, gracious hospitality, I will regrettably only have time for one quick glass of your wonderful tea today." Al-Kassem needed to transact his business with the cagey old jeweler as quickly as he could and be on his way, but he would have to accept at least one sip of the shopkeeper's steaming brew. In Pashtun culture, to do otherwise might easily be perceived an egregious insult. "I have pressing matters that must yet be tended to back home in Peshawar this evening if I am able to finish my business with you soon enough to catch a timely return flight."

Yafai al-Kassem, was a much-revered elder of the Afridi tribe of northern Pakistan who had become a relatively wealthy man through many years of successful trading in new and used vehicles to the Pashtun tribesmen, Taliban militants, foreign terrorists and myriad other groups of individuals populating the Hindu Kush—the mountainous region bordering Pakistan and Afghanistan, where the Indian subcontinent and central Asia converge. Every three months

4

for the past twenty years, al-Kassem had regularly traveled from his home in Peshawar—the ancient city that sits at the eastern entrance to the fabled Khyber Pass—to Islamabad, some 170 kilometers away, where he always attended a big auction at one of the largest vehicle marts in the country.

The seemingly endless conflict of the region surrounding Peshawar was an economically unfortunate fact-of-life for many who called that part of Pakistan home, but not for al-Kassem. He was a survivor. Where most merchants in the historically war torn area struggled simply to remain in business, the wily vehicle trader flourished, finding numerous ways of doing business with the disparate factions perpetually fighting for control there. If anything, the region's turmoil more often than not precipitated situations that accelerated the need for people to replace their vehicles. Regular treks to Islamabad to replenish his rapid-turning inventory of cars and trucks were thus essential to al-Kassem's business. His reason for visiting the upscale jewelry merchant today, however, had little to do with the buying and selling of vehicles.

"By all means, my friend, by all means," responded the shopkeeper as he filled two small glasses of steaming green tea from an ancient-looking brass samovar. "I am disappointed we cannot visit longer, but I understand. I always do so look forward to our conversations though. May I presume you're here to once more avail yourself of our financial services?"

"That's correct. I need to send money to my son in Germany again."

"More support for the budding engineer, heh? He fares well with his studies, I trust?"

"Yes! Yes, he does, but the cost of tuition and fees, room and board, and books seems to increase with frustrating regularity."

"Well, I have never experienced your plight, my friend. Alas, *Allah*—may he be praised forever—has never blessed me with children. Yet, I can readily believe what you say is true." The balding, bespectacled, old jeweler grinned and shook his head sympathetically. "Same instructions for delivery as before, I would presume, Hamburg, Germany at our earliest opportunity?"

"Right, but this time, I need to transfer the equivalent of ten thousand Euros instead of our usual five."

"My, that is an increase, my friend. It indeed appears to be a big commitment for one's children to study abroad. Does it not?" Wajihuddin wished he had more occasions to handle transfers like those that al-Kaseem regularly transacted through him between Rawalpindi and Germany. The volatile exchange rate between Euros and Pakistan Rupees accorded the old merchant frequent opportunity to augment the usual one and one-half to two percent fees he charged for this type of transfer with an additional profit. Punching some numbers into a laptop computer sitting on his customer counter, Wajihuddin's brow furrowed as part of a much-practiced look of resignation. "Hmm, let me apologize in advance, my friend, but it would seem our country's many conflicts and upheavals during the past year have continued to greatly devalue our Rupee in the European market. We are at 168 Pakistan Rupees against the Euro today."

"No explanations needed, Mr. Wajihuddin. I knew that would be the case and have come prepared for that."

"Very well, my friend, I just wanted to forewarn you," said the old money mover looking back at his computer. "However, using the figures shown here, it appears as though we will need 16.8 Lakh PKRs for the transfer and another 25,200 PKRs for our one and one-half percent fee, kind sir.

"Fine, as I said, I came prepared for that." The heavily bearded al-Kassem reached under his Jubba, the traditional ankle length outer garment worn by many of the Pashtun tribesmen in his home area of Peshawar, and reversed the

6

cloth belt around his waist to reveal a large pouch he had been wearing in the small of his back. Removing a sizeable stack of large-denomination Pakistani currency from the pouch, he carefully counted out the requested amount using mostly mustard-colored 5,000 PKR denomination bills, and handed them over to the expectant Wajihuddin.

By comparison, the quarterly transactions usually conducted between al-Kassem and the Islamabad auto mart he had done business with earlier that day were most always handled using conventional bank transfers. Yet, for these international transfers to his son, al-Kassem preferred to use the kind of service someone like the old jeweler provided. It was much faster, and considering the occasional failings of the Pakistani banking system, in many ways far more secure. Cash was needed to transact business in this manner, however, and al-Kassem was always nervous about having to carry around large amounts of it in some places he had to frequent on his buying trips. Life might be tenuous at best were any number of the unsavory characters he typically encountered along the way ever to find out what he was carrying. This also explained the Glock 19 in the shoulder holster beneath his Jubba—and his heavy sigh of relief upon entering the shop

Wajihuddin made a deliberate show of not recounting the money given to him in front of al-Kassem. To be sure, the amount would later be verified by machine, but in the interim everything regarding the business they were about to transact would be based on trust, an inviolable trust that neither dared breach. "And how will your son identify himself to our Hamburg associates this time, Mr. Kassem?"

"Same method as before would be fine with me."

"Excellent!" The old merchant reached into a drawer under his customer counter, withdrawing a U.S. one-dollar bill. Tearing it equally in half, he handed the right portion to al-Kassem, pointing to the duplicate serial numbers in the upper right and lower left-hand corners of the bill. "As always, communicate the serial number on your half of this bill to your son at your earliest opportunity, Mr. Kassem. Using it, he should be able to pick up his money at just about any time from tomorrow morning on."

"Will the place of delivery be the same as well?"

"Yes, my friend. We always use our associates at Halbmond Jewelers at Altes Steinweg 53, in downtown Hamburg, which coincidentally happens to be an affiliate of ours. As you know, most often that is not the case. Again, all your son need do to receive disbursement of the funds is to properly identify himself as the recipient by accurately reciting the serial number I have just shown you on your half of this bill."

Nodding curtly, al-Kassem turned to leave the shop, stopping briefly at the door to thank the money mover. "*Shoo kran*, Mr. Wajihuddin, *Maa as-salaam*."

"*Allah Yi sull mak*, Mr. Kassem. I shall look forward to your return. Perhaps you will have time to share more than one glass of tea with me next time."

Returning to his laptop, Wajihuddin quickly typed out an e-mail message via a free, online Gmail account to his counterpart at Halbmond Jewelers in Hamburg, Germany. The amazingly truncated message was limited to simply stating the serial number he had just given to al-Kassem, followed by the amount being transferred. It was all Wajihuddin's counterpart in Hamburg needed to know to complete their part of the transfer.

Settlement for this particular transaction would indeed be far simpler than most. As he had indicated to al-Kassem, Halbmond Jewelers in Hamburg was an affiliate of Wajihuddin's shop in Rawalpindi, both being subsidiaries of PAK Metals, Ltd., an international company owned by the well-known and influential Nasir family of Karachi. The next shipment to Hamburg of gold jewelry designed and handcrafted by Pakistan-based Nasir artisans would be under-invoiced to provide for the appropriate credit from one profit center to the other. Even though it was an intra-company transfer, company policy still required each office to account for such transactions in the same way they would have had they been with a non-related entity, as was far more frequently the case.

◊◊◊◊

MAHMOUD NASIR, patriarch of the Nasir family and sole owner of PAK Metals, Ltd., was a devout Sunni Muslim whose ancestors had been movers of money for many generations before him. Theirs was the business of *Hawala*, the ancient form of financial service embraced by residents of South and Central Asia and parts of the Middle East since the days of the Great Prophet, Muhammad.

For centuries, members of the *Ummah*—the body of true believers constituting the whole of Islam—have relied upon the system of hawala as a way of doing business throughout the commercial worlds of their day. Transcending great distances and political boundaries through amazingly simple methods of transfer and settlement, ancient practitioners of hawala were providing a form of private banking to their clients long before such a concept was ever envisioned in the world of modern finance. Arab caravans during the time of the Great Prophet used the system to avoid robberies on the Silk Road, while other ancient societies like the Chinese with their system of *Fei Chien* or Flying Money, or Thailand with its system of *Phoe Kuan*, used similar methods to ensure the security of financial transactions within their cultures.

Engendering the trust of the people they serve by adhering to strict confidentiality and the Islamic principals of honesty and strong family relationships, providers of such services—known as *Hawaladars*—have always purposely functioned in the shadows. Yet, as many countries have begun to realize the monetary size and reach of such informal systems of value transfer, governments have instituted regulations aimed at controlling their activity. As a result, most countries have started to require the registration of all such entities—now collectively referred to as Money Service Businesses—along with the detailed reporting of nearly all transactions processed through them.

Hawala is nevertheless a system that still clings to a rigid, centuries-old culture of confidentiality. So, it is not rare to find many hawaladars around the world today who have chosen not to register, hiding their involvement in the trade behind business facades that can both mask and compliment money transfer operations, choosing instead to function outside the confining, currency-reporting laws and regulations of modern banking and finance.

Principally aiding in the transfer of money worldwide for both commercial and personal business, the methodologies used by the hawaladar have remained much the same throughout history. Only the tools and speed by which they are now able to transact business for their clients have changed. Modern technologies such as faxing, Internet communications, smart phones, and social networking have empowered their netherworld of parallel banking, while at the same time debilitating the efforts of those who would desire to regulate the type of business they transact.

Clients served by the system of hawala are predominantly small businesses and individuals, but in some instances may just as likely be governments or those involved in a multitude of nefarious activities, such as terrorism or money laundering by criminal elements. To the traditional hawaladar, the purpose of the transaction is by and large of little concern. No questions are typically asked beyond those necessary to complete the transaction at hand —and cheating is beyond comprehension. To defraud a client would not only bring on an irreversible loss of face, but possibly as well the dreaded designation of *Kafir*, or non-believer, for the offending hawaladar. Such a breach of trust would be equivalent to signing one's own economic—or perhaps sometimes physical—death sentence.

Transactions are simple. A hawaladar in one city or country will receive cash or its fungible equivalent from a client, along with a request for the transfer of that sum to an individual in another distant location, who properly identifies his or herself as the designated recipient. Verbal agreements or temporary chits substitute for written proof of the transaction. Although larger operations may involve memorizers who may serve as arbiters in cases of later dispute, generally no written records of any significance are maintained. Simple messages of one sort or another called *hundi* are then dispatched by courier, fax, e-mail or sometimes the social media of today, to hawaladars near the place of final delivery. Seldom, if ever, bearing any names for the purpose of identification on either end of the transaction, these hundi convey such details as the amount of money being transferred, the time and place that amount is to be delivered, and the method by which the intended recipient can be identified. Amounts may vary, but transactions can range from a small amount of money to pay for the educational expenses of a student engaged in foreign study, to millions of dollars in cash to fund other far more involved or delicate transactions.

Fees charged for the services of the hawaladar may range from one to five percent of the amount transferred for modest transactions, to levels that can well exceed ten to fifteen percent for matters of particular sensitivity. Where financial transactions processed by way of the conventional international banking system may easily entail many days to complete, and involve a well-documented audit trail along the way, hundi can often be delivered in utmost privacy on the same day using modern technologies available.

For those hawaladars most trusted, and accordingly most successful, the system of hawala has become a source of great wealth and prestige—and the Nasir family of the Pakistani city of Karachi was one of the oldest in the business.

The HAWALADAR

CHAPTER ONE

THE BISTRO Le Francais, a well-known restaurant located on the Galernoya Alitsa, a major thoroughfare in Saint Petersburg, Russia, had always been one of Dr. Aleksandra Lebedev's favorite places to dine whenever she was in the city. Dinner for two at the restaurant could be horribly expensive, but the cost was of little concern to her this evening. The statuesque, sophisticated-looking redhead knew she would not be paying for the meal. Her dinner companion would be picking up the tab.

The Bistro was a very popular place for both intimate and business-related dining. It was almost always crowded, secluded booths were dimly lit, and space between the tables was well-distanced, making it particularly conducive to private conversation. That was important to the lady scientist this evening since she was more than just a little apprehensive about her meeting with the likes of her host. The popular restaurant seemed to her the perfect location for the two to meet.

Dr. Lebedev's dinner companion, Demitri Fomin, knew perfectly well what his attractive dinner guest was trying to accomplish by selecting such a place for their rendezvous. The restaurant was the same sort of secure, neutral location he would have chosen for their meeting had he been in the same situation as she. So, he feigned complete satisfaction with the doctor's choice and suggested they reserve a table for 10:00 p.m. He knew the hour to be late, but was relatively certain she would agree with his recommendation as to time. Like many high-quality Saint Petersburg eating establishments, the Bistro Le Francais was open for dining until the early hours of the morning, making 10:00 p.m. one of the restaurant's more active times for business. The din of chatter amongst the patrons and the noise of serving them would not only drown out the rather delicate nature of the couple's conversation, but also offered a certain level of comfort to a woman dining alone with someone she was perhaps a little unsure of.

"You have excellent taste, Doctor, I come to this place often. The French cuisine here at the Bistro is excellent. If you had asked me beforehand, this would have been one of my top five choices in the city," and Dimitri Fomin knew all the best restaurants in Saint Petersburg. As head of the Russian *Mafiya* there he had the resources to dine out as often as he wanted, and at whichever restaurant he chose. "If you like roast duck, let me recommend their *Canard á L'orange*. It's excellent."

"Whatever you suggest is fine with me, Mr. Fomin, but let's order our dinner right away, and get on with the discussion at hand, if we could. We can visit as we eat. I'm on a bit of a tight schedule this evening." Dr. Lebedev actually had nowhere else she needed to be, but she was not really in the mood for small talk. She wanted this meeting over as quickly as possible and had little appetite for sharing some long, drawn out dinner, playing nice with someone she really did not care much for. Dimitri Fomin was former KGB. She knew him in a prior life, disliked him immensely then and would not have been having dinner with him now were it not out of necessity. She was in possession of a very sensitive product she wanted to sell, and Fomin and his unsavory associates were necessary intermediaries for getting that product to the highly select group of people who might ultimately be interested in purchasing it—and at the price she wanted.

"Fine, doctor, I'll order for us immediately, and then we can get down to business." Fomin motioned for one of several waiters standing against the wall across from their table, quickly ordered the roast duck for the both of them along with an appropriate bottle of wine, and then returned to the conversation. His tone of voice, however, now sounded far more serious and subdued than it had been previously.

Ah, there's the old Fomin I remember, thought the doctor as she observed the change in the mobster's expression. *Cold, insidious bastard.*

The well-dressed, attractive, middle-aged woman, still looking far younger than her age, and the cheap-suited, bull-necked, crew cut old former secret agent, obviously every bit a man in his late sixties, made for an odd-looking couple. Their table was the subject of much speculation around the dining room.

The past near twenty-nine plus years since the fall of the former Union of Soviet Socialist Republics in 1991 had been a long and difficult period for Dr. Lebedev, but things just might finally be starting to look up for her. Before the communists were ousted, the then brilliant, young biochemist with a recent PhD from the University of Moscow had been one of the most widely respected, up-and-coming members of the special research arm of the *Biopreparat* ("the System"), which was the organization in charge of the old USSR's Biological Warfare program.

For nearly four years, Dr. Lebedev had run a highly secret program located on *Vozrozhdeniye* ("Rebirth") Island, situated in the western part of the Aral Sea, a body of water divided by the border between Kazakhstan and Uzbekistan. Between 1936 and 1992, when it was closed down, Vozrozhdeniye was one of several such sites of its kind located around the USSR, where a great deal of research and open-air testing occurred on the use of such infectious diseases as Smallpox, Anthrax, Tularemia, Plague, and Ebola for use as weapons of mass destruction.

During her time on Vozrozhdeniye, she established quite a name for herself with breakthrough research in genetic alteration. Government officials for whom she worked made sure of that by putting her front and center at seminars and symposiums all over the country, publicly touting the unclassified portions of the work she did for them. It was part of their deal with her. They would pay her well and give her enough exposure to make a name for herself in the scientific world, and in return, she would devote the best years of her life to the USSR's bio-weapons program.

Most of her more significant work, however, was far too classified for open discussion with peers, and known only to but the few to whom she directly answered in the Biopreparat. During her time on Vozrozhdeniye, for example, not only had she overseen the research unit responsible for developing and placing into arsenal a virulent, weapons-grade strain of *Variola Major*—or Black Smallpox as it was more commonly referred to by the unscientific world—but she also came quite close to successfully altering the genetic makeup of both the Ebola and Smallpox viruses in such a way as to provide a workable recombinant chimera for use as a biological weapon. Had the program on Vozrozhdeniye Island not been shut down when it was, one of the most dangerous weapons ever known to humankind might well have found its way into the Soviet arsenal.

When Vozrozhdeniye was closed, Dr. Lebedev was transferred by the new Russian Federation to a somewhat similar position within the Scientific and Production Association located in Novosibirsk, Russia, but it was an arrangement where both her level of responsibility and compensation within that organization were much diminished from that which she previously had held on Vozrozhdeniye. Worse yet, funding for the kind of research she was most involved in previously was no longer a high priority to the cash-strapped, new Russian Federation. The position in Novosibirsk ultimately proved tenuous, with her eventually being let go to join what was then an ever-burgeoning crowd of unemployed, former Soviet scientists, technocrats, and apparatchiks.

Many of the doctor's former associates, who experienced the same fate as she, failed to see what was coming, but not the bright, young lady biochemist. She had predicted the whole, inevitable turn of events, and had made special plans to ensure her future. She had given up way too many things personally in deference to her career and to accommodate the demands of her former overseers, to be relegated to frittering away the remainder of her life in some low-paying, nondescript industrial job like she and most of her former associates—who were lucky enough to even find positions—were having to accept in recent years.

At 56, Aleksandra Lebedev was intelligent, well-educated, still very attractive, and had many good contacts in both the public and private sectors. So, why not put those assets to good use now for personal benefit? The lady scientist had worked extremely hard for most of her career but had nothing much to show for it financially since the former USSR became part of the dustbin of history. To her way of thinking, she had earned the right to eventually enjoy some of the good life, and now that the Russian Federation had ushered in full-blown capitalism, there was tremendous opportunity out there for a bright entrepreneur with sufficient Rubles to invest. After carefully biding her time for the near thirty years since her days with the Biopreparat, Dr. Lebedev was certain she had a sure-fire way of getting some of that money.

"All right, young lady," began Fomin in a voice now lowered to a sinister whisper. "Let's get right to business." It was difficult for Dr. Lebedev to hear him over the chatter and background music within the restaurant. "My associates and I understand through a mutual acquaintance that you are in possession of a fairly sizable amount of a certain rare commodity you wish to sell. A commodity that has supposedly never existed from a program that never was. Is that correct?"

"Mr. Fomin, please. You and I both know that you have not been KGB for many years, and we both know what you do now. So, let's quit talking in riddles. It will waste far less of your time and mine if we simply speak candidly and keep our voices quiet enough that no one else can hear us." She saw Fomin's eyes narrow. He seldom tolerated disrespect of any kind. "I have in my possession a substantial amount of weapons-grade Variola pathogens, which I am prepared to sell to any interested buyer willing to pay my price. I understand your organization knows of some potential purchasers, and that you might be able to move them for me. Is that correct?"

"Variola?"

"Yes, Smallpox, Mr. Fomin, Black Smallpox," she snapped back, "but then you knew that."

"My, Doctor, you do have a way of cutting through all the smoke in this room, don't you." Many Russian restaurants still accommodated the tobacco habit.

Fomin studied the set of his dinner partner's jaw. It was obvious she was nervous, but she still exuded a level of confidence that was admirable under the circumstances. With her intelligence and good looks, there is no doubt he could have used someone like her on his team back in his KGB days. *Too bad it's only business she has in mind this evening*, thought Fomin. *She looks great.* Unaware of how repugnant she actually found him to be, Fomin would have been interested in making the evening a lot longer had he felt her willing—or perhaps in a situation where she had no place to run.

"I have little time for niceties. Am I correct in my understanding, Mr. Fomin?"

"Yes, that's possible. My associates and I may indeed be able to make a market for your product, but that depends on your price. We're talking about a very delicate transaction in a multitude of ways. The handling of such material is very sensitive, so costs will be high. Depending on what you're asking, the margins on resale could be tight." Fomin found it difficult to be direct. He always spoke in the abstract, the effect of nearly thirty years in the KGB. "That being said, I have heard several figures from others about what price you may be asking for this very special commodity, but I would like to hear that directly from you. How much are you looking to receive? Can you please share that with me?"

"Mr. Fomin, to begin, I have no intention of negotiating with myself. I'm well aware that there are perhaps only two stockpiles of such a 'product,' as you call it, which may yet remain in the world. One we believe to be in the hands of the United States military, and the other is held by us Russians under very tight security, with both countries claiming not to have them. So, although I do not want to appear greedy in this matter, I also know the value of what I have to the right party, and I do not plan to part with that which is in my possession without someone paying a price commensurate with its, shall we say, rarity. Therefore—and this is not negotiable—the successful purchaser will pay absolutely no less than $2 Million wired net to me at the time and place of my choosing before they take delivery. Further, with respect to timing, since I already have two other parties that are quite interested in doing this deal with me at this time, the date by which I wish to have this transaction completed is no later than seventy-two hours from now, with payment being made to a numbered Swiss account that I will provide the information on just prior to delivery."

Fomin's jowly, pockmarked face flushed red. He didn't care for his dinner guest's tone, but he remained calm and businesslike. "Well, Doctor, as I stated a moment ago, the margin on this transaction will be quite tight if you insist on a price at that level, but you are nevertheless correct. It is a near one-of-a-kind situation. We are interested. So, we should be able to come to some sort of agreement this evening. I am, however, curious. Are you at all concerned about what type of person or organization may be the end purchaser of this product you are trying to sell, and what perhaps their agenda may be?

"That's not my concern. I've held onto and nurtured these pathogens for nearly thirty years now, letting the trail as to their source cool, and patiently planning on them to provide me with a comfortable, early retirement. I'll let you worry about who the ultimate purchaser may be."

"Enough said, my dear. Asked and answered on your price. Let's now enjoy our meal and allow me to catch up on what you have been up to during the intervening years since we last saw each other."

It was easy for Fomin to be gracious. He had no plans to pay the scientist's price or anything like it. The dinner was simply a ruse to make sure she was in possession of the pathogens. Within fifteen minutes of their parting, Fomin's men would be picking her up, and they had special talents for extracting information from even the most reluctant of individuals. They would find out the exact location of the deadly pathogens from Dr. Lebedev well before the seventy-two-hour deadline she had previously prescribed. After that, it would be better for all concerned were she to permanently disappear.

CHAPTER TWO

SAALIM NASRALLAH had been in Saint Petersburg for
three weeks now on an international visa, arriving there in
mid-October as a crew member aboard the Aurora Crescent,
an ocean-going cargo vessel owned by a U.S. company
named Aurora Transportation, Inc., sailing under Liberian
registry.

Nasrallah was in a hurry. He had disembarked and
stayed behind under the pretext of important personal
business while the Aurora Crescent made the circuit of
several other Baltic ports. The ship was now, however, due
back into Saint Petersburg's Port of Kronstadt within three
days. He needed to finish his business in the city and be
ready to leave when it arrived. The Aurora Crescent would
spend only two days taking on additional cargo, and then it
would sail straight for the Canadian Port of Montreal and its
entrance to the Saint Lawrence Seaway. If all went well with
the purchase Nasrallah had been working to consummate
during his time in Saint Petersburg, he would need to be on
board again as a member of the crew when the Aurora
Crescent departed, to ensure safe delivery of a very
important cargo to its ultimate destination through the U.S.
Port at Calumet Harbor in Chicago, IL. Once there, and the
sensitive cargo successfully offloaded into the hands of the
right party, he would be free to either continue on with the
Aurora Crescent to its next destination, return to his home
country of Liberia to await his next engagement, or remain in

the Chicago area to take part in a very important operation that a little-known Muslim organization—to which he now belonged—was planning soon to undertake there. As an ardent jihadist, he had already made his choice in that regard.

It had taken Nasrallah only a few hours in Saint Petersburg to locate Demetri Fomin, the man he had come to see in that city, but it took another two days to arrange a meeting. Finding the man was the easy part. Everyone seemed to know him. Arranging a meeting with him was another matter. Fomin's people had checked Nasrallah out thoroughly before the meeting was agreed to. The jihadist was impressed with their security. Once he was able to get together with Fomin and his associates, however, things progressed well with their negotiations.

Operating on knowledge garnered from messages passed to them, both by word-of-mouth and a complex network of Internet websites, Nasrallah's fellow jihadists had learned that certain parties in Russia were in possession of a substantial amount of weapons-grade Smallpox pathogens, and that those individuals were willing to part with some of the materials at an acceptable price. Properly utilized with good planning, such a weapon could do much to further the goals of the organization to which he belonged. So, they sent him to consummate a purchase.

Negotiations for the bio-weapons were, to say the least, an experience that Nasrallah would never be able to forget. In their first meeting, Fomin explained to Nasrallah how his criminal organization had come into possession of the Variola pathogens through some poor, out-of-work, female Russian.

"Name of Lebedev," said Fomin, as he recounted the story of how he obtained the pathogens to Nasrallah, "a brilliant female scientist with looks to match, but a little greedy, if you ask me. She apparently lifted these pathogens from one of the biological weapons stockpiles she had supervisory control of prior to the fall of the Republic. Had it stashed away in a private, personal lab she maintained at a country dacha that had been in her family for years. Held it for going on thirty years, waiting to sell it for big money. Her one tragic mistake was thinking she would squeeze us in the process."

Nasrallah had little interest in how Fomin and his mafiya people had obtained the pathogens, but he could tell a megalomaniac when he met one. It had taken him much longer than he had anticipated getting to Fomin and beginning negotiations for purchase of the bio-weapon his organization very much wanted to obtain, and time was of the essence. So, as uninterested as he might be, it appeared as though he would have to suffer through Fomin's recounting his acquisition of the pathogens in order to complete negotiations for the purchase he was sent to Saint Petersburg to make.

"This Dr. Lebedev had the unmitigated gall of thinking she could exact a ridiculous price from me and my associates in her attempt to market this product of hers, but we decided, shall we say, to use some time-honored bargaining techniques to satisfactorily resolve the matter," Fomin recounted with a sadistic chuckle.

The mafiya boss then went on to show Nasrallah video snippets of his men extracting information from the woman regarding the location of the Smallpox pathogens, matter-of-factly describing how the torture had taken place over approximately twelve hours of painful interrogation. Fomin seemed particularly proud that his men were "especially skilled at such things," sadistically showing how they purposely kept the young woman alive long enough to eventually be used as a "human guinea pig" in testing the virus' effectiveness once they had it in their possession.

Fomin sadistically studied Nasrallah's reaction as he showed him another video of the tests. With Dr. Lebedev having barely recovered from the ordeal of her interrogation,

Fomin and his henchmen had taken her and three other unfortunates—men who Fomin claimed had wronged him in one way or another—and caged all four in an airtight, stand-alone building where they were then exposed to a small amount of airborne Smallpox virus. Over the course of what Fomin rather coldly explained was about a three to four-week period, the video graphically depicted each stage of the disease's horrible progress. What followed was perhaps one of the most gruesome, sickening things that Nasrallah had ever witnessed.

Looking and sounding much like a Discovery Channel documentary, voice-over in Russian described how the four hapless souls had been infected with but a "minute amount of the airborne virus." Clinically explaining how the infection only required but "a few virions introduced into the mucosa of the respiratory system," the narrator detailed how "the infection worked its way to the lymph system over an approximate three to four-day period, and from there on to the spleen and marrow of the bone." Sadistically filming each stage, viewers were shown the ravages of fever and toxemia around the eighth to ninth days, told how the virus attached itself to the "leukocytes in the bloodstream", and then "migrated on to the small blood vessels in the skin, nose and mouth." By the fourteenth day, all four victims of the disease were in the throes of high fevers, with ugly rashes beginning to appear on their faces and upper bodies. By the eighteenth day, only the woman scientist was left alive, but even she was no longer recognizable as the attractive Slavic beauty that Nasrallah had seen at the beginning of the video. With all visible areas of her swollen face and body covered with darkened pustules, the only thing that hinted to the viewer who the individual in the film might be was the mane of auburn-colored hair still attached to the head of the person now struggling for each additional breath. The grotesque "marketing piece" ended with the viewer being shown the lab building engulfed in flames, with the narrator explaining how the fire resulted from "a highly accelerated blaze utilized to cleanse the facility of contamination," and destroy any evidence of the grisly test that had occurred there. Nasrallah had been inoculated with Smallpox vaccine prior to his trip to Russia as a safeguard for his part in this transaction. That was reassuring considering the nature of his mission, but it did nothing for the extreme nausea he experienced while viewing the video.

"Assuming we can agree upon a suitable price, Mr. Fomin, how and in what form would we take possession of the pathogens?" Nasrallah took several long sips of the espresso the Russians had provided him at the start of the viewing of the video, knowing it would do nothing to settle his stomach. *These are people I would not want to cross*, he thought. *The sooner I am done with this disgusting bunch of thugs, the better.*

"As we previously stated in our e-mail exchanges during the last two months, our price for the product is $2 Million, and that is non-negotiable." Fomin smiled with satisfaction as he thought about how the price he had just quoted Nasrallah was exactly the same as that which the recently departed Dr. Lebedev had quoted to him before she met her untimely demise, and it was for only part of the weapons supply he and his men had been able to extract from the lady scientist.

"That price is exorbitant, but we do not wish to quibble at this point. How do we proceed?"

"That's simple. Pursuant to your specifications, the pathogens you requested have been suspended in an appropriate medium, and encased in aerosol containers labeled to look just like over two hundred other cases of four-ounce containers of Russian-made, commercial bathroom air freshener. Adequately marked so they can be identified from the others, ten cases of twelve canisters each have been loaded into the middle of a shrink-wrapped pallet in a warehouse at the port authority here in Saint Petersburg."

"How do we tell those containing the pathogens from the others?"

"The ten cases containing the special aerosol containers have each been stamped with a small red 'X' on the bottom to identify them from others in the shipment, and the bottom of each of the canisters in those cases has been similarly marked. I wish to emphasize, however, that no other controls beyond that have been used. So, you will need to take great care once you have taken possession."

"When can that be?"

"When satisfactory payment is received, we will provide you with the appropriate bills of lading, the pallets will be loaded on the ship you designate, and then control of the product will be in your hands. Any problems that occur thereafter with respect to the handling of this delicate cargo will be on your shoulders."

"We are prepared to pay one-half of the requested $2 Million purchase price once the cargo is on board a freighter flying a flag under Liberian registry, named the Aurora Crescent, which is currently docked at the Port of Kronstadt," responded Nasrallah. "$1 Million in cash will be available to you just as soon as you hand over the bill of lading to me. When the special cargo arrives at its U.S. destination, $1 Million more will be hand delivered to you either here in Saint Petersburg, or any other location of your designation."

"That suits us just fine, Mr. Nasrallah. I will meet you on board your ship tomorrow morning at 10:00 a.m. So you are forewarned, however, I will be accompanied by several of my associates when I arrive. This is a delicate matter. So, they will be present to see that all goes smoothly. The first $1 Million will be in our hands before you receive the necessary papers to leave with the cargo, and the second $1 Million will be delivered in a timely fashion before one month has passed, or the U.S. Department of Homeland Security and the security agencies of most of its allies will somehow receive word of the transaction and as much information as we can provide on you and all of your associates. Do I make myself clear?"

"You do indeed, Mr. Fomin."

◊◊◊◊

WHEN THE Aurora Crescent departed Saint Petersburg, Russia the day after his meeting with Demitri Fomin, Saalim Nasrallah was once again on board as a crew member. A forty-four-year-old Liberian Muslim, and a third-generation mariner with over twenty years of experience on the high seas, Nasrallah was on his third pilgrimage to the Saudi Arabia city of Mecca in 2012—or *Hajj 1433* according to the Muslim calendar—when he first met the recruitment team of the infamous *al-Qaeda* terrorist organization and was enlisted by them into their ranks. The al-Qaeda had adopted a relatively low-lying operational posture since the supposed halcyon days of post 9/11 and Osama bin Laden, but they were still a preeminent force with which to be reckoned.

Nasrallah's recruitment had not been a hard sell for the al-Qaeda. The career seafarer came from a long line of strict *Wahhabi* Muslims who had been waiting most of his life for such a call to come. Having always envisioned himself as one day becoming *Shahid*, or martyr to the cause of Islam, it was his thinking al-Qaeda might well be Allah's tool in that regard.

Al-Qaeda had likewise for some time been looking for someone with Nasrallah's profile when he came to their attention. The terrorist group was always much in need of dependable couriers. To be able to recruit a person with Saalim Nasrallah's background and capability into that capacity was in the words of one Ayman al-Zawahiri, leader of al-Qaeda since the death of bin Laden in 2011, "a gift from Allah."

Nasrallah was not only a master seafarer registered with the Liberian International Ship and Corporate Registry, but because of such registry he also possessed a legitimate international visa. In fact, he was one of the first to be issued

27

that organization's new, hi-tech biometric identity card that accompanied his Seafarer's Identification and Recordbook when they were first issued in February 2002. This new system of identification used a 2-D bar-code technology, which included a data strip that contained one or two fingerprint templates, a digitized version of the cardholder's photograph and several pages of encoded personal information on the registrant. It was considered virtually counterfeit proof, since the technology of the card doesn't capture actual fingerprints, but instead creates a unique template that utilizes mathematical algorithms. An optical fingerprint scanner compares stored fingerprint templates with the cardholder's live fingerprints and then matches the bearer to the registry on the spot. With such credentials, he could enter, exit and enjoy extended stays in most ports-of-call countries with little problem, making him the ideal operative to both purchase and accompany a sensitive shipment of cargo.

Nasrallah's al-Qaeda overseers had, therefore, asked him to do just that with the purchase and handling of the shipment of sensitive materials now bound from Russia to the United States and the ports of Chicago, Illinois. Following safe arrival, and successful delivery of the very special cargo to its ultimate destination, he was to consider himself under operational control of a fledgling, al-Qaeda affiliate terrorist organization with respect to his future disposition, should he desire to remain.

CHAPTER THREE

SITUATED ON LaSalle Street, in the midst of Chicago's canyon-like, downtown financial district, the main offices of Global United Bank of Chicago, N.A., were second to none with respect to opulence. Regularly derided by competing institutions as a "gauche expression of extravagance," the bank's headquarters were in actuality the envy of most of its competitors. The building's interior had a classic motif, richly decorated in a warm, traditional style reminiscent of a bygone era of business in the town poet Carl Sandburg had called "the City of Big Shoulders."

Millwork of heavy, dark-stained, cherry wood adorned walls, doors, desks and under-counters. Strategically placed, delicately hand-woven Persian rugs also complimented the soft-colored Berber carpet found throughout the offices and customer service areas within the bank. A rich Verde marble accented every area wherever it could tastefully be used. Were it not for the ubiquitous flat computer screens found at literally every workstation in the organization, customers might easily imagine themselves entering the offices of a turn-of-the-twentieth century financial institution, instead of those of a modern, fast-growing organization that was steadily setting itself apart from a goodly portion of its competition.

Logan Hart, Global United's newly appointed Executive Vice President, Chief Operating Officer and Senior Lender, remembered having the same impression the first time he entered the bank's new headquarters facility sometime during the latter part of 2009 when ownership of the bank was in the process of changing hands. At the time, Hart was a senior partner with Holland & Associates, Ltd. of Park Ridge, Illinois, one of the country's preeminent bank consulting firms. Global United had retained him and his organization to conduct a thorough review of the bank's policies, procedures, and financial performance to aid in some much-needed strategic planning. With that mindset, the opulence of the bank's headquarters had initially seemed to Hart as being just a little over the top, but that impression was quickly dispelled when he learned of the special circumstances surrounding the bank's acquisition of the property. Apparently, Global United had managed to negotiate a greatly discounted long-term lease on the posh facility with a very distraught landlord, whose prior tenant—a large regional bank that had fallen on hard times earlier that year—failed to renew its lease. Much in need of funds from the U.S. government's then recently instituted Troubled Asset Relief Program, the regional bank had been asked to reorganize and divest themselves of certain facilities as one of the requirements for receiving their TARP funds. One bank's problem was clearly another's opportunity during times of financial unrest.

Having only recently joined Global United after spending seventeen years on the consulting side of the commercial banking business, Hart was excited about the prospect of returning to active banking. Never far from the fray during his career as a consultant, Logan, as he preferred to be called, had worked hard during his time with Holland & Associates to build and maintain a reputation as someone with a wide range of knowledge in commercial banking, and he had been most successful in that regard. There were few major financial institutions that either hadn't used the services of him and his firm or were at least well aware of their reputation. A goodly number of banker friends would be watching with interest, to see how successful Logan would be now that he was returning to the banker's side of the desk, so to speak.

Logan had resigned from Holland & Associates to accept the new position with Global United in early September, after a lengthy period of negotiation. The move had partly been made to fulfill a promise he had given to his recently deceased wife, Melanie, who had passed away a little over a year before after a very long bout with cancer.

Logan and Melanie Hart had been high school sweethearts, growing up together in the same small town in North Carolina. At one time, Logan had thought perhaps the U.S. Army might be his career, and as always, although she had tremendous private misgivings about the matter, Melanie had stood behind him in that regard. Secretly, she despised the military for all of its forced separation, and the constant worry that burdened nearly every Army spouse during the days of the first Gulf War—the period during which Logan was on active duty—but she was still supportive.

Logan had been a Special Ops Infantry officer, Airborne, Ranger-qualified and a veteran of combat command during the days surrounding Desert Storm. He and Melanie had married in 1988, only weeks before he had entered Officer Candidates School at Fort Benning, Georgia, and although that tour of duty was supposed to be "unaccompanied," Melanie had joined him there, taking an apartment in nearby Columbus to help "push hubby through."

As with most of their contemporaries, Logan and Melanie's military days were concurrently some of their happiest, and yet most trying. They made many wonderful friends with whom they stayed close over the years, but Logan saw a great deal of action during the 1990-91 invasion of Iraq, ending up being severely wounded during a clandestine operation somewhere just south of Baghdad on

31

the eve of the ceasefire. The whole ordeal had been a sobering experience for both of them. Although he received a promotion to Captain after returning to limited, post combat duty as a Ranger instructor at Fort Benning, he was still unsure of his ability to recover sufficiently from the physical injuries he had incurred overseas. So, when the choice arose, Logan declined promotion, left the service and returned to graduate school at the University of Georgia in nearby Athens. Melanie was secretly delighted.

Logan obtained his MBA while in Athens, graduating with honors in 1994. Afterward, he and Melanie returned home to North Carolina, where he found his first financial position with the Bank of the Carolinas, a regional bank headquartered in Charlotte. While there, he was eventually elevated to the office of Senior Vice President, Commercial Banking, before leaving the company in 2002 to accept a position with Holland & Associates.

Logan's years with Holland & Associates had been very rewarding with respect to career. Promoted to full partner within three years, he was not only able to finely hone his banking skills during his time as a consultant, but to further develop a network of powerful friends and acquaintances within the industry that would serve him in good stead during years to come. Worry nevertheless was also a constant companion while he was with the firm, making his tenure there a period of tremendous struggle on a personal level.

Shortly after their arrival in northern Illinois, Melanie was first diagnosed with a slow acting form of leukemia that would plague her on and off for the rest of her life. During the period that Logan was with Holland & Associates, she was diagnosed as being in remission from the disease no less than twice, receiving extensive chemotherapy prior to both occasions. When informed by the doctors for the third time that her cancer had returned in a much more aggressive form, however, Melanie declined any further treatments.

Knowing the prognosis not to be good, her comment had been "I just want to enjoy some quality of life for the short time it appears Logan and I have left together, and he needs me right now too." Friends thought the oft-repeated latter part of that comment strange considering her ongoing personal battle with cancer, but simply attributed it to Melanie Hart's always positive strength of character. Little did they know how close to true it was.

During the years following Logan's release from active military duty, hard work toward a successful career, a wonderful marriage and a maniacal regimen of regular, recuperative exercise and conditioning had greatly minimized certain physical and mental problems Logan was burdened with that were so common among veterans with a military history similar to his. Shortly after Melanie's cancer diagnosis, Logan had himself begun to experience a worsening of certain symptoms of his own that would eventually be diagnosed as Post Traumatic Stress Disorder, or PTSD, as his mandated Veterans Administration shrink so nonchalantly preferred to call it.

On September 11 of the year prior to Logan's joining Global United, *a date synonymous with the horrible events in 2001 at the World Trade Center,* Logan remembered thinking, Melanie Hart finally lost her long battle with the dreaded disease that had burdened her so long.

For many years prior to Melanie's death, the Harts had vacationed as often as they could in the northwoods of Minnesota, finding the solitude of the U.S./Canadian Boundary Waters one of their favorite places to visit during troubled times. Toward the end, Logan would take Melanie there as often as her health would allow. So, it was no surprise to him when she asked that her final resting place be somewhere near there, and he had promised to make it so. It had taken him quite a while to gather the fortitude to follow through on his promise, but after a very long wait, Logan had taken one week off prior to the day in October when he assumed his new position with Global United and had driven to Split Rock Lighthouse just north of Duluth, MN. The picturesque landmark was one of his and Melanie's favorite places along the North Shore of Lake Superior. There he released her ashes into the blue waters of the lake on just the kind of sunny, crisp, fall day that both he and Melanie most enjoyed.

◊◊◊◊

"IN EARLY again today, Mr. Hart?

"What? Uh, yes…yes, I am," Logan responded with a start, smiling sheepishly at his secretary, Myrna Brock, as he looked up from the credit file he had been poring over. "Good grief! Sorry, for my startled reaction, Myrna. I didn't hear you come in. Little jumpy, I guess."

"No, I'm the one who should be sorry, Mr. Hart! I didn't mean to startle you. I should have knocked."

"No, no, no, that's fine. I was just deep in thought and didn't hear you come in. Did you need something?"

"Uh, n-nothing special, I just wanted to let you know I'd made a pot of coffee, planned to have a cup for myself, and thought I'd get you one, if you'd like." After only four weeks as an administrative assistant for Logan Hart, Myrna Brock finally felt comfortable enough with her new boss to pop in on him unannounced, although she probably would have done so anyway, had she felt like it. She was rather sure of herself that way. As the only employee with over forty consecutive years on the staff of Global United, she was no wilting flower. The tightly coiffed, prim, career executive assistant did not really feel she needed to be. Having spent most of her time with the bank as personal assistant to the now deceased former Chairman of the Board, old Harold Flannery, Jr., and later his son, Harold III, she was on a first name basis with most of the bank's largest clients, and a favorite of nearly all the bank's board of directors. Very few staff members failed to show her tremendous deference. Myrna was old school, with a work ethic second to none in the organization. She was nearing seventy years old, but few employees arrived in the office any earlier or left any later than she. At least that was until Logan Hart had arrived. He was almost always there when she came in each day. It was one of the many traits she rather admired about him, and Myrna Brock had some pretty high standards.

"Sure, Myrna, thanks much! I would appreciate that. I had a cup on the train this morning, but I could perhaps use a little more fortification before this day actually gets going."

"Not fretting your meeting this morning with the OCC examiners, are you? Shouldn't be all that bad. I'm sure you're prepared; and that nice Mr. Trotter is leading the exam team. He hasn't been in the bank for years, but was part of the team from the Office of the Comptroller of the Currency who worked with us when we changed our bank's charter from state to national back in 2009. He seemed really nice to work with back in those days."

"Yeah, I've known Paul Trotter for a number of years myself, mostly in his capacity as Deputy Comptroller here in the OCC's Chicago office, however. You may not remember, but my former firm did some consulting for this bank around that same time. Some of it related to obtaining the national charter. Got to know him some then and ran into him from time-to-time in subsequent years. He's a regulatory stickler, but he's always been fair to deal with—tough, but fair." Sipping his coffee, Logan removed his reading glasses, leaned back in his chair and smiled at this senior staffer he had taken such an immediate liking to upon his arrival. "I was rather surprised to see Trotter out here on a job like this though. I spoke with him in passing the other day, and I guess he's retiring. He apparently relinquished his regional position to his successor already and asked as a parting request that he be allowed to spend his last few weeks leading an exam team at one of the larger banks in the area. Said he wanted to be 'in the field just one more time' before he was done. A rather strange request, wouldn't you say?

Guess they were apparently hard-pressed to turn him down though."

"Oh, I don't think that's so strange, Mr. Hart." Myrna was always painfully formal, never addressing a member of senior management by their first name, no matter how familiar she was with them. She had been trained that way early in her career. "I'm nearing retirement myself, and I think I understand what Mr. Trotter's going through. Sort of an old-times-sake thing for him, I would imagine"

"You're probably right." Logan smiled knowingly. He had already been clued in that retirement was a sensitive subject with Myrna. It was widely understood that she was thinking about calling it quits because she was mentioning it a little more frequently to some of her closer confidants in the bank. Everyone knew enough, however, to leave it up to her to bring the matter up if it was to be discussed at all. She was well past average retirement age, but continued to work, even though Logan had heard it wasn't exactly all that necessary for her to do so. Myrna was apparently a very astute personal investor, and word was that she had been successful enough in that regard that she only continued to work because she wanted to.

"Oh, the meeting will probably go just fine," said Logan, "but being so new here at the bank, I'm interested in hearing what the OCC's findings are to date. I have never really taken much of an adversarial approach through the years when it comes to dealing with regulators. So, I'm otherwise not really all that apprehensive about the situation."

"Well, I know they can be tough to deal with sometimes."

"Indeed, particularly in these days when the government wants to stick its nose into most everything we bankers are doing. You know, Dodd-Frank and the like. It's simply a matter of attitude in how you approach them. Follow laws and regulations as closely as you possibly can, be reasonably cooperative when they're in your bank looking things over from top to bottom, and most examinations should go reasonably well. They have a tough job and a very real purpose in the banking process. There are admittedly a few bureaucratic jerks here and there, but we also have more than our share of such folks on this side of the business too."

"You can say that again!" Myrna had a succinct honesty about her. It was one of the things Logan was also beginning to appreciate about her.

"Well, it's been my experience that most examiners sincerely want to help the bank and protect the depositor, and Lord knows how gun-shy they are after the events of the last decade or so. I've learned that a genuinely positive, proactive approach when responding to their findings goes a long way with them. Besides," he chuckled, "I'm new enough that maybe they'll go a little easy on me this time. It's next year when I'll have no excuses where they're concerned."

Myrna had been correct in her assumption as to why Logan had come in so early, but only partially so. He had indeed been spending the better part of the last few evenings preparing for his first critique session with the OCC since taking over his new responsibilities at Global United. In his opinion, getting started on the right foot with the regulators was as important as it was with senior management and the board of directors. He had made some of his own assessment as to asset quality and the overall safety and soundness of the bank before and after coming on board at Global United, and he was now anxious to see whether the examiners would agree with respect to those findings. But that wasn't the only reason for the early start. Logan hadn't been sleeping well again for quite some time now. Old memories die hard and have a way of making restful nights a precious commodity.

CHAPTER FOUR

"LADIES AND gentlemen, if I could have everyone's attention, please. It's 7:00 a.m. on the dot. So, let's get this meeting started." Scott Kruse, President and CEO of Global United Bank of Chicago, was an early riser who had a penchant for break-of-dawn staff meetings, and he insisted on promptness at any he called. It was he who had suggested such an early hour to Paul Trotter, Senior Examiner-in-Charge of the OCC's currently ongoing Safety and Soundness examination of Global United, as the start time for a first conference between the bank's management group and Trotter's team of examiners to discuss progress and initial findings of the OCC's review. A few of the participants from both sides of the table had complained a little about the timing of the meeting since many lived out in the Chicago suburbs, and that meant a short night for some if they were to arrive at the appointed hour. Yet, no one had indicated they couldn't make it. Sessions between examiners and bank management were something you didn't miss if at all possible.

Scott Kruse, like Logan Hart, was also a relatively new arrival at Global United, having assumed his position as President and CEO at that institution only eighteen months before he and the bank's board had approached Logan about joining the bank. Like Logan, Kruse was also a career banker with over thirty years of experience in the business, half of those years spent as CEO of three successive commercial banks in Minnesota and Wisconsin. Tall, rather professorial looking, and always impeccably dressed in Armani suits accented with signature bow ties, Kruse's bearing suggested a vaulted self-opinion. Rumored to be a bit of a ladies' man, a great deal of Kruse's time was spent burnishing his image and cultivating relationships with major shareholders, directors and key customers of the bank—with an obvious preference for those who were female and attractive. So far, the jury was out in Logan's mind as to whether he and Scott Kruse would ultimately make much of a team in the future. Scott was perhaps somewhat more politically oriented and hands-off in his management style than Logan usually felt comfortable with, but it was a little early yet to form any real firm opinion about him.

Scott liked to call himself a "visionary," openly claiming his best talent to be an ability to surround himself with many good people who could carry through on the myriad ideas he was always coming up with. Logan had worked with people like Scott before, and more often than not, such doublespeak masked a proclivity for letting unfortunate subordinates pay the price when the so-called visionary's ideas went south. Logan hoped it would not be that way with Scott.

As part of his due diligence on Global United prior to joining the organization, Logan had learned that Scott Kruse had taken the position of CEO at the bank after having parted with his previous employer under somewhat unpleasant circumstances. It seemed Kruse had helped a number of investors in a Minneapolis suburb successfully establish a bank under a new charter, only to lose the position of CEO after completing that task, having developed major differences with the bank's board of directors as to what the long-term strategic direction of the bank should be. Word was that when Kruse resigned, the bank's board had also differed with him regarding the applicability of a cushy severance agreement he had negotiated with them prior to joining their team. A nasty suit was still pending.

"I don't believe that all of us here this morning have had the chance to become acquainted with each other yet. So, let us begin the meeting by going around the table and introducing ourselves to ensure that everyone is well aware of who is responsible for what within our separate organizations. The meeting will perhaps run a little smoother that way. We'll start with the bank team on my left first, and then you can make the introductions for your group, Paul. For those of you with the OCC whom I haven't had the opportunity of meeting, I'm Scott Kruse, President and CEO for Global United. Logan…"

With Kruse motioning to his left, introductions proceeded around the conference table beginning with Logan. Among members of management present was Rosemary Shindler, the rather stern-looking, petite, fifty-something head of Retail Banking who, Logan had noticed, typically preferred talking more about her golf game than banking. As the first female president of a small suburban golf country club—where the bank perennially picked up her membership—it was seldom she didn't find a way to mention that fact to all with whom she came in contact.

Following her on the trip around the table was Leland Tucker, the buttoned down, balding, little Pillsbury Doughboy-type Senior Vice President in charge of Trust and Wealth Management, who usually slept through half the meetings he attended, particularly when they were as early as this one. To his left, whispering to each other in the Middle Eastern language of Farsi were Saud "Sammy" al-Dajani, the very confident, smooth-talking, Senior Vice President of Bank Operations, and Mairaj "Raj" Haifa, Senior Vice President of the bank's new International Banking department. Both Sammy and Raj were rumored to be young protégés of the bank's Chairman and principal shareholder, Tariq Nasir, who had been quite instrumental in recruiting them from competing banking institutions. Logan had taken an early liking to Raj, who was always quite pleasant, and ex-military. The jury was, however, still out a bit on Sammy. Logan had developed a good track record in trusting his gut when it came to people, and thus far his gut had been telling him to hold off in passing judgment on Sammy al-Dajani until he knew more about the man, and he planned to do just that.

Also present were three younger female officers who Logan had found early on could nearly always be depended upon for solid informational input where needed: Patricia McGill, Senior Vice President and Controller; Colleen Murphy, Vice President in charge of Bank Audit and Compliance; and finally Jennifer Goodell, Vice President in charge of Human Resources. This hard working trio of friends were often referred to by some of their far less capable—and accordingly less successful—counterparts around the bank as the "iPad Pals." It was a good-natured jibe resulting from their penchant for constantly punching notes into identical, hand-held electronic tablets during meetings of this sort, sometimes surreptitiously inserting snide text messages to each other when the ineptitude of others reared its ugly head. Rounding out this already substantial representation of bank management were also the lead lenders from each of the bank's loan divisions, primed each one for the always dreaded problem loan discussions.

Aside from the computer tablets held by each of the iPad Pals, on the table in front of nearly every bank officer and OCC examiner alike was a lineup of individual laptop computers. Those belonging to bank officers were tied to the bank's intranet for informational reference in discussions, and all the OCC's computers were wirelessly connected to their central computer system for immediate, online update of findings during the examination and related discussions. Logan noticed with some amusement, however, that even though Paul Trotter was equally equipped with online connectivity, he still appeared to be reading from and making reference to notes written on 5x7 cards of various colors in the same manner used by regulators in years past.

Logan could tell by looks on the faces of the examiners that they perhaps considered such a large gathering of bank management a bit of overkill, but Scott Kruse had claimed that he wanted no questions from the examiners left unanswered. As he put it in the e-mail sent to everyone regarding the time and place of the meeting, "The more we're able to take care of in this one session with examiners, the better off we'll be in the long run."

After introductions of bank management, the conduct of the meeting was essentially turned over to the OCC, with Kruse indicating that Paul Trotter would function as moderator in his capacity as Senior Examiner. Trotter then reciprocated with an introduction of each of his examiners, explaining which areas of the bank they had reviewed and would be discussing. "With apologies beforehand," said Trotter, "I should begin by telling all of you that I would expect this meeting to last a goodly part of today, but since most of us with the OCC need to leave early this afternoon to attend a special function, our discussions could very likely extend over into next Monday. We have a great deal to go over."

"Sounds fine, Paul," Scott replied. "These meetings are as important to us as they are to you." Expressions on the faces of bank staff in the room suggested universal doubt as to Scott's sincerity in that regard. Examinations were never pleasant, and several had heard him previously bemoan having to deal with bank regulators.

"Great, let's get started, and try to free up as many of your bank team as we can, as early as possible," continued Trotter. "To do that, I'm suggesting that we spend the first few hours of the meeting discussing the results of our investigations into those areas of safety and soundness where we have fairly well completed our work and found little concern. Then if time permits, I would like to spend whatever is left of the morning discussing some questions we have regarding certain insider loan and account relationships under Federal Reserve Regulation O, the Financial Institution's Regulatory and Interest Rate Control Act or FIRA and the bank's handling of its requirements under the Bank Secrecy and U.S.A. Patriot Acts—the latter of which as I'm sure you all know had certain portions amended and extended in 2015 by the Freedom Act.

"BSA and Anti-Money Laundering, Paul? You know, Reg O and FIRA I understand, but I admit to being surprised at hearing you and your crew were looking at BSA and AML-related matters here at the bank with this visit. I've been meaning to talk with you about that since your arrival. Those are areas of bank regulatory compliance aren't they?" Scott Kruse sounded perplexed. "Isn't that normally part of a separate examination?"

"Yes, you're correct about that, Scott; and I'm glad you asked. The exam that we are currently conducting is indeed a review of safety and soundness, not regulatory compliance; and Global United most assuredly is scheduled for a full compliance examination sometime around the second quarter of next year. Nevertheless, BSA and Anti-Money Laundering compliance are such continuing hot-buttons with the Comptroller and other agencies of government these days that we've been asked to still have a look-see at how the bank is handling things in those areas of concern while we're here. So, we've been doing that and we'll need to discuss some of our findings there as well," answered Trotter.

"Never mind, that's fine if it's what you feel you need to do. It was just my understanding that was typically part of a separate compliance exam, and it had made me curious when I heard you were also looking into those areas of the bank this time around. Any idea as to how long that part of our discussion will take?

"Oh, I would say if our questions regarding those and

43

other non-lending areas of the bank don't lead us too far afield in getting the answers we need, we should be able to finish most of that this morning. That being said, I suppose if it helps and you folks have no reasons otherwise, I would think any members of your management team here having to do with the lending side of the bank could feel free to go back to work until we're ready to call them back in. But I'll leave that up to you."

"I guess I'll defer to Logan here on that," answered Scott with a quick glance at his new number two.

"And you think you will be finished with the non-lending areas by noon, do you?" Logan asked.

"Yes, I would think so, Mr. Hart, but I must regrettably repeat that even if our discussions relative to the lending side of the bank get started by then, I feel certain they will definitely take more time than we have to cover today. Considering your recent arrival and the process you are overseeing with respect to changes in lending policies, procedures, and operations, etc., there is much we need to go over regarding the lending function here at Global United; and we have a substantial number of larger credit relationships about which we have questions. Based upon how all that goes we will no doubt also need to spend some time discussing the adequacy of the bank's Allowance for Loan & Lease Loss Reserve."

"Well, that's a lot to discuss," said Logan. So, maybe our lending people here really should go try to accomplish something constructive now until we need them later this afternoon. "

"Probably best," added Trotter, "because there's even a possibility we may not even be able to start our lending discussions until Monday if very much of the subject matter we plan to talk about this morning carries over into the afternoon. Unfortunately, to make matters worse with respect to how far we may get today, we examiners are going to have to call it quits sometime around mid-afternoon today to enable most of us to attend a special function this evening. So, we may not even get to the lending discussion today."

"Sounds fine with me, if that suits you, Scott," said Logan as a number of the bank's senior lenders started exiting the room. He had been sincerely pleased to hear the depth at which Trotter and his examiners planned to look into the loan side of the bank. Deliberate was better as far as Logan was concerned. "And you're right, Paul. As new head of lending here at Global United, the areas you mentioned are of significant interest to me also. I've been reviewing pretty much everything you mentioned as much as time has permitted since my arrival, but there have been only so many hours in the day in the short time I've been here at the bank. Your team's independent review will perhaps be a big help in targeting future efforts. We'll be glad to spend whatever time is required."

Logan could tell from the look of consternation on Scott Kruse's face that the bank's CEO didn't perhaps much share his enthusiasm. Generally speaking, Global United's loan portfolio had thus far appeared to be of reasonably high quality to Logan, but vestiges of the past recession still plagued many financial institutions around the country with some still experiencing economic distress of one sort or another, and this was still of grave concern to bank regulators.

Beginning with the bursting of the residential real estate bubble in 2008 and 2009, the U.S. banking industry had entered a period of record bank failures with over five hundred institutions closing during the previous decade. Peaking with the failure of over one hundred and fifty institutions during 2010 alone, bank closings had tapered off to an insignificant level in recent years, but concerns remained for some major areas of exposure to risk in the industry. Commercial real estate loans for example had been particularly hard hit as a result of the recent COVID-19-related downturn; and that category of loans constituted a significant part of Global United's balance sheet. So, Trotter and his OCC crew had zeroed in on that portion of the bank's loan portfolio during their current review, and there was much to discuss.

Thus far, based on Global United's own assessment of loan quality, it appeared as though the bank's underwriting approach relative to commercial real estate and commercial operating loans had resulted in few non-performing assets to date. The OCC, however, was infamous for its stringent approach to loan grading, and there was always the possibility that regulators might take issue with the bank's ratings on loans heretofore considered borderline substandard by Global United's analysts. Scott's trepidation hadn't gone unnoticed by Trotter and his examining crew either.

◊◊◊◊

AS TROTTER had predicted, he and his team of examiners were able to dispense with numerous, minor concerns regarding various issues of safety and soundness by the end of the morning. They were just beginning their discussion of Global United's handling of bank transactions covered by Federal Reserve Regulation O and the Financial Institutions Regulatory and Interest Rate Control Act—which deal with business between the bank and its principal shareholders, directors and executive officers—when it was decided to break for lunch. At Scott's suggestion, lunch had been ordered in so that the OCC could continue its review right on through the noon hour. Everyone served themselves, and then Trotter began his discussion of the OCC's review of insider transactions while the group was eating.

"As hopefully most of you are aware," began Trotter, "FRB Reg O and FIRA establish much stricter requirements for bank-related business with Directors, Executive Officers and bank shareholders with either direct or indirect ownership of ten percent or more of the bank's outstanding stock, and during the past few years of regulatory oversight, past and present Comptrollers of the Currency have been quite insistent that this area of concern be closely reviewed. To that end—and I'm not sure how you would like to handle it, Scott—I do have some questions I would like to discuss regarding the bank's handling of its various relationships of business entities owned or controlled by your board chairman and largest shareholder, Mr. Tariq Nasir. He is, as you know, the 'insider's insider' here at Global United, whether it's by way of his official capacity here at the bank or his controlling stock interest in the bank and other related entities."

"Why, what's wrong there?" Scott Kruse acted incredulous, becoming noticeably animated for the first time since the meeting began. "We've always tried to be quite circumspect with everything we do relative to Mr. Nasir's personal and business relationships."

Trotter was somewhat taken aback by Scott's defensiveness, a reaction seemingly shared by just about everyone in the room, including Logan. Scott's red face, and the near panicked sound of incredulity in his voice suggested the examiners finally had his full attention for the first time that morning.

"There's no cause for alarm, Mr. Kruse. These are, by and large, routine questions that I'm certain you'll be able to answer easily, but I do need to ask them." During a long, storied career as a regulator for the OCC, old Paul Trotter had seen this same reaction from many a bank CEO when faced with a need to scrutinize principal insiders to whom they perhaps answered, like Global United's Mr. Nasir. It was the type of reaction, however, that always made him immediately suspicious. The CEO of a bank closely held by one individual, such as was the case between Scott Kruse and Nasir, sometimes only kept his or her position by staying in the best of graces with that principal shareholder. It was a built-in potential for conflict of interest with which only the most forthright and principled of individuals were often able to contend. "Interestingly enough, I met Mr. Nasir early on in our examination when he was in the bank on some business," continued Trotter, "and he seemed to be a very capable, straightforward businessman. Nevertheless, he and his various other companies do a great deal of business with Global United—as they certainly should if all is handled according to regulation—and I would simply like to better understand his organization, what parts of it do business with the bank, and how the bank handles that business with respect to the requirements of Reg. O, etc."

"Fine, what would you like to know?" the still obviously perplexed Scott Kruse snapped back.

"Well, from what I can tell, Mr. Nasir appears to handle most all of his business operations through a holding company he and his family own by the name of AmeriPAK, Inc., I believe it is," said the old regulator, looking down at his notes. "The company appears to have a rather complex corporate structure consisting of a number of subsidiaries that are, shall we say, interestingly eclectic in nature."

"That's correct," responded Kruse, still looking a bit perplexed by the subject at hand.

"Yes, well, from what we've been able to determine from an organizational chart we found in an accountant-prepared statement in the AmeriPAK file," said Trotter, "the company's subsidiaries would appear to include six corporate entities: Aurora Development, Inc., a Chicago real estate development company that Mr. Nasir must have purchased from his father-in-law's estate some years ago; Aurora Transportation, Inc., a domestic trucking and international shipping firm; Aurora Tech, Inc., a computer hardware and software provider; AuroraNet, Inc., a regional Internet service provider; Aurora Vending, Inc., a company that apparently owns and very successfully operates vending machines and electronic game rooms at a multitude of locations throughout the Chicago area; and finally PAK-West, Inc., an international precious metals operation that also owns a number of well-located, high-end jewelry stores in several major cities around the country. They're named Crescent Jewelers, I believe. All the companies except for the technology outfit seem to be rather profitable operations, and all the companies, including the technology concern, have very strong balance sheets. Each of them also appears to have established deposit and loan relationships with the bank. Are we correct in all of that?"

"Sounds correct," Scott responded, "but what do you need to know about those relationships that you maybe don't already? There should be fairly complete write-ups in all the files."

"Yes, we found the very write-ups to which you refer, and they were quite helpful." Trotter was trying not to be confrontational. "And from our review, it would appear as though the bank has accommodated AmeriPAK and each of its subsidiaries with fairly substantial lines of credit."

"Absolutely! And that's as it should be, wouldn't you think, Paul, seeing as how Mr. Nasir owns most of this bank?" Scott added, even more defensively.

"Look, again no need to be concerned here, Mr. Kruse. We're only recapping our observations here with respect to credit arrangements. We have found that when the total of the lines of credit granted all the AmeriPAK companies are aggregated—as they must be since Mr. Nasir is near sole owner of all AmeriPAK, Inc. shares and a major shareholder of Global United as well—the resulting number would exceed the regulatory lending limit as a percent of bank capital were it not for the fact that you correctly arranged for participations of the excess credit authorizations or overlines to various upstream correspondent banks. So, no problems appear to exist in our initial review of the credit side of these relationships."

"Well, we're glad to hear that," Scott retorted with an air of condescension, "but I'm not surprised. We have always taken great care in that regard."

"We figured you would be." Trotter smiled sympathetically. "We do still have a few routine questions regarding some covenants in your loan agreements with the AmeriPAK group, but aside from that I would repeat that we have little problem with how Global United has handled the credit side of its AmeriPAK relationships."

"Well, if I might interject, I'm glad to hear that too," added Logan. "AmeriPAK, Inc. is one of our larger, more involved credit relationships."

"Yes, I'll bet you are, Mr. Hart." Trotter hesitated a moment while making prolonged eye contact with Scott and then looked back at his notes before continuing. "And we would essentially be done with AmeriPAK, were it not for the fact that it appears we also need to discuss their deposit relationships and some services the bank provides Mr. Nasir's companies on the operations side of the bank."

"What might I ask could be of concern with the AmeriPAK group of deposit accounts?" Scott asked, shaking his head in rekindled exasperation. "They're simply standard business checking accounts set up with sweep features to accommodate some related cash management arrangements. It's all an automated function similar to that which we've established with a multitude of other commercial customers. We've always been quite careful to charge them our standard fees, and to show no preference with respect to overdraft procedures, etc."

"Look, we really have no problems whatsoever with either the type of accounts AmeriPAK has with the bank, or thus far anything about account fees. What we would like to visit about instead, however, has to do with the bank's Cash Transaction Reporting procedures with respect to Mr. Nasir's accounts."

"And what may I ask is wrong there?" Scott was again on the verge of becoming confrontational. Logan was more than just a little disappointed at Scott's attitude, and Trotter and all of his examiners appeared somewhat put-off as well.

It was a side of Global United's CEO that Logan hadn't seen before.

"Well, nothing that we're sure of yet, Mr. Kruse. We've simply noted that except for a couple, the bank has placed most of Mr. Nasir's companies on its Cash Transaction Reporting Exempt List—exempting them from regular reporting of large cash transactions to the federal government—and we want to ensure that your organization has exercised sufficient due diligence in that regard. Some AmeriPAK subsidiaries appear to be quite heavy users of cash, and some are not. So, we would like to discuss the bank's methodology for determining the eligibility of those that have been listed as exempt."

"Well, from what I understand, our policies and procedures covering the Bank Secrecy Act and Anti-Money Laundering regulations are quite comprehensive, and have never been brought into question in previous examinations by the OCC," said Scott, "particularly as they have related to Mr. Nasir's companies. Why all the sudden concern this time around?"

"Well, Mr. Kruse, as I am trusting you are very much aware and as I alluded to earlier, BSA and AML compliance have been areas of intense regulatory scrutiny for a very long time now," responded Trotter, "but it just so happens to also be a real hot button for our new Comptroller, Carter Bennett. As a result, all district offices of the OCC recently received directives from him demanding that they all approach their oversight of those areas of regulatory compliance with renewed vigor in all banks within their jurisdiction. So, with all due respect, what we may or may not have done in past examinations here at Global United when it came to our reviews of those areas of concern, must and will be of little consideration this time around."

"Okay, look, I suppose I understand," Scott interrupted, "but if you don't mind perhaps we could leave our review and discussion of Mr. Nasir and his AmeriPAK companies on this matter until later this afternoon. Better yet, since you have already indicated this must be a short day for you and your crew, perhaps we could even set it for the first thing Monday morning, depending on how long you think you may need to visit about the questions you have in this situation. Mr. Nasir is very concerned about confidentiality in all circumstances relating to him and his companies. So, I would rather we had this discussion at a later time when we can have a slightly more private meeting between say just me, perhaps Mr. Hart here, and you and your examination team, if that's okay. Typically, only a few of our management team with a 'need-to-know' have familiarity with matters concerning Mr. Nasir and his businesses. He prefers it that way. So, if we could wait until later and handle the discussion of his situation in that manner, I know that Mr. Nasir would be most appreciative."

Logan noticed Trotter bristle for the first time that day, but the old regulator remained polite and in control. Stifling obvious consternation, Trotter hesitated a moment before replying. "I suppose that would be okay with respect to our initial discussions, Mr. Kruse, but please understand that should we find any irregularities or feel that any questions have not been adequately answered, we will involve anyone and everyone from your organization necessary to obtain the answers that we need. I hope you realize how essential it is that we be made comfortable in matters such as this that involve a major shareholder like Mr. Nasir."

"If we are going to be discussing our compliance with the Bank Secrecy Act, or our Anti-Money Laundering efforts and related reporting, shouldn't I perhaps also participate in those discussions, Scott?" Sammy al-Dajani, head of bank operations, spoke up for the first time that day. "I'm in charge of the bank's ongoing compliance with BSA and AML requirements. I've helped develop most all of our policies and procedures along those lines, and I'm also well aware of our handling of Nasir-related accounts in that regard. I could perhaps save everyone a great deal of time in providing Mr. Trotter the answers he needs."

"Uh...sure, you're probably right Sammy," Scott replied. "It might be a good idea for you to also join us. You could perhaps more readily answer a goodly number of the questions Mr. Trotter and his team might have on the subject."

"Fine, Mr. Kruse, we'll wait until Monday morning to discuss those matters, and leave it up to you to decide who participates in those discussions," said Trotter, "but please ensure that the necessary people are there to answer our questions regarding your BSA and AML reporting policies and procedures. We have a number of questions in that area." Trotter pushed his still half-full lunch plate aside, removed his glasses and scooted his chair back. "Well, I guess if that's the route we're going to go, folks, what say we take a fifteen-minute break. When we resume, we'll begin our review of the rather long list of commercial loans about which we have questions, and anyone who isn't essential to those discussions is free to return to his or her job, with our appreciation for giving us your entire morning on such a busy day."

Sammy al-Dajani seemed in a particular hurry to leave the room, with Scott Kruse close on his heel. On his way out, Scott explained that he had "some important matters to take care of that may preclude me from taking part in much of the loan discussion, but I'll try to get back in here before the afternoon is over, if I can."

Logan thought that strange. Sammy and all non-lending-related officers weren't really needed for the afternoon meeting, but the bank president's presence was always a plus during loan discussions, and that's what befuddled Logan just a little. Scott had told Logan as they were walking into the meeting just that morning that he had set aside the whole day to meet with the examiners without interruption. Scott's reactions during most of the morning

53

meeting, and the fact that he and Sammy al-Dajani seemed to share a nervousness regarding the OCC's regulatory review of the bank's management of the BSA and AML-related activities for the AmeriPAK accounts bothered Logan a great deal. In the few short weeks since he had joined Global United, it had become very apparent that Scott's relationship with the bank's Chairman, Tariq Nasir, was a close one, far closer than what most bank CEO's might have with an outside director, regardless their controlling ownership in the company. It seemed as though Scott made very few major decisions without first conferring with Nasir. Scott's response when Logan asked him once about Nasir's heavy involvement in day-to-day affairs of the bank was, "Tariq's an extremely sharp guy and our largest shareholder. I simply have a great deal of respect for his advice, and like to use him as a sounding board on any number of things regarding the management of the bank."

Fairly early on in his new position at Global United, it had become quite apparent to Logan that a number of the bank's officers, specifically those of South Asian and Middle Eastern origin like Sammy al-Dajani, had far more direct contact with Mr. Nasir than one might think normal for people of their position within the bank. Thus far, Logan had perceived nothing sinister about the situation. He just simply felt it a not-so-positive management aberration that could easily become the source of future "chain of command" issues. *More than likely a cultural thing worthy of keeping one's eye on*, he remembered thinking.

CHAPTER FIVE

FOR THE better part of three generations, Global United Bank of Chicago's predecessor institution had been the quintessential Chicago neighborhood community bank, with all of its operations limited to a headquarters and two branches located on the city's near northwest side. In 1924, Harold Flannery, Sr., an industrialist, and grandfather of one of Global United's current shareholders, Harold Flannery III, was quite exercised at having recently been turned down by another local bank for a loan to expand his manufacturing business. Vowing that would never happen again, he decided to establish a new bank that would be slightly more entrepreneurial in nature, and a little more sensitive to the needs of its customers. Flannery gathered together eight other northwest side community leaders—all of Irish descent—and talked all of them into making an investment of $25,000 each, to form what was originally known as Guarantee Bank of Chicago

Guarantee Bank was a conservatively managed institution from its founding, with steady growth and profitability during its first several years of operation, and that was fortuitous considering the uncertainty that would eventually occur during the Great Depression, when the bank was temporarily closed along with all other financial institutions in the country during the banking moratorium of 1932.

As with its peers, Guarantee's doors were required to

remain closed at the time, until they could sufficiently prove up the safety and soundness of their institution to federal regulators. The bank was one of the first allowed to reopen three days later, however, after a number of the directors met with regulators and informed them that there would be an infusion of $300,000 in capital by way of an unsecured loan from one of its directors. Harold Flannery provided that loan.

$300,000 was a large sum of money in the 1930's, and its source was the subject of much conjecture at the time. A misguided consensus was that more of the money had perhaps come from bootlegging during the days of prohibition than from manufacturing, but few questions were asked at the time in that regard. Whatever the source, Flannery had the money that was needed when others did not. Considering the press of the national financial crisis at that time, bank regulators required little explanation, and the bank was allowed to continue its service to the community.

When it came time for the loan to be repaid, Flannery asked that the repayment be in the form of newly issued stock instead of money. The investors gladly complied, and those new holdings, along with purchases of stock made from financially struggling directors during the remainder of the 1930's, gave Mr. Flannery ownership that would eventually exceed seventy-five percent of the bank's outstanding common stock by the end of the decade. In 1940, Flannery sold his manufacturing businesses, became the full-time Chairman and CEO of the bank, and the rest became history until Flannery's grandson, Harold Flannery III, finally decided his interests lay elsewhere.

◊◊◊◊

IN 2009, Tariq Nasir was on a lot of Chicago area short lists. At forty-three years of age then, he was fast becoming one of the most talked about young business and cultural leaders in the city. A naturalized Pakistani-American and devout

Sunni Muslim, Nasir had arrived in Chicago in 1990 at the age of 24, shortly after receiving an MBA from Harvard and marriage to Melissa Hardesty, a recent graduate herself from the Harvard School of Law. A native of Chicago, Melissa was the daughter of Lawrence Hardesty, owner and CEO of Hardesty Development, Inc., a successful downtown commercial real estate development firm.

Nasir began his business career as a securities broker in the Chicago office of Harnish & Fager, the large, international investment-banking firm. There he specialized in the sale of initial public stock offerings and was an early success in that market. His specialty was holdings in companies or investments compliant with Muslim Sharia law. As a result, he was particularly strong in sales to the more financially successful members of Chicago's growing South Asian and Middle Eastern immigrant communities, a niche that made him the envy of many of his contemporaries with respect to his level of sales and resulting compensation. He was almost certain for early advancement had he stayed, but such was not to be the path of his career.

A seemingly devoted husband to Lawrence Hardesty's daughter, Nasir ingratiated himself early on with his new father-in-law; and from the start, Hardesty was impressed with Nasir's intelligence and business acumen. So much was it the case that only two years into his career with Harnish & Fager, Hardesty made Nasir an offer to join his development firm as an understudy to Hardesty who would eventually take over the business.

Lawrence Hardesty had only three daughters, and none were interested in the real estate development business. The oldest daughter, Margaret, was a Catholic nun who had spent several years as a missionary to Costa Rica; the youngest, Maureen, was a budding artist with an internship at the Chicago Art Institute; and Melissa, Nasir's wife and Hardesty's middle daughter, was only interested in pursuing a legal career or raising a family—and not necessarily in that order. Hardesty had always wished for a son to take over. Perhaps a son-in-law would have to do. It wasn't long after his daughter, Melissa, married young Tariq Nasir that Hardesty began to realize his new son-in-law might have more than just a passing interest in the lucrative world of Chicago real estate development. Hardesty made an offer for Nasir to join his firm. It was quickly accepted.

In 1994 two years after Tariq Nasir joined Hardesty Development, Lawrence Hardesty died tragically, a victim of an apparent hit-and-run driver in downtown Chicago. There was a great deal of talk about the incident. Hardesty was innocently crossing one of the very quiet side streets in the prestigious area that surrounds Water Tower Place just off North Michigan Avenue. The traffic there is typically very subdued. Onlookers claimed it was a yellow cab that fled the scene at a relatively high rate of speed, but no one was able to get the number of the vehicle.

Just prior to the incident, Hardesty had only recently worked out a detailed buyout agreement between him and his son-in-law that essentially transferred control of his development company to Nasir in the event of his death. The agreement utilized an intricate combination of key man insurance proceeds and the purchase of any amount remaining on the stipulated purchase price over time, by way of payments to an irrevocable family trust.

Once he was in control, Nasir was quick to make changes. Within one month of assuming ownership of Hardesty Development, he had formed a new holding company named AmeriPAK, Inc., into which he transferred one hundred percent ownership of Hardesty. AmeriPAK was incorporated in Luxembourg, a country known for the secrecy of its corporate and banking systems. Tariq Nasir held seventy-five percent of the ownership in AmeriPAK, and the remaining twenty-five percent was registered in the name of Nasir's father, Mahmoud Nasir, who although still a resident of Pakistan, was now a frequent visitor to the United

States and Chicago.

Over the course of the next twenty-five years, following a strategic plan envisioned with the help of his father while in grad school years before, Tariq Nasir's business empire grew with more companies added under the aegis of the AmeriPAK holding company. No expense was spared in seeking out aggressive talent to run the subsidiaries, with nearly all key positions filled with management talent of South Asian extraction. It was evident this staff of talented, well-educated and typically professional looking young executives had an undeniable flair for business. The financial success of the AmeriPAK group of companies was phenomenal, but one important element of the plan was still missing.

For some time, owning and operating a federally insured U.S. commercial bank had been a coveted acquisition for Tariq Nasir, and this was in spite of how problematic an investment of that sort was for such a devout Sunni Muslim as he. In nearly every respect, the concepts of modern finance as practiced by western financial institutions disqualified them as investments that were compliant with the dictates of the *Holy Qur'an* and *Sharia* law in every way.

Very basic to the business of western banking, for example, is both the paying and receiving of *Riba*—or interest—on nearly all forms of qualified investment, a practice that is *Haram*, or strictly forbidden to all Muslims under Sharia law. Citing a long-term plan of eventually converting any bank purchased to a totally compliant Islamic banking institution, however, Nasir claimed temporary dispensation from the requirements of Sharia, covering such a purchase under a loose interpretation of the Islamic concept of *Taqiyya*. This special provision in part allows that any Muslim may deviate from the requirements of Sharia law, or even deny their faith on a short-term basis, to either protect oneself from dire persecution or when such an act results in the long-term furtherance of the faith. Nasir thus

59

felt little constraint in pursuing such an investment.

◊◊◊◊

TARIQ NASIR had long been desirous of owning either all or a goodly portion of a privately held, Chicago-based commercial banking institution. It was part of a long-term strategic business plan that guided nearly every major business decision on his part.

For many years Nasir had been an investor in bank stocks, but that ownership had always been restricted to minority holdings in a fairly diverse portfolio of publicly traded institutions, mostly larger national or regional banking organizations. There had been a number of opportunities to buy into a privately held institution, but none of the banking organizations he had looked at were of the size and location that interested him.

That all changed in 2009, however, when Nasir received a call from Oliver Tandy, a representative of Clayton McGruder, Inc., a Chicago-based boutique investment house that specialized in negotiating the sale of smaller, Midwestern bank holding companies, and making a market for their stocks. McGruder kept a list of acquisitive corporate and individual investors, and Tariq Nasir had been on it for some time.

"We think we've just come across the type of investment opportunity we know you've been looking to find for quite a while, Mr. Nasir," gushed Tandy. "We were just this morning contacted by Harold Flannery III, Chairman and principal shareholder of Guarantee Bank of Chicago, an old line, independent Chicago financial institution. He's indicated to us that he may perhaps be interested in selling a goodly portion of his family's holdings in that bank."

"I'm listening, Mr. Tandy," said Nasir, feigning initial ambivalence. "Tell me a little bit about it."

60

"Well, sir, Guarantee's a commercial bank with about $2 Billion in assets. It's a sound institution, been well run for many years, and has very strong capital. What we think may be of particular interest to you, Mr. Nasir, is the fact that they have four locations in Chicago. Three offices are on the near northwest side of the city, where the bank started back in the 1920's. And then, get this, they've only recently opened a new, very attractive office downtown."

"Where about downtown?"

"Right in the middle of the financial district. I guess they moved into approximately 30,000 square feet of space on the first three floors of the Trainor building on Lasalle Street, in the midst of the financial district. Subleased the space from one of the big regional banks that wanted to close a few offices, from what I hear. It's exactly the kind of situation that you described to us sometime back. Think you might have any interest?"

"Perhaps I might," Nasir responded in his usual controlled manner, but he was more than interested. "How much of their stock are we talking about? You know I prefer to only buy into corporate situations where I am acquiring control."

"Well, only up to twenty-five percent of the outstanding stock is being offered for sale at the present time, Mr. Nasir, but we think there may be an opportunity to make a pitch for more either now or later. We're uncertain that Mr. Flannery is necessarily interested in staying real active with the bank. He has some other ventures going at present that appear to be of greater interest to him. Could we arrange a meeting and at least see where discussions might lead?"

"Certainly, I'm always willing to talk. I'm leaving this afternoon for Europe on business, but I will only be gone for about four days. Perhaps we could meet sometime the first of next week, if Mr. Flannery is interested. If you would like, you can make the arrangements while I'm gone with my assistant, Falanna Kristoff. She keeps my schedule, and I check in with her at least a couple of times a day, no matter where I am. She'll get to me with any questions that may arise."

"That's wonderful, Mr. Nasir. I really think we may have something here. I'll talk with Mr. Flannery and get back to you as soon as possible."

◊◊◊◊

THE 2009 meeting that the investment bankers at Clayton McGruder, Inc. set up between Tariq Nasir and Harold Flannery III regarding the purchase of ownership in the then Guarantee Bank of Chicago ironically went far better than Nasir expected it would. Clayton McGruder's Mr. Tandy had been quite correct. Harold Flannery III did have very little long-term interest in banking, and he was greatly in need of money, having a number of downtown commercial real estate ventures of far more interest to him at the time.

The meeting began with the premise that only twenty-five percent of Flannery's family bank stock holdings was available for sale, but before it was over, a much different outcome would unfold. Nasir controlled the timbre of the meeting from the start. "Mr. Flannery, I am very much interested in obtaining ownership in your bank," said Nasir, "but I've always made it a personal rule to never acquire an interest in any business that was less than fifty-one percent of the company. I'm willing to discuss an offer that would be some kind of multiple of book value, but not unless you're willing to sell that much or more of the stock."

As always, Nasir had done his homework. He was well aware that Flannery enjoyed the prestige and notoriety of his bank title, but badly wanted cash for the commercial real estate ventures in which he was far more interested. "Oh, and one thing further," said Nasir. "If we can reach a deal, I'll need you to stay personally involved for at least the next few years in your current position as Chairman of the Board. I will want to be involved in major strategic decisions, but I have far too much going on in my other businesses at present to be greatly involved at the bank on a regular basis."

That comment hit a note of accord with Flannery. He was single, the last surviving member of his family, had no one to whom he wanted to pass along the business, and inasmuch as he was quite adept at banking, hated to give up the challenge and prestige of his ownership and resulting position so abruptly. Such a gradual exit over time would make the sale of controlling interest far more palatable. The President and CEO of the bank primarily handled the day-to-day operations of the institution, so Nasir's offer had great appeal. Flannery could have his cake and eat it too, so to speak. "I was really only interested in selling up to twenty-five percent of the bank's stock at this time, Mr. Nasir, but everything has its price," said Flannery. "There may be some steps we'll have to take with respect to your offer and minority shareholders, but if we can agree upon a price that's attractive enough, I would certainly be willing to look at selling more."

As was Nasir's suspicion, Flannery was not a driven negotiator. Before the one meeting was over, Nasir had succeeded in reaching an agreement to purchase what would ultimately amount to initial ownership of over sixty percent of the outstanding common stock of Guarantee Bank.

Nasir had been truthful in saying that he preferred to stay out of the limelight where the bank was concerned, at least initially. As far as the public and bank regulators knew, Harold Flannery and the bank's then current President and CEO were the go-to people at Guarantee Bank during his early years of ownership. Tariq Nasir was simply one of nine directors. Behind the scenes, however, the situation was far different.

Managing in short order to subtly, but sufficiently, endear himself to both Flannery and the CEO, Nasir was able to make numerous changes to his liking, using both men as his proxies wherever needed. To begin, a holding company was formed named Global United Bancorp, Inc. that would be the corporate entity used to consummate Nasir's initial tender offer to Flannery and all other shareholders for the purchase of their remaining stock in Guarantee Bank, by making it a wholly owned subsidiary of the holding company. The proposal further called for the bank to change its charter to that of a national banking organization, and concurrently changing its Guarantee name to Global United Bank of Chicago, N.A. just as soon as was allowed by regulation after completion of the purchase. Minority shareholders would have the option of either retaining their stock in the bank by converting it to stock in the new holding company or selling for cash. Flannery chose the latter for the bulk of his remaining ownership, and many minority shareholders followed suit, leaving Nasir in a strong position of majority ownership.

Almost immediately, the corporate persona of the new Global United Bank of Chicago began to take on an international flavor. By early 2010 the bank had greatly expanded its stodgy, old Trust Division to include new Private Banking and Wealth Management operations, and an International Banking department was established that would grow its outreach at a pace previously unparalleled by that of any other bank in the city. Special emphasis was also immediately placed on marketing to Nasir's many affluent friends and acquaintances in the South Asian and Middle Eastern Islamic communities in the Chicago area. A special, new Islamic Banking Services Division was in the works.

CHAPTER SIX

AHMED KHALID, alias Ismail Hamadi, worked two jobs for a supposed living, driving a cab and working as a crew supervisor for a growing Chicago area building maintenance contractor. He was a highly educated and degreed individual who could have under more normal circumstances found far better work for himself, but the anonymity of the more menial positions he had chosen far better suited the covert objectives of his current situation.

Khalid had entered the United States illegally, making his way to the city of Chicago, Illinois sometime during the middle part of 2016. Clandestine entry was difficult, but not impossible. The then current U.S. President and his administration had little interest in policing the country's borders with its neighbors, both north and south.

Khalid's journey to the U.S. had been long and arduous, however. Aided by exquisitely forged passport documents provided at each step along the way, his trip to Chicago had started six months earlier in Jakarta, Indonesia, and then had followed a circuitous route that consisted of lengthy layovers in: Frankfurt, Germany; London, England; and Toronto, Canada, to arrive eventually in Dearborn, MI.

The latter part of the journey which included traversing the U.S. border with Canada without documentation, was particularly delicate. He accomplished that portion of the trip by stowing away for over twenty-four hours in the trunk of a new Chrysler 300—one of several models produced at a plant in Brampton, Ontario—and loaded on a semi-trailer bound for distribution warehouses in Dearborn. Once Khalid made it there, the worst part of the trip was over. Home to one of the largest and fastest-growing Muslim diasporas in the U.S, it would be easy for someone like Khalid to blend in; and Chicago, Khalid's ultimate destination, was also but a few hours easy drive away by automobile.

An Egyptian born Muslim, Khalid had lived most of his young life in Dubai, one of the United Arab Emirates. As the privileged first son of medical professionals—his father an oncologist and his mother an accomplished obstetrician— Khalid had moved to Dubai with his parents before the age of two. Much in demand as personal physicians to numerous members of the very wealthy ruling families of Dubai and the other six Arab Emirates, his parents' practices were lucrative but very time-consuming. Both his father and mother doted on Khalid and his two brothers. So, their childhood lacked for nothing materially, but very busy schedules allowed both his mother and father little time for parenting. A good deal of the boys' upbringing was, therefore, delegated to a number of old mullahs who ran the Islamic preparatory schools, or *madrassas*, their parents required them to attend; and nearly all the mullahs were Wahhabi fundamentalists whose special interpretation of their faith envisioned a pan-Islamic state or Califate, attained through whatever means was necessary. Young Khalid was an enthusiastic student who particularly took the fundamentalist teachings of the mullahs to heart.

While still in his twenties, after graduating from university with a bachelor's degree in bioengineering, family wealth allowed Khalid to fulfill the requirements of Hajj. Last of the Five Pillars of Islam, Hajj mandates that all faithful Muslims who are financially capable undertake a pilgrimage at least once during their lifetime to the Saudi Arabia city of Mecca, to worship at *al-Masjid al-Haram*, a mosque built around the *Ka'aba*, a black obelisk believed by Muslims to contain the first house built on the face of the earth for the worship of Allah, and the holiest of all Islamic shrines.

Lacking little in the way of financial resources, Khalid was able to remain in Mecca for weeks beyond the ten-day ritual of *Dhul al-Hijja* that is observed by all the pilgrims who journey to Mecca for Hajj. There, between periodic fasts, performing ablutions and praying to Allah five times daily as required by the *Salah*, Khalid passed much of his time sipping espressos in the Azahar Coffee Shop of the Intercontinental Hotel and developing several associations that would change the course of his life.

Over two million worshipful Muslim pilgrims from literally all around the world visit Mecca each year in observance of Hajj. For most believers who come, their time in the city is spent as a period of affirmation in their faith. For a few that are a bit more zealous in their beliefs, however, the pilgrimage can sometimes fuel simmering fires of fanaticism that burn within. Khalid was one of the latter. Naturally drawn to other radical young fundamentalists like himself, Khalid was an easy sell for the many individuals and organizations present in the city anxious to make him an acolyte.

One such organization, started by an idealistic band of wealthy young Saudis, was a fledgling group calling itself *al-Sahaba*, or "Companions of the Prophet." Augmented by lesser educated and somewhat disenfranchised young Egyptian, Pakistani and Afghan fundamentalist pilgrims, these Muslims espoused a radical brand of Islamic dogma calling for *Jihad*, or Holy War, against all faiths other than that which followed the teachings of Muhammad the Prophet and the Holy Qur'an. Khalid found kinship with al-Sahaba and was quick to join.

Zealous in all that he did within the faith, and useful because of his wealth and education, Khalid was quickly embraced by the organization's inner circle. Initially, his involvement was strictly limited to fund raising for the organization, spending most of his time entertaining wealthy pilgrims on Hajj, appealing to them for their financial support of supposed charitable programs that al-Sahaba claimed to sponsor, and proselytizing for the organization wherever possible.

Assuring them that al-Sahaba would be a conscientious steward of their contributions, devout Muslim contributors were promised by Khalid and his associates that their funds would be utilized in ways that fulfilled the donor's obligations under the teachings of az-Zakat, the fourth Pillar of Islam requiring that a certain percentage of every believer's assets be set aside to help those less fortunate, and to spread the teachings of Islam.

Once in the hands of al-Sahaba, however, the better part of these contributions tended to find their way to far more nefarious activities. Justifying such a diversion on the premise that successful Jihad against all non-believers would eventually lead to a world far more supportive of the downtrodden under the rule of Islam, al-Sahaba used very little of the funds donated to their organization for charitable purposes—and donations were plentiful. Khalid was a very successful, charismatic, young pitchman.

Ahmed Khalid was also a capable leader. At six foot four, very muscular and darkly handsome, the young zealot had a commanding presence that belied his age. Outspoken, articulate and thoroughly familiar with the Qur'an, all related Hadiths, and Sharia law, Khalid had a way of rallying fellow jihadists to nearly any cause when the need arose. He was fast becoming a dominant figure within the leadership structure of al-Sahaba as the organization gained stature in the underground of radical, Islamic fundamentalism. Organizations such as the Islamic Brotherhood, Hamas, Hezbollah, and al-Qaeda were always looking for new talent and yet relatively unknown smaller groups with whom they could work. Early on in their existence, Khalid and his al-Sahaba were asked to align themselves with the efforts of these and other like organizations. The al-Sahaba chose to become direct associates of al-Qaeda.

In the early part of 2011, Khalid and a number of the al-Sahaba inner circle were invited by al-Qaeda to travel to the mountains of northern Pakistan for a series of highly secretive meetings with Dr. Ayman al-Zawahiri—at the time Sheik Osama bin Laden's second in command—and much of the hierarchy of the al-Qaeda organization. He was informed that Mr. bin Laden, still alive at the time, was in a secret location known only to but the highest levels of al-Qaeda command for purposes of his security. Communications with him were limited to either written or taped messages delivered back and forth via courier.

Discussions lasted for several days, eventually culminating in Khalid and his associates agreeing to undergo paramilitary training at a camp run by al-Qaeda in the mountains to the north of the city of Kabul, near the Pakistan border. At this camp, the young al-Sahaba acolytes were taught such skills as the use of weapons and explosives, hand-to-hand combat training, infiltration, concealment, clandestine operations and communications, and self-sacrifice. Khalid distinguished himself by the skill and enthusiasm he brought to the training.

Upon completion of their indoctrination, Khalid and his associates once again entered into another series of planning meetings with Dr. Zawahiri and his command group. These lasted yet another month. At the end of those sessions, plans and agreements were made, and organizational alliances established. Al-Sahaba would keep its separate identity but would function as an arm of the al-Qaeda alliance. The burgeoning coffers of al-Sahaba were to be also surrendered to the elaborate financial infrastructure of the al-Qaeda organization for future management.

Choosing aliases under which to travel, everyone within al-Sahaba's inner circle was provided with necessary travel documents bearing new, assumed names, and all departed for destinations known only to them and the command group of the al-Qaeda organization. Khalid's chosen alias was Ismail Hamadi, with his ultimate destination three years later being Chicago, IL, by way of Jakarta, Indonesia and points in between.

◊◊◊◊

"*AS-SALAMU ALAIKUM*, kind sir. My name is Ismail Hamadi. I'm here to meet with either Mr. Tariq Nasir or Mr. Yussef Ibrahim if I could please."

"*Wa-Alaikum-ud-Sallam*, and peace be unto you also, Mr. Hamadi. I am Youssef Ibrahim, president of Crescent Jewelers, and it is my sincere pleasure to meet you. I very much regret, however, that someone may have grossly misinformed you. Mr. Nasir is not available at this location, and normally would not be."

"Why is that, Mr. Ibrahim?"

"Well, our jewelry chain is indeed one of many businesses owned by Mr. Nasir's holding company, but he is not directly involved in day-to-day management of this concern, or for that matter, any of the several companies owned by his holding company. He is far too busy with larger matters and tends to leave the running of his companies to others, such as myself. I was told to expect you, however, and am here for the express purpose of meeting with you, Mr. Hamadi. How may I be of service?"

"My apologies for the confusion regarding Mr. Nasir. I had the privilege of meeting him on Hajj a couple of years ago, and I was hoping to get to meet him again, but perhaps another time? I apologize for my ignorance regarding his organization."

Oh, no problem, no problem indeed, Mr. Hamadi. That is a mistake made by many in the past."

"Well, thank you, for explaining that to me, Mr. Ibrahim. I am disappointed I will be unable to renew my acquaintance with Mr. Nasir, but it is nevertheless a pleasure to meet you, sir. If you were expecting me, then you must already know that I am in the market for a special item of jewelry, which I understand from a mutual friend you may have recently imported from the United Arab Emirates. If that is correct, and the piece you have is what I am looking for, then you and I may be able to do some business."

"Yes, perhaps your friend is correct, Mr. Hamadi. We import a great deal of our jewelry from various precious metals dealers and artisans across South Asia and the Middle East, and we did just take shipment on a number of items from Dubai a few days ago. Many of the dealers we do business with by the way, including the one in Dubai, are also quite frankly owned by Mr. Nasir's father, Mahmoud Nasir. So, it is very difficult to find any better assortment or prices anywhere. I am certain we can find something to please you."

"That's wonderful, Mr. Ibrahim. The mutual friend I mentioned contacted me this morning by e-mail and told me that you and he had visited about this matter. He provided me with this supposed catalog reference number for one item that he said both you and he felt might be just what I am looking for."

"Excellent, if you'll let me have that reference number, Mr. Hamadi, I'll have one of my associates pull the item from our stock along with a few pieces like it for purposes of comparison, and then we can discuss your purchase in my office over a cup of coffee."

Khalid reached into his pocket, removed a small piece of paper upon which was written a number, unfolded it and handed it to Ibrahim. The balding, thick-set, well-dressed jeweler, in turn, removed a neatly folded sheet of paper from his lapel pocket, compared a number on it to the information Khalid had provided, and nodded approval. He then passed the paper on to a nearby clerk, quietly whispering some instructions as he took his young customer by the arm, led him up a set of stairs to a well-appointed mezzanine office overlooking the showroom, and closed the door behind them.

"Now that we are alone, Mr. Hamadi, perhaps we can get down to business. The communication that I received this morning indicated that a customer of ours in Dubai wishes us to ensure delivery of $75,000 to you at our earliest opportunity. We have that amount already prepared for you here this morning." As Ibrahim spoke the clerk entered the office and placed both a jewelry display case and a large envelope on Mr. Ibrahim's desk. "The currency is in this envelope, Mr. Hamadi. If you wish to verify its amount, I will draw the blinds for privacy".

"That will not be necessary, Mr. Ibrahim. My associates and I are confident that you would never slight us in any way. Besides, trust is the essence of hawala. Is it not?" Khalid's matter-of-fact tone was ominously dismissive. He was sorely disappointed and a little embarrassed at being misled regarding the accessibility of Tariq Nasir, and it showed. He had been looking forward to the opportunity of making his acquaintance once again for various reasons. Besides, the cologne the pinstriped hawaladar was wearing was overpowering and most unpleasant. *I've had all I need of this self-important old fop*, thought Khalid.

"You are absolutely correct, Mr. Hamadi, and you can always depend on the Nasir organization. Hawala has been a family profession for generations."

"That's good to hear. My associates and I may very likely have a number of similar transactions in the very near future that we may wish to have the Nasir family assist us with."

"Should that be the case, you can rest assured we both can and will always be most reasonable to deal with. By way of example in that regard, your people earlier today paid our representatives in Dubai the money they wished to transfer to you in Arab Emirate Dirhams. At the time they brought the money in, the currency exchange rate for

Dirhams by way of conventional banking channels was approximately .275 U.S. dollars per Dirham. We were, however, able to provide the same amount of money to you today for 30.5 cents per Dirham along with a very reasonable 1% fee for our services. By my rough calculation, when you compare what the cost would have been for a similar transaction through a traditional bank, we saved you and your associates nearly $2,300 on this one exchange alone. We also accomplished in one morning, in absolute confidence and with total accuracy, what would probably have taken better than a week to go through a bank. We hope everything is satisfactory?"

"It is indeed, sir. My associates and I thank you for your assistance. We may need your help again in the very near future."

"We will be anxious to be of service," Ibrahim responded.

Hamadi placed the envelope containing the currency in a canvas briefcase, shook hands with the jeweler and quickly headed for the exit. Escorting his young client to the door, Ibrahim observed Khalid climb into the driver's side of a yellow cab, and quickly disappear into a sea of downtown Chicago traffic. This Hamadi made Ibrahim uncomfortable. Intense young zealots on missions from Allah, which Ibrahim presumed Hamadi to be, were very unpredictable. Ibrahim had seen too many others like him in recent years, and he was never completely comfortable working with any of them. Give him some poor Muslim working stiff sending a few bucks home to help the folks to do business with any time.

CHAPTER SEVEN

EACH FRIDAY, devout, dedicated congregants begin arriving at The Islamic Institute of Greater Chicago—the *Masjid* or mosque located on North Michigan Avenue—long before *Dhuhr*, the regular span of time during midday when *Jumu'ah* or Friday prayers are observed. As the *Muezzin* issues his call to prayer in hauntingly melodic tones over a state-of-the-art sound system located in a modern-looking minaret atop the roof of the one time, downtown commercial structure, the faithful perform their ablutions, bathing in the manner prescribed by the Hadith. Each worshipper enters the mosque's main meeting hall shoe-less to jockey for the nearest prayer rug position remaining available adjacent to the outer wall of the hall, or *Qibla*, oriented exactly in the direction of the Muslim holy city of Mecca.

Kneeling in tight, orderly rows facing the Qibla, the worshipers quietly and reverently recite their *Sunnah*, or personal prayers, as they await the start of the service. At precisely the prescribed moment, the Institute's Imam mounts the steps to the *Minbar*, the platform where he will later deliver his typically fiery *Khutbah*, or Friday sermon, and begins the service by singing out the *Adhan*, a call to the faithful to join him in prayer. The congregation responds with respectful *'a-salaams* and then listens in rapt silence as the Imam admonishes them to rise to new heights of devotion to Allah.

The mosque housing the Islamic Institute is located in

what was once an empty shell of a building that previously served as a warehouse distribution center for a long since defunct cosmetics company. In early 2006, the then dilapidated, but well located, structure was brought to the attention of some of the more affluent members of Chicago's Islamic community by one of its leaders, downtown real estate developer, Tariq Nasir. Having purchased the building on options just prior to its being condemned by the city to make way for development of another sort, Nasir had paid the cost from his own pocket to bring in one of the Middle East's more preeminent religious architects from Saudi Arabia to offer renderings of what could be done to transform the old building into a place of worship that would not only "bring glory to Allah," but would also create the "right kind of image" for a group of the faithful whose prominence within the community was growing by the day. Concurrently appealing to both the religious zeal and personal egos of this Islamic leadership group made the idea an easier sell. What was once a downtown eyesore was now a beautifully renovated example of classic Middle Eastern religious architecture, complete with a golden dome and minaret that was fast becoming a local landmark. The project accomplished everything that Nasir and his group had wanted for Chicago's Islamic community—and it made a tidy profit for Nasir's development company in the process.

The monthly meeting of the *Dars-e-Qur'an*, or Islamic study group, at The Islamic Institute was always held on the fourth Friday of every month. Led by a different Qur'anic scholar each time, the group usually met in one of the comfortable *Mihrabs*, or meeting rooms, just outside the mosque's main prayer hall, immediately following Friday prayers. Ostensibly, anyone within the congregation interested in attending was welcome to join the faithful at the Dars-e-Qur'an, but in practice, most of those who typically attended were, by and large, the more celebrated congregants. That was at least until the arrival of a group of several young zealots during the latter part of 2018 that made it clear from the start they considered it not only their sacred right, but duty as well, to attend; and they were now doing so once a month without fail.

From day one of their arrival, it was quickly evident to everyone else in the study group that these new attendees were not your average, run-of-the-mill Muslim worshipers. A couple of the young men claimed to be U.S. citizens, but most of the group were apparently recent immigrants. Ironically, all eight claimed to be involved in very unassuming occupations, such as cab drivers, waiters, and janitors. Yet, none of them looked or acted anything like what they claimed to be. Well dressed, well groomed and well spoken, they appeared to always have money, and handled themselves in a manner suggesting excellent educations, both religious and secular. Seemingly well versed in both the Qur'an and a multitude of the Hadiths, none of the eight was shy about participating in religious repartee. Each of the young men went out of their way to appear respectful in how they addressed the many community leaders that regularly attended the study group, but were steadfastly adamant regarding their fundamentalist approach to religious dogma, unafraid to take on any of the other congregants about such things when they felt the need arose.

The eight also claimed to be strangers to each other prior to joining the study group, but at the same time displayed a familiarity that belied that story. From the day they first began attending, they could nearly always be found gathered in an intense conversation in a nearby coffee shop following the adjournment of the lecture and discussions, acting nothing like the strangers they said they were.

"WERE ANY of these infidels really to know the reason our group meets here over lunch each month, I am certain they would lose a great deal of their appetites." sneered Bakir

Abdullah, the Saudi-born leader of a group of al-Sahaba sleepers headquartered in Detroit, Michigan. At twenty-seven years of age, Abdullah was the youngest cell leader within the command structure of the U.S.-based al-Sahaba, "I find it thoroughly disgusting how smug they are in their disbelief. I remain hopeful their day of reckoning will come soon."

"You're correct, Bakir, and I share your desire to hold this nation of dogs accountable for their unforgivable sins, but none of us has the luxury of taking any action on our own. I have been assured, however, that something very important is ultimately being planned for us in the scheme of things," responded Ahmed Khalid, leader of the U.S.-based al-Sahaba. Known only by the alias of Ismail Hamadi to all the young cell leaders seated around the table, it was part of Khalid's job to control the fervor of the young zealots until the established time for the activation of any initiative on their part. That was in itself, however, proving to be a nearly full-time job. "The success of the *fatwa* we are tasked with facilitating is far too important, and American intelligence and security forces far too vigilant these days for us to be careless or complacent about anything we say or do until we receive final instructions as to what next awaits us."

The group of eight young jihadists stood out very little from the usual lunch crowd at Spiros' Family Restaurant. The little Greek coffee shop was located on Ontario Ave. about three blocks from the Islamic Institute. The group of eight had become a monthly fixture at the restaurant, regularly getting together at that location following Friday services, and there were always numerous members of the congregation who frequented the establishment at the same time. The eight young men were unfailingly pleasant and polite to the waiters, tipped well, and went out of their way to portray an appearance of conviviality, smiling, laughing and conversing in low tones as they ate their lunches and downed large amounts of black coffee.

77

Usually requesting a table to the back of the restaurant, the eight young men would stick to themselves, speaking in near flawless English only when there was a need to communicate with one of the restaurant staff. Otherwise, they conversed exclusively in languages of South Asia or the Middle East, such as Farsi and Urdu, figuring it highly unlikely anyone other than another patron of similar background as they would understand a word they were saying. To be sure, they always took great care in that regard.

Each member of the group was gainfully employed in their respective cities of operation. Bakir Abdullah, the young Saudi-American cell leader from Detroit, used his given name. Abdullah had entered the United States legally in 2010 on a study visa to attend the Graduate School of Engineering at Michigan State University and had made an extra effort to become a U.S. citizen five years later.

Two more of the cell leaders, Nagif Fadallah and Muktar El Amir, like Abdullah also of Saudi background, typically flew in monthly for the meeting from their respective bases of operation in Seattle and Dallas. Contrary to Abdullah, however, both of them were currently residing in the country on work visas.

Assem Rafiq, the oldest of the group at age forty-two, who originated from Pakistan, flew in monthly from New York to attend the meeting. Rafiq was the only other one of the eight besides Abdullah who had attained U.S. Citizenship, having given his so-called oath in that regard but a mere six months before.

The three remaining cell leaders: Allaidan Hussain Alwan from Washington, D.C; Muhammad al-Zanati from Los Angeles; and Barzan Ibrahim Hussan from Miami were of Egyptian birth like their leader, Ahmed Khalid. Having arrived in the U.S. at the same time three years before, all were in possession of permanent resident green cards.

At age twenty-eight, Khalid was one of the younger

members of al-Sahaba's U.S. organization and a recent arrival, but there was no question as to his leadership. As a principal member of al-Sahaba's international leadership council and that organization's currently pivotal affiliation with al-Qaeda, his was a position of great influence within Jihadi circles. Intelligent, sophisticated and very well informed, Khalid could be ruthless in his exercise of authority. He considered every aspect of whatever the current mission was to be ordained by Allah, and no situation or person, whether friend or foe, could be allowed to stand in the way of its success. Unless and until someone breached organizational etiquette or security, or disobeyed an order, he could in all respects be as loyal and attentive a friend to his al-Sahaba comrades as they could hope for, but let one of those things happen, and the reverse ruled the day. Khalid was trained to take the life of another person in a multitude of ways, and there had never been any hesitation on his part when the mission was threatened even the slightest.

"A time of testing will soon be upon us, my brothers." Khalid addressed his fellow al-Sahaba in Farsi, the language of choice for the day. "We have worked hard and planned much for the day when we will bring the judgment of Allah to this abode of Satan, and you have all been patient in that regard. So, I am excited to inform you that the sword with which we shall finally strike this nation of vipers will soon be in our hands."

"When, when will that be, Ismail?" Allaidan Hussain Alwan, the Egyptian-born leader of the Seattle, WA al-Sahaba cell, excitedly asked, voicing the question that was on the mind of every member of the leadership council present. "Most of the brotherhood assigned to our respective teams have been in this country, training, and planning for months, some for years—and most of them with untenable immigrant status. It is now nearly two decades since our al-Qaeda brothers delivered their 9/11 blow to the heart of this evil nation. It's also the better part of a decade since this wretched country exacted its vengeance on Sheik bin Laden for his planning and execution of that event—may he be revered forever—and the best we have been able to muster by way of response here in this country has been rather pinprick actions like those two idiot Chechens running amok with homemade bombs in Boston back in 2013, or some half-wit fanatics deciding on their own to shoot up a nightclub, run a few people down with a car or some such thing. It is time for a much larger statement from the brotherhood. No one is taking these American dogs to task in any significant way for the retribution they have wreaked upon our brothers around the world in recent years. Look at what they have done and continue to do to our brothers across the Levant even as we speak. The Islamic State was attempting a comeback in Syria and Iraq, but leaders of this country still brag at having eradicated that organization. They must be held accountable. If we are able to deliver a significant blow at this time, then we must. I speak what I know is on everyone's mind here, Ismail. When do we strike, and how?"

"Yes, I understand and sympathize, my friend. So, I think you will all be pleased with what I have to tell you." Khalid glanced around the room and lowered his voice. "Look, the situation with respect to immigrant status for most of us is becoming increasingly tenuous since this new administration began its crackdown over the past couple of years. I myself am an illegal alien of the highest order. Those above us know that and have thus indicated that it might be best for us to act sooner rather than later with respect to any plan of attack envisioned for our future as an operative group."

"We couldn't agree more," Alwan quickly retorted. "Yet, we've heard that sort of thing before. If that is indeed the case, then be more exact. Tell us when.

"Well, Mr. Alwan, in an effort to do just that, let me just say that we are soon coming to that time of the year when people like this whore of a waitress here, and her fellow vermin that inhabit this despicable country most clearly demonstrate the depth of hypocrisy so inherent in their way of life." Khalid nodded his head and smiled mockingly at the young, blond waitress who was pleasantly filling the group's cups with fresh, steaming coffee. He knew she couldn't understand a word he was saying. "The Christmas and Hanukkah seasons will soon be upon us. It is that time of year when both the modern-day Christian 'crusaders' and many Zionist pigs who inhabit this country demonstrate most clearly how decadent their society has truly become. It is repugnant to me how they feign worship and don mantles of piety while engaging in all manner of commercial avarice and evil merriment. Hordes of people will be crowding major cities and airports as shopping, spending and travel are at their annual heights. It is that time of year when this country and much of the western world is most vulnerable. So, it is the thinking of those above us..."

"This Christmas season, Ismail? You're saying it's this Christmas that we're finally going to execute our long-awaited operation against these swine?" Alwan excitedly interrupted in a low voice, glancing furtively around the room. He could tell from their expressions that his fellow al-Sahaba cell leaders shared his excitement. "Please forgive our incredulity, Ismail, but each of our cells has been in place and preparing for so long now that it is hard for us to believe what you are now finally telling us. Are we truly to understand that the time has finally come for us to deliver a real blow to the heart of this evil country—a blow that matters?"

"Yes, my brothers, the time has now indeed arrived when you and those who have been placed in your charge will see the purpose of everything you have been asked to do over the last couple of years. I have known for many weeks now the intended timing of the attack, and that we of al-Sahaba would be the point of the spear, so to speak, for this operation to come. Yet, I could not inform any of you of this until I was certain everything would be in place by the time we needed it. Now that I know for sure that the weapon with which we will strike this blow for Allah is on its way to us, and the approximate time of its arrival, we can begin final planning for the attack in earnest."

"This is wonderful news, Ismail!" Assem Rafiq from New York exclaimed, as the group hugged, slapped one another on the back and rendered high-fives.

"This time, we shall not stop with just the City of New York or Boston my brothers!" Khalid placed his arms around the necks of the young men to his right and left, as he leaned forward, glanced around the table and in a low voice whispered, "They will be pin pricks by comparison. Our attack will bring this entire evil country to its knees."

"Can you tell us more, uh, be more specific with details?" Rafiq asked.

"That is all I can say for now, gentlemen, but be prepared. I may need to ask you all to return to Chicago on short notice when it is time to act. Until then, that will have to do for information," said Khalid

People in the restaurant smiled. It looked like the group of eight was having a good time.

CHAPTER EIGHT

PAUL TROTTER was a veteran bank regulator who had spent his entire regulatory career with the OCC, and he was convinced he had pretty much seen it all. Trotter had examined good banks and bad, large and small, and his experiences had made him the proverbial regulatory cynic. The highlight of the stocky built, grandfatherly, little regulator's career had occurred in 1984, when he was assigned at a relatively young age to the position of senior examiner in charge of the investigation into the Parkside National Bank failure in Tulsa, Oklahoma.

The Parkside failure was such a large workout project for the OCC at the time of its closure that Trotter became a near full-time resident of Tulsa for almost two years, and a staple for several months on the national evening news. Parkside had been a prolific seller of large participation loans to upstream correspondent banks, many of which it turned out had not been very well vetted by the purchasers. Parkside itself was only $450 Million in asset size at the time —a community bank of relatively insignificant size by today's standards—but thanks to the near $2 Billion in participation loans it had sold several larger institutions, its demise precipitated problems of a systemic nature for the banking industry, significantly taxing the Bank Insurance Fund at the time of its closing. Trotter and his team had to sift meticulously through the entire records of a financial morass created by years of gross dishonesty and mismanagement on the part of both members of the board and senior management of Parkside, and in some cases, complicit officers of the upstream banks. The Parkside failure would pale by today's standards of failed institutions, but in its day, it was a major financial debacle. It took many months of painstaking audit reconstruction and loan analysis by a team of nearly one hundred examiners to get a handle on the overall condition of both Parkside and the upstream banks to which it had sold so many loans. Trotter's final report of examination and testimony before a federal grand jury would eventually result in indictment upon indictment being handed down against a number of previously high-flying bankers, putting them behind bars for many years to come.

What bothered Trotter most though, and left him a zealot for banking propriety for the remainder of his career, was the human financial tragedy he witnessed as a result of the actions of the Parkside Bandits—as Trotter and his team referred to those whom they eventually helped send to prison. Federal deposit insurance covered the little depositor who had kept their deposit balances below the maximum coverage threshold of $100,000 at that time, or knew enough about the workings of deposit insurance to structure multiple account coverage. However, not all customers were so fortunate. Many small businesses, numerous little old retired folk and other customers of a similar nature who had dealt with Parkside for generations before the Bandits had purchased the institution—and still trusted the bank enough to ignore limits of insured coverage—lost great amounts of money. For a lot of those customers, the losses were devastating. Trotter's required involvement in many emotional sessions with such depositors left him affected for the remainder of a dedicated career, a career that was soon to an end.

Trotter planned to retire at the end of the current month. December 1st. would be exactly forty-four years to the day from his hiring by national banking regulators when he was just six months out of DePaul University with a new accounting degree. Most of Trotter's contemporaries had either resigned or retired after twenty to thirty years of service at best, but Trotter loved his work. So, he stayed far longer than most, and his decision to finally call it quits was an emotional one.

As Assistant Deputy Comptroller in charge of Specialties/Operations for the Chicago District Office of the Comptroller of the Currency, Trotter had enough clout within the OCC after his many years of service, to not only fairly well hand pick his own successor, but also to make a special request to step down from his Deputy Comptroller responsibilities thirty days in advance of his actual retirement. His reasons for requesting this concession were, in his words, to "assist my successor in her transition, and to once more, for old time's sake, join a team of young examiners in the field on an actual bank examination before I'm done."

The powers that be within the OCC felt the request a little strange, including the Comptroller himself, but nearly everyone recognized it as classic Paul Trotter. The current U.S. Comptroller of Currency, Carter Bennett, who had himself been a young assistant of Trotter's on the team that handled the clean up of the Parkside debacle, was said to have laughed when told of the strange request and responded, "Look, if that is the way Paul wants to spend his last thirty days with us, then so be it."

Global United Bank of Chicago was thus chosen as Trotter's final assignment after he had suggested that was where he wanted to go. It was not only close to the OCC's downtown offices on LaSalle Street, where Trotter would still be needed from time to time for transitional purposes during his last month, but it was also an operation that held some special interest to him. He had commented. "Look, Global United has been one of the fastest growing banks in our district during the last few years, and they are doing some new and innovative things, such as introducing Islamic-based financial services. Any time you see that, you know that there has to be much that warrants scrutiny. Just the kind of project I would like to sink my teeth into one more time before I leave." Trotter was a legendary regulator of sorts, who was not only looked up to but also extremely well liked throughout the OCC. So, the entire group welcomed his presence on the team of fifteen young examiners that descended on Global United at the outset of the three to four-week regulatory examination occurring between October and November.

The first of a number of events being given in honor of Trotter's impending retirement was to take place at 6:30 p.m. on the same Friday in November as the OCC's first meeting with bank management. As predicted, the rather long loan discussion with Global United necessitated adjournment until the following Monday, early enough for the examination team to make its way to the festivities. A come-and-go reception was planned at the home of a now retired fellow former Deputy District Comptroller in the town of Barrington, a northwest suburb of Chicago, and the community where both the retired regulator and Paul Trotter lived. To make it on time, Trotter needed to leave Global United's offices early enough to shower, change, and pick up his wife, Eunice, or there would have been no way he would have called it quits that early in the day, considering some of the interesting items he had come across thus far in his review of Global United. He had a number of questions that he wanted to ask management, but perhaps they could wait until Monday.

Trotter had always been frugal to a fault. It was an agency joke. A fellow Deputy Comptroller had once described him before a gathering of District management as being "tighter than the bark on a log," leading most of the office to in a good-natured fashion tag him with the nickname "Old Woody," used whenever they wanted to give him a bit of a hard time about being so cheap.

More often than not, Trotter preferred commuting from his home in the northwest suburban city of Barrington to his work at the downtown Chicago offices of the OCC by way of the METRA commuter rail service, as opposed to driving. The METRA was far less of a hassle. He was able to work while traveling and most important of all to Trotter, it was by far the least expensive way to go. Today was a slightly different situation, however. He needed to be home early and had a couple of errands to run along the way. So, it had been far more convenient to take his car.

The cost of parking downtown was exorbitant. So, true to his tight-fisted reputation, Trotter always made special parking arrangements for whenever he drove into the city for work. Spader's, a perennially trendy, downtown restaurant known for its German cuisine, was located near the OCC's offices on LaSalle Street. Otto Bachmann, owner and operator of the restaurant, was a close friend of Trotter's and a former OCC examiner himself, who unlike Trotter had taken early retirement and invested in Spader's as a second career. Trotter dined at Spader's nearly every day he worked downtown, and Bachmann would invariably join him at his table.

Whenever there was cause for Trotter to drive his old 2010 Toyota Camry into the city, he would leave Barrington at an early hour, drive straight to Spader's, pull the car through an alley alongside the restaurant, and park it next to the dumpster at the rear of the building. The parking spot occasionally smelled of garbage, but it was always free. Typically, on the rare occasions when Trotter availed himself of this parking arrangement next to Spader's, he would usually stop in for a beer and some friendly banter with Bachmann after work, but this Friday evening in November was different. Bachmann was invited to the barbecue later in Barrington, and Trotter knew he would see his good friend there. So, he headed straight for his car.

With his mind on the quickest route home, and

determined to beat as much of rush hour traffic as possible, Trotter threw his over-sized briefcase in the back seat of the old Camry, jumped behind the wheel and was about to insert the key in the ignition when the first muffled shot from the silenced Sig Sauer P239 nine-millimeter automatic pierced the window on the driver's side of the car and slammed into his left temple. Blood, brain matter and parts of Trotter's skull splattered all over the inside of the car, as the second and third shots entered his chest in a close pattern over the heart.

Knowing that he had little time, the assailant moved quickly. Opening both doors on the driver's side of the vehicle, he first rifled through the large, black pilot-style briefcase in the back seat, removing Trotter's laptop computer and a goodly portion of the examination files that were inside, throwing them into a large, black garbage bag for ease of carrying. He then returned to the front seat and removed Trotter's watch and wallet, to ensure that the attack had the appearance of a vicious robbery. It was all over in under a minute. The assailant struck silently and was gone without any witness to the attack. Ten minutes later, the restaurant owner, Bachmann, would find his old friend's body as he too was leaving to attend the Trotter retirement function.

People were shocked with disbelief as they were informed of the incident later when they arrived at the gathering in Barrington. No one wanted to believe that something as horrendous as this could happen to so dedicated a friend and public servant, literally at the outset of a much-deserved retirement. The Chicago Tribune, Sun Times and other outlying newspapers would all carry front page articles about the incident for days, with editorials clambering for a crack down on street crime and Chicago's skyrocketing murder rate, the city's existential scourge.

CHAPTER NINE

CASSANDRA PRICE, or Cass, as her close friends and colleagues knew her, was a rising star in the Office of the Comptroller of the Currency. At forty-eight years of age, she had built a first class reputation for herself within the agency as a capable, no-nonsense banking regulator, in spite of numerous obstacles along the way. Although typically far more capable, and often better qualified than most counterparts she encountered over the years, whether male or female, the tall, statuesque and remarkably attractive, blond regulator had still been plagued for the better part of her career by all the typical stereotypes associated with someone of her looks.

Cass possessed an undergraduate degree in accounting from Northern Illinois University—a school critically acclaimed for its accountancy program—and a law degree from Georgetown University, the latter of which she attained summa cum laude while working full-time as a young regulator in the main offices of the OCC in Washington, D.C. Until only recent years, making a success of it in what had historically been a relatively male-dominated government agency had been a struggle in spite of the agency's posturing about its record of Equal Opportunity and Affirmative Action.

Until Cass was promoted to a sufficiently lofty position within the OCC to shield her from such things happening, just about every new, eligible young male regulator she encountered within the organization routinely attempted to hit on her. It typically happened only once in each case, however. With seemingly no time for anything in life but her career, Cass usually met any such advances with cryptic, icy rebuffs that sent more than one panting, young regulator packing with, as they say, his tail tucked between his legs. Over time, a rather large group of badly bruised male egos ended up collectively dubbing her the "ice maiden," with those spurned finding solace for their failed advances behind what they all concurred had to be a "total lack of any personality" on Cass' part. Some more sorely offended even went so far as to make rude suggestions about her sexual orientation, but none of this, of course, was ever within earshot. They were crude, but not quite that stupid.

Little would any of them ever know, however, how tempting many of their offers had been to Cass over the years. She wanted all the same things that most young women wanted and seemed to find time for in their private lives, but she was more driven than her average female counterpart. Somehow, she had just never found a way to sufficiently balance personal desires with career goals, and make them happen concurrently.

Cass' biggest career break came when she was transferred to the OCC's Chicago District Office in late 2017. There, through the mentoring and sponsorship of Assistant Deputy Comptroller, Paul Trotter, she was able to advance with some swiftness. Trotter was one of the more special people Cass had encountered in her career. He possessed years of background and experience, and quite different to many of his generation, was for all intents and purposes seemingly blind to gender, race or political persuasion when it came to offering a leg up or unselfishly sharing what he knew.

When Cass first arrived in Chicago, it was Trotter who came to her rescue when she was initially ostracized by many of her fellow regulators in that office for being a suspected Washington mole. They had heard that Cass had been one of the Comptroller's fair-haired girls in Washington, and she had arrived in Chicago just at a time when the office was being criticized for what had become a huge backlog of work on the table. Even though it was widely known that the backlog was due to an understaffed situation—the actual reason Cass was sent to Chicago—many in the office were still a little paranoid that she had perhaps been sent there to review performance and keep the headquarters group in Washington informed. Paul Trotter knew better, however, and he went out of his way to demonstrate through his actions that Cass was a welcome, new addition to the OCC's Chicago staff. Thanks to his universally respected intercession, initial suspicions soon passed and Cass was quickly accepted.

Cass' friendship with old Paul Trotter eventually went well beyond the office. Even though Trotter and his wife, Eunice, had a large family of their own, with five children and sixteen grandchildren, it wasn't long before the entire family had all but adopted Cass. Knowing that both of Cass' parents were deceased, and that she had little family besides, the Trotters were insistent during the first holiday season after her arrival in Chicago that she not celebrate the holidays alone, and it had been a wonderful time for her. The entire Trotter family had the same open, generous approach to life as had their parents. There were several little gifts for her on Christmas, and she spent most of the day with delightful little children crawling all over her. It was one of the best holidays she had spent in years. The Trotters filled a void in Cass' life that had been there for some time. The more time she spent with them, the more she realized how much she was missing in life as a result of her single-minded pursuit of a career.

It also took little time after her arrival in Chicago for most of her associates in the Chicago office of the OCC to realize how truly bright and capable Cass really was. Her first assignment had been to analyze staffing and work flow in that office, and then to oversee a restructuring of the organization there to optimize efficiencies and eventually bring the agency's regional oversight program back on schedule. Although many in the office were initially suspicious of what the results of her work might mean with respect to their futures, most would eventually embrace her final recommendations as insightful. Add the results of that effort to the prodigious work ethic, analytical skills and investigative talent that Cass demonstrated during the couple of years she had been in Chicago, and it ultimately came as no surprise to anyone when she got the nod to replace Paul Trotter upon his retirement as Assistant Deputy Comptroller for the Chicago district of the OCC.

Paul Trotter's death at the hands of some suspected thief or drug crazed mugger was devastating not only to everyone in the OCC system, where he was known and loved by many, but it had also been quite a blow to a multitude of admiring counterparts in numerous other federal and state agencies and bureaus around the country. Words of shock, disbelief, and condolence poured in by telephone, fax and e-mail from people all over the country during the days immediately following his death. He had positively touched a lot of lives during his career.

Cass was also heartbroken but would have little time to grieve over Paul's death. As the newly appointed Assistant Deputy Comptroller, there was much to be done. The violent nature of how Paul died, coupled with his high-ranking capacity within an important government agency, drew a special kind of attention. Cass split her time over the weekend following his murder trying to help console Paul's grieving widow and family, while fielding numerous phone calls from people such as Carter Bennett, current U.S Comptroller of the Currency, many of his immediate subordinates, and a whole raft of other high ranking representatives from the offices of such agencies as the

Federal Bureau of Investigation, Federal Deposit Insurance
Corporation, Federal Reserve and so on. The consensus
thus far was that Paul Trotter was simply in the wrong place
at the wrong time, but considering his professional history
and the sensitivity of his official position and responsibilities,
the situation of his death warranted a full investigation.

◊◊◊◊

ON THE Sunday morning following Trotter's murder,
Comptroller Bennett called a hurriedly convened weekend
meeting in the downtown Chicago offices of the OCC. Flying
in early that morning with two of his key administrative
assistants, Bennett had requested that a special contingent
of Chicago-based regulatory and law-enforcement
authorities join him there to discuss Trotter's untimely death.
Attending at his behest were: Cass Price and her immediate
superior, Jarred Levine, Chicago District Deputy
Comptroller; two representatives from the Chicago offices of
the FBI, agents Jim Seilor and Lon Erickson; and Maurie
Cronin, a senior staff member in the Chicago office of the
FDIC and an old friend of Paul Trotter's from their younger
days when both he and Comptroller Bennett were involved in
the workout of the Parkside Bank failure in Tulsa during the
80's. Bennett had never been all that fond of Cronin during
their time together on the Parkside affair, but one would
never have known it considering the warmth of his greeting
of Cronin at the meeting.

"My profound apologies to all of you for needing to pull
you in on such short notice over the weekend," began
Comptroller Bennett, "but I felt this horrible thing that
recently happened to our good friend and colleague, Paul
Trotter, warranted special scrutiny considering the violent
nature of his death, and the important positions he has held
within our agency. I hate to pick on you boys from the FBI

93

right out of the box, but what, if anything, agents Seilor and Erickson, have you folks thus far found out about what took place with Paul on Friday that you can share with us?"

"It's rather soon to provide a great deal of detail, Mr. Bennett," responded Agent Seilor, "We weren't called to the crime scene for several hours into the investigation of Mr. Trotter's murder, but when the Chicago police eventually found his OCC identification card in his jacket pocket, they called us in right away. We brought in our forensic people to assist the Cook County Coroner's office, which they seemed to appreciate a great deal, but we have only scant information as to their findings thus far. Initial thoughts were that Mr. Trotter was perhaps the hapless victim of some stoked-up crack-head looking to get some quick money for a fix, or some such thing, but we aren't fully comfortable with that conclusion just yet. Certain aspects of the crime scene bother both the police and the bureau."

"What kind of things?" Bennett asked.

"Well, for one thing, sir, the more we study the murder itself, the more it looks for all the world like a professional hit, as opposed to a killing by some street criminal."

"Professional hit?" Cass exclaimed incredulously. She became nauseous, experiencing a sudden chill.

"Yes, that's what I said. Mr. Trotter was shot once in the head and twice in the chest at close range by a nine-millimeter handgun, and even though there was a great deal of pedestrian traffic in that area at that time of the afternoon, no one has yet come forward who says they heard any shots. Street noise could easily mask gunshots in a back alley during those hours of the day, but ballistic analysis is telling us that a silencer was used. And that certainly isn't the kind of thing we find in the commitment of a street crime."

The room grew silent as the agent continued his comments. Cass found herself choking up. Paul Trotter was a dear friend. She started to apologize for her show of emotions as she used a tissue to wipe her eyes several times during the discussion, but the expressions on the faces of all those present told her that there was little need to do so. She wasn't alone in her grief and anger.

"The second thing that also puzzles us," continued Seilor, "is the way in which Mr. Trotter's rather large briefcase was rifled. Members of his examination team, whom we talked to last evening, recollect it to have only contained Mr. Trotter's laptop, along with files and work papers relating to the examination that he and his team were conducting of Global United Bank at the time. Instead of finding the contents of the case strewn all over the car, as someone would expect if some thug were only looking for money or valuables, we instead found the case empty of most of its contents. One might expect the laptop to be missing. That's worth a little something. But for the life of us, we can't figure out what some street criminal would want with a bunch of paperwork he probably wouldn't understand, anyway."

"So, what are you insinuating, Agent Seilor? Are you trying to tell us that Paul Trotter's death was in some way premeditated?" Bennett's expression and that of all the other regulators in the room reflected both anger and disbelief.

"You can't mean that you really think someone purposely killed Paul?" Cass interjected. She felt herself getting sicker by the minute. "Why, he was liked by everyone. I'm certain he didn't have an enemy in the world."

"Well, it may have nothing to do with enemies, Ms. Price," responded special agent Seilor. "Was there anything he was perhaps working on that might have made someone concerned enough about him to want to take his life?"

"No, I can't imagine that Paul was working on anything that was particularly sensitive." Comptroller Bennett explained before Cass could respond. "He was quite close to his retirement. So, he contacted me a few weeks ago and requested that I allow him to relinquish his Assistant Deputy Comptroller's position in Chicago to Cass here in advance of his actual retirement date. He said he felt it would give her an opportunity to transition into his position while he was still around for a while. He then said he also wanted to go back out in the field one last time with a group of young bank examiners before he was finished. We thought it was a strange request, but we were hard-pressed to say no in light of his past dedication to the OCC. The examination of Global United Bank of Chicago was a nearby engagement that had already been scheduled. So, he went along with a bunch of our younger examiners on that engagement. I'm told that everything was going reasonably well with that situation from what we know. I can't imagine his death would have anything to do with that. Would you, Cass?"

"No, I can't either, Mr. Bennett. I talked with Paul on Friday afternoon, and he alluded to nothing of significant concern relative to that examination. He did say that he was meeting again with bank management on Monday morning to go over a few BSA carry over issues and that they had a few loan relationships left to discuss with bank management, but beyond that, he didn't seem to indicate that there were any significant problems with the examination." Cass stopped to blow her nose before continuing. "I asked him if he thought he would be finishing on time, and he said that they should be done in the bank by the middle of next week. So, no, I can't imagine it would have anything to do with the examination at Global United."

"Well, I'm not too sure from the sound of things that we have the luxury of assuming that, Cass." Maurie Cronin of the FDIC was weighing in on the conversation for the first time that morning. "Paul's murder is, in my opinion, something that we can't just simply dismiss without looking further into everything that he was involved in at the time of his death. Sorry, to be injecting myself. I know you've only requested my attendance here this morning as a courtesy to me as an old friend of Paul's, and perhaps a heads-up to our office, but I really think the OCC needs to make sure that

Paul's work at Global United had nothing to do with his death. Don't you?"

"Yes, Maurie, we plan to do that." The OCC's Central District Deputy Director, Jarred Levine, felt the need to say something assertive. The head of the OCC's Chicago-based operations could tell by Comptroller Bennett's red face that he hadn't appreciated Cronin's remark. Cronin's presence at the meeting was indeed only a simple courtesy at this time. The FDIC had the authority to inject itself into the situation at any time, but they would normally only need to be involved in the examination of a national bank if some threat to the Bank Insurance Fund reared its ugly head, and there was not even the slightest hint of any problems of that sort known at present. "We want to make certain as well. What I think Cass is trying to say is that we would all be quite surprised if Paul's death had anything to do with the examination he and his team were conducting at Global United, but we will, of course, be conducting a full investigation."

"Mr. Levine and Ms. Price, if you don't mind, the FBI also needs to be kept closely apprised of anything questionable that you may find in your examination," Special Agent Erickson interjected. "To that end, both Agent Seilor and I will more than likely drop in at the bank ourselves tomorrow for a chat with some of their people and yours. We need to see if anyone there might have any insight into what Mr. Trotter may have been doing during the final hours of his life."

"Look, I think we all need to keep each other informed as to any information garnered through our separate investigations," said Comptroller Bennett. "If it's okay with everyone here this morning, what say we agree to all of you here in Chicago meeting periodically, until we have assured ourselves that there is nothing more sinister about Paul's horrible death than the fact that he was anything more than a target of opportunity."

"Sounds fine to us," Agent Erickson responded. "And

just to make everyone comfortable with any coordination we may need back and forth, we'll see the U.S. Attorney tomorrow and obtain an order from a Federal Judge covering a joint investigation, authorizing us to work together on the matter to whatever extent necessary."

"I obviously really don't need to be a part of those meetings going forward folks, but I would appreciate you keeping the FDIC informed through me if anything you think might be of later concern to us were to come up. Paul was an old and dear friend of mine," Cronin injected once again.

"We'll try to do that, Maurie," Comptroller Bennett responded. It was somewhat evident he was less than pleased the FDIC had even been made a part of the meeting, but he knew from having personally worked with them both many years previous that Cronin and Paul Trotter did indeed go way back. "And Jarred and Cass, I'll try to make myself available via telephone or video-conference from my office in Washington, if you wish, for anything you might need from me until we're satisfied with what may have happened here. Getting to the bottom of all this is extremely important to all of us, I think."

"Thank you, Mr. Bennett, we appreciate that." There was apology coupled with apprehension in Levine's voice. It had been he who had invited Maurie Cronin to the meeting that morning, and he had sensed the Comptroller's agitation. He would probably hear about it afterward.

"In the meantime, let's all hope and pray that either the police here in Chicago or you fellows over at the Bureau find some information that helps you nab this guy," added Bennett. "We need to get someone like that off the street before they do something like this again."

CHAPTER TEN

"STARTING THIS week out the way you ended it last Friday, aren't you, Mr. Hart?"

"Huh?" Logan whirled around, thinking he was alone in the office. His assistant, Myrna Brock, seemed to be making a habit of popping in on him unannounced, particularly during the early morning hours when he was trying to get a head start on the day. "Uh, yeah, I guess so." He chuckled.

"You were in early like this last Friday too. Kinda getting to be a regular thing for you, isn't it?"

"Yes, but for the same reason as last week, Myrna. If you'll remember, we're supposed to meet with the examiners early again this morning, to finish what we started Friday." Logan plopped his overloaded briefcase on his desk and sat down rather hard on his desk chair. Leaning back in his seat, he smiled a bit. Myrna was probably the person who really needed admonishment regarding early hours. Here it was, 6:30 a.m., and she had once again beaten him into the office. He knew she lived in a nearby condominium, only a few minutes from Global United's downtown offices, but there was really no reason that she needed to feel as though she had to be in the office so early every morning. Logan took the Metra into downtown from his home in the northwest suburbs nearly every morning at 5:30 a.m., so that he could get a jump on the activities of the day, but that didn't necessarily mean she always had to be there. He made a mental note to talk with her about that when the right opportunity arose.

"Did you have a nice weekend?"

"As a matter of fact, I had a fantastic weekend, Myrna. How about yours?"

"Oh, I suppose it was okay."

"Somehow that doesn't sound too convincing." Logan picked up on the hesitance in her voice. "And just why are you also in here so early on a Monday morning?"

"Oh, I did remember that you were meeting with the examiners again this morning, and thought you might need some special assistance before then, considering all that took place over the weekend."

"Why, what do you mean? Something special happen in the last couple of days I ought to know about? I went hunting in Wisconsin over the weekend. Got back late last evening."

"You mean you haven't seen the news," Myrna answered incredulously.

"No, I've been a bit out of touch. Purposely avoided any news. Didn't turn the TV or radio on or even buy a paper this morning. Napped on the way in. What's up?"

"Oh, my, you mean you didn't hear what happened, Mr. Hart? It's just horrible!" Myrna dabbed at her eyes with a tissue. Logan could now see she had been crying a bit. "It's been all over the news for most of the weekend. Big articles on the front page of all the newspapers, and they've been talking about it on all the television news shows"

"Talking about what?"

"Oh, it's that poor Mr. Trotter, the very person you were supposed to meet with this morning. They found him shot dead in his car Friday evening, just a few blocks from here."

"The heck you say!" Logan was truly dumbfounded.

"Yes, can you believe that? Right here in downtown, probably not long after he finished his meeting with you folks.

I often walk right by where it happened. Paper said it happened in the alley behind Spader's, that German restaurant just down the street. The police think he may have been the victim of a robbery. It's so sad. He was just in the process of retiring you know."

"Whoa, that's horrible! Paul Trotter was a decent guy. I rather wonder if the examiners will even be here this morning, considering that turn of events."

"No, it's quite to the contrary, Mr. Hart. They're already here. They arrived in force, and early. Someone was letting them in at about the time I got here. Some lady by the name of Price, Cassandra Price I believe it is, stuck her head in here only about ten minutes ago." Myrna handed Logan a business card. "She left her card. It indicates she's an Assistant Deputy Comptroller for the OCC here in Chicago. She said that she'd like to meet with you and Mr. Kruse, just as soon as both of you are in."

"Sure, fine. I would think Scott ought to be here shortly if he isn't already. He was supposed to be part of the same meeting that Trotter had set up with us for 8:00 a.m. this morning anyway." Logan shook his head in disbelief at what he had just heard. "Boy, this one ought to be interesting."

◊◊◊◊

"THANK YOU, to everyone here for meeting with us this morning." Deputy Assistant Comptroller, Cassandra Price, had a straightforward, no-nonsense approach to any meeting she conducted, and this particular meeting was to be no exception, in spite of all that had happened the previous Friday. "As I think you folks may be aware, we had a very tragic event take place over the weekend with the violent death of our Paul Trotter, one of the people you were supposed to meet with this morning."

"Yes, we heard about it. Horrible thing to have

101

happened! We quite frankly didn't think you folks would be in here this morning." Scott replied.

"I'm sure you didn't, but for a number of reasons of our own, we felt it imperative that the examination continue as it was, in spite of what took place with Paul."

"Sure, whatever you folks say," Scott responded. "But wasn't Mr. Trotter supposed to be a big part of what we were going to discuss here this morning?"

"Yes, indeed he was, and you have a very good point, Mr. Kruse, but we'll have to do the best we can. We're not really sure about everything that he was planning to discuss with you today either since both his laptop and most of the paperwork he had prepared in anticipation of getting together with you were stolen in the incident where he lost his life on Friday. We were hoping, however, that you might be able to shed some light on that, and accordingly felt it imperative we go ahead with this meeting."

Cassandra Price's name hadn't rung any bells with Logan when Myrna first mentioned her to him earlier that morning, but he recognized her immediately the moment she walked into Global United's third-floor board room. Ms. Price had given a speech on current regulatory issues at an Illinois Banker's Association conference Logan had attended only a few months prior to joining the bank. He sat next to her at the luncheon that day and visited with her at some length. He wasn't sure if she would recognize him or not. He was still an independent consultant then and had no affiliation with Global United Bank at that time. Her presence this morning, along with the serious looking entourage that accompanied her, assured the meeting was going to be something more than what had been planned at the end of the previous week. He knew Cass Price was one of the OCC's heavy hitters, but the telltale bulge of concealed weapons under the coats of the two more serious looking men accompanying her and the other examiners that morning gave rise to conjecture. He had a suspicion as to who they might be, but knew for sure that they were hardly bank regulators. Logan could also tell by Scott's edginess and uncharacteristic silence, that he sensed the same.

"Let me start by introducing everyone I have here with me this morning," Cass continued. "First of all, as I believe I mentioned when you folks from the bank joined us here this morning, I'm Cassandra Price, Assistant Deputy Comptroller for Central District Special Operations here in Chicago. Joining me are Latisha Caldwell, whom I think you already know as assistant to Paul Trotter during our examination here at Global United over the last few weeks, and Special Agents Jim Seilor and Lon Erickson from the Chicago offices of the FBI."

Just as I figured, thought Logan.

"FBI!" exclaimed the excitable Scott in seeming disbelief. "What on earth's going on here? Why would the FBI have any interest in operations here at Global United? I mean no offense to these gentlemen, but I can't imagine anything we might be doing here in our organization that is of the sort that would necessitate the agency's involvement here at our bank."

"Don't get concerned, Mr. Kruse," Agent Seilor quickly interjected. "Our presence here is simply an extension of our investigation surrounding Mr. Trotter's murder. He was a senior federal regulator, and your bank was one of the last places he was seen alive before he was killed. We've simply asked to be part of this discussion in an effort to rule out his activities here on behalf of the OCC as being related in any way."

"Agent Seilor's correct," Cass continued. "All we want to do at this meeting is to understand more clearly what Paul was working on here at the bank at the time of his death, and what areas of concern, if any, he had as a result of that work. Ms. Caldwell has told us that she recollected the agenda for the meeting this morning was to cover a few questions that Mr. Trotter had regarding the bank's compliance with insider-related requirements under Reg O, FIRA, and perhaps some questions on BSA and AML operations, and then they were going to finish up our loan discussion with Mr. Hart and his department heads. Is that correct?"

"That's right, Ms. Price," Scott responded. "Mr. Trotter claimed he had some concerns about Reg O and BSA, but didn't really go into them much. Then we were going to continue our discussions about a few additional credit relationships that your folks didn't have enough time to discuss with us on Friday. Beyond that, he didn't indicate there was much of anything further on his mind. Isn't that your recollection, Logan?"

"Yes, that's essentially my recollection as well," Logan answered, again wincing a bit at Scott's defensive posture and effort to downplay the meeting of the previous week. He knew Paul Trotter's intentions were a little more specific than what Scott had just described. He said nothing more, however. Perhaps that would come out in further discussion without him having to embarrass the bank's president with any further elaboration.

"Well, you can rest assured that every member of the bank's board, management team and staff will cooperate in every way possible to ensure your satisfaction that Mr. Trotter's work at Global United had nothing to do with his death." Scott appeared sincerely concerned. "And I'm confident that will be the case. What would you all like from us?"

"Well, we had thought that we would be wrapping up our examination over the next couple of days," Cass continued, "but it now, regrettably, looks as though some of us will need to be here a little longer than that. We know those areas of bank operations here at Global United that Paul reviewed himself, but as indicated, some of the results of his review are now missing. He should have backed up his work like our procedures call for, but Paul was old school and often ignored such requirements. So, it appears that we will need to reexamine those areas again. We're sorry about the inconvenience of that, but it is something that must be done. Latisha and her crew will hopefully finish up their loan discussion with Mr. Hart and your loan people by the end of today, and then they will be available to assist me and my crew in other areas of the bank that we are re-examining. With a concentrated effort, and barring any unforeseen circumstance, perhaps we can be out of here in the next week to ten days or so."

"We'll help you in any way we can," Scott repeated. He wanted nothing more than to see the regulators gone. The whole affair was making him increasingly nervous by the moment.

"Thank you, Mr. Kruse. We can use it. Here's a list of those areas of the bank that we think at least for now we will need to review again. There may be more, but this will be it at least for now." Cass handed both Scott and Logan an Excel spreadsheet listing several areas of bank operations. "If you and your people could get together, decide who the best person is to work with us in each of these areas, assign them the responsibility of doing so and then get that list back to us right away, maybe things can move along quite quickly. Preferably, if you can arrange it, we would like to have the same people assigned who worked with Mr. Trotter when he reviewed those areas before, but if it must be someone else, then please let us know who it is, and why it is different."

"We'll have this list back to you by mid-morning, Ms. Price," said Logan, rejoining the conversation as he perused the document Cass had just handed them. "Then I and my loan department heads should be available to finish up on the loan discussion at say 10:30 a.m. if that works for you."

"Thank you, very much, Mr. Hart. We appreciate your help." A smile of recognition crossed Cass' face for the first time that morning. "By the way, I'm sorry for the circumstances surrounding this meeting, but it's good to see you again after our acquaintance at the IBA conference last spring, Mr. Hart. Looks like you decided to get out of the consulting business and back into banking, huh? It's nice to see you here. I look forward to working with you."

"Same here, I'm sorry it had to be under these circumstances, but it's nice to see you again too." Logan recalled how easy Ms. Price was on the eyes when he first met her months before at the IBA conference. *Not much has changed in that area*, he thought.

Logan immediately headed to his office to review the list Cass had supplied to bank management that morning, and to begin working on which officers to assign the responsibility of working with the OCC in their extended review of Global United. Noticing that Scott Kruse seemed upset and completely distracted by the end of the meeting, Logan had volunteered to prepare a list of assigned officers for the OCC as they left the boardroom.

Scott appeared relieved to have the help, telling Logan in parting, "Thanks, I appreciate your willingness to assist with that, Logan. I have a number of things going this morning. Look me up, if you would please, however, before you provide the list to the examiners. I would like to have some input into which people we've assigned what responsibilities. Uh, perhaps we can communicate via e-mail on the matter, and then I'll have the list on computer for reference. If I'm not in my office, I'll be somewhere in the building until at least a little before noon. Have someone call me if you have any need to talk to me direct."

"You got it! Just remember though, Scott, Ms. Price did indicate she wanted the list of those assigned the same as before wherever possible. We're probably going to need some good explanations wherever those with assigned responsibility vary from the original." Logan was beginning to wonder a bit about his CEO. He had not previously realized how readily excitable Scott could be.

"Yeah, yeah, I know!" Scott did little to hide his exasperation.

CHAPTER ELEVEN

"MR. HART, two FBI agents are waiting outside your office, and they would like to visit with you for a few minutes if you have the time."

"Sure, what do they need?"

"Don't rightly know. They said they just want to have a short conversation with you by way of follow-up to your meeting of earlier this morning." Myrna Brock acted concerned. The presence of the FBI bothered her. "Is there a problem, Mr. Hart?"

"No, Myrna, no, I don't think so at all. If its agents Seilor and Erickson, they're probably just here as part of their investigation into Mr. Trotter's death. Pretty much routine, I would think. I would be happy to visit with them. Send them in."

Logan was no stranger to dealing with government agents. He was quite comfortable in doing so. During his time as an active duty U.S. Army officer, and even during several subsequent years of active reserve involvement, Logan had specialized in the area of intelligence gathering, both at a tactical and strategic level. That involvement had paired him on more than one occasion with representatives of numerous agencies of the government involved in the intelligence gathering process, both domestic and international. Thanks to the Internet, he maintained friendships to this day with several acquaintances in the U.S. Departments of State, Defense, and Justice that he made during his years of involvement with the military. In the wake of the 9/11 tragedy, monitoring the functioning of the nation's security and intelligence gathering processes had become a bit of a hobby for him. He liked to stay informed and visited often with many of his old friends in government.

"Come in gentlemen," Logan said to his guests, guiding them away from the side chairs next to his desk toward a conversational arrangement of sofa and overstuffed chairs at the rear of his office. "Let's use these seats over here or perhaps the conference table if you would like. Both are a little more comfortable and far less formal." Logan seldom visited with people while seated behind his desk. He used it only for paper work. When he arrived at the bank weeks before, he had insisted on his office being outfitted with both a seating area and conference table arrangement. He had explained that it put people on an equal footing when you visited with them around a table and sometimes over a cup of coffee. He felt it far less intimidating for customers and made them a great deal more comfortable than when you sat behind your desk staring at them over your glasses. "Can I have Myrna bring you both a cup of coffee before we start?"

"Oh, no, Mr. Hart, thank you very much. I think we're both coffeed out. Wouldn't you say, Lon?" Agent Lon Erickson, typically the quieter of the two, smiled and nodded in agreement as he and Agent Seilor both chose to sit on the sofa. "We apologize for taking more of your time this morning, Mr. Hart, what with all that's going on for you folks here at the bank after our earlier meeting. We did nevertheless want to have a little chat with you separate from the others before we left."

"That's fine, gentlemen. How can I help you?" Logan seated himself in an overstuffed chair opposite the agents.

"Well, first of all," continued Seilor, "we were told to look you up by someone who claims he's an old friend of yours, Special Agent in charge of our Chicago office, Merritt

Daimler. He says you and he go way back."

"Yes, we do indeed!" Logan smiled in recognition.

"Merritt told us you were both in the same class when you went through Ranger school some years ago while you were in the Army. He says you're new here at Global United, but that you have a great deal of banking savvy. He also thinks, considering some of your past background and experience, that you might be able to help us do an early wrap up on the Global United part of our investigation."

"Yeah, Merritt and I have been friends since the 80's. We pounded a lot of ground together when we were in the service. He's a great guy, and he's right. I'm more than willing to assist you in whatever way I can. This thing that happened to Paul Trotter last week is really a horrid situation. I got to know Trotter some through the years, and I both liked and respected him very much. I really feel for his family. I lost my wife not long ago myself. It wasn't easy, but I at least had a few years to prepare for that loss. I can't imagine what the sudden and violent nature of Paul's passing must be like for the Trotter family. I want to help in any way. What can I do for you?"

"Well, to begin," explained Seilor, "Lon and I don't want you to mistake any of the questions we're going to ask as being disparaging in any way with respect to Global United Bank of Chicago, but we do want to develop a reasonable understanding of the kind of financial institution Global United is, and more specifically a better feel for the players involved. We eventually plan to visit with Mr. Kruse regarding these things as well but thought after the way he reacted to some of our comments and questions in our meeting this morning that we might be better served saving that for later. We didn't sense that he was any too pleased with the OCC's extended examination, and even more so the FBI's involvement in the process."

"I know," Logan responded. "I sensed the same thing. Look, I am not trying to make any excuses for him, but any

110

examination can be rather trying for a bank's CEO. I'm sure he, like all of us, was just a little disappointed with the fact that the OCC won't be exiting the bank this week like we thought it would. He has a lot on his mind, but I'm confident he'll be as cooperative as he can when all is said and done."

"We're sure you're right, Mr. Hart," injected Agent Erickson, finally joining the discussion. "But for now we thought we might be better served to save our questioning of Mr. Kruse for later, and just enlist your help, if we could. So, in that regard, what can you tell us about your Chairman and principal shareholder, Tariq Nasir?"

"Mr. Nasir? Uh, probably not too much, I'm new enough around here that I'm still getting to know him myself. Why, what questions do you have about him?"

"Well, as I think you know, since it is our understanding that Paul Trotter was examining insider regulatory compliance here at the bank at the time of his death, and it is our further understanding that he was, in that regard, spending no small amount of time looking at Mr. Nasir and his relationships with the bank." Erickson paused before continuing, showing some trepidation about what it seemed he wanted to say next. "So, we really don't want you to misunderstand us, and we would certainly appreciate your keeping this all in the strictest of confidence, but we'd like to get your take on Mr. Nasir, and to the degree you can his dealings here at the bank."

Logan studied the agents for a brief moment before responding. He wasn't all that comfortable where this might be heading. "Well, like I said, I'm still just getting to know him on a personal level, and I probably have only limited knowledge of his relationships here at the bank, but I'll do what I can."

"Great, thank you, we appreciate that." Erickson hesitated, looking at the floor for a moment before continuing. "So, what can you tell us about him, Mr. Hart? How well do you know him?"

"First of all, please call me Logan. Your boss would."

"Fine, Logan, thank you, we will." responded Erickson, "And please, you can also feel free to use first names with us. As we were saying, however, what can you tell us about Mr. Nasir?"

"Well, my first exposure to Mr. Nasir occurred back in 2009 and 2010 when he obtained controlling ownership in the old Guarantee Bank of Chicago, the predecessor of Global United. The firm that I worked for, Holland & Associates, a bank consulting firm out in Park Ridge, was retained by Mr. Nasir to consult on the acquisition. My direct involvement with him, however, was rather limited at that time. Then about one year ago, long before I joined Global United and still a partner at Holland & Associates, we were retained by Global United once again to consult with the bank on a redux of their lending policies and procedures, with an eye toward their offerings of certain authorized Islamic banking services, something our firm had no small degree of expertise in. I led the team that worked on that engagement, and as Chairman of the Board for Global United, and Chairman of the bank's Audit and Compliance Committee, Mr. Nasir was very involved in that project."

"What were your impressions of him, and how was he to work with at that time?" Seilor asked.

"Well, it was immediately evident to me when I first met Mr. Nasir that he was a very bright individual. To my understanding, he's a naturalized Pakistani-American who received most of his higher education in the U.S. I'm told he holds an MBA from Harvard, and apparently also possesses a Juris Doctorate from the University of Chicago, a degree I guess he obtained in recent years."

"Yes, that's what we understand. What do you know about his family and businesses?"

"Oh, I guess he married a Chicago girl some years back, became a naturalized citizen in the process from what they say. He and his wife—Melissa I believe her name is—

112

have two kids, boys to my knowledge. Never been there, but they live out in Evanston, I think. As to his businesses, well, I have studied that quite a bit. Over the last twenty-five or six years or so, Mr. Nasir's apparently built a very successful group of companies he runs under the umbrella of a holding company he calls AmeriPAK, Inc. As evidence I suppose of the international nature of his business involvement, I believe AmeriPAK is a company that was incorporated in Luxembourg. According to our files, Mr. Nasir owns about 75% of AmeriPak, and his father, who still lives in Pakistan most of the time to my understanding, owns the other 25%."

"What can you tell us about AmeriPAK?" asked Agent Erickson.

"Well, AmeriPak's sole shareholder of several very successful, regional, national and international subsidiaries in varied lines of business. None of these companies have any affiliation with Global United Bank, however, other than by virtue of Mr. Nasir's common ownership. I understand all of Mr. Nasir's shares in Global United are held by him personally, or in family trusts for the beneficial interest of his two sons that are separate and apart from his ownership in AmeriPAK, Inc, and under which he retains power of direction. The numbers would seem to indicate his holding company is quite profitable and rapidly expanding." Logan paused before continuing. "I guess I would have to say that my impression thus far is that, for his age, Mr. Nasir appears to be one of the more financially astute individuals I've met in my years in this industry."

"That's what everybody says. We understand he's a pretty impressive businessman. What kind of guy would you say Mr. Nasir is personally though? For example, what, if anything, do you know about his political or religious philosophies?" Agent Seilor lowered his voice and leaned forward in his seat for emphasis as he asked this question.

"Very little I would have to say," Logan answered, sensing where the agents might be going in this regard. "On a personal level, Mr. Nasir has at all times been polite, gracious and considerate, and he is an extremely well informed, articulate individual. There isn't much in the way of business, politics or religion that I've ever heard anyone ask of him that he hasn't had an extremely intelligent and reasoned response for; but I really don't have much knowledge about his religious or political philosophies. I know he's considered a leader within the Muslim community here in Chicago, but that's never appeared problematic for him in his dealings with anyone not of that faith in or out of the bank, at least not to my observation. "

"And the political?"

"Political? Well with respect to his political leanings, I suppose I'd have to say that I'm a bit uncertain there. I know that he's well connected politically, but I've never heard him declare himself as Democrat, Republican, Independent or otherwise. From what I know, he gives to candidates in both major parties from time to time." Logan grinned impishly. "But remember, guys, this is Chicago, and Mr. Nasir is a very astute businessman. So, I would imagine you might find he's been a little more generous to Democrat politicians around here than most others." That comment elicited an understanding chuckle from both agents.

"Look, you've asked me some questions, gentlemen. Now let me ask a couple of you if you don't mind." Logan shot back. "Is there some particular information you have on Mr. Nasir that leads you to ask all of these questions? Is there something that I as a senior officer here at this bank, where he is the major shareholder, should be concerned about?"

"Oh, no, we have no immediate concerns regarding Mr. Nasir, Logan, at least not that we know of yet," answered Seilor. "It's just simply an unfortunate fact that at this point in time in our nation's history, Mr. Nasir falls into that category of individuals about whom we as protectors of national security need to satisfy ourselves that there is nothing to worry about with respect to his political and religious proclivities. No doubt, when all is said and done, he'll do just fine with respect to any investigation we may conduct here at Global United. Nevertheless, when you consider the circumstance of Mr. Nasir's background and affiliations, and couple that with the violent nature of Mr. Trotter's death while specifically looking into Mr. Nasir's dealings here at the bank, I think you can see where we would at least feel compelled to look his situation over a little more closely before we simply dismiss any possibility of his or anyone else's having been involved in the Trotter matter, whether knowingly or unwittingly. And I say that with all due respect."

"I suppose you're correct, gentlemen. It's just hard to imagine you will find any culpability on Mr. Nasir's part as it relates to Paul Trotter's ghastly demise."

"Oh, we're sure you're right," answered Agent Seilor, as he and Agent Erickson rose to leave, "but we'll have to wait and see what our combined investigation with the OCC turns up. In the meantime, we would not only appreciate your keeping the jest of this conversation to yourself, but we would further like to know that we can perhaps look to you for assistance from time to time in the conduct of our investigation. We think you have a multi-faceted skill set that could be most helpful."

"I will certainly do what I can, guys, as long as I am neither asked to break any laws or regulations, or participate in any ethical compromise, I'm here to help. I know I'm preaching to the choir when I say that to the FBI, but then I'm also sure you can see where I am coming from in that regard."

"We do indeed, sir. We respect you for that, and we'll do everything in our power to ensure that's never a problem for you," responded Seilor. "You are everything the boss said you were. We'll be in touch."

◊◊◊◊

"TARIQ, SORRY I missed you, but we need to visit sometime today if at all possible. Call me when you arrive in the office." Scott Kruse despised answering machines, but Tariq Nasir regularly screened all calls to his private number in that fashion. "I don't know if you caught the news over the weekend, but the examiner I mentioned to you on Friday, the guy who was supposed to visit with us here first thing this morning—in part about your account relationships at the bank—was that Paul Trotter who was murdered downtown later that evening. All heck appears to have broken loose. Most of the examiners appeared to have finished their work here at the end of last week, and we were supposedly only having a wrap-up meeting of sorts this morning. That is all changed, however, and they now appear to be back in here in full force. A full-blown assistant deputy director from the OCC just arrived this morning, apparently to take Trotter's place. Would you be available to meet me for lunch? I could perhaps fill you in on what's cooking with the OCC at that time. I'd suggest the Federation Club at noon if that works for you. I'll probably be tied up with the regulators for a goodly portion of the morning. So, if your gal, Falanna, could confirm lunch with my secretary, Lynda, I'll check with her later this morning. Look forward to visiting with you if you can make it. We really need to talk!"

CHAPTER TWELVE

"MR. HART, this is Cass Price. I'm calling from the conference room you provided our team on the third floor. Am I interrupting anything important?"

"No, no, that's perfectly alright. I was just busying myself trying to get ready for our meeting at 10:30. What can I do for you?"

"Well, if you don't mind, I would like to change our plans for that meeting if I could."

"Sure, you're calling the shots on that. When and where do you want to meet?"

"Well, I seldom do something like this, but would you perhaps be free to have lunch with me away from the bank today at noon? There are a few things about our exam that I would like to discuss with you confidentially, and I really would like to meet with you about it away from the bank, if you're willing."

"Well, sure, I suppose I can do that, but what about the meeting we had planned for later this morning? Are we still on with that?"

"No, right at this time I think I would prefer to meet with just you, and as I said to do so away from the bank for now."

"Alright, is there any specific place you'd like to meet?"

"I would defer to you on that. I only ask that you make it someplace where it is highly unlikely we might run into someone from the bank. I really want this meeting to be strictly between the two of us if it's at all possible."

"Well, let me see, if you don't mind say a ten-minute cab ride or so, there's a great little place called RoSario's over in Little Italy, twelve hundred block of Taylor, I think. We can go separately and meet there around noon if that works for you. I know the hostess there pretty well, and I'm sure she can find us a quiet corner."

"That sound's fine. I'll try to be there as close to noon as possible. And I would appreciate your not mentioning this to absolutely anyone else in the bank, please. I really want this meeting kept confidential. These are some very sensitive issues that I want to visit with you about."

"Sounds rather ominous, but you got it. I'll contact everyone who was planning on getting together this morning at 10:30 and cancel that meeting. I'll also keep our later meeting just between us—won't mention it to a soul. See you at RoSario's at noon."

Admittedly, the Paul Trotter incident and now this whole extended examination thing had Logan a great deal on edge. He had taken this new position as EVP at Global United because it provided the opportunity for a much-needed change at a rough time in his life following the loss of his wife, and he had hoped new challenges within a growing organization would give him a fresh start. Now, however, no more than a matter of weeks into the new position and he was finding himself embroiled in murder investigations and regulatory intrigue. FBI agents were crawling all over the place, asking him to snoop for them, and now this—not all that unattractive—lady examiner was calling, asking him to meet her in some out-of-the-way place to chat about "sensitive matters". *Just what the heck is going on here?* He wondered. *I'm not exactly sure this is what I really thought I was buying into when I joined this outfit.*

◊◊◊◊

"GOOD AFTERNOON, my name is Cassandra Price. I'm supposed to be meeting a Mr. Hart here for lunch. I believe he may have made a reservation for two?"

"Yes, Ms. Price, Mr. Hart has already been seated. He told us to expect you. Please follow me." The attractive, raven-haired hostess, who spoke with a pleasant Italian accent, led Cass to a table in the rear of RoSario's Italian Ristorante. "We seated Mr. Hart in the back of the restaurant. He said that you needed privacy to discuss some business. I hope the location will be satisfactory."

"I'm sure it will be just fine." Cass followed the hostess to the back of the restaurant. She could see Logan motioning to her from the farthest booth. The back up of people waiting to be seated, the aroma of the Italian dishes being delivered to the various patrons, and the ethnic ambiance of the place—right down to the red and white colored tablecloths and large, basket-covered bottles of Chianti—suggested RoSario's as being a great place to eat. *Too bad*, she thought. *Were it not for the unpleasantness of the task at hand, this luncheon would have the makings of a delectable respite.*

"Hello again, I'm glad you were able to find this place. It's small and out of the way, like you requested, but the food is also fantastic here. I can personally vouch for that," said Logan, smiling as he rose to shake his guest's hand. *She's better looking than your average bank examiner. Soft, slender hands too*, he thought to himself, instinctively admiring the lady regulator's good looks for the second time that day. That thought had no sooner crossed his mind, however, than he felt a sudden, slight twinge of guilt at the realization of why he found her so appealing. Cass Price handled herself with the same pleasant, self-assured manner as his recently departed wife, Melanie. She also remotely reminded him of Melanie in looks.

"Oh, this is just great! And the aromas coming out of that kitchen smell delightful." Cass commented, as she slid into the booth across from Logan. She was pleased he had taken a seat on the side of the booth facing the door. Just that much less likely someone might identify her. "But please, before we go any farther, let me repeat the request I made to you and your staff this morning. Please, make sure you call me Cass instead of Ms. Price, as you were earlier this morning. It'll make me feel a lot more comfortable."

"Fine, I'll do that if you'll reciprocate. My friends and most everyone in the bank call me Logan. I don't stand much on formalities either." They smiled in agreement with each other as Logan handed Cass a menu. "Look, I don't know what your schedule is or how long you need for this meeting, but I blocked out two hours to visit with you. I hope that will be sufficient?"

"Oh, yes, that should be more than enough time, and I thank you for adjusting your schedule to meet me like this today. I realize we examiners aren't making your days any easier, looking into everything at Global United for a second time the way we are and all."

"No apologies necessary, I'm sure that you folks wouldn't be poking around the bank all of this additional time, if you didn't think it necessary. Look, I got to know Paul Trotter on a personal level myself through the years. He and I worked on a few projects together for a number of banking associations, etc. He was a decent guy, and a capable, reasonable regulator to work with. I really can't imagine anything he was doing at the bank would be behind the horrible way he died, but I can certainly understand your need to be sure of that. I'm more than willing to do anything I can to help." He looked down at the menu. "But first let's order shall we. They always have some wonderful lunch specials here. If it's okay with you, I'll get the waiter for us. We can place our order, eat and then perhaps have our talk."

The two only engaged in small talk while they were

121

waited on and then picked through their entrée. The food was quite good, but both were apprehensive about the discussion to come. Using the time to size each other up, neither finished their meal. Passing on dessert, Logan asked the waiter instead to bring them cups of coffee. *Shared coffee tends to offer relief to moments of tension* had always been his thinking.

"Well, Logan, I'm sure you're curious as to why I wanted to meet with you like this. Aren't you?"

"Yes, I guess you might say that. This is somewhat of a first for me. I've never had a bank regulator, in the midst of examining a bank that I worked for, ask me to meet them for lunch, and then further insist on top of it all that our meeting be in a location where others in the bank would be likely not to see us together. As I said when you called to set up this meet this morning, sounded ominous to me."

"Does all seem a bit mysterious and melodramatic, doesn't it?"

"You might say that." Logan took a deep breath, shook his head and smiled. "So, let's cut to the chase. What's this all about, Cass? What do you need from me?"

"Well, I'll explain things before we're done, but first let me ask you a few questions by way of background, if I might."

"Ask away!"

"You joined the bank, what about two months ago?"

"Yes, that's correct, but you probably already knew that from your review of minutes from meetings of the bank's Board of Directors or my personnel jacket, if you decided to look at those before this meeting. Why do you ask?"

"Well, I'd like to get an idea of what led you to accept your present position as EVP of Global United Bank of Chicago. I'm told that you were a full partner in a very successful, lucrative bank consulting firm. How did you come to be offered your new position, and what led you to accept it?"

"First of all, you are correctly informed. I was a partner at Holland & Associates, a bank-consulting firm located in Park Ridge, IL."

"Yeah, I've heard of them. They're well-known, and now that you mention it, I remember your telling me that when we first met at that IBA conference sometime back. Fine company from what I understand. Why would you want to leave them?"

"Well, I was part of that organization for about seventeen years, and had a very satisfactory career going for myself there. Last year, however, I lost my wife after she succumbed to a long, hard fought bout with cancer, and I just decided that I needed a change. I was a banker before I joined Holland & Associates and thought I'd perhaps give it another whirl before my career was over."

"Oh, I'm so sorry to hear about your wife. I wasn't aware of that. I'm sure that was a tough thing for you."

"Yes, it was a little rugged. Melanie and I were married for nearly thirty years before she passed away, and we were quite close. She's actually the one that suggested I make the change. She knew she was terminal and was fully aware that her death would probably throw me for a loop—which it did a bit. So, she made me promise I would make a change after she was gone. Bugged me about it almost daily toward the end, said she figured I might need a new challenge."

"It sounds like your wife was a remarkable lady. Did you have any children?"

"No, she was never able to have children, but she would have been a great mother."

"I'm certain she would have. So, did you approach the bank, or did they approach you?"

"No, they coincidentally contacted me. I had done some consulting work for Global United around the end of last year, and the Board of Directors was apparently sufficiently impressed with my performance on that project that they thought of me when they set out to find someone to fill the number two spot at the bank."

"How involved was the Board of Directors in your hiring?"

"Well, I was initially contacted by the bank's CEO, Scott Kruse, informing me that the bank was looking for a new EVP, and that led to a first meeting over dinner with he and the bank's principal shareholder and Chairman of the Board, Tariq Nasir, to discuss the proposal."

"And that apparently must have gone fairly well?"

"I guess you could say that. Almost immediately thereafter, Scott set up a whole series of meetings with various members of the bank's Executive Committee, bank HR people and a few key individuals within the organization."

"And those meetings went okay?"

"Yes, the chemistry seemed right with nearly everyone I met. They eventually made a particularly attractive offer. The position appeared to have the kind of challenges I was looking for, and I needed the change. So, to shorten a long story, I accepted the position. Pretty much the standard approach for situations of that nature, I would say."

"Did you negotiate a hiring agreement with the bank?"

"Yes, I did. I learned the hard way quite some time ago that a person is wise to negotiate the circumstances under which he or she can be terminated with as much attention to detail as they would those under which they are hired. I negotiated a fairly comprehensive severance agreement, but I think you'll find that nothing about the agreement is outlandish or onerous for the bank. Greed was not my reason for taking the job. I simply wanted a change."

"I surmised that was probably the situation, but I just wanted to get a feel for what led you to join Global United. What kind of due diligence did you do on the bank before you joined it, and what did you think of your dealings with Mr. Kruse and Mr. Nasir during the time you were being interviewed? Can you give me some insight there?"

"Well, I conducted a rather thorough analysis of the

bank, looking at many of the same things you folks might review in your regulatory assessment of the organization's safety and soundness. I did a fairly extensive review of Global United's ownership, governance, organizational and management structure, and to the extent I could, I thoroughly analyzed a five year history of the bank's balance sheet and income statements, looking at such things as capital adequacy, quality of earnings, liquidity, overall asset/liability management, etc., developing a comparative set of ratios I studied for weeks. I would also have loved to have reviewed their last couple of Reports of Examination by you folks before I joined, but as you well know banking laws and regulations would bar them from sharing such information as that with me until I became an authorized officer of the bank,"

"Yes, you're right in that regard, but I would say it sounds as though you did a fairly thorough job, anyway. May I ask, however, what impressions you had as a result of your investigations into bank ownership and the bank's Board of Directors? Did you, for example, look into the backgrounds of Mr. Nasir, Mr. Kruse and various other board members? If so what were the results there?"

Logan began to sense where Cass' questions might be heading. Leaning forward the way she did with such a serious look on her face when she started questioning him about Tariq Nasir, Scott Kruse and various other directors of the bank, told him a great deal. She was obviously after information on them, and he wondered why. It was becoming reminiscent of his conversation with agents Seilor and Erickson earlier that morning.

Logan had already begun to develop some minor apprehensions of his own about a few of the key players at Global United and how the bank was run since he joined the organization, but he had come to no decision yet as to whether there was anything to be concerned about. So, he decided for the moment to move with caution in answering

Cass' questions. He had a reputation for being forthright with regulators, and he was determined this case would be no different. Yet, he also had no desire to perhaps unnecessarily undercut those at the bank for whom he worked by commenting on yet unfounded suspicions. Logan had found no reason thus far to doubt anyone within the organization, and until he did, he would do what he could to remain as loyal as possible. When it came to such things, Logan from time-to-time liked to quote a favorite, turn-of-the-twentieth-century writer/philosopher named Elbert Hubbard, *"When you work for a man, work for him..."*

"Well, you know, interestingly enough I answered a similar question from your two FBI buddies, Agents Seilor and Erickson, just this morning, and I'll tell you the same as what I did them. Yes, I did indeed look some into the backgrounds of Mr. Nasir, Mr. Kruse and certain members of the board, to the extent that I was able to find information. Mr. Nasir often distributes a biography of sorts that I presume some marketing types prepared for him, and that pretty much tells the same story as what little I was able to dig up about him on my own. He's a naturalized American citizen who was born in Pakistan and educated at some of the best schools in the U.S. He's got an MBA from Harvard, I believe. Married a Chicago girl and fellow Harvard grad and then moved here in the early 80's. He spent a couple of years in the investment business and then eventually joined his father-in-law's real estate development company, which he apparently took over after the father-in-law died. Using a great deal of savvy, he then leveraged that business into the corporate empire he now calls AmeriPAK, Inc. Mr. Nasir claims to have a net worth of around $2.4 Billion, a number he regularly calculates and loves to expound on with little provocation, I might add. I'm told, for example, that he carries around a relatively current personal financial statement in a spreadsheet on his smart phone, and updates it almost continuously. It's sort of a status thing with him. It takes very little urging to get him to pull it out and quote a current net worth. He's also quite proud of the approximate seventy-five percent ownership in Global United that he acquired in recent years. Kind of likes to talk about that too. Don't blame him much, I guess."

"What do you know about his company, AmeriPAK, Inc.?"

"Oh, I know that Mr. Nasir has put together a fairly diverse group of what appear to be mostly successful companies under the AmeriPAK umbrella, and they're all seemingly making a great deal of money for him now. As near sole shareholder of AmeriPAK, those profits appear to be making him a very wealthy man. Before I joined Global United, I also tried to find out as much as I could about AmeriPAK and its subsidiaries, but what I was able to garner was fairly limited. Being a closely held private corporation, there is little publicly available."

"Where did you get your information?"

"Well, the bank has access to financial statements and tax returns prepared by Nasir's people, but I wasn't privy to those either prior to joining Global United. I had to satisfy myself with what little I could dig up from the public domain before then—which wasn't much. AmeriPAK has a website that I checked out, and I managed to get hold of some Dun & Bradstreet information on the various AmeriPAK companies, but you and I both know that information is essentially only comprised of what his people are willing to release, what with the company being unlisted and closely held."

"I completely understand, but what have you determined about Mr. Nasir since you became part of Global United?"

"Once again, not all that much. As I told you earlier, Tariq Nasir deals primarily with Scott on a day-to-day basis. So, my exposure to him has been limited to a few luncheons and my attendance at monthly meetings of the Board of

Directors and various committees of the board where he has been in attendance. I have reviewed the credit files for his various companies. They're profitable, what debt they have is well managed, and they're all fairly flush with cash."

"I think I begin to get the picture, but you're a reasonably sharp, intuitive individual, Logan, and you've been with the bank now for two months. So, what at least is your gut feel about Mr. Nasir to date?"

"Well, like I said, my exposure to Mr. Nasir has been limited, and he is a hard guy to read. Nevertheless, I would have to say he thus far strikes me as an extremely bright individual, with a natural eye for business. Most everything that he undertakes seems to turn out successful. He is unusually astute in financial matters. He can analyze financial statements at a glance and tell you quickly just what problems if any a borrower or potential client may be experiencing. He's a real asset on the bank's loan committee."

"Sounds like you are quite impressed with him, but is there anything about him that doesn't seem quite right to you, anything at all? What about his character or personality for example?"

"Well, no, I wouldn't say there was anything I have thus far observed about his character that concerns me, but I guess you might say his personality is a bit different."

"How, so?"

"Well, let me be perfectly candid," Logan responded, pausing for a sip of coffee and pensively biting his lower lip before continuing. "You only have to be around him for a short time before it becomes apparent that Mr. Nasir's towering intellect and business acumen are equally matched by his ego. He has a tendency, for instance, to dominate meetings in which he participates. He rather likes to hear himself talk, you might say."

"Well, isn't that a trait, Logan, that one might find rather common among self-made, successful businessmen like Mr. Nasir?"

"Yes, I guess you could say that, but with Tariq Nasir the trait is not always an endearing one. He has that South Asian way of being patronizingly polite when he talks to you, but still demanding in a way that leaves some people with the feeling he's talking down to them a bit."

"Have you experienced this directly yourself?"

"No, thus far he has been rather cordial and solicitous of me."

"Why do you think that is?"

"Well, I believe it may be for a couple of reasons. First of all, I think Mr. Nasir senses I know enough about this business that I'm not all that intimidated by him. Quite frankly, right now the bank may need me more than I need the bank, and I think he knows that."

"What do you mean?"

"Well, for one thing, as again you probably know, Global United has been in the process of introducing an array of Islamic banking services to the Muslim community here in Chicago by way of a new department they've organized at the bank. They're just getting started with it, but as you may or may not further know, that is an area where I've developed some level of expertise in recent years, and I'm rather certain it was a major factor in their hiring me to the position I currently hold."

"Yes, I was told about your familiarity with Islamic banking just this morning, and I may be interested in visiting some further with you about that in the near future, but that's not necessarily what I'm most interested in visiting about now. Before we go to that, however, you said there was a second reason you figured Mr. Nasir has given you a certain level of deference. What might that second reason be.

"Well, second of course, is a perception I have that Mr. Nasir feels the need for a strong second-in-command behind Scott, overseeing some things Scott Kruse is responsible for, but often appears not to have the time to do.

So, my take thus far is that as long as I am doing that satisfactorily, and don't run too much afoul of where Nasir thinks things should be going with respect to bank performance, he will probably allow me a certain degree of management latitude. Things may change when I have a little more time under my belt and perhaps begin to make changes he doesn't quite agree with, but for now, as I said, he has been most solicitous."

"Hmm, that's interesting." Cass was quiet for a moment as she appeared to be thinking over Logan's answers. "Let me follow up just a bit on something you just said about Scott Kruse, however. You said something about him having things that tended to pull him away from his CEO duties from time to time. Could you just elaborate on that a little?"

"Well, I really don't mean to cast any aspersions on Scott as the head of Global United's day-to-day operations. He seemingly tries to stay on top of everything required of a CEO. It's just that by nature Scott is not a detail person. He tends to leave such things to someone like me to cover for him in that regard. He's also the primary point of contact with Mr. Nasir and the board of directors, which seems to take a goodly portion of his time. I rather get the feeling that Mr. Nasir can be rather demanding of Scott on a regular basis. So, I guess you might say I was hired with the idea in mind of me being his proxy in areas where he might be spread too thin."

"Yes, I see. Now that we're on the subject of Mr. Kruse, however, let's talk a bit more about him for a moment if we might. Since he would be the principal person you might regularly answer to in the position you now hold, what kind of due diligence, if any, did you undertake regarding him prior to joining Global United; and what is your bottom-line assessment of him as bank CEO since joining the organization?"

"You know, Cass, I admit to being a little

130

uncomfortable with where this is all going. Both Mr. Nasir and Scott Kruse are my superiors at Global United, and I would have to say that I haven't really developed any tremendous concerns about either to date. So, I'm a little reluctant to answer these questions without knowing your purpose in asking them."

"Look, what we discuss here today, Logan, is strictly between you and me. I will do everything I can to avoid putting you in a compromising position when it comes to the people with and for whom you work. I am just trying to put some perspective on a few of the key players within Global United's organization before I dig as deeply into the bank's operations as we plan to do with this extended examination."

Logan sighed, sat his cup down and leaned back in his chair, studying the disarmingly attractive lady regulator once again. He could tell this was no ordinary bank examiner sitting in front of him. He knew she was after more than she let on. If there was something she suspected about either Tariq Nasir or Scott Kruse, he needed to know what it was before the luncheon was over. He took a few sips of his coffee and waited for what seemed an interminable amount of time before responding.

"Well, I said I would do whatever I could to help, and I will. But I expect you to be open and above-board with me in return. Before we're done here today, Cass, I expect you to at least give me some idea of what all this cloak and dagger is about, and what concerns if any you may have about bank ownership. If there's something going on at the bank about which I should be aware, I would hope you might be willing to fill me in. I want to know what I may have gotten myself into."

"That's a deal, but let's continue if we could. I have a number of additional questions I'd like to ask, and neither of us should probably be gone from the bank any longer than absolutely necessary. I don't want to arouse any suspicions. Now, tell me more about Mr. Kruse."

"Well, yes, I also did do some prior investigation into Scott's background before joining Global United, but I found nothing of great concern about him either, or I wouldn't have taken the position he was offering. People that I talked to largely gave him reasonably good reviews. He and I have a somewhat different approach to management, but I understand he's run a couple of decently successful commercial banking operations in southern Minnesota and Wisconsin."

"How do you mean different approach to management? What about his approach differs from yours?"

"Well, as I somewhat indicated before, Scott describes himself as being an 'idea person' or 'visionary,' somebody who is continuously thinking up new programs or initiatives he wants the bank to embark upon, but looks to others to devise and implement those initiatives. Scott's success through the years has seemingly then been due in great part to his ability to surround himself with capable bankers who could take all of his ideas and make them happen. Whereas, I tend to be much more hands on in my management approach."

"That's interesting. I've seen a number of people like that in my day too, and it's been my experience that they are often, shall we say, quite political. When an idea is successful, they are front and center to take the credit, but when the plan runs afoul, they will often lay a great deal of the blame off on some of those same people who were doing their best to turn their visions into reality. Is that the way you see Mr. Kruse functioning at Global United?"

"I think Scott's a relatively competent banker, but I certainly wouldn't mind seeing a little more leadership and independence of thought out of him than what I have seen demonstrated thus far. Perhaps I could stand to be a bit more politically sensitive than I am, but to my way of thinking Scott is, as you say, a little too political. He is pretty much joined at the hip with Tariq Nasir, making few decisions of any import without Mr. Nasir's blessing."

"Do you think that the relationship between Mr. Nasir and Mr. Kruse is a constructive one when it comes to running the bank?"

Logan paused again and looked around the restaurant for a moment before answering. Cass could see she had touched a nerve. Scott's relationship with Nasir was one of the things that had bothered Logan since he joined Global United, but he would still take care in how he answered Cass' question. "Well, let's put it this way. Mr. Nasir most certainly has a controlling ownership in the bank, and as such he should have a right to influence how the bank is run, but not perhaps in the way I perceive he does it. As Chairman of the Board, he purports himself to be active at board level only, taking no part in day-to-day management of the bank, but that is not necessarily what I see taking place. Scott makes few decisions without first talking to Mr. Nasir, and I really don't think in the long run that is what the Board of Directors should be looking for from their CEO. To be sure, all of us in bank management have a responsibility to Mr. Nasir and other shareholders of the bank to see that Global United grows and prospers, but we have an even greater responsibility to our depositors and other customers of the bank to protect their interests by seeing to it that the bank remains a safe, sound, well-administered place in which to do business. I guess I've wondered at times how much Scott would share that view when the interests and needs of Tariq Nasir might be a consideration. Don't know that for a fact, just feel he's inclined that way to some degree."

Cass furiously wrote notes as Logan talked, nodding her head and only occasionally glancing up as he answered her questions. She really was not much surprised with what Logan was saying, but it bothered her nonetheless. "Are you suggesting that you think Mr. Nasir's influence on senior management is undue and inappropriate?

"No, not that I have seen thus far. I would just say that I plan to be rather vigilant in that regard. Mr. Nasir may be quite bright, and an astute businessman, but he is not a full-time, professional banker, and great care needs to be taken relative to any new and different direction in which the bank may be taken. So, I hope to be a voice of reason when I feel management is departing in any way from regulatory requirements and accepted, prudent banking practice. It is my concerted opinion that is what the Board of Directors hired Scott Kruse, me and other members of senior management to do."

"You're quite right, and as a regulator I'm glad to hear you say that." Cass closed her notebook and laid her pen down, looking intently at Logan. He could tell she was thinking carefully about what she had next to say. "You know, when we started this conversation, I told you I'd fill you in before we were done about why I wanted to meet, and I shall, but I really need your assurance that none of this gets back to quite frankly any of your associates at Global United at this time, not Mr. Kruse or anyone you work with, and for sure not Mr. Nasir. This is all highly confidential for now."

Logan waited a moment before answering. He was beginning to wonder altogether about this new association with Global United Bank of Chicago. He had hoped the new position would be the kind of change he needed after Melanie's death, but instead what he had gotten thus far were exotic and mysterious major ownership, an obviously politically motivated boss, a murdered regulator and government agents all over the place. He wasn't sure that he hadn't gotten more than he had bargained for in this whole process and wondered whether he actually wanted to hear what she had to say. Curiosity overrode any concerns he had along those lines, however. "You have my word. Now, what do you think is going on?"

"Well, we're not all that sure that anything is, as you say, going on just yet, but we intend to find out."

"Wait a minute, what do you mean by that? Explain yourself, if you don't mind—and define we."

"Well, when I say we, I mean the Office of the Comptroller of the Currency, the FBI and other agencies within the Office of Homeland Security."

"Office of Homeland Security? Whoa, I don't like the sound of that at all. Why in the deuce would DHS be involved in this? Are you insinuating there's something about Mr. Nasir or Global United Bank that would be of concern with respect to national security? I realize Nasir is of Pakistani origin, and I know he still has strong connections in both South Asia and the Middle East, but he also seems like a painfully straight arrow in most respects. Is there something you know about him that the rest of us do not?"

"No, I can honestly say there is nothing we yet know about Mr. Nasir at this juncture that has proved to be of any concern from the standpoint of either sound banking practice or national security. Yet, there are certain circumstances about Mr. Nasir, Mr. Nasir's companies and his involvement with Global United Bank, NA, which we think bear scrutiny considering all that has taken place in the last week or so, starting with the death of Paul Trotter."

"What circumstances, and how do I fit into all of this, anyway?"

"Look, Logan, Jim Seilor and Lon Erickson of the FBI visited with us later this morning and told us that you had agreed to assist them where you could. We in turn want to inject ourselves into that loop. We at the OCC need your help too."

Logan was becoming increasingly uneasy. "Yeah, I've agreed to help the FBI where I can, and I am, of course, willing to assist you all from the OCC as well, but only to the extent that such assistance is both legally and ethically sound. That's important to me."

I appreciate your concerns, and we would expect no less from you. I can assure you that we would be respectful

135

of your concerns in every way."

"And I would hold every one of you to that, Cass, but I also like knowing why I am doing things, and this all is going a little beyond anything I've previously experienced in any banker-regulator relationship. What can you tell as to why you think you might end up needing some higher level of assistance from me other than that which I should by all rights be giving you, anyway?"

"I know, I'm sure this all does sound rather foreboding. So, let me see if I can summarize the situation in some way that doesn't come off sounding too melodramatic. Perhaps I can put it this way." Cass paused for a few seconds before continuing. "Uh, these days we at the OCC find ourselves in a regulatory world which like it or not is heavily influenced by current world affairs that are tenuous at best, with all the layers of concern that entails. Case in point, here we are looking at a wealthy Pakistani-American businessman—to wit one Tariq Nasir, who is a recognized leader within the Chicago Muslim-American community—that not only owns a fast-growing international business conglomerate, but also controlling interest in a newly formed, fast-growing banking organization with international operations. The OCC's in the guy's bank doing a routine examination, and a soon-to-retire, senior banking regulator is murdered while examining that man's bank. Wouldn't those general circumstances possibly give you a little pause for thought, and make you want to do a little digging if you were us, Logan? Well, it certainly does me!"

The more Cass went on with her explanation of the situation, the more animated and vocal she became. Logan couldn't help but find this good-looking lady examiner increasingly fascinating. "So, what you're intimating with that long dissertation, Cass, is that you, the FBI and all of these other governmental agencies you refer to think Tariq Nasir may be involved in some sort of untoward activity, such as terrorism or some such thing? Boy, I certainly hope you all would want to be sure of yourselves before you head down that road."

"Well, that's exactly it. We do want to be sure of what the situation is with Mr. Nasir and Global United before we would ever think of making any accusations about him or anyone else at the bank for that matter. We have no reason whatsoever to be overly suspicious of Mr. Nasir at this time beyond the strange, overall set of circumstances I've just mentioned; but the situation all around does warrant a bit of cogitation, and a careful, deliberate approach to the remaining work we have to do at Global United. Wouldn't you say?"

"Yes, I guess I can appreciate where you're coming from. Perhaps if I was in your shoes, I might have some of the same suspicions and concerns. So, you're simply looking to me to help you in the process of easing your minds along those lines?"

"I suppose you might say that. We could very much use someone inside that we can confide in and depend upon, who knows something about the inter-workings of the bank, and who is willing to work with us to make sure there is nothing about Mr. Nasir, or any other person or situation at the bank that might be connected to Paul Trotter's untimely death, or about which we should be concerned from the standpoint of sound banking practice or national security. We don't expect you to compromise yourself in any way, but you're an extremely knowledgeable banker with very little historical baggage in the bank; and you're a person who is no stranger to sensitive matters such as this. To put it bluntly, FBI tells me that unlike most of the rest of us, you are also someone who is no stranger to some element of danger or intrigue, and considering what happened to our Paul Trotter that is something to be concerned about. How about it, can we count on you to help us?"

Elbows on the table, Logan put his chin on clasped hands and stared at Cass over his glasses. He really hated to admit to himself that the suspicions she had just outlined to him had been at the back of his mind to some small degree after Trotter's demise, but they had indeed, and he too was interested in finding out whether there was any basis for concern. "In what way do you want my help? And if I do this, how can I work with you in such a way that suspicions aren't aroused at the bank?"

"Well, what we really need is someone to whom we can look that will truly cooperate in helping us quickly get the answers, and not obfuscate at every turn. Mr. Kruse has previously indicated that you would be our principal contact at the bank when it comes to our examination. So, there should at least initially be no suspicions. If it is all right with you, I'll plan to meet with him again at my earliest opportunity, and ensure that arrangement continues."

"How do you plan to do that? Scott could easily decide to assign someone else to the responsibility of working with you people, maybe even take the job on himself. He's extremely nervous about this whole thing with you folks. He calls me continuously to check on how things are going."

"Oh, I wouldn't worry about that. When I finish describing the type person we need, and what we will want that person to do, only one individual on his senior staff will fit the bill, and that person will be you. He'll want to have you continue as the bank's point man with us, let me assure you of that."

Logan smiled. Somehow he believed this feisty little lady could probably accomplish most anything she set out to do. She truly did remind him of his late wife's self-assuredness and determination, and Cass was the first woman he had run across since Melanie's passing that had struck him that way. It was refreshing. "Fine, I'm already in the process of overseeing the gathering of a great deal of information for you folks. What you ask is a natural expansion of that. I'll cooperate in whatever way I can."

"Great, now before we wrap this up, inasmuch as

we've both been gone from the bank far long enough, I'd like to ask you for a couple of additional things. First of all, as I've just told you, there's a lot of ground we're going to have to plow again at Global United in order to reconstruct our work before Paul Trotter's demise. So, if it's possible, and we have enough time left yet this afternoon, I would like to relay that message in a short meeting with your staff and enlist their help in trying to complete our work as quickly as we can. Do you think you could put together a quick meeting this afternoon to do that?"

"One similar to the meeting you called off this morning?

"That's correct, one to replace the meeting we asked you to cancel for 10:30 this morning."

"Yes, I think I can. Why don't we shoot for say 3:30 this afternoon, and I'll get right to work putting that together just as soon as I get back. And now, I believe you said there were two things you wanted?"

"That's right, Logan." Cass seemed hesitant with her next question. "You know, I hate to ask you this after having already taken so much of your time here today, but there are still a number of additional things beyond what we have thus far discussed that I would appreciate the opportunity of talking further with you about. Do you think you might be able to meet with me a second time away from the bank during the next couple of days? There's more I'd like to visit with you about."

Logan liked the idea of that. Another meeting with the pretty regulator would not be hard to handle. "Sure, be glad to. If you would like, and you wouldn't find it too much of a good thing, so to speak, perhaps we could meet here again tomorrow evening. Say around 7:00 p.m. if that would work for you."

"Sounds great, their food's wonderful here. It's a date, 7:00 p.m. it is!" Cass caught herself blushing just a little. What she had just blurted out was totally unintentional. She hadn't had what one might call a real date in years. This Logan Hart was admittedly the kind of attractive man she actually wouldn't mind having a real date with if the situation was right, but there was a real business purpose in her need for a second meeting. She hoped he would take no offense with what she had next to say. "Oh, and I hope you won't find it too imposing, but Special Agent Jim Seilor of the FBI and I were talking some late this morning about the possibility of my perhaps needing to meet with you a second time, and he's asked if he couldn't join us were we to decide to get together again. Hope that will be okay with you."

Logan hoped his disappointment at hearing they were going to be joined by Agent Seilor didn't show too much. *There goes an opportunity out the window*, he thought. "Sure, no problem, more the merrier! With that, however, guess I better scoot if I'm going to be able to put that quick meeting of staff together for you yet this afternoon. So, I'll see you again this afternoon at 3:30, and both you and Seilor here at RoSario's again tomorrow evening at 7:00."

"Thank you, Logan, I really appreciate all of your cooperation. See you with whatever staff you can put together at 3:30 this afternoon."

CHAPTER THIRTEEN

SINCE ITS founding in 1879, the venerable Federation Club
of Chicago has been synonymous with power and prestige.
Considered one of the leading private clubs in the city, it has
always been one of the key places movers and shakers of
that community go to get things done, brokering the power
and prestige each brings to the table from their respective
spheres of influence. Even when a person has no more
important objective than simply to fill his or her belly, it is still
considered by many a good place to be seen.

Both Tariq Nasir and Scott Kruse were members.
Nasir's father-in-law, Lawrence Hardesty, had proposed him
for membership shortly after he joined Hardesty's
development firm back in 1992, and Nasir had used the club
as a preferred place to do business ever since. Nasir then
also introduced Scott for membership when he joined the
bank, with Global United picking up his membership as a
perquisite. Whenever Nasir was in town, the two would meet
there over lunch at least once a week.

The Federation Club prides itself in its recognition of
members, pampering them with staff specifically trained to
recognize them by name whenever possible and to cater to
their every need. Nasir was a big tipper. So, he was treated
like royalty. A regular table was reserved for him on a daily
basis in the oak trimmed main dining room on the sixth floor.
On days when the table wasn't used, the club by
arrangement would still bill Nasir for two of the club's

specials of the day, along with a twenty percent gratuity for whichever waiter was assigned to the table that day, as a way to ensure that the table would always be there for him. Today, however, his regular table would not be used. Nasir's secretary had called to make more private arrangements. Lunch for two would instead be served in one of the small private dining rooms on the eighth floor; and by special request, an Iraqi born waiter, who had Nasir to thank for his job, would serve them.

"Well, Scott, what worries seem to be plaguing you this week?" Nasir studied the visibly nervous Scott Kruse. "I've heard nothing negative from anyone I've run into from the bank as of late, and I thought the bank's regulatory examination was going reasonably well. So, tell me you're a harbinger of good news, and not bad, my friend."

Scott studied the busy waiter, and signaling an apology to his host, delayed answering Nasir until after the waiter had completed serving the sumptuous Federation chicken Caesar salads both men had ordered and departed the room. "Well, Tariq, if you'd have asked me that a few days ago, it would have been nothing but good news for me to report right now, but that was before the happenings of last Friday evening. As I stated in my phone message to you of earlier today, all heck did for sure break loose when someone murdered that OCC examiner. He wasn't just your average regulator. He was a very powerful, well-known OCC official, who was 'out with the troops' one last time before he was to retire, or some such silly thing. Whatever the case, it is our great misfortune that he was in our bank at the time that someone chose to rub him out."

"Look, I don't want to sound unsympathetic, but what on earth does this man's murder at the hands of some mugger, as tragic as it may be, have to do with either Global United or me? The two situations are totally unrelated. Aren't they? I wouldn't think that incident should have anything to do with the progress or outcome of the bank's examination

142

by the OCC."

"I know that, and you know that, Tariq, but try to convince the OCC and the FBI that it doesn't—at least until they prove otherwise. It's their very nature to be suspicious. When the OCC lost a powerful, well-loved member of its organization, murdered on his way home the very night he was supposed to be feted at a party in honor of his retirement, it sent them all into a total tizzy. They were back into the bank this morning with a vengeance. There is no doubt they're going to be all over us now; and what has me particularly worried is that one of the key items Trotter wanted to visit with us this morning, had he still been there, had to do with the bank's relationship with you and your companies as an insider. I fear they may be really inclined to double-down on anything like that now. We may have to jump through our wazoos to prove nothing he might have been working on at Global United has anything to do with his death."

"Look, Scott, our trust surely hasn't been misplaced by having selected you as CEO of Global United, has it?" Nasir had a piercing, furrowed eyebrow-type stare whenever he was trying to size up a person or situation that was intimidating to many people, Scott Kruse in particular. "There is absolutely no way any of my relationships with the bank should come into question; and we pay you a great deal of money to take care of situations such as this. You were chosen for your current position over a multitude of other qualified banking executives, in great part because you claimed to be experienced in the handling of such matters. You act as if you think they will find something. I could take offense at that."

In truth, Nasir's conclusion that Scott was someone who could be controlled and manipulated had actually weighed far more into his getting the job as CEO of Global United than any influence Scott might or might not have with bank regulators. Scott looked as though Nasir had just kicked him in the gut.

"Oh, no, Tariq, I didn't mean anything like that," Scott stammered. "I just meant that until the OCC examiners prove to themselves that this Mr. Trotter's work at Global United had nothing to do with his death, they're going to be a real headache to contend with in my opinion, and just when we thought we were about done with them."

"Look, Global United is running quite nicely these days, and I have nothing about which I am worried regarding the relationship of me or my various companies with the bank, Scott. So, quit worrying. All that can serve to do is make matters worse. Everything regarding either my personal or corporate business with the bank is in order. Isn't it?"

"Yes, by all means, that's absolutely correct!"

"I would hope so! At all times, I have insisted both verbally and in writing that sufficient upstream loan participation agreements be arranged so that my companies can avoid any possibility of regulatory overline situations, and you have always assured me that has been the case. If you will recollect, it was at my behest, that the bank's Controller, Patricia McGill, developed the automated insider relationship worksheet that is used daily, to my understanding, to calculate the total loan exposure to any insider, like me and my companies, and ensure that all loans outstanding to those companies remain in compliance with regulatory lending limits. We have reviewed those at our board loan committee meetings on a monthly basis as they relate to my companies and me. Those reports to us have been accurate, have they not?"

"Oh, absolutely Tariq, they have been.

"Well, I fail then to see where I and my AmeriPAK companies might have a problem."

"Yeah, well you're right with respect to our loan arrangements for you and AmeriPAK, but as I indicated when I called you last Friday afternoon, Mr. Trotter wasn't just looking at lending limits. He was also poring over all of your companies' deposit accounts, looking at our cash transaction reporting mechanisms and testing how well we have complied with regulations having to do with such things as the Bank Secrecy Act and the USA Patriot or Freedom Act, all of which have for years now been perpetual hot buttons with the examiners." Scott thought he noticed a flicker of concern cross Nasir's always very composed face at his reminding him of that information. "Please, I mean no offense, Tariq, but as you are well aware, many of your companies are involved in international trade, and much of that is over in Asia or the Middle East. On a regular basis, certain of your companies both send and receive numerous, large international transfers and a great deal of the time most of them handle goodly amounts of cash. Add all of that to your insider status, and you, AmeriPAK and Global United become immediate targets for closer scrutiny as it relates to both loan and deposit account activity, whether we like it or not."

"Well, at the risk of repeating myself, Scott, that's where I expect you to ensure that we never stub our toes on matters such as that." Nasir's increasing consternation showed in his voice. "It's up to you and your staff to keep us on the straight and narrow when it comes to the business that we do through the bank and any related regulatory compliance. That sort of thing has always been of major concern to me. Look into this immediately, and keep me informed with respect to how, where and when we may have gone awry, if indeed we have. Am I clear in that regard?"

"Yes, you can count on me to do that, Tariq. It's just that I get the feeling these regulators are laboring under some ill-conceived suspicion that there's a connection between this Mr. Trotter's murder and his involvement at our bank, and I think that may be coloring their approach to some of these other issues. I just thought we should meet and give you a heads-up on just how intrusive they are going

145

forward."

"And I appreciate that Scott, but it is imperative you take this all in stride. Accept my assurance that your regulators will find nothing irregular in their investigation of my accounts whether personal or business, or any transactions domestic or international. I still don't suppose, however, that it would hurt for you to keep me informed." Nasir reached into his pocket, pulled out a small generic-looking smart phone, and slid it across the table to Scott. "Look, let's make sure we have no problems. Here is a new prepaid cell phone that was purchased this morning by one of my people. Destroy the one that I previously gave you, and use this one exclusively in the future whenever you wish to call me about anything outside of normal bank business. Keep me informed as this special investigation progresses, but discuss nothing you feel is sensitive in any way with me by any other method than this cell phone. If the regulators find anything unexpected, let me know right away. Try also to include me where you can in any future meetings where the examiners look as though they are really going to take the bank to task on some sensitive issue. Tell them that you want to include some representatives of the board in the discussions to keep us informed. Don't make it obvious, but involve me where you can. Perhaps you could insist that the Audit and Compliance committee, which I chair, be involved. Whatever the case, Scott, I want to be kept informed as to what is going on with any of this we've been discussing. I want no surprises."

◊◊◊◊

ACROSS TOWN at the same time that Scott Kruse and Tariq Nasir were having their discussion at the Federation Club, a somewhat related gathering was taking place. Melissa Hardesty-Nasir, Tariq's wife, and her sisters, Margaret and Maureen Hardesty, usually tried to meet for lunch at least once a month, but it had been more than ninety days since they had last gotten together. "This is simply unacceptable," Melissa's phone message of the day before had said to both of her sisters. "Here we are. All three of us living in the same city, and we can't see each other at least once a month for lunch. That's nuts! I'll accept no excuses this time. I want to see you two. I've reserved our usual table at The Sandhill Crane on North Michigan tomorrow at noon, and I really need for you both to be there in the worst way. Look, I miss you guys! So, I'm turning off our answering machine until after we see each other tomorrow. That way, neither of you will be able to leave me some lame excuse about how you can't make it. I'll be waiting on you both, so please be there."

The Hardesty sisters had always been close. There was exactly three years difference in age between each of the three girls, and while growing up, what one did, the others were never far behind. Melissa Hardesty-Nasir had always been the more aggressive one of the three. Valedictorian of her class at Our Lady of the Angels Catholic girls school in an Irish neighborhood on Chicago's northwest side—where she and both her sisters graduated— she attended Notre Dame University to get her pre-law undergraduate degree, and then went on to graduate magna cum laude from Harvard University's School of Law. Her family was convinced she had everything going for her, but that had been thrown into doubt in the eyes of at least her sisters when she met and fell in love with the guy her youngest sister, Maureen, had always privately referred to as the "brother-in-law from Hades," Tariq Nasir.

Melissa was aggressively recruited and hired by a prestigious, downtown Chicago law firm almost immediately after she graduated from Harvard. To the disappointment of nearly everyone in her family, however, particularly her sisters, she only worked there for six months after joining the firm. That was when she married Tariq Nasir, the supposed "love of her life" who had attended Harvard with her, and who

147

was soon moving to Chicago to start a new position in investment banking.

Nasir was not at all interested in having Melissa pursue her career after they married. He wanted to start a family immediately, but it took Melissa several years to become pregnant with their first boy, Faoud. She had always figured she could handle both a career and family, but Nasir would have none of that after the birth of Faoud, and to that end somehow managed to persuade her to become a full-time, strictly stay-at-home mother. Melissa's response to anyone who questioned her decision in that regard was to quickly inform them that being a wife to Tariq and mother to any children they might have would be sufficiently fulfilling until those children were old enough for her to return to the practice of law. To a great degree, she was relatively successful in convincing both herself and everyone else that would be the case—everyone that was except her sisters.

Neither Margaret nor Maureen Hardesty had cared much for Tariq Nasir from the start. First of all, there were the religious differences. The Hardesty family were all devout Catholics, and Tariq and his family were even more devout Muslims, who in spite of their outward western appearance, still clung very clearly to many traditions of South Asia and the Middle East.

To be sure, Nasir was strikingly handsome and intellectually almost overpowering. At six foot three, and bearing a strong resemblance to an Omar Sharif in his younger days, it was easy for the Hardesty girls to see the physical attraction that their sister, Melissa, might have for the man, but for at least Margaret and Maureen that was where attractions stopped. For some inexplicable reason, neither of the two trusted him. Nasir initially worked so hard at being nice to everyone in the family that it made both of the sisters uncomfortable. The way he fawned over Melissa's parents appeared to the sisters, for all his effort, to be both disingenuous and patronizing. Margaret and Maureen questioned their sister's decision to marry Nasir only once, and her reaction dissuaded them from ever trying again. They knew from the tone in her voice how futile it would be to do so, and they loved her way too much to let the matter cause any irreconcilable difference between them. Like their parents, the sisters would do their best to embrace their new brother-in-law.

Melissa Hardesty's twenty-eight-year marriage to Nasir had produced two handsome, dark-eyed boys, Faoud and Hassan, who were now in their late teens, and the apples of their aunt's eyes. Their nephews were the one result of their sister's union with Nasir about which Margaret and Maureen Hardesty could absolutely find no fault. Both sisters doted on the boys, and to the extent they were allowed, did everything in their power to prove that fact by lavishing every kind of attention on them whenever the opportunity arose. When the three sisters got together, the first half hour was always spent catching up on how the boys were doing. As Margaret often commented to her sister, Maureen, "No child can choose his or her parents, and these beautiful boys are a perfect example of that fact. I plan to spoil them in any way I can."

"Lissa, thank you so much for calling us," Margaret Hardesty whispered, as she and Maureen embraced Melissa before being shown to their table at The Sandhill Crane restaurant, a venerable Chicago eating establishment on the near north side of the city. The Hardesty sisters had been lunching there nearly every month for the last twenty years. The folks at The Sandhill Crane knew them well enough that they were almost always seated at the same table, table number eleven if it was available. This was one of those times.

Melissa had arrived at the restaurant a full half hour before her sisters and was there to greet them upon their arrival. That in and of itself concerned both of the sisters. Melissa was usually always the last one to arrive. They could tell that something was awry.

"You look beautiful as always, babe, and it's great to see you, but if you don't mind me saying so your message yesterday bothered me a little." Sister Margaret had never been known for being very diplomatic. After twenty years as a nun, she was the personification of directness. She could tell something was wrong with her sister, and she had every intention of finding out what it was before this luncheon was over. "You sounded rather vexed. Can't be anything to do with the boys, they're always such sweethearts. What's the matter, things not so rosy these days with your rich, Arab knight?"

"Oh, come on, Margie, Tariq provides me with everything I need. The boys are doing fine, and I am doing fine. I just needed to see you both." Melissa looked across the room and fidgeted with her napkin as she answered her sister. Not being able to look someone in the eye when she was struggling with the truth was a habit of Melissa's that was always a dead giveaway to her sisters. "And he's not an Arab, he's of Pakistani origin," she muttered with downcast eyes, "but then you both know that.

"Oh, sure, Lissa, every thing's just hunky-dory with you, isn't it?" Maureen joined her sister, the nun, in grilling Melissa. "You've always been a poor liar. It's good your legal specialty is corporate law. You'd sure as hell be a horrible courtroom attorney. Your face telegraphs everything that's on your mind."

"Easy, Maureen!" Sister Margaret had an aversion to even the hint of profanity, and that was always a problem with her sister, Maureen.

"Well, I'm sorry, that's the way I feel, Margaret. But no kidding, Lissa, we're your sisters here now. What's cooking? Things not so good with Tariq?"

"Oh, what am I thinking? I never could lie to you or the folks very well. I know that." Melissa sighed, and with teary eyes, looked again at her lap as she took a sip of the glass

150

of wine she had ordered while waiting for her sisters to arrive. Her devout Muslim husband allowed no alcoholic beverages around the home. So, she usually treated herself to a glass or two of wine when the sisters got together. "No, things aren't all that good at home. As you both know, the first few years of my marriage to Tariq were wonderful. We had our differences of course, not the least of which was my refusal to convert to Islam, but he knew that would be the case when we married. He was gracious about it at first, but after the boys were born that difference has gradually become a deeper and wider chasm between us. He provides extremely well for me and the boys, but for some years now, we have really been husband and wife in name only."

"Oh, sweetheart, we've all surmised that for some time now." Sister Margaret answered. "I hope you won't get angry with Maureen and me when we say to you that it was always our fear that things might turn out this way. Tariq's effort to be a good brother or son-in-law were always a little too over the top during the first years of your marriage. It never ever seemed real. You could tell even then that what really mattered most to him was the almighty dollar, and how many of them he could make. To be sure, the change in his personality certainly accelerated when the boys were born, but I really think we all began to see the kind of person he truly is when dad died in that accident years ago. That's when we began to see the real Tariq Nasir."

"I know you're right about how things were when Tariq and I first got together, Margaret. I suppose I should have listened to you both before he and I got together, but you know how young people are. I was so very much in love at the time. I suppose my judgment was really not the best in those days."

"You can say that again, kiddo." Maureen chided. "You really bit both of our heads off when we questioned what you were doing before you got married."

"I realize that, but like I said, you know how young

151

people are when they think they're in love." Melissa dabbed at her eyes with her napkin as she continued. "But you both are wrong about when the real Tariq Nasir began to come out. Certainly, the loving husband thing was history years ago, but since the events of September 2001 and this whole Islamic thing became such a hotly debated issue, he has become someone even I can hardly recognize anymore."

"What do you mean, Lissa?" Maureen asked incredulously. "We know that Tariq has family in Pakistan and that he's Muslim, but you're not somehow implying that he had anything to do with that horrible situation, are you?"

"Oh, heavens, no! Where did you get that? That's not what I mean at all." Melissa retorted. "Why, he more than ever now goes out of his way in every respect to prove he's a loyal American. He's paranoid that anyone would think otherwise. He is becoming an increasingly magnanimous benefactor of charities; he purposely involves himself wherever he can in community matters; and he gives generously to political candidates of any persuasion where that generosity can gain or maintain influence and depict him as being patriotic. It's just that it seems like he now leads two lives."

"How do you mean, sweetheart? What do you mean two lives?" Sister Margaret asked.

"Well, for the better part he immerses himself more than ever in his various businesses, but that isn't something admittedly all that strange for him. He's always claimed he was 'building an empire'. The big difference now is that he seems to have found this higher level of renewed devotion to Islam. Where he used to rarely attend Friday services at his mosque, he now does so weekly without fail. Why, he's even built this sort of mini-mosque in his office building. He and his Islamic employees pray there throughout the day. Although one would think he could hardly have the time, he now almost always prays five times daily, and he studies the Qur'an with regularity."

"Well, hasn't he always been somewhat that way?"

"No, not really. During the first part of our marriage, in spite of his upbringing, he never seemed to be that committed to his faith or seemingly that connected to his family back in Pakistan. He's always been close to his father in the past, usually calling him about once a week prior to '9/11', but since then he now communicates with his father almost daily, via telephone, fax and e-mail. Oh, and I dare not say anything that could be construed as besmirching his faith in any way. It sends him into unbelievable fits of rage."

"Well, I suppose some of those things are understandable, considering all that's happening in the world these days, including Tariq's home country of Pakistan.

"How do you mean?" Melissa asked.

"Well, you name it and Pakistan has it, earthquakes, their economy, all the political upheaval. You know, all that terrorist stuff up in the north part of their country, the Taliban, suicide bombings and all. Then we muddy the waters with things like drone strikes and actions like the raid to take out bin Laden several years back. They were none too happy with us for that one." Sister Margaret responded. "And then there are all the headaches across the Middle East and North Africa and such. You name it, Libya, Iran, Egypt, Somalia, and now all this folderol again in Iraq and Syria with that ISIS outfit of terrorists. They're a bunch of crazies! You can't listen to the news anymore without hearing about any one of those things and more. Most of Tariq's family is still over there. It's his homeland, for heaven's sake. All of this, rightly or wrongly, makes for a goodly amount of distrust of Muslims in this and other countries around the world these days, and that has to worry Tariq a great deal, considering the financial and social aspirations he has never tried much to hide."

"Serves the son-of-a bitch right!" Maureen hissed.

"Come on, Maureen, please, let's watch our language," admonished Sister Margaret. "I'm no great fan of

Tariq's either, but Lissa here is still married to the man, and we do have the boys to think about."

"I know, I know," said Maureen. Obviously frustrated, she had never been one to hide her feelings. "But the way Tariq has treated Lissa all of these years has always galled me to no end. Romances her until she marries him and he becomes a U.S. citizen, and then kisses up to Mom, Dad and the rest of us until Dad takes him into his business and eventually turns it over to him. It's a little hard to watch the way I talk."

Melissa made no effort to respond to Maureen's caustic commentary, choosing instead to stare tearfully into a cup of tea that had just been set before her, no longer as hot as she usually insisted it be.

"Well, look, let's calm down some and forget about Tariq for now. Things are what they are." Sister Margaret said, placing her finger to her lips and speaking softly in an attempt to quiet things down a bit. "We're here to enjoy each other and be of support to you, Lissa. Maureen and I will always be there for you and the boys if you need us. You'll never be alone, no matter how bad things may seem in your marriage. You know that."

Melissa nodded and smiled weakly while the three women held each other's hands. "Now," said Sister Margaret, "let's get a waiter over here and order. Shall we?"

CHAPTER FOURTEEN

"MR. HART, Mr. Al-Dajani, thank you for agreeing to meet yet again this afternoon. We appreciate everyone here for taking time out of your busy schedules to visit with us further today about Global United's overall program for managing its compliance with the Bank Secrecy Act, Anti-Money Laundering requirements, and Office of Foreign Assets Control laws and regulations." Cass Price glanced around a room full of what she knew all too well had to be very unhappy bank officers as she started the OCC's meeting with Global United's bank operations division. Attending were representatives from nearly every area within that part of the bank. Prior to the meeting, Logan Hart had informed Cass that everyone in attendance well knew that contrary to what they previously expected, the wrap-up session the group had been told would happen that day would not take place. They had been told the examination would instead continue for an undetermined additional amount of time, with the bank being subjected to an even more thorough second review of many areas of bank operations. A principal concern would be the bank's BSA/AML programs.

 "To begin," continued Cass, "I've been told that most all of you have been informed we will be taking 'another kick at the dog' so to speak in our review of many areas of bank operations, in particular, the ones I've just mentioned. I'm certain it has to be frustrating for you folks to have gone through this all once before with Mr. Trotter and our crew, only to have to do a great deal of it again with us, because of what happened to Paul." There was a pause as Cass struggled to maintain a business-like composure. She was still struggling with the tragic loss of her friend and mentor. "As I explained to Mr. Hart when I asked for this meeting, the results of Mr. Trotter's review of the bank's BSA and AML programs were apparently on the hard drive of his laptop together with a great deal of information from other areas that he reviewed when he was here. Unfortunately, his laptop and those papers were stolen when the horrible incident occurred last Friday where he lost his life.

"Excuse me, Ms. Price, I apologize for interrupting, but might I ask a question that I know is on everyone's mind here?" asked Sammy al-Dajani. "Wouldn't any of the other examiners on your team have had copies of the information Mr. Trotter was working on, either hard copy or on computer?"

"Normally, that would be the case, Mr. al-Dajani. Our procedures call for all our examiners to back up such information online to our servers at regular intervals throughout the day when we are working in any bank, but for whatever reason, Mr. Trotter had not done that with this and other specific information for several days prior to his death. That was most unacceptable, and contrary to numerous OCC policies for him to have done that, but as is sometimes the case with certain of his generation, Paul was a little less computer literate than most of our younger staff. So, he didn't pay as close attention to some of our IT procedures as he perhaps should have. So, here we are, needing to go over much of this once again. All of our staff has learned a lesson from the experience, and of course, Paul isn't here to grouse at about it, but that doesn't eliminate the situation. We're going to have to go through some of these things again." Cass could see her explanation was eliciting very little sympathy from the bank staff, and she guessed she couldn't really blame them in that regard. She knew her team of examiners would encounter this reaction in every area of the bank where the OCC needed to take a second look at any work previously done, but she and they all still had a job to do.

"Please, don't misunderstand my asking that question, Ms. Price. I think we all were simply wondering why we had to retrace our steps. We understand, and appreciate your telling us why." Sammy was doing his best to take the edge off the situation and yet sound supportive of his staff, and it seemed to work as several of his subordinates around the room nodded in agreement. "I think I speak for all of us here in bank operations in telling you how disturbed we are at the tragic loss of Mr. Trotter. We understand your need to look a second time into anything he may have been working on while he was here. If you will tell us what questions you have or what information you need and don't already have, we'll do our very best to forthwith supply you with the answers."

"Thank you, Mr. al-Dajani, we appreciate that. It'll make this difficult task much easier." While Cass spoke, one of the examiners stood up and began passing out a document to each of the staff members present at the meeting. "Latisha Caldwell, who will manage our examination team here going forward, is passing around a list of most of the information we think we'll need to conduct our re-review of the bank's compliance with BSA and its related report activity. Much of this information you will probably see is a repeat of what was included in the pre-examination packet that you would have been provided at the start of our earlier examination, but with this new request, we are in many cases asking for expanded information. Hopefully, this will not be too difficult to pull together."

Everyone tried not to show it, but the whole process of this re-examination of the bank's operations was a source of irritation. Bank examiners had been climbing all over Global United now for more than five weeks, and most of the bank's staff thought the examination was essentially complete. As one uncaring staff member rather crassly summed it up for a few confidants, "It looked like the OCC was about to leave, and then that old examiner gets bumped off by some drugged out street person, and here we go again!" Whether or not they were right, many members of bank staff had it figured that Trotter's death had nothing to do with his examination of Global United, but that mattered very little. Until someone convinced the regulators of that, it appeared the bank was destined to have the OCC in their shop for a great while longer.

For a number of years now, the Currency and Foreign Transactions Act, or Bank Secrecy Act as bankers more commonly know it, had been the method by which the U.S. government has attempted to monitor such activities as drug trafficking, money laundering, and terrorist funding. In November 2001, shortly after 9/11, these regulatory controls were even further strengthened by the passage of the U.S.A. Patriot Act. Though on each occasion the subject of much political debate, that act had been renewed or extended several times, the last being in June 2015—this time, however, known by its new moniker, the USA Freedom Act. Since then, and particularly in just the last few months because of increased tensions around the world, scrutiny of compliance with both regulations had been a hot button for all bank regulators, in particular, the OCC. When it was, therefore, determined these were the areas being examined by their associate, Paul Trotter, just before his death, they became a top priority to the OCC with respect to their extended examination of Global United.

Sammy al-Dajani and the group of managers he had assembled for this meeting quickly glanced over the list of information the OCC said it needed. Except for some requested updates and minor additional materials, they appeared essentially to be the same as those requested at the original start of the OCC's examination. It was standard operating procedure for the bank to keep a second copy of all information it provided regulators throughout their examination. This was one time when that practice could prove to be a godsend. *Maybe this won't be all that bad*, Sammy thought as he and everyone at the meeting perused the list. *I may have most of this in my office right now.*

"As you can see," Cass explained, "we'd once again like to have a complete copy of the bank's policies covering its efforts to comply with the Bank Secrecy and U.S.A. Patriot or Freedom Acts, along with all materials proving up its adherence to those policies. What you would have given us before we believe was part of the material stolen when Mr. Trotter was attacked. To make things hopefully easier for you, we are asking for basically the same reports that were used in the last go-around, which was printed with an as of date of September 30. Understanding that you keep records of all such things on your computer system, we will want you to once again provide all records relating to any sales of monetary instruments or deposits made by non-exempted businesses and individuals during the past year, the source of which is cash in amounts between $3,000 and $10,000 inclusively. We will also want similar information covering the same period on all transfers of funds over $3,000, where the bank acted as the originator, recipient or intermediary for the transfer. We currently only want to review the aforementioned information for the past year, but depending on what we find in that regard, we may ask to go farther back, since you are required to maintain at least five years' worth of records on this information."

"What about the actual Currency Transaction and Suspicious Activity Reports, we have on file, Ms. Price?" asked Rosemary Schindler, head of Retail Banking. Her expression typified those of other staff present who seemed rather put out at having to redo work previously submitted. "How far back will you want to go with that?"

"Please, everyone call me Cass if you wish. I really stand little on formality." Cass was doing her best not to appear too officious, but she could tell from the frustration registering on the faces of many of the Global United people that her efforts were having little effect. "In answer to your question, if you will note from the printed information given to each of you here today, as with the transactions using cash we ask for all historical information going back one year to begin with, but we reserve the right to have you go back further if needed. To that end, we will want to see all records or documentation, whether written or digital, of the following: Suspicious Activity Reports or SAR's - Form 111s; Currency Transaction Reports - CTR Form 112s; Foreign Bank Account Reports - FBAR Form 114s; Foreign Transaction Reports - Form 105s. Oh, and in particular, we want to review all Form 110's for each of your accounts you've Exempted from Reporting that were filed with FinCEN. Inasmuch as it is our understanding that you keep such records electronically, we will be more than happy to accept all the information I've just indicated in that fashion. Getting it that way would more than likely save us a great deal of time. If we see something in reviewing that information which is of sufficient interest to us to make us want to do so, we may then decide to go further back in time."

The Financial Crimes Enforcement Network—or FinCEN as it was more commonly known in government, regulatory and financial circles—was a unit of the U.S. Department of the Treasury, set up by the government to link the law enforcement, regulatory and financial communities, to aggregate, analyze and share all such information in an effort to detect and prevent financial crime.

"We just updated our list of companies, individuals, and organizations we currently exempt from reporting at the end of last week," Sammy added. "So, it may differ from the one we provided Mr. Trotter. Since you've asked for that on your checklist, which one do you want to see, the one we provided Mr. Trotter or our new list?"

"If you have an updated list, why don't you provide us

with both the old and revised lists? We'd like to see what changes they made and know why they were made." Cass noticed Sammy grimace slightly. That didn't appear to be the answer he was perhaps hoping for. "But we're getting ahead of ourselves a bit here," she continued. "Let's once again go down this list of information needed if we could, and then I'll answer any questions you have. To summarize, what we really want to accomplish with this review is to determine how Global United's supervision of BSA compliance is organized, and how well it is managed as a result. We will want basically to look at all of your anti-money laundering policies, procedures, and systems. Who's responsible for what, and who reports to whom relative to those compliance programs, and we'll want to know that information as it relates to all products and departments of the bank. We need to develop a thorough understanding of the bank's system of internal controls, and what kind of independent testing you do of those controls if any. For example, when it comes to Cash Transaction or Suspicious Activity Report monitoring and submission, we must know which parts of your system in that regard are manual, and which parts are automated. We also want to assess the bank's volume of transactions by product, and will want to know all of this information for every location and market that the bank is in."

"Every location and market?" Sammy looked surprised. "I don't, uh, believe that Mr. Trotter asked for all of that."

"Oh? I would hope he would have, but whether he did or did not, I certainly will want to see that information before we're done here. I'm told that Global United has three offices here in Chicago, nine offices in other major cities across the U.S., and has, I believe, over the last few years added offices in fourteen foreign countries. So, the program you've established should take all of that into consideration as it comes to collecting information. Before this is done, we will want also to review transactional samplings for accounts in your private, trust and international banking areas, and look at transactions handled for nonresident aliens, international bordered deposits, and foreign correspondent accounts, particularly if such activities occurred in countries on our high-risk country list. That list is provided in your packet for reference. Any accounts with significant international cash or wire activity are of interest to us; and if you have any relationships with any Money Service Businesses or Private Investment Companies, we will want to know that. If your program is as it should be, you ought to be able to provide all of this information for every location. That isn't going to be a problem is it?"

"No, no, most everything you've mentioned is automated within our system, and we have, uh, regular downloads of information such as that which you're asking for here from all of our offices," Sammy answered while feverishly taking notes. "We keep copious records along these lines and should be able to have most all of this for you right away. It's just that you appear to be taking things a little further than Mr. Trotter did last time around."

"Look, if any of you have any questions about what we are asking for here, I and my examining team will try to answer them for you now. Once we've completed that, all we OCC folks here will leave the room, and then your team can continue the meeting to determine who needs to do what to get this information for us. We would like to obtain as much of this material as you may already have available, just as soon as you can get it to us. Any other information you don't have right now, you can give to us as you manage to pull it together. We want to get started with our review just as soon as possible. The sooner we can get the information we want from you all, the sooner we can wrap things up and get out of your hair here at Global United."

"Ms. Price, for your information, I informed our CEO, Scott Kruse, that we were having this meeting, and he asked that I express to you his regrets at not being able to be here.

He said that he unfortunately had a number of conflicts that prevented his attendance. In his absence, he's asked that I please assure you for him that senior management realizes how important your work here at Global United is considering all that has happened over the last few days. He further wanted me to assure you that every officer of the bank and any resource available to us will be at your disposal to see that everything about your extended examination here goes smoothly." Logan Hart had been a quiet observer until now, but he had been asked to express management's commitment of cooperation, and this seemed like the opportune time to do so.

"We appreciate that, and please pass that along to Mr. Kruse, if you would, Mr. Hart."

"I'll do that."

◊◊◊◊

SAMMY WASTED little time getting back to his office after the meeting. The examiner's list of things needed for their new review of the bank's handling of BSA and other anti-money laundering requirements for the bank was daunting, and there was much to do if he was to meet management's expectation of a timely response and still accomplish some much needed surreptitious editing of the information requested.

Much of what the examiners had requested from the bank would be easy for Sammy to provide. Global United had fairly specific policies and procedures related to BSA and CTR reporting, and each bank location kept detailed records regarding all transactions involving cash, or transfers of funds sufficient in type and amount to require that it be reported to FinCEN.

Unless it was originated by a company or individual appearing on a list kept by the bank that exempted them from that requirement, any deposit, withdrawal, exchange of currency or other payment or transfer processed through the bank that involved currency in excess of $10,000, had to be reported to FinCEN regularly with a Currency Transaction Report, Form 112. Global United, submitted these reports on a weekly basis to FinCEN using that agency's online, e-File electronic submission system.

Every branch location within the Global United network processed all daily transactions handled by that office in a real-time, online basis, communicating directly with the bank's central server. Any transaction that had the potential of precipitating a required report to FinCEN was recognized by codes specifically designed for that purpose and submitted on a daily basis to the bank's Chicago headquarters via either the Internet or the bank's inter-office network. Digital copies of the forms submitted were kept at branch level as backup until a predetermined suspense date. Following parameters outlined by bank policy, once all necessary branch reports reached Chicago the information was scrutinized one last time by designated personnel, sometimes Sammy himself, and then transmitted online to FinCEN as required.

Subsequent to having originally provided Paul Trotter with all the information previously requested regarding Global United's BSA and AML programs, Sammy began to worry that some of the methodology used to compile the bank's list of accounts exempt from regular required CTR reporting might come into question—primarily those related to Tariq Nair's AmeriPAK group of companies. So, he had after the fact changed the old list, returning the AmeriPAK-related accounts to non-exempt status. It was his thinking if these accounts could skate by without being criticized in the earlier examination, then it perhaps it would be better were transactions from those accounts treated as non-exempt in all future reporting. He was now, however, second guessing having made such a move. To be criticized for the mistake of exempting the AmeriPAK accounts from reporting in the first place was one thing, but to admit you perhaps knew better by now making them non-exempt was a totally separate matter. The original position was the lesser of two evils.

CHAPTER FIFTEEN

"MR. NASIR, this is Saud al-Dajani once again. Please forgive my many calls. I regret bothering you, but you had requested that I keep you informed about the regulators' ongoing examination activities here in the bank, and I have just exited a meeting with the OCC where they have once again requested certain information that I thought you might want to know about before it was provided to them."

Sammy had Tariq Nasir to thank for the position he held with Global United, and his career advances to date. In return, he was one of Nasir's most dependable sources of inside, confidential information, keeping him aware of as much as he could without damaging the chairman's carefully crafted image of being removed from day -to-day management. Sammy knew that Nasir had several others like him salted throughout the Global United organization, but he was unaware of who those other people might be.

"No, Mr. al-Dajani, no need for apologies. I appreciate your keeping me informed. What do you have for me?" Nasir always portrayed an air of unflappability in such situations, but Sammy felt this was one instance where Nasir might be well advised were he to act just a little more concerned.

"Well, it looks like the OCC's planning to take a new, and perhaps even more thorough look this time into our reporting of large cash transactions, international transfers and such-the-like; and I have to say I'm a little more worried this time about that, sir."

"I have also been informed of what you say from other sources within the bank," said Nasir, "but go ahead. I would nevertheless appreciate your take on the situation too."

"Well, as you know, that Mr. Trotter who was murdered last week spent a goodly amount of time looking over much of our BSA information here at the bank before he was killed. He appeared to be particularly interested in our list of companies and individuals exempt from regular reporting, dwelling in particular on the fact that a number of your companies were on that list. If you will recollect, Mr. Nasir, I called to let you know about that when he began to grill me along those lines. I told him I knew little about your companies other than that they regularly used a lot of cash, but I don't believe that much satisfied him. He was still investigating that situation when he was killed."

"Now see here, Mr. al-Dajani, don't get too riled up. You were able to handle everything that their Mr. Trotter was throwing at you before. So, I have every confidence you'll be able to do the same with these other people."

"I wish I could be as confident as you are about that, sir. He really hadn't gotten back to me yet with many of his concerns and observations on the matter before he was killed. So, I'm really not all that sure what questions or criticisms he may have been planning to raise before he left for that fateful weekend. Now that the OCC is looking into the matter even more thoroughly, I have even heightened concern as to what they may come up with in their investigation of those areas of our operations. The regulators can get pretty prickly these days when they're looking into just about anything related to BSA and other areas of related compliance."

"Well, all I can suggest is that you stand your ground on this matter, Mr. al-Dajani. You're right on the money—no pun intended. Most of my companies do indeed utilize substantial amounts of cash as an integral part of their operations and on a regular basis. So, in my opinion, they quite rightfully should appear on your list of exempt businesses. My people and I are prepared to respond to any inquiry. Call on us if you need."

"Well, with regrets in advance, I may have to do just that, sir. I rather have the feeling they may think I... er we, were perhaps overreaching some in our exempting a couple of your companies from regular reporting."

Well, I'm not all that sure I would agree with you on that, but let's just wait and see. If they start to push on the matter, let me know. As I just said, my AmeriPAK people and I will be more than pleased to get involved."

"Thank you, sir! I appreciate that. I may need to call on you for assistance before this is all over. I hope you don't mind me bothering you so much on this, but it has me nervous right now."

"No, no, you were quite right to call. This is exactly what I want you to do. Just as with the first BSA go-around under that Mr. Trotter, I do want to be kept informed of any future concerns they may have in that regard. A few of my companies have some very important transactions pending, and I want no surprises that might cause any interruption of that business as a result of some unwarranted investigation."

"I shall, Mr. Nasir. I appreciate all that you have done for me. I will keep you informed regarding any part of the examination in which I am involved."

"That's great. I thank you for that. Oh, and by the way, you are talking to me right now on the cell phone that I provided to you sometime back, aren't you?"

"Yes, sir, I am."

"Good! I would prefer you use the prepaid phones I'll provide you from time-to-time over any landlines or even your personal cell phone when you feel the need to call me on matters such as this—whether you are at home or at work. Confidence on anything of this nature is of paramount concern to my associates and me. Am I understood?"

"Yes, sir, I understand you perfectly."

"Good, I appreciate this kind of loyalty. The day will come when I shall reward you handsomely for it."

Still only thirty-nine years of age, Saud al-Dajani was the youngest member of Global United Bank's senior management team. The youthful-looking, diminutive, 5' 6" bachelor held an undergraduate degree in finance from the University of Illinois, and similar to Tariq Nasir, the man he considered his mentor, an MBA from Harvard.

To even the dullest of observers, it was readily apparent that al-Dajani was on a fast track within the bank in terms of career, and that frustrated many who had been part of the operations division of the bank far much longer. For sure, there was begrudging respect for Sammy's uncanny grasp of all aspects of bank operations, systems, and technology, but jealousies were still abundant. It was difficult for many older subordinates to reconcile themselves to taking orders from the curly-haired, boyish-looking senior vice president, when most of them had put in far more years than he—some going all the way back to the days of Guarantee Bank of Chicago—in hopes of sometime holding the position he now occupied within that organization. Education and obvious intelligence aside, it just did not seem possible to them he could leapfrog everyone in the division to become its manager unless favoritism was surely in the mix. Some who felt slighted were inclined to attribute al-Dajani's advancement to his being one of Tariq Nasir's "favored Muslim protégés," an opinion you could be certain was expressed by the disgruntled in only the most discreet and private of settings.

Were any of his Global United subordinates to have had even the slightest inkling of Sammy's "other life", however, it would have shocked them to the core. Raised in the home of a wealthy, Islamic fundamentalist, Sammy had remained a strict observer of the faith from the day he arrived in the United States as a nineteen-year-old U of I freshman in early 1999.

Despite all the distractions and temptations western culture offered, Sammy had but three goals in mind after his arrival: get a top-notch education; find and develop a career befitting that education; and spend whatever time remained of his life dedicated to the service of Islam, awaiting whatever higher calling that dedication might entail. Such a call came in 2015 during Sammy's seventh year at Global United, when he was back home in Saudi Arabia for his annual pilgrimage to Hajj. It was there that he met and came under the influence of a charismatic representative of the al-Qaeda splinter group calling itself al-Sahaba.

◊◊◊◊

"JUST AS soon as you get that BSA information we've requested from Mr. al-Dajani, Latisha, I want you to let me know." Latisha Caldwell was Cass Price's second in command on the extended examination at Global United. "I want to be part of our review in that area of the bank."

"Sure enough," Latisha responded. "Tell me, though, are you still expecting we will find a lot of problems in that area of the bank? I mean, you know, you're asking that I pick four people to work on just that project. That's a good-sized crew. We have a lot to do, and we rarely assign that many people to review compliance with the Bank Security Act in a bank this size, particularly when our charge in this examination is safety and soundness, and not compliance."

"I don't know, Latisha. Call it intuition or whatever you wish, but I just have the feeling that we should review that area of this bank far more closely this time around."

"Can you confide in me what it is your intuition is telling you?"

"Look, I'll tell you a little of what's bothering me, but I don't want you repeating any of this to anyone because if you do, I will deny it."

"You have my word."

"Well, at the risk of sounding as though I'm profiling, as they say, the way I see it this bank is primarily owned and controlled by an international businessman of South Asian, and furthermore Islamic extraction. The man still keeps very close ties and does significant business with people all over that part of world, the Middle East, South Asia, and so on and so forth. Additionally, within the last four years, Global United has opened up no less than nine new domestic branches and eighteen new foreign branches, many of the latter being in major cities throughout the areas I just mentioned. I'm sorry, but with all that's going on in the world today, that piques my curiosity."

"Is it just his ethnicity or religion that bothers you, or do you have some other information about him that gives rise to suspicions?"

"No, nothing further at this moment about Mr. Nasir personally, I just for reasons of my own think it might be a good idea to look at all of his personal and business relationships here at the bank, and as we do that also look closely at the bank's BSA and anti-money laundering systems. You and others here on our original examining team have all said that Paul was personally reviewing that area of the bank prior to his death and that admittedly also drives some of my curiosity regarding Mr. Nasir."

"Wow, that all has a sinister ring to it. You're beginning to make me wonder what we might find."

"Like I said, I hope we find absolutely nothing, but I want us to look at the matter closely. We'll attempt to do it in such a way that we take care not to offend either Mr. Nasir, any of his Muslim associates here at the bank or any of the many Muslim customers the bank has developed in recent years—but we are going to look into this just the same."

"Based on what all you've just said, is Global United's rather aggressive offering of various new Islamic banking services somewhat bothering you?"

"No, not necessarily, the bank has seemingly made every effort to coordinate their offering of religiously compliant banking products with all the necessary regulatory agencies, we at the OCC included; and they've since been making quite a name for themselves in that regard in most of the markets they're currently serving, particularly within the Islamic community here in Chicago during recent years. As you know, this Islamic banking thing's also a new animal for us regulators, but they appear to be falling over backward to accommodate all of our requests as we try to grow into a level of oversight that is fair to all concerned. So, we want to do nothing that will damage all that the bank has done in that regard. Actually, as long as they appear to be doing everything they can to comply with the regulatory requirements we've placed on them with respect to their offering of Islamic banking services, we would want to encourage their efforts. So, although I want us to be aggressive in this extended examination we're doing, I still want us also to be as polite and culturally sensitive as we can in the way we go about it."

"Hopefully, I can help some in that regard. As you may remember, Cass, I attended a regulatory session the Fed put on about a year ago where a knowledgeable big shot out of our Washington offices talked about the emergence of Islamic banking in this country. Guess all the agencies, including the OCC, are struggling to know how to adequately regulate the offering of financial products vastly different from those offered by our traditional system of banking."

"That's true, but with an Islamic population of well over three million in this country and growing, enterprising banks like Global United here are gearing up to tap that market. Some institutions, including this one I understand, have jumped in full force in the offering of services specially designed to satisfy nearly every kind of financial need for their Muslim customers, and still meet the requirements of their Qur'an. Sort of a 'bank within a bank,' so to speak.

Didn't you folks look at that when you first arrived?"

"Yes, I believe we did, but once again it was Mr. Trotter and two Islamic banking specialists out of our Washington office that he brought in for a couple of days that examined that area of the bank. I offered to help because of some training I've had but he said he and the specialists had it covered. He said there wasn't a huge book of that sort of business on the books of the bank yet, anyway. You know, as I think of it, however, maybe Mr. Trotter shared some of your suspicions along those lines, Cass."

"How do you mean?"

"Well, it appeared just about anything the bank was doing by way of product offerings for its Muslim customers, he was treating as kind of hush, hush. None of us much got involved in that while he was with us. Rather makes me wonder now, what with all you've just said."

"Well, we may or may not be onto something, Latisha. I'll need to review whatever I can find of Paul's work in that area and perhaps look up the two specialists you say he worked with and see what they have to say to make any determination. I believe the team he brought in to review those operations made a report that was filed with our downtown office, but Paul always kept personal examination notes on whatever he did. He didn't happen to share or leave any of his examination notes on any of those areas of Global United with you kids while he was still with you?"

"No, not really. He kept most of his stuff on most everything he was looking at in written notes, etc. He did put some information on his laptop, but I understand that was apparently stolen when that horrible thing happened to him last week. Right?"

"Yeah, shoot, that's what I figured, and unfortunately Paul wasn't too good about backing things up online like we're all supposed to do. So, we may all have to become experts on this Islamic banking thing before everything is said and done here. Could be we might get a pretty good read of what the results were in our previous look-see into that area of the bank by talking with the team that came in here and assisted Paul in his previous review. I'll get in touch with them and see. We may want to have them come back."

"Maybe I can still find some of my materials from that session I attended on the subject a while back. Perhaps there's someone listed in there that we might use as a resource."

"Great, I'd appreciate that. Then also, I know we regulators have been throwing a lot at him regarding this expanded examination of the bank, but we might bear in mind that Logan Hart, the bank's Executive V.P., apparently knows a goodly amount about Islamic banking, and he has also been overseeing a thorough review of that area of Global United since his arrival here a month or so ago. Apparently, he developed much of his expertise regarding the proper establishment of Islamic banking operations by banks such as Global United as part of his previous work with the bank consulting firm he formerly worked for. Guess he consulted along those lines with many banks around the country before he joined Global United. I understand it is one of the reasons the bank offered him the position he now holds here at the bank. To our good fortune, they have also appointed him our principal liaison with the bank on matters related to our examination here. I'm sure he'll be happy to give us all the help he can on such matters."

"Fine, I'll remember that too."

"Oh, and again, make sure you let me know right away when Mr. al-Dajani gives you the BSA information we requested from him. I want to be involved in every bit of our review in that area of the bank. Stay on him about it. It shouldn't take him long to provide the information. He said in our meeting earlier this afternoon that he still had copies of most of the information he had provided Paul Trotter before. He should be able to at least provide you that much right away."

"I hope so." Latisha shook her head.

"What's the matter, Latisha? You don't care for Mr. al-Dajani?"

"Well, no, not really. You can have Global United's Mr. al-Dajani. He isn't all that easy a guy to deal with. He doesn't seem to like women. Kind of a supercilious bastard, if you ask me. I don't know, maybe it's a cultural thing there too. I'll do as you ask though."

CHAPTER SIXTEEN

ALL OF Tariq Nasir's AmeriPAK companies were headquartered in Chicago, and the situation Scott Kruse had just described to him over lunch made it once again abundantly clear why he had arranged it so. It was seldom that the CEOs of all the AmeriPAK subsidiaries got together as a whole, but when they did, having most of them ready at hand was always helpful. When meetings of the "executive committee"—as Nasir called such gatherings—occurred, nothing short of near-death circumstances excused an executive's absence. Every CEO was expected to have wireless Internet communications at their disposal at all times, and AmeriPAK headquarters in Chicago was equipped with the technology required to video-conference any of them in from just about any place in the world using satellite communications, if the executive could not be present in a physical sense.

Following the conversation between Scott Kruse and Tariq Nasir, each of the AmeriPAK subsidiary CEOs received one of those rare phone calls informing them that an executive committee meeting was to take place at the company's Chicago headquarters in the afternoon of that same day, and as always, attendance was mandatory.

On this occasion, Faud Arif, President and CEO of Aurora Transportation, and Mustaffa Agha Khan, President and CEO of PAKWest, Inc., Nasir's precious metals trading company, were both out of town. They would use the company's state-of-the-art technology via the Internet to take part in the meeting.

"Gentlemen, I thank you all for making yourselves available on so short a notice. I felt there were some things we needed to talk about immediately and thought them important enough to interrupt your various involvements." Nasir started and ran all meetings with an air of solicitude and conciliation, but there was never any doubt who was in charge. "If our cameras are working adequately, Faud and Mustaffa, who are out of the country on business, should be able to clearly see that the CEO's of all our companies, are present with me now in Chicago. Is that the case gentlemen? We can certainly see you both perfectly on this end?"

"I can see and hear you all most clearly, Mr. Nasir." Faud Arif responded from his hotel room in Stockholm where he was attending an international shipping conference. "There is a slight bit of delay in both sound and picture, but beyond that everything is clear as usual."

"It's the same for me, sir," Khan added from his location in Dubai. "I never cease to be amazed by today's technology. My reception here is quite good. It feels as if I were there in Chicago with all the rest of you."

"Fine, then let's get started." Nasir continued. "I have asked all of you to attend this meeting this morning to inform you of an event that has occurred which may bring somewhat greater scrutiny on our organization than what we normally experience—or I prefer. I felt it extremely important that each of you know of this so you could take whatever steps are necessary to ensure that the secrecy and confidentiality which I insist surround all the dealings of each of our companies are thoroughly maintained."

"What is the problem, and how can we all be of service, Mr. Chairman?" Abu al-Madi, President and CEO of the holding company, was Nasir's cousin and one of those individuals who liked to hear himself talk. Ostensibly second in command within the AmeriPAK organization, al-Madi was the stereotypical, sycophantic toady who nearly everyone of importance within the organization secretly loathed. "You know that you can always depend on us to help in any way. Just tell us what situation has arisen."

Nasir seldom acknowledged al-Madi's superfluous ramblings. "As you're all well aware, for several years now since I obtained a controlling interest in Global United Bank of Chicago, we have all had to be very careful about any business our companies, or any of us personally, does with the bank. As I have said on occasions too numerous to mention, the bank differs greatly from any business in which any of us has ever been involved. It is heavily regulated and overseen by a plethora of government agencies and is by its very nature quite closely accounted for. In the instance of every transaction that it touches, there is an audit trail. So, although we have important 'special business' to conduct for which it is helpful from time-to-time to have a close affiliation with a conventional financial institution, it is nevertheless extremely important that we take great caution to ensure that any business we process through the bank appear circumspect at all times. I have gone so far as to have even instructed all of you and several key, mid-level managers in the nuances of various bank regulations, so as to give us all greater insight into how we must structure any business we need to conduct through Global United to avoid scrutiny of our other, non-bank business dealings. Each of you has, I know, been heretofore very careful in that regard, but if ever there was a time when we as an organization need to be on our guard along these lines, that time is probably now."

"Sir, don't we have a few close relationships on staff at the bank who typically work quite closely with us to ensure that we encounter no problems?" asked Agha Kahn from his office in Dubai. "I would think we would be fairly well covered on such matters. What has happened, may I ask, to make things more sensitive than usual now? We have always been extremely careful in everything that we do with the bank."

"Well, gentlemen," answered Nasir, "on last Friday evening, after meeting with officers of Global United supposedly to wrap up an examination of the bank by the office of the U.S. Comptroller of the Currency, one of the OCC's examiners was murdered by someone while on his way home from the bank. Perhaps some of you may have read or heard about the incident in the news over the weekend."

"That is unfortunate, but what would that have to do with us? This is Chicago, IL, and murder is not unusual in this decadent cesspool of infidels." Ahmed Khalil, President of Aurora Vending was the company's resident Muslim fundamentalist. Nearly every reference he made to or about any non-believer was disdainful in some fashion. "Why, in some parts of the city where my people go, they themselves even carry weapons. This is a very rough community."

"I well know that, Ahmed, but it just so happens that this gentleman was reviewing all of our companies' relationships with the bank at the time of his death, and for whatever reason, the bank's president thinks that may have generated extra suspicion on the part of the bank's regulators. I understand that the OCC has extended its examination, and it involves even the Federal Bureau of Investigation. When you consider the extent to which each of your companies is from time-to-time involved in my family's special business of hawala, the last thing that we certainly need is for some government agent to come sniffing around. By design, ours is an unregistered operation. It would be disastrous if they determined we were in the money service business and were not following federal law, etc."

"We have always taken great care, Mr. Chairman, to avoid any trail leading back to the hawala portion of our businesses," interjected Abu al-Madi, feeling as though it was time for him to add his two cents again. "Our accounting operations know their job well. We maintain accurate records on all transactions of the holding company, and by and between each of our subsidiaries, but we maintain no records beyond the traditional minimum on any hawala transactions conducted on behalf of our clients worldwide. We use our time-tested cadre of 'memorizers' in dealing with most of our larger, more sensitive transfers, and all hundi connected with any transaction are destroyed after we are certain they have satisfactorily completed the transfer. Our IT people also take great care to regularly scrub all PC and server hard drives with special software, to permanently delete all traces of any information that might relate to a hawala transaction. Our in house accountants are also well trained in disguising any hawala activities as part of normal business. Further, the high cash nature of certain of our companies has been perennially convenient in masking transfers and the excellent profits we make from this very important part of our business."

"I am well aware of all of that, Mr. al-Madi. If you will recall, I played an important personal role in designing all the security procedures used in the hawala portion of our business, and there is no place in our organization for anyone who cannot use them properly. So, I don't need you to inform me of what I already know."

The rebuke stung al-Madi. Considering himself subordinate to no one in the corporation except the Chairman, Nasir's condescending tone was an embarrassment. He would talk to his cousin when the opportunity arose, but knew better than to press the matter at this time.

Hawala was the underpinning of all the companies under the aegis of the AmeriPAK umbrella. Each had its own business niche, but whatever business that might be was designed and organized in such a way as to complement the conduct of hawala anywhere in the world Nasir and his family had established relationships—and there were few countries where relationships did not exist.

PAK-West, Inc., Nasir's precious metals trading business, for example, had far-flung international operations, and few of its affiliates around the world were not part of its hawala operation. Over or under invoicing when either buying or selling precious metals or finished jewelry products, whether for the company's Crescent Jewelry chain or for non-affiliated precious metals customers worldwide, was a way of accommodating and camouflaging hawala transfers that occurred almost daily. The same was also true regarding the international sale of software products by Aurora Tech, Inc. If logistical problems ever arose in the physical transfer of funds, or for that matter any other sensitive product or materials, Aurora Transportation was there to assist. If the need was there to move cash either into or out of the banking system, Aurora Vending, Inc., one of the largest users of coin and currency in the Chicago region, was a convenient conduit.

To be sure, pretty much all the AmeriPAK subsidiaries turned in regular annual profits based solely on the core business of each; but the unrecorded earnings every member of the group made from their involvement in the shadow world of hawala made them far greater contributors to the AmeriPAK's true profitability than what was reflected on company records. AmeriPAK subsidiary CEO's didn't just occupy their positions within the organization strictly based on business acumen. Each one had to possess years of experience in the business of hawala. Like Tariq Nasir, most all were descendants of long lines of hawaladar families. None, however, possessed his exclusive pedigree. The house of Nasir had a reputation that spanned centuries.

"All I am saying, gentlemen," continued Nasir, "is that we may be entering a delicate period for the way in which we do business, and I insist that all of you take whatever steps are necessary to ensure that everyone in our organization involved in any part of our hawala operations be on his or her guard with respect to security."

"You know, that is always uppermost in our minds, Mr. Chairman," injected Mahbubal Rehman, President and CEO of Aurora Development. "In all due respect, I think every one of us knows how important such things are to our organization."

"Yes, I'm well aware of that, Mr. Rehman, and I appreciate everyone's diligence in that regard. Yet, I think world events dictate we continuously remind each other of our needs along those lines. The government under which we live attempts to monitor and control nearly every endeavor in which we are involved, and the need they feel to do so is only heightened by all that has occurred in recent years. Pick your crisis, you're all well aware of everything that is happening around the world today. Take the recently decimated Islamic State for instance. As it attempted to spread its caliphate tentacles across the Levant and Middle East, places like say Syria have imploded, bringing in opportunistic interlopers like the Russians, Iranians, and Hezbollah. Claiming for example they are simply in the mix to halt the advance of organizations such as ISIL and al-Qaeda, every move made by the Russians in the last couple of years has instead been designed to prop up the likes of that megalomaniacal idiot-of-a-dictator, Assad. That situation and others like it in the Mideast have precipitated mass migrations of refugees like no one has seen in generations, flooding to any place willing to take them; and many of the nut cases I mentioned are for certain traveling right alongside them with no good intent in mind. That situation and others like it around the world puts many of the countries in which we do business on edge. With that comes scrutiny of the sort we look to avoid with a passion gentlemen, and that is why I have asked you all here."

"We're here to listen, Mr. Chairman," Rehman added.

"Well, what I'm trying to say," continued Nasir, "is that international geopolitical unrest of the sort I just mentioned, always causes an equal upset in the business world, and this places many government agencies, particularly those that monitor the financial industry and the movement of money around the world on full alert. As you all know, the U.S. Government and many other governments in countries around the world where we do business have definitely made the regulation of money service businesses top priority. Most countries, in particular, the U.S., now expect all hawaladars to register their operations. They're also required to keep records similar to regular banks, and report transactions for nearly all their clients, so that government oversight may be attained." Nasir's tone sounded contemptuous. "We are one of the largest sources of hawala services in the world, but that is a little-known fact, and we want to keep it that way. For my father, Mahmoud, and his fathers before him—peace be upon them all—confidentiality has always been the underpinning of every transaction undertaken, and we must allow nothing to compromise that. It has required centuries for my family to develop the level of trust and respect we enjoy in this business. I will countenance no breach of confidentiality or anything else that might damage that reputation."

"I and Yussef Ibrahim, President of our jewelry chain, probably handle thirty-five to forty percent of all of our hawala transactions, Mr. Chairman," Agha Kahn, head of PAK-West metals, once again interjected. "We have many small to very large transactions pending worldwide at any given point in time, and we always take great care to ensure the privacy of those clients. Some of our clients, however, are a rather sensitive lot, and I wonder at times what their true objectives may be, if you understand my meaning, sir."

"I am well aware of that fact, Mustaffa, and that kind of thing is just what the government is trying to sniff out regularly. This makes our taking great care in all we do related to our business of hawala all the more important these days. Look, gentlemen, there should be no problems regarding the money transfer side of our business if we are discerning as to who we do business with and never vary from time-honored methods and procedures that have been in place for generations. It matters not to me what the cause or business venture of our clients may be as long as they are willing to pay for services rendered. It has always been that way, and to the best of my ability it will always stay that way. The situation of vastly increased scrutiny that may now have arisen by way of my holdings at the bank and the situation arising out of the murder of the old regulator may yet, however, be another matter. We will need to be particularly vigilant in all that we do with respect to our hawala operations until that situation has passed. What say we use the next hour or two to discuss those areas of our operations where we are most vulnerable in that regard. If any of you have other plans for now, I suggest you change them."

◊◊◊◊

"OK, LATISHA, what do you and the gold dust twins here have for me as a result of your afternoon's work relative to our look-see into Global United's BSA compliance? What did your Mr. al-Dajani give us to work with here?"

"Well, 'our Mr. al-Dajani,' as you call him, has actually provided us with quite a bit of information to go over here. As usual, he wasn't the most pleasant of people to deal with, but he at least got us most all of what we were after." OCC examiner, Latisha Caldwell, and her two young assistant examiners, Craig Garrett and Barbara Howell, had computer printouts, stacks of photocopied information and file folders spread all around them on a conference table in the third floor conference room at Global United's downtown offices. "It's going to take us a while to go through all of this." Latisha shook her head as she thumbed through the stack of information.

"Well, to begin, did we get everything we asked for? Did you all compare everything you got here with what we requested on our list?" Cass could often come across as an inquisitor.

"We were just finishing that when you walked in, but so far it appears as though most of what we've asked for is either in this room or accessible by computer." Latisha made a sweeping gesture at all the materials piled around the room. "Policies, procedures and organizational materials related to the bank's BSA, AML and OFAC programs are in that pile over there; and detailed information on all Cash Transaction, Foreign Bank, and Suspicious Activity reporting are spread across this table here. We're really lucky too that the bank has apparently digitized most of that type of activity, making it available on computer. They've given us online access to all of their information, along with data disks and hard copies of all the same. I believe their system allows us to do some direct comparisons with FinCEN to determine if there are any differences between what the bank is reporting to us now versus what they electronically submitted to FinCEN previously."

"Sounds great, Latisha. I'd like to use the bank's computerized records to the greatest extent we can, might help with the speed of our investigation."

"Well, it would appear we have that now, and if needed, all related information can also be downloaded to just about any analytical format we wish to use, Cass." Craig Garrett, a 24-year-old, first-year examiner with the OCC was a whiz with his laptop. "We can manipulate their information several ways to assist in analysis."

"Great, then I'll tell you what let's do to begin with. Pull a sampling of say every fifth SAR and CRT that the bank has compiled during the last couple of years for customers or account holders that do not appear on the bank's exempt list. Look to see if you can find anything that looks suspicious. I think you know the kind of anomalies we're looking for, such as corporate accounts that have deposits or withdrawals primarily in cash as opposed to checks; retail businesses or check cashing services that hardly ever request cash from the bank; businesses that have multiple accounts where they transfer funds frequently between those accounts, and so on. Better yet, pull out your examiner's manuals and refer to your BSA checklist. Let's leave no stone unturned. I want to hear about anything that you think is even just a little out of the ordinary, in particular where those situations seem to establish a pattern of any kind." Cass slid a sheet of paper across the table to each of the young examiners. "I would also like to have you three look at all transactions of that sort for any of the companies that appear on this list. It's the list of businesses exempt from reporting that Mr. al-Dajani provided. I want you to conduct a thorough review in their case. You know the drill."

Latisha and her helpers scanned the list Cass had given them. "These appear to include all of Mr. Nasir's companies," Latisha observed. "Think we're going to find some problems with them?"

"No, not necessarily," answered Cass. "It's just that Mr. Nasir is probably the most significant insider we have in this bank, and some of his companies are on the exempt list. Perhaps everything is just fine with the bank's handling of those companies in that regard, but let's make sure we agree that they should be exempted. I want you to get right on this and inform me of the results at your earliest opportunity."

◊◊◊◊

LOGAN HART was authorized to access Global United's mainframe computer system from home, using encrypted methods. Such remote access was available to senior management of the bank only, to allow them the capability of working on important bank matters from the comfort of their homes when needed. Until now, Logan had used this capability only once to prepare for an upcoming meeting of the bank's board of directors. He preferred not to take too much in the way of work home from the bank with him. The special work he was now doing on the quiet for the OCC, however, was changing all of that. In that case, he planned to use the system a great deal to assist him in reviewing all the bank's credit accommodations and other related information for Nasir's AmeriPAK group of companies.

The system that Global United had set up for off-site access to bank information was impressive. Any bank officer with proper authorization and adequate computer capabilities could literally view any information resident on the bank's mainframe or peripherals from any remote location. Part of this remote capability included access to the state-of-the-art digital imaging system Global United had installed sometime in early 2012, years before Logan joined the bank. Included in the data available by way of the combined system were: bank balance sheet and income statement information; details of the bank's general ledger and entire chart of accounts; all deposit and loan subsidiary trial balances; full access to the bank's central information file on all customers; and imaged copies of all credit files within the bank active at any time since they installed the system.

Originals of all notes, collateral, and key security documentation were kept in a large records vault at the bank's main, downtown office, but beyond that little in the way of hard copy loan documentation was kept any longer. All documentation relating to any loan was instead digitally scanned on a daily basis, and placed into proprietary cloud storage for ease of retrieval wherever and whenever needed. All Logan had to do to look at a credit file for any loan relationship was to access the bank's imaged system from his remote location, put in his identifiers and then electronically "thumb through" the loan file of his choice. The system would be a big time-saver for Logan when reviewing the Nasir accounts.

Logan spent the evening of the Monday prior to Thanksgiving reviewing all the information he could find in Global United's records on Tariq Nasir's business empire. He started with the AmeriPAK, Inc. holding company file, beginning first with a perusal of imaged annual credit reviews, showing a thorough summary of everything about the company and the bank's relationship with it. Included in the very lengthy write-ups was full information on ownership and management, a company history, a historical analysis of the company's financial performance that included a comparative spread of the most current five years worth of financial statements complete with performance ratios, detailed facts and figures regarding every outstanding loan the company had on the bank's books as of the date of the review, and an overall risk analysis and rating as to the quality of that asset as an investment.

One of the first things that Logan noticed in his review was that all the AmeriPAK companies' financials, except for interim statements that were internally prepared, were fully audited with unqualified opinions as to the validity and accuracy of the information provided. The accounting firm of Jibril, Dharr, and Associates, Chicago, IL did the audits. Jibril, Dharr was not only the accounting firm for Mr. Nasir's companies but also for Global United Bank of Chicago. This somewhat troubled Logan.

Edward Jibril, senior partner of Jibril, Dharr was an extremely close personal friend of Mr. Nasir's. Logan had first met Mr. Jibril at a reception the bank hosted when he initially joined the bank. Logan remembered thinking when he conducted his preemployment analysis of Global United how strange he thought it was that the bank had decided only two years before to sever relations with a much larger, national accounting firm in favor of signing an audit agreement with Jibril, Dharr. From everything that Logan could determine, Jibril, Dharr's only other banking clients at that time were a couple of new, smaller single-bank holding companies in the northeast Chicago suburbs. Hardly the experienced accounting firm one would expect to find auditing a bank with over $10 Billion in assets and both national and international banking operations.

Global United used a seven-point loan grading system, where scores for loans and credit relationships were rated anywhere from a loan grade of "1", where little if any loan risk existed, to a loan grade of "7" that signaled the investment was a "Loss." The latter required that bank management immediately charge the loan off to credit reserves, and if possible later collect the money owed by whatever legal means remained available. Logan noted that Global United's credit review department had rated all the AmeriPAK companies a "2", indicating all of those companies were of "Good Risk", a rating well above most on the bank's books. There were very few loan relationships within the bank able to garner ratings of that quality, perhaps also a bit of a red flag that Logan might want to later look into. He jotted down a reminder to himself.

Everything relating to AmeriPAK's credit accommodations and those of its subsidiaries, at least on initial review, appeared to Logan to be structured and documented the way they should have been. Current participation agreements were in each company file showing that the bank had made the requisite arrangements to participate—or sell to upstream correspondent banks—those portions of Global United's credit authorizations to the AmeriPAK companies that exceeded the bank's legal lending limit. Built within the bank's loan accounting system was a control mechanism that aggregated on a daily basis the outstanding balances of all loans authorized to the related entities of the Nasir organization, and even those that might be unauthorized, such as an overdraft in one the companies' accounts. Whenever that number exceeded preset lending limits, the excess would then be sold off to the correspondent bank that had committed to the pre-authorized purchase of the loan overline. As required by bank policy and regulation, digitized copies of the calculations aggregating total Nasir-related company credit authorizations and outstanding balances as of the end of every month, were in each company's imaged file. Logan had thus far detected no technical violations of either bank policy or regulation in his review of the loan files for the AmeriPAK family of companies, but something told him he perhaps ought to look a little further. Maybe further review of their financial statements?

Each of AmeriPAK, Inc.'s five subsidiaries had $7 Million revolving lines of credit that were used from time-to-time to augment capital for varied purposes, depending on the short-term needs of the company. In the case of Aurora Transportation, Inc. for instance, their line of credit served as a backup for international trading purposes, letters of credit, bankers acceptances, and so forth. For PAK-West, Inc., Nasir's precious metals trading and jewelry store company, they used it for foreign and domestic purchases of precious metals, gems and finished jewelry. For Aurora Tech, Inc., the line was used to purchase and carry inventories of computer hardware and software for both domestic and international sale; and for Aurora Vending, Inc., it was used to purchase vending machines, electronic gaming machines and ATMs located in restaurants, pubs, and arcades all over the Chicago area. With Aurora Development, Inc., the company originally started by Nasir's father-in-law and the basis for Nasir's empire, their credit arrangements were far more involved. Credit accommodations for Aurora Development consisted of not only a similar $5 Million line of credit for temporary operating capital in its construction company, but also included $100 Million in fixed-term loans for the purchase and development of commercial real estate properties it continually added to its ever-growing portfolio located throughout Chicago and many other major cities of the U.S.

In auditing the AmeriPAK loan reviews, Logan looked for, found and verified calculations in file that aggregated all Global United loans outstanding to Tariq Nasir, AmeriPAK, Inc. and the five AmeriPAK subsidiaries, as would bank examiners, to determine whether their total exceeded the regulatory lending limit for loans to an Insider and all of his or her related interests as defined by Regulation "O", the Federal Reserve ruling that governed such matters. For purposes of his calculation in that regard, Logan knew that the legal lending limit for total loans to such a borrower by a federally regulated U.S. national bank was a number not to exceed fifteen percent of combined capital and surplus reserves of that bank. With total capital at Global United Bank of Chicago standing at $900 Million, this placed the bank's legal lending limit to any insider and their affiliates at $135 Million. Bank records showed that Nasir personally had no loans outstanding with Global United, but total AmeriPAK-related loans and authorized lines of credit on the books of the bank totaled no less than $180 Million. Logan knew this would be a violation of insider regulations without documented, prior arrangement by Global United to participate those portions of the AmeriPAK loans that exceeded the legal lending limit to other banks. He was relieved to find everything in order in that regard, but did notice certain other anomalies on the balance sheets and income statements of the AmeriPAK family of companies that aroused his curiosity to some degree as he read through the files.

While analyzing the balance sheets of all the AmeriPAK companies, one piece of information nearly leapt from the computer screen during Logan's review. Apparently, beyond two relatively small documentary letters of credit through Global United's International Banking Department on behalf of Aurora Transportation, none of the AmeriPAK companies currently had any outstanding draws against their authorized operating lines of credit, and the only debts outstanding on the books of any of the companies were very well secured longer-term loans, most of which were financed by lenders other than Global United. To the contrary, all of Tariq Nasir's companies had highly liquid statements with large amounts of cash on their balance sheets, something almost unheard of for firms of the size, complexity, and types of business as those beneath the corporate umbrella of AmeriPAK, Inc.

Putting it mildly, nearly everything Logan was finding regarding Tariq Nasir and his AmeriPAK group of companies since joining Global United was an amazing study in contradictions, not the least of which was the fact that Nasir was Muslim, and to be more specific a Muslim strictly observant of his faith. As such, it was difficult to reconcile Nasir's involvement in much of the business he conducted, in particular Western style banking in any form.

According to the dictates of the Qu'ran and Sharia, all Muslims were strictly prohibited from the taking or giving of interest, or *Riba*, regardless of the rate or purpose of the underlying debt or obligation. An Islamic owner of capital, or *rabbul-mal*, could invest such capital in a business venture and share in the profit or loss of that business, but never should a member of the Ummah collect Riba from anyone. *How, could a practicing Muslim such as Tariq Nasir be principal shareholder and chairman of the board of a western style bank such as Global United, where all of those things are done?* Logan wondered. *An investment in such an organization would be Haraam, or non-Sharia compliant.*

Understanding what he did about Islamic banking, Logan found this very large inconsistency baffling. Early on in his tenure at Global United, he had the opportunity to discuss the matter with both Raj Haifa and Sammy al-Dajani one morning over a cup of coffee. Questioning how Nasir, or for that matter they themselves, were able to rationalize their involvement with Global United considering the teachings of Islam regarding the concept of interest paid and/or received, Logan was told by both men that they ascribed to Nasir's interpretation of the situation. Supposedly, in Nasir's way of thinking, his involvement with Global United was more of a matter of return on investment, or rabbul-mal, than it was an instance of paying or receiving interest. Nasir explained that even though modern Islam was divided on the subject to begin with, at no time had he "ever personally executed a loan, or paid or received any interest." As he put it, "My ownership of stock in either Global United or even my holding company, AmeriPAK, Inc., is strictly an investment which fully satisfies the dictates of Sharia. Besides," said Nasir, "our long-term goal is to ultimately convert Global United to a conforming Islamic banking institution anyway." In Logan's estimation, however, this seemed situational ethics at its most extreme, a circumstance that only compounded his uncertainties regarding Nasir and some of the players at Global United. How could, for example, Nasir's AmeriPAK holding company and all of it subsidiaries be parties to such complex, traditional credit arrangements as were on the books of Global United and other institutions and not be in conflict with the dictates of Islam? It was something Logan knew he would have to discuss with Nasir sometime in the future.

Scrolling through AmeriPAK's file, one exhibit attached to the holding company's latest review immediately caught Logan's eye. It was an organizational chart depicting the corporate structure of AmeriPAK, complete with all subsidiaries, related entities and the names of key management figures responsible for each. Logan printed it out for reference. It would save tremendous time by helping target his review. He figured the OCC and FBI might also appreciate a copy. He made a mental note to scan and send one to both agencies via e-mail attachment.

Overall, the financial condition of all the AmeriPAK companies appeared quite strong. Balance sheet and income statement ratios exceeded industry peer performance in nearly every category of measurement. The companies were growing fast, but earnings and capital were easily keeping pace. In nearly every area of measurement their performance appeared to out pace industry norms.

What about Nasir's companies is so all-fired different to others in the same field? Logan asked himself.

Two anomalies Logan thought particularly strange when he compared the financial statements of AmeriPAK and its various subsidiaries to industry standards for companies involved in similar businesses, were the relatively high levels of cash and inter-company liabilities that seemed to exist on nearly all of their balance sheets. The situation didn't make much sense. *Its almost as though the companies are trading cash back and forth*, thought Logan, *and they're awash in that. When they want to borrow money, they seldom look to the bank. They seem to instead borrow from each other. What's their thinking?* He asked himself. *They've all got plenty enough operating capital to pay off those liabilities between each other. There's no logical reason for the companies to owe each other money like that. That's really strange?* Financial ratios for all of the companies were still excellent—bordering on fabulous—but Logan nevertheless made a note to himself to discuss the oddity of the high levels of cash and what appeared to be unnecessary inter-company liabilities with Scott Kruse and perhaps a couple of the AmeriPAK CEO's he had become acquainted with. The situation might also be worthy of mention to Cass Price and some of the investigators she was working with.

One other question I wouldn't mind asking either Nasir or someone of responsibility within the AmeriPAK organization about sometime when I have the chance, thought Logan, *is what in the devil their logic was for acquisitions. One has to wonder what the symbiosis is between real estate development, shipping and transportation, precious metals, computers, software and Internet service; and then of all things, vending machines?* Logan made a mental note to ask Mr. Nasir about that at the next opportunity he had.

CHAPTER SEVENTEEN

THE REGULAR monthly meeting of the Board of Trustees
for the Worldwide Islamic Charities Foundation usually
convened on the fourth Tuesday of each month following
midday prayers at the Islamic Institute mosque in downtown
Chicago, where most WICF trustees were members of the
congregation. Nearly all WICF board meetings were held in
the corporate offices of Tariq Nasir's AmeriPAK, Inc. holding
company, located not far from the Islamic Institute. So,
whenever a WICF trustee was in any way pressed for time,
they were invited to offer up daily prayers prior to the
meeting in a very nice facility provided for that activity at
AmeriPAK headquarters, if they so desired. Over time, the
latter became the option most preferred by WICF trustees
on meeting day.

AmeriPAK's headquarters were housed in a
renovated, four-story, turn-of-the-twentieth-century office
building located in the 500 block of Grand Avenue in
downtown Chicago. The building was in a very dilapidated
condition when Nasir purchased it in 1997, but after a great
deal of architectural planning, and extensive renovation at
the approximate cost of $8 Million, it had become
AmeriPAK's palatial corporate home base.

AmeriPAK's boardroom was located on the building's
fourth floor, along with Tariq Nasir's personal suite of offices.
Used as a facility for both meetings and receptions when
opened up by way of two large double doors in between, the

boardroom doubled as an elegant entrance to what was essentially a private mini-mosque, or *Masjid Saghir*, complete with its own Qibla wall. Five times a day, in accordance with the *Salat* and whenever any Muslim was present in the building—which was usually 24/7 during a normal business week—the faithful were remotely called to prayer over a loud speaker by the Adhan of the Muezzin at the Islamic Institute, electronically piping his melodic pronouncements into every office in the building.

Whenever the boardroom was not in use for AmeriPAK, Inc. board meetings, special gatherings of company management or outside groups like WICF's board of trustees, all Muslim faithful on staff were encouraged to observe their prayers within the Masjid Saghir to the extent space was available. Facilities were made for the storage of the personal prayer rugs, or *Sajjadh*, of individual staff members, or if needed company-owned rugs were always on hand for individual use. An in-house Imam usually presided. Whenever boardroom scheduling conflicts arose, an announcement to that effect would always precede the call to prayer. The faithful were then required to vacate the Masjid Saghir within ten minutes following the end of prayers. To the extent any believers felt too constrained by this limitation, all were given the option of observing midday prayers within their offices.

"Welcome, gentlemen! Please, if I may, let me call our meeting to order right away. We have several important matters to discuss and make decisions on this afternoon, and I know that all of you want to get on with your schedules." As chairman, Tariq Nasir was always very punctual in calling any meeting of the WICF to order. As expected the November monthly meeting was well attended. There were several important business items on the agenda, but it was a holiday week and everyone was in good spirits. "First of all, let me thank each and every one of you for making this a month of full attendance for our foundation board meeting, particularly so close to a major national holiday. Normally, we would have changed the date, but the grant requests we have to consider this month are rather time sensitive. So, changing the date or canceling was a bit out of the question this time." Nasir always ran every meeting in a strict, business-like fashion. He usually allowed the foundation's twelve trustees no more than fifteen minutes in which to visit following midday prayers before he would request that they take their places at the conference table to begin the meeting. Today was no exception in spite of the board's festive mood.

The WICF as an organization was originally the brain-child of Imam Abdul al-Hakim, the deeply fundamental, Egyptian-born congregational leader of the Islamic Institute of Greater Chicago. The Imam was a long-time member of the Egyptian-based Islamic Brotherhood, and a schemer by nature, who was always hitting on his wealthier congregants for financial support of one form or another. On one such occasion in September 1995, al-Hakim invited most all of the more successful business and professional leaders in his congregation to a special meeting following a Friday service where he first delivered a particularly fiery Khutbah on az-Zakat. Looking directly at those whose financial help was most wanted in establishing the foundation, his words were, "As promised in the Holy Qur'an, your possessions will be purified by setting aside a small portion for those in need. Like the pruning of plants, this cutting back will balance and encourage new growth in your lives."

The old Imam's religiously flowery entreaty was effective. Foundation organizers included all sorts of professionals: doctors, lawyers, educators, government officials and business leaders. They, in turn, convinced nearly everyone else in the congregation to give, as they never had before. Chief among al-Hakim's targets for leadership involvement in the activities of the new foundation was the aggressive young congregant, Tariq Nasir. The

Imam knew Nasir was the natural leader he needed to reach initial fund-raising goals. Once he assumed ownership of a project, its success was usually assured. Appealing to Nasir's legendary ego by telling him he was the only person within the congregation "who has the leadership and organizational skills to help this new foundation reach its initial fund-raising goal of $3 Million." The Imam convinced him to chair not only the steering committee, but to also organize and chair the original fund drive itself. Under Nasir's leadership, the drive was far more successful than the old Imam had ever suspected it would be, raising $4 Million, thirty percent over target by the time initial fund-raising was complete. As a result, Nasir was unanimously made Chairman of the organization's first Board of Trustees, and had continued as such until present.

"Gentlemen, we've dispensed with all of our administrative duties for today, and essentially handled most of the grant funding requests for which you received packets, but I am told we have one more item of business before we're done." Gesturing toward the board's lone cleric after pretty much every business item on November's agenda was completed, Nasir explained. "Imam al-Hakim has informed me that he has one more request he would like for us to consider before everyone heads home. Imam, you have the floor."

"Yes, thank you, Tariq." The Imam rose and began distributing a rather thick sheaf of papers to each trustee around the long conference table. "Please accept my apologies, gentlemen, for the fact that you did not have an opportunity to see this information beforehand, but we received this request far too late for the written presentation to go out in your packets, and we really don't want it to wait until next month."

Grant proposals to the WICF nearly always consisted of a standard written, three-page summary outlining certain specifics, such as the amount of the request, the intended recipient, qualifying information and if necessary, supporting financial and statistical data. There were audible groans from some recipients as the Imam handed a copy to each trustee.

"My, but this one passes the weight test, I would say," Charles Boulos, owner, and operator of a very successful, high-end Chicago area grocery chain, commented sarcastically as he hefted the thick presentation. First groaning and then whistling out of the corner of his mouth as he raised his eyebrows, Boulos stared at the amount of the request in general disbelief. "Mr. Chairman," he exclaimed, looking across the table at Nasir, "this is a significant request to be throwing at us so late in the meeting if you are expecting an answer this evening. This amount far exceeds the aggregate of everything else we have previously authorized today. Are you expecting us to pass on this proposal this afternoon?"

"Yes, Charles, that is regrettably what the Imam tells me he needs," Nasir answered for the Imam before he had a chance to respond. "So, let me suggest that we all adjourn for a half hour to give everyone a chance to familiarize themselves with the request and glance over the attached data. If anyone also needs to take a bathroom break, they may do so at this time. We can then reconvene let's say at 3:00 p.m."

"Mr, Chairman, if you don't mind, I would like to begin our discussion of this request by making a few observations if I might." Edward Jibril, Senior Partner of Jibril, Dharr and Associates, a highly respected Chicago area accounting firm, was first to speak after the WICF trustees had finished the break in their meeting. During that time, he and several members of the board had commiserated in the men's room about the lateness and size of this final request that was submitted. Many of the trustees had been becoming disenchanted as of late with the growing tendency toward such last minute requests, and it hadn't gone unnoticed that most situations of that sort were usually presented by Imam al-Hakim. "First of all, this request for $500,000 is far more than what we usually consider to only one charitable endeavor, and as if that was not enough to be concerned about with so little time to review the situation, it is also money destined for a Muslim orphanage in the city of Saint Petersburg, Russia, supposedly to help pay for food, room and board, and schooling of needy, young Muslim men."

"Yes, Edward, and a very worthwhile endeavor it is." The imam responded. "It's just the kind of thing our organization is supposed to be supporting."

"Well, I'm not all too sure of that. What are we thinking gentlemen? Any financial institution would be obligated to report a transfer of this sort to the authorities, and a grant of this nature could result in all sorts of unwanted scrutiny of our foundation at a most inopportune time. The government is really looking closely anymore at organizations like ours, and at sizable grants or gifts of this nature that have foreign destinations, particularly when the money being transferred is from one Muslim organization to another—and destined for Russia, of all places."

"We can't let the U.S. government's paranoia stand in the way of this foundation and its contributors fulfilling their obligation to Allah under the rule of Zakat, my friend." The Imam was getting defensive, and when that happened, he almost always used az-Zakat as a cudgel. "So, what are you inferring?"

"I infer nothing, Imam. I am only asking the kind of questions required of any responsible fiduciary. What do we know about the intended recipients of this grant, and what kind of accountability will we receive for how the funds are administered? We're not funding a bunch of fundamentalist Madrassas, are we? I am horribly apprehensive of this one. Don't we have plenty enough deserving causes that meet our criteria here at home that could use this kind of support?"

"I am surprised at your lack of concern for our beleaguered brothers elsewhere in the world, Edward," the

Imam shot back. "The worst of the lot here in this country live like kings by comparison."

"We mean no disrespect, Imam." Jibril was also starting to bristle. "But you of all people must surely know how much charitable Islamic foundations such as ours have been under the microscope in recent years. There have been several instances where trustees of organizations like ours have been arrested, and some imprisoned, for the supposed funding of terrorist organizations when all they claimed they knew they were doing—just like you are suggesting here—was helping out the needy somewhere else in the world. Homeland Security agencies will follow this money every inch of the way, and both we and the recipient will be looked at very closely. Do we want that?" There were nods of agreement as other trustees muttered amongst themselves around the table.

"We have a higher calling my friends." Imam al-Hakim answered. "We cannot be dissuaded from that which the Qur'an bids us do to aid fellow believers in need."

"Gentlemen, please, let's have order here." Nasir tapped the table with the end of an expensive-looking Mont Blanc pen. "Imam, first of all, explain to us, do we have something to be concerned about with this organization? What do they call themselves?" Nasir questioned, looking down at the presentation summary. "Uh, World Islamic Youth Fellowship?"

"That's correct, Mr. Chairman," answered the Imam. "This is a chain of orphanages and schools located in several countries across Europe, the Middle East, South and Southeast Asia, where by and large mostly secular education is emphasized. To be sure, attendance is limited to Islamic young people of all ages. Study of the Qur'an and Hadiths is, therefore, part of their curriculum, as I think we all would want it to be. Secular studies, however, predominate. So, we really don't think one could describe these schools as Madrassas. If you will also observe, a far greater part of these funds will go for support of the Youth Fellowship orphanages, than for their schools. We have investigated this agency fully, gentlemen."

"In what way?" Farouk Kubriti, Dean of International Studies at the University of Chicago looked both disconcerted and skeptical. He was one of the Board's more regularly outspoken members. "Has our due diligence regarding this World Islamic Youth Fellowship, for example, included any on-sight visits to confirm the substance of these operations? I would think with all that has been said here this morning, and considering the size of this grant, that we should at least do that before proceeding."

"No, Farouk, we have not as yet visited any of the Fellowship's locations, but the organization's operations are administered by a number of clerics I have known and trusted for many years, and they have assured me it is a well-balanced operation in terms of administration. Attached to the back of this request, for example, are the resumes of members of its governing body, and as you can see it also includes many secular individuals, well-known businessmen, etc."

"Given that you are even correct with what you say in that regard, Imam, there are still other aspects regarding this grant request about which I worry more." Kubriti was not one to back down. "We can't, as my good friend, Ed Jibril here, said a moment ago, just dismiss the attention an international transfer of this magnitude will bring to our organization in these times. If any of this money were ever to go for any activities other than those described in this grant application, there would be tremendous ramifications for us all."

"That would be true, Farouk, were we to use traditional banks as a means of transfer," answered the Imam.

The room fell silent.

"You're not implying are you, Imam, that we use a

money transfer agent, a hawaladar say, to transfer a sum of this amount? Surely we wouldn't want to entrust the transfer of so great an amount to any medium other than the international banking system."

"Yes, gentlemen, I am suggesting that. All of us here have used various hawaladars to move money around the world to loved ones. Who here has ever, and I repeat ever, had a problem in getting that money to the intended recipient?" There was no reply. "Your silence tells me a great deal, gentlemen. $5,000 or $500,000, the principal and methods are the same. I contend that one can use the system of hawala faster and more dependably than one can via the international banking system. Most of you know how corrupt some banking systems are in certain countries where we are active."

"I do admit, Imam, you are not totally incorrect in what you say regarding the relative dependability of a reputable hawaladar versus what we know the banking systems to be in many of the countries mentioned with respect to this grant," said Edward Jibril, rejoining the discussion. "However, even the simple act of disbursing an amount like $500,000 from our accounts at Global United could easily give rise to reports being filed by the bank, unless it is connected with some more routine business matter."

"Tariq made the same comment to me earlier this morning when he and I discussed this grant request, Edward, but after giving the situation some further thought, I think he has come up with a rather innovative way of avoiding a lot of unnecessary government concern about this much needed gift. Tariq, would you mind telling the other trustees what you told me?"

"Certainly! Look, gentlemen, as Chairman and principal shareholder of a federally insured commercial bank, I must, of course, be very careful with what I say. I'm not necessarily fond of the laws and regulations that govern cash transaction reporting in the banking system, but our bank still goes out of its way to avoid criticism by strictly reporting large money transfers that the government says it wishes to know about. So, what I am going to say, I will adamantly deny if any of you brings it up in the future."

"You know, Mr. Chairman, perhaps I should excuse myself from this discussion," said Edward Jibril. "My firm audits both your companies and your bank. Maybe this is something you wouldn't really want me to hear."

"That may be a good idea, Edward. I wouldn't want anything I have to say to compromise anything for you ethically."

Jibril rose quickly, leaving all of his board materials on the table, as it was the custom for all members to do. Smiling and nodding at his WICF associates, he quietly coupled a traditional salutation with another greeting of the day. "*Wa 'alaikumus Salam*—peace be upon you all, my friends—and have a wonderful Thanksgiving!"

The rest of the trustees had no idea just how fully familiar Mr. Jibril was with Nasir's often cavalier approach to general accepted accounting principals. The task of hiding many of Nasir's off-the-book business activities often fell to him and his firm as the primary accountants for the AmeriPAK group of companies. So, whenever it appeared as though Nasir was beginning to once again blur the lines between acceptable modern business practice and functioning of the ancient financial netherworld of hawala, Jibril would invariably find some reason to excuse himself if the discussion was public in nature.

The transfer of $500,000 half way round the world from one party to another was a great deal larger than the average transaction usually handled by most Money Service Businesses around the U.S. It was not, however, all that unique a situation for Yussef Ibrahim, President of Crescent Jewelers and chief money transfer agent for the Chicago portion of Tariq Nasir's hawala operation, to handle.

The Nasir hawala organization was an unregistered

money service business, in spite of U.S. laws regulating MSBs. It had never been registered, and it was the Nasir family's intention to never do so if it could be avoided. Like other more traditional practitioners of hawala, secrecy and confidentiality were bulwarks of every Nasir financial transaction. It had been so for generations, and Tariq Nasir was determined he would not be the first to make any changes in that regard, despite the more traditionally structured nature of his other banking operations.

Nasir's plan to hide the WICF's transfer of $500,000 to the intended recipient in Saint Petersburg, Russia, was really quite ingenious, and some trustees were impressed with its simplicity. "For the past two years, gentlemen," said Nasir, "my construction company, Aurora Development, has been making progressive renovations to the downtown offices of the WICF that we were eventually planning to treat as contributions. We will simply bill the foundation in the amount of $500,000 for those improvements, and then the foundation can cut us a check in that amount. We will in turn ensure that those same funds are transferred to Saint Petersburg by way of a very reputable hawaladar at our earliest opportunity.

"How soon can this be done, Tariq?" Imam Abdul Al-Hakim asked.

"In a relatively short order, if everyone here is in agreement. My construction company will have no problem providing the necessary documentation to back up such a billing. We can draw up our minutes for today's meeting so they exclude any discussion of this grant request and instead enter a discussion of a billing for 'construction services rendered' by my construction company in the amount of $500,000 as requested by this worthwhile cause. My company will generate backdated invoices to the foundation equaling that amount, which the board can then authorize payment by resolution today. We will find the right hawaladar and see to it that amount makes it to the World Islamic Youth

Fellowship in Saint Petersburg as requested. No one will be the wiser regarding the grant."

There was a noticeable silence in the room. All the WICF board members were well aware of how hawala transactions were handled, but looks on some faces showed that many were uncomfortable with what was being suggested. "What about your construction company's books, Tariq? Won't what you've described here create a taxable event on your books that you will need to account for," asked Charles Boulos again.

"Under normal circumstances, yes," replied Nasir. "That, however, will be a matter for me and my people to contend with."

"Do our intended recipients in Saint Petersburg have access to the Internet, or are you in touch with them by phone, Imam?" Nasir continued.

"Yes, I've been communicating with them regularly by way of e-mail."

"Great, if we can then come to an agreement as a board this afternoon regarding this matter, our accounting department for Aurora Development will begin work on putting together the invoices and backup documentation on such a situation before today is out. We can probably have this done within the next twenty-four hours, and the WICF can cut us a check at that time. By then we can also have coordinated the necessary instructions on how, when and where the money can be picked up in Saint Petersburg, and you can e-mail that information to your contacts there with the World Islamic Youth Fellowship. They should have their money within the next seventy-two hours or so." Nasir smiled. "We could perhaps make it sooner, but today is just about gone, and then there's the holiday, gentlemen."

"So, by way of summary Mr. Chairman, are we to be given to understand that this foundation is going to grant this request through some surreptitious back channel without ever recording any official resolution regarding the matter, and then mask a transfer for that amount through some convoluted series of transactions between it and one of your companies?" Dr. Faris Haifa, M.D., a soon-to-retire professor of medicine at Northwestern University, had been a soft-spoken, thoughtful member of the WICF board of trustees since its inception. Extremely well respected by many in Chicago's Islamic community, his membership on the board had always been a great benefit to the foundation from a public relations standpoint, but his insistence on propriety was regularly a source of irritation to some of his more aggressive fellow trustees. "If that is indeed the case, then I must vehemently protest."

Based upon the expressions of many of the trustees around the room, it appeared more of the board had been enjoying the intrigue of the whole affair than deploring the duplicitous aspects of the proposal. Haifa's comments were not well received.

"As a matter of fact, gentlemen," Haifa continued, "I have been becoming increasingly concerned with our foundation's penchant for such actions as of late. I would be extremely regretful to have to do so, but I, unfortunately, feel as though I would need to resign from my position on this board of trustees if we were to pursue this matter as proposed."

"Would we be able to depend upon you holding our discussions of today in the strictest of confidence if you were to leave," asked the Imam?

"Yes, it is the least I could do after all these years with the foundation, but I would still have to leave, nonetheless."

After another moment of awkward silence, Tariq Nasir looked slowly around the table at each of the trustees and spoke as though he represented the entire group. "Your counsel has been extremely valuable to this organization for many years, Faris. You will be sorely missed in the future."

◊◊◊◊

207

IMAD FAYIZ Mufassa was as nervous and pumped as any time he could remember in his twenty-five short years of life on earth. Never in his wildest dreams could he have ever imagined himself playing such a pivotal role in an operation he had been assured was of epic import to the furtherance of worldwide Islamic jihad.

At the start of the workday on the third Tuesday in November, Mufassa, a semi-tractor operator for Chicago's Dominion Janitorial Supply, Inc., was forewarned that somewhere, sometime during what would otherwise be a rather normal day of pick-ups and deliveries, he would be performing a task or tasks that could potentially be pivotal to a major tactical operation soon to be undertaken somewhere in the United States by the yet unknown al-Sahaba terrorist organization. Beyond that, however, Mufassa knew little more than general rumors as to what that operation might be.

Although unconfirmed by any of Mufassa's al-Sahaba superiors, conjecture had it that the yet unknown operation had been originally planned for execution by a consortium of al-Qaeda-related affiliates sometime around the middle of the coming year. However, the operation had instead been moved up to sometime around the end of the current year as part of a coordinated response to steadily increasing military operations by the United States and various of its allies across the Middle East and South Asia. This stepped-up attack had been assigned by al-Qaeda to its fledgling al-Sahaba affiliate in direct response to an urgent request by the dregs of the Islamic State, which was still on life support but attempting a comeback. The United States had been bragging for some time how it had totally vanquished ISIL, and the al-Qaeda felt it was time to prove otherwise.

Beyond these rumors, Mufassa was largely in the dark about what form such retribution would take. Yet, the feeling that it was he and only he upon whom the success or failure of this yet unknown operation might well depend, gave him great pride. He apparently had only to remain calm, cool, collected and go safely about everyday tasks inherent to his job as a driver to complete what was expected of him—and this was his final load for the day.

"Are you a companion of the Prophet," asked the stranger as he jumped into the passenger side of Imad Mufassa's Peterbilt tractor?

"Uh, yes, uh…it is to him that I owe all!" Mufassa stammered. He had not been told that anyone would be joining him at any time during the execution of his duties that day, but he still had the presence of mind to quickly recognize one of the highly secretive greetings used by one fellow member of al-Sahaba to another. The situation left him feeling queasy and lightheaded. He was nervous to begin with, but was now taken completely off guard by the stranger's sudden appearance. Not always the best under pressure, Mufassa was relieved he had been able to remember the correct response. Had he hesitated in the slightest, or even to any small degree failed in an exactly worded response, his life could easily have ended on the spot. The stranger's right hand was tucked into the left side of his jacket. Mufassa figured it held a weapon at the ready.

The stranger's hand and jowled, pockmarked face both relaxed. He spoke in Urdu, Mufassa's hereditary language from Pakistan, but with an accent Mufassa couldn't quite place. *Possibly west African*, Mufassa surmised. *How did this man know to address me in Urdu?*

"I am Saalim Nasrallah. Your final cargo pickup for the day is, I think, now on board this truck, and I believe you are in possession of related bills of lading. I saw the customs people stamp them for you, my brother. If you don't mind, I will look over your shipping documents while you're driving, but in the meantime let us leave this place with utmost dispatch—and drive with care, an accident could prove disastrous for us now."

Mufassa put the Peterbilt in gear and slowly moved

away from the loading docks at Chicago's Calumet harbor. "I was not told anyone would be joining me, sir, but I welcome the company."

"You now know my name, my young friend," Nasrallah continued. "What may I ask is yours?"

"I'm Imad Fayiz Mufassa." The young al-Sahaba operative proudly responded as he drove and at the same time tried to study his passenger more closely. "I saw you get off the ship as they were loading my truck. Did you just arrive in country?"

"Yes, young man, it was a long journey. I've been babysitting one of the cargos you just picked up for a few weeks now. I shall be glad when it's delivered into the hands of its next caretaker. Where are you taking us?"

"I will be delivering this entire truckload to a company called Dominion Janitorial Supply here in Chicago. Our people run it. The trip should only take about thirty to forty minutes. Little more than half an hour and your responsibilities are ended, Mr. Nasrallah."

"Not really, my friend. Once I have seen this shipment safely into the hands of your superiors, I will be returning again to the Aurora Crescent, the ship this cargo came in on. From here I will then be working my way back to New York. Once there, I will be joining our brothers in that city for my next assignment."

"Do you know the details about what is going to be happening, Mr. Nasrallah? I too am to take part in whatever the operation is that's being planned, but many of us know little in the way of details at this time. Word has it that we are to all be part of an operation that will dwarf all previous attacks that have taken place in this nation to date, including the great victory that occurred when al-Qaeda hit the World Trade Center on 9/11."

"We should not be talking about any of this, and you should not be asking such questions, Mr. Mufassa. You can't be certain as to who I am, and even if you were, I would not be at liberty to tell you any more than what you already know at this time. All you need to know is that we have something on board that is very important to those above us here in this city. I am certain you will be informed of more just as soon as your superiors are able to tell you. For now, however, it is best that you concern yourself only with the task at hand, and get this load safely to its destination as quickly as you can."

◊◊◊◊

PAUL TROTTER'S funeral was also held at St. Peter's Catholic Church near his northwest suburban home in Barrington, Illinois on the last Tuesday in November, four days after his death. The service was a large one. He was well-known and loved in his community, active in his church, had a huge family, and there was a significant amount of media attention that resulted from his notoriety and the nature of his death. Cass Price was asked along with a few family members and former associates to give a brief eulogy at the service. She felt honored to be asked, and had graciously agreed to take part in the ceremony. There was little time to prepare considering all of the activity she was now involved in as a result of her duties with the OCC and work at Global United, but speaking extemporaneously about someone as wonderful and well-liked as Paul was not difficult.

The HAWALADAR

CHAPTER EIGHTEEN

"GOOD AFTERNOON, Mr. Nasir, Saud al-Dajani calling here again from the bank. I apologize profoundly for calling you so late in the day and bothering you as much as I have been lately, sir." As instructed, Sammy was calling Nasir using the burner phone Nasir had provided him with quite some time before.

"No, apologies are necessary, Mr. al-Dajani. As I heard once said, your friends don't need them, and your enemies will never believe you anyway." Nasir cordially responded. "And you are a friend, aren't you?"

"Uh, yes, most assuredly, sir!" Sammy laughed nervously. He always found Nasir's rare displays of conviviality disarming. He could never quite tell when he was serious, and when he wasn't.

"What can I do for you this afternoon?"

"I simply wanted to bring you further up to date on where we are relative to the OCC examination, sir."

"And just where are we this time, Mr. al-Dajani?"

"Well, yesterday we provided the examiners with most all the information they requested for their second look at our bank's compliance with the Bank Secrecy Act and our Anti-Money Laundering program."

"If you will excuse me, Mr. al-Dajani, you had already forewarned me yesterday after your meetings with the OCC that you were going to be doing that. Why are we discussing it again today?"

"I know that sir, but I thought you might want me to fill you in a little further by letting you know that the people from the OCC definitely appear to be expanding their examination this time around. They've requested much more information than the time before when that Mr. Trotter was looking at that area of bank operations. This time they asked for complete transactional histories for certain account relationships with the bank, and AmeriPAK and all of its subsidiaries were included on that list."

"What's so different about that? Wasn't Trotter looking into some of those same areas of the bank at the time he died?"

"Yes, he was, sir, but he was just getting started. He had come to me the day that he died and had asked for some of this same information, just not as much as they've asked for this time. I never got around to providing it before we were informed of his death."

"I rather remember back to your calls to me prior to Mr. Trotter's death. I recollect you also being concerned then about what he was looking into. You seemed rather obsessed about the situation at that time, and now you appear to be again. Why, pray tell, are you so continually worried that the examiners are going to find some problem with the way we are handling our anti-money laundering efforts at Global United?"

"Well, sir, like I believe I told you back when Mr. Trotter was looking at this same situation, I was just a bit worried about the exemptions from currency reporting the bank has given a few of your AmeriPAK companies in the past. The examiners have shown a great deal of interest in the significant number of cash transactions and money transfers your companies generate, and the fact that we exempt them from a great deal of the reporting that we require of others."

"Give me more details, Mr. al-Dajani."

"Well, they've asked for example how much trouble it

would be for us to pull together all the records regarding cash transactions for your accounts and a number of others on our exempt list going back as far as four years instead of the two Mr. Trotter had asked for. Additionally, they want to know what criteria we used in deciding which companies to include on the list of those exempted from reporting, including all the AmeriPAK subsidiaries. From the start, we treated Aurora Transportation and Aurora Vending both as non-exempt organizations, because their types of business activities were most clearly listed as those of entities strictly forbidden status that would exempt them from reporting; but all of your other companies were shown as exempt. So, the OCC wants a full report on the methodologies used to determine them as such. It is their thinking that some of your companies hardly appear to be of the sort that would have enough cash business on a regular basis to qualify for exemption. I think they're going to really give our determinations as to exempt status a good going over."

"I believe I see what you mean. I am admittedly none too pleased at having the regulators making it some special crusade poring over our accounts. I really don't need that at this time." Sammy sensed Nasir's voice finally beginning to sound uneasy. "I suppose it is too late into this situation to take those of my companies you exempted off of the bank's exempt list?"

"You know, back when Mr. Trotter was looking at most of the same information I actually started to do just that, but after giving it a great deal of thought I decided we absolutely could not do that at this time. It is far too late for that now, sir. To have changed the status of those accounts at this time would have raised all sorts of red flags. It would suggest we question our previous actions in that regard. In my opinion, the removal of any of your accounts from the exempt list now would look far more suspicious to them than if we simply left things as they are."

"You are no doubt correct about that, Mr. al-Dajani.

Forget I ever mentioned it. What to your knowledge will be their action if they indeed determine any of our AmeriPAK company accounts to have been improperly exempted?"

"Well, sir, they would probably then look very closely at any and all cash transactions processed through those accounts, perhaps all of your accounts. If they found nothing suspicious about what took place with respect to the history of those accounts, and they don't take any great issue to our having exempted any of them, then they would probably just simply cite us for some regulatory violations, demand we clean up our act, and that would be all."

"And if their findings are more serious than that, Mr. al-Dajani?"

Al-Dajani took a deep breath and paused before answering. "Well, I don't really believe from what I know thus far that things will happen this way, but if any violations they find are considered serious and pervasive enough, they could decide to take some far more serious disciplinary action on the bank."

"Such as?"

"Well, such as perhaps a Memorandum of Understanding where the entire board would have to sign off on both an explanation for how and why the violations occurred, and what steps the bank will take to ensure it never happens again. Then they would probably examine that area of the bank quite closely again in the near future to ensure that things were being done the way we said we would. And then there's also always the potential for pecuniary penalties. They really mean business with stuff like this anymore."

"Fines, monetary fines?" Nasir asked incredulously.

"Yes, sir, in some cases where they feel a bank has been particularly negligent or shown a careless disregard relative to their compliance with BSA/AML regulations, they have been known to assess fines, some of which can be fairly hefty." Sammy began to sense that Nasir was now somehow playing with him with respect to some of his questions. He was certain Nasir knew a lot more about all of this than he was letting on.

"I see." There was an unmistakable pause in the conversation while al-Dajani waited for Nasir to make further comment. "Well, to say that I am displeased at this turn of events would be the understatement of the year, but I suppose there is nothing we can do about it now. I rather wish, Mr. al-Dajani, that if you had any concerns about this sort of thing that you would have talked to me sooner about them, but I suppose it is a little late for that now." Nasir sighed. "Look, I am confident the examiners will find nothing inappropriate about any AmeriPAK transactions, but what, just for my information, are the penalties when they do find so-called gross negligence in a bank's handling of its cash transaction reporting?"

"That is something, sir, neither you nor I want to have happen. The last I heard, any business, individual or bank that was deemed to be involved in any egregious violations of BSA could face not only criminal action but could also be subject to fines in the range of $500,000 or more. I have even read of situations where the government has for example assessed fines ranging up to twice the amount of the transactions involved. It's all pretty serious stuff to my recollection. I don't want to be an alarmist. Thus far, sir, we've been fortunate, but I worry when they look so long and hard at such matters."

"OK, let's not panic at this point in time, Mr. al-Dajani, but please keep me informed of any more developments in this situation. I appreciate this additional call, and after further thought, believe it might not be a bad idea if you perhaps touched bases with me say at least once a day to keep me posted until we get past all of this. You may even call me more if you need, but do keep me informed. As I have said before, Sammy, I want and will tolerate no more surprises. Do I make myself clear?"

"You do indeed, sir!"

"Oh, and I shouldn't have to remind you of this, but again always secure calls using only the special cell phone I gave you. Do you hear me?"

"Yes, sir, I understand. I have done so with this call, and as you ask will do the same in the future."

◊◊◊◊

IMAD FAYIZ Mufassa was greatly relieved when he pulled his Peterbilt semi-tractor rig into the warehouse Dominion Janitorial Supply rented in an old industrial area near downtown Chicago. Mufassa wasn't exactly sure what it was his truck was carrying, but he knew it perhaps to be an important element in a large operation al-Sahaba was planning to conduct across the United States sometime soon. He was quite relieved that this Nasrallah guy, who had jumped into the passenger seat of his truck earlier that afternoon, was who he said he was. A proper al-Sahaba password exchange had identified Nasrallah as friendly to the cause, but it was still a little embarrassing as to how quickly and easily the man had been able to enter his truck. Mufassa wasn't sure what their leader, Ismail Hamadi, might have to say about the whole affair. Hamadi was not fond of surprises and countenanced little in the way of laxity on the part of his people.

Mufassa had no sooner pulled his truck into the warehouse than he heard the overhead door quickly being lowered. Several al-Sahaba operatives immediately surrounded the vehicle with automatic weapons, aimed at both Mufassa and Nasrallah. While they were held at gunpoint, four men leapt into the tractor cab and pulled the two men out of the truck and roughly threw them face down on the floor.

"What is this all about, Mufassa? Who is this with you? Answer, and answer quickly for both your sakes."

Mufassa recognized Khalid's voice. "I can explain, Mr. Hamadi. I can explain," responded Mufassa.

218

"Well, then do so, and be quick about it."

"I had just finished picking up my last load at Calumet harbor and was pulling away when this gentleman jumped into the cab of my truck. I asked him to get out, but it was evident he had me covered with a weapon held under his jacket. I could tell that. He, uh, told me to exit the terminal area right away, and then that was when he did it."

"Did what?"

"Identified himself."

"How, did he identify himself, Mufassa?"

Whoever it was that had his knee in Mufassa's back was pushing his face hard against the cement warehouse floor. Mufassa would note the person who let him up when this was all over, and that person would soon pay. "He identified himself as a Saalim Nasrallah and then used one of our al-Sahaba passwords. He knew it exactly. Please, believe me, sir. I would never have brought him here unless I was sure."

"Let them up, gentlemen."

Mufassa and Nasrallah could feel the knees in the middle of their backs let up. Rough hands grabbed them and helped them up, brushing them off by way of apology.

"You must understand, Mufassa, we can be none too careful at this delicate point in time. We are indeed regretful of the way you were also treated, Mr. Nasrallah, but surely, you can put yourself in our shoes. What were we to think, seeing you ride in with Mufassa? He was supposed to be alone.

"'I understand completely, sir."

"Well, if you do, then you won't mind relinquishing that weapon you're carrying under your jacket. Will you?"

Nasrallah was hesitant. He didn't much like the idea of giving up his weapon but thought better of the situation looking down the barrels of the Kalashnikovs the men in front of him were carrying. "I suppose not," he replied, reaching into his jacket and pulling out a vintage Walther

PPK that he handed to Khalid.

"My apologies to you as well, Mr. Mufassa. I am regretful we had to handle you in that fashion. You've actually performed very well today, but we had to take these precautions. Now, why don't you find yourself a cup of coffee or a soft drink or something, while I take Mr. Nasrallah to my office for a further conversation? I have some questions to ask you, Mr. Nasrallah. Please, follow me."

Khalid led Nasrallah up an open staircase to an enclosed mezzanine-level office above the warehouse floor. Neither of the two communicated until they were in the office and the door was locked. "Nasrallah my friend, I am so glad to see you again after these many months. I hope you will forgive that complete charade." Khalid and Nasrallah kissed each other on both cheeks as was the custom of respect when friends greeted each other in that part of the world where both men originated.

"You have a strange way of showing it, Mr. Hamadi."

"I know, I know! I really am sorry we had to treat you that way, but I wanted to teach my young operative a lesson or two, and I also didn't want my people to know that we are former acquaintances."

"Yes, I figured it was something like that. A little rough way to say hello, my friend, but perhaps excusable considering what you say."

"Yes, I am sorry my brother. Thank you, for playing along. I purposely didn't tell him that you would be meeting his truck. Mr. Mufassa has been one of my weaker young operatives. He often talks too much. I have been worried how he might react if he were ever taken into custody by any homeland security forces."

"I would have to say, Ismail, that your young Mr. Mufassa concerns me too."

"How is that, my friend?"

"Well, he actually handled himself reasonably well when I jumped into the cab of his truck unannounced, even

220

though it was easy to do so. I used one of our password phrases, and he answered me impeccably. I would say he generally handled himself fairly well up to that point. It was what he did later thereafter that really concerned me."

Why, what did he do?"

"Well, on our way back, and once he thought he knew that I was on his side, he began to question me about what he termed the 'upcoming operation'. He was fairly insistent about the matter. You know, Ismail, we really can't have our people talking about such things. Can we?"

"No, I should say we cannot," Khalid responded curtly. "Please, wait here. Have a seat and a cup of coffee for a few minutes. I need to go have a talk with our young Mr. Mufassa."

Khalid exited the office and descended the stairs two at a time. Mufassa was sitting in the employee lounge drinking a cola and talking with a couple other al-Sahaba associates. Mufassa saw the other operatives look up, and heard Khalid's footsteps behind him as Khalid entered the room, but saw nothing of what was next to come.

Grabbing an approximate three-foot length of flat nylon crate binding as he entered the room, Khalid was on Mufassa before he knew what was happening. Wrapping the nylon strap a couple of times around both hands as he approached Mufassa from behind, Khalid without warning crossed his hands and formed a reverse loop, slipping it quickly over Mufassa's head and pulling it tight around his neck as a knee was pressed against the back for leverage. The two men across the table looked on in stunned silence as Khalid pulled tighter and tighter. Mufassa thrashed about kicking over furniture and all sorts of objects in the room as he gasped for air. With his face turning first red then purple in an effort to breathe, Mufassa strained his neck backward looking up into the eyes of his attacker. The onlookers could see the surprise and confusion in Mufassa's eyes as they heard his hyoid and trachea pop like a light bulb. Mufassa was clawing and pulling at Khalid's hands as his body gradually went limp. Khalid pulled at the garrote for what seemed like another full minute before he let Mufassa's body flop to the floor. Looking at the two al-Sahaba operatives, he could tell that this was the first time they had seen anyone killed. "Clean this room up and dispose of this refuse immediately, gentlemen. And let this be a lesson to you. This man violated our rules of secrecy. Anyone who does anything close to the same will pay in similar fashion."

Khalid threw the now bloody nylon strap at the two shocked al-Sahaba operatives, turned immediately on his heel and left the room. He had not seen his friend, Saalim Nasrallah in some time. They had some catching up to do.

CHAPTER NINETEEN

"YOU WANTED to see me again, Mr. Hart?"

"Yeah, Raj, come on in and shut the door behind you, if you would. I appreciate your taking the time to visit with me." Logan was a member of Global United's International Banking Committee, but beyond that, he had very little day-to-day exposure to Raj Haifa, the head of that department of the bank. He was nevertheless still very much impressed with the young Senior Vice President.

Raj was a second generation Asian American, whose father and mother were both soon-to-be-retired college professors. A proud American, Raj had "paid his dues," as Logan liked to put it. After graduation from Northwestern University with a degree in economics, and then receiving an MBA from that same institution's Kellogg School of Business Management. Raj served four years in the U.S. Marines with a tour in Afghanistan before entering the field of international banking with a large Chicago regional. Within five years after his arrival Raj had worked his way up to the number two position in that bank's international banking department when Tariq Nasir successfully recruited him over to Global United to help start that bank's international department. Bringing with him a well-known reputation in international banking circles and Chicago's Muslim-American community with the help of excellent family ties, Raj achieved early success in developing a great number of new account relationships for the bank. Logan had pegged him early on as quite bright and a real "straight shooter". He liked him very much.

"How's the International Department been faring thus far with the OCC examination, Raj?"

"Well, so far, so good, I would say. They gave us a good going over in the weeks before all the hubbub with the examiner getting killed and all, but thus far they haven't been back in to see us on this extended review they're doing." He raised his eyebrows and grinned at Logan. "Maybe they don't need anything more from our department."

Logan's weak, return look of chagrin suggested he knew better. He liked this young son of Pakistani immigrants. Logan felt he had a lot in common with the tall, well-muscled, no-nonsense ex-marine. Raj's respect for Logan's like military and banking backgrounds made the feeling mutual. More than once, the two had ended up sharing military experiences. "I'm sorry, Raj, that was a loaded question. I'm afraid you're not really going to be that lucky. I can't believe they haven't talked to you again already."

"Oh, great, I was fearful of that. What have they got cooked up for us that you know about?"

"I'm not totally sure. There's a chance it may not be all that much, but we can't guarantee that.

"How do you mean?"

Well. they indicate that you provided them with a full listing of customers when they first arrived, and they apparently reviewed a sampling of transactions the bank handled for those customers over the last year. Am I correct in that?"

"Yes, that's basically correct. And this time?"

"This time I understand they have another list of customers that they want to review transactions for, but they want to go back four years instead of two, and they are requesting information on both foreign and domestic customers. Depending upon what they find, they may want to go back even further. Are you going to be able to accommodate them without too much trouble if they need all that?"

"Sure, no problem! We have far more than four years of transactional information accessible on computer, and we're required by regulation to keep all the same information for transactions handled through all of our foreign branches available here at our home office, specifically for examinations. Do you know, however, which accounts they will want to look at?" Raj leaned forward with his elbows resting on his knees, looking Logan intently in the eye.

"Yes, as a matter of fact, I do." Logan handed Raj a sheet of paper. He watched as Raj read slowly down the page to a point where he did a double-take and looked back at Logan again over the top of a pair of stylish horned-rims.

"I see where Mr. Nasir and all of his companies are on this list. He wasn't on the original list they gave us last time, and I admittedly wondered why, what with him being an insider and all. This time though, he and his companies appear to be front and center. Do you think that's suggestive of problems they're expecting to find there?"

"Well, that remains to be seen, I guess. At this point, I just think they're trying to cover all the bases. Aside from being our principal shareholder, Mr. Nasir is also one of our biggest international clients, and I would imagine that they are including him and his companies this time for that reason alone. I am also quite frankly surprised they left him off your list the first time around if that is what you say they did."

"Yes, that was the case with the first list they gave me, but that may be because their first request was just a perfunctory part of the pre-examination checklist, and I was just dealing with a couple of the younger examiners on the OCC's initial review of our department. I'm not surprised they're asking for that information this time around though. I haven't really told this to anybody since, but just before he was killed, that Mr. Trotter got involved some in the review of our department. He came in and asked me to give him a

225

printout on the activity of Mr. Nasir and the AmeriPAK companies for the last year. I started putting it together for him but put it on hold after he was killed, thinking I would wait until Ms. Price or someone like her got back to me. Maybe I was wrong not to have inquired about the matter, instead of waiting for them to come to you with this."

"Oh, I don't think you necessarily did anything wrong, Raj. Did Trotter give you any reason why he wanted the information or why they left Nasir and his companies off the list the first time around?"

"No, he didn't get a chance. Our conversation was on the morning of the day he died, and he was of course in meetings all that day. I assumed, as we've discussed, that it was because of Mr. Nasir's insider capacity, and the fact that his companies do use our services a great deal. As you say, they are perhaps one of, if not the biggest, international clients we have. I figured Mr. Trotter was well aware of that."

"What kind of transactions do you mostly handle for Mr. Nasir, Raj?"

"Well, we do a few wire transfers here and there for Mr. Nasir personally, mostly to his family in Pakistan, but the bulk of what we do is for his AmeriPAK companies. As you know, the AmeriPAK group does a lot of international business, so they use many of our services. We provide his companies with such products as documentary letters of credit, bankers acceptances, some foreign exchange business and again international transfers, but there is nothing that I've ever seen that looks particularly suspicious with any of it, pretty standard stuff for our department." Raj looked at Logan and laughed nervously. "Is there something you're not telling me? Should I be looking at the business we do with Mr. Nasir and his companies a lot closer?"

"No, Raj, just put together the information that is requested, be as complete and exacting as you can, and don't worry about it until the examiners ask to discuss the matter. Let's just assume it's all routine at this juncture. I would, however, ask one favor."

"What's that?"

"Well, if you don't mind, Raj, let's keep this all between you and me for the time being.

Let me know when you have the information assembled, and then we will meet with the examiners together."

"What about Mr. Kruse? What if he asks me?"

"Mr. Kruse is the bank president. If he asks you anything specifically about this matter, you should answer him fully and accurately. He has a right to know. Just don't volunteer anything much about the examination of your international banking department unless he does ask. In particular, I would ask that you not bring up the fact that examiners have asked for all of this information on Mr. Nasir and his companies unless Scott specifically questions you about that. It's the one area about which he tends to overreact just a bit. Answer any specific questions he has on that matter fully, but just don't bring anything up regarding that subject unless he does—just for now at least. I have my reasons."

"Fine!" Raj paused and looked over his glasses at Logan again. "You know, Logan, I believe I know what your answer is going to be, but can you tell me why you would prefer I not mention any of this to Mr. Kruse unless he asks?"

"Yes, I can. It's because—and I think you're aware of this already—anything you tell Mr. Kruse will get back to Mr. Nasir before the day is out. You and I both know how sensitive Mr. Nasir is about such things. So, there's no need to rile him with the details about what the examiners may or may not be looking into concerning him and his companies, unless and until it's absolutely necessary."

"That's what I thought, sir. Thank you for confiding in me. You can count on my discretion."

◊◊◊◊
WHEN LOGAN arrived at RoSario's on the evening of the
fourth Tuesday in November, he glanced across the
restaurant looking for his dinner party. When he located
them, he saw not one, but two FBI special agents seated at
a table with Cass Price, both Jim Seilor and Lon Erickson.
He remembered how disappointed he had been when Cass
had told him the day before that Agent Seilor would be
joining them for dinner, and now here was Erickson to boot.
That's the pits, he thought! All three stood to greet him as he
approached the table.

"Good evening, Logan," said Agent Seilor. "I hope you
don't mind that both Lon and I are crashing your little dinner
meeting with Cass here this evening. I visited with Cass
yesterday and told her that I wanted another opportunity to
visit with the both of you together about a couple of important
matters. She told me that the two of you were planning to
meet this evening over dinner and that I would be welcome
to join you if I wished. She said she would take care of
informing you that I would be joining you, but that didn't
include Lon here. I later took the liberty of asking Lon to
come along with me, hoping neither of you would mind. He's
been part of this investigation all along, and I thought at the
last minute that he ought to be included again here too. I
hope you both will forgive our presumptuousness."

"No, guys, that's great!" Logan lied through his teeth.
Both Seilor and Erickson were people he liked, but he had
secretly been looking forward to time alone again with the
attractive lady examiner. "The more the merrier!"

"We've had some very important things come up that
we thought you both needed to know about and a slew of
questions we wanted to ask you both, or we wouldn't have
barged in," Seilor added.

"No, it's perfectly okay by me, gentlemen. Cass told me yesterday that you would be joining us, Jim, but I can also certainly see the advisability of you being here too, Lon. Glad to see you both again." Logan shook hands with Cass and both agents before taking his seat.

The agents could tell by the look on Logan's face that he was probably not being all that truthful with them, and they could hardly blame him. *Were either one of us single and meeting with a gal as good-looking as this one*, thought Erickson, *we probably wouldn't be all that happy to have a couple of interlopers like us barging in either.*

"What's so important that would take you both away from your families on an evening like this, though?" Logan asked, smiling at both agents. "As single folk, Cass and I have an excuse for eating out. We had agreed to meet away from the bank if the need arose until the OCC finished with its examination, and both of us don't much like cooking for just ourselves. So, RoSario's seemed like a mutually acceptable solution. Right, Cass?" Cass nodded and returned a sheepish smile. She had been rather looking forward to dinner alone with Logan as well. "You two, however, could no doubt be enjoying a nice home cooked meal. You must definitely have something important to talk about."

"You're right there," Seilor responded. "You can believe us. We wouldn't be here butting in if we didn't really feel the need to."

"Jim and Lon were both waiting on me when I got here, Logan." Cass smiled and touched Logan's arm by way of emphasis as she spoke to all three of the men. It was a perfunctory gesture on her part, but the agents could tell by the flushed look on Logan's face that he enjoyed it. "You both looked awfully sober when I got here," she said to the agents. "So, what's cooking'?"

"Well, we do have some serious matters to talk to you both about," said Seilor," but let's order something first before we get into it. We're probably all hungry, and we would really prefer we not be interrupted once we start our conversation. Now, what's good on this place's menu, Logan? Cass told us before you got here that this is one of your haunts."

"Well, you can hardly go wrong with anything on the menu," answered Logan, "But one of my favorites here at RoSario's is their eggplant parmigiana. Comes with a salad and side dish of pasta. It's fantastic."

"Sounds great to me. What about you, Lon?"

"Yeah, I think I can go with that." Agent Erickson answered. "What about you, Cass? What looks good to you?"

"Oh, why don't we make it easy on the waiter tonight. The eggplant also sounds fine to me. I'll go with Logan's recommendation. He didn't steer me wrong when he and I ate here yesterday."

"Fine, and just to get one other thing straight before we go any further, Lon and I are the ones who invited ourselves here tonight. So, we're buying."

"Whoa, that's not necessary, guys." Logan protested. "I rather thought I would take care of this."

"Nope, Lon and I'll hear nothing of it, and you really shouldn't argue with us. We FBI guys are usually packin', you know."

Logan laughed somewhat strangely. "Well, if you put it that way. I've been shot before, and it's not fun. I certainly wouldn't want it to happen again over a lousy plate of eggplant."

The other three glanced at each other questioningly at the aside from Logan about being shot, but no one seemed inclined to pursue the comment.

"Good, now that that's settled," said Seilor, "maybe we can have our waiter bring the food, and then we'll tell him we don't want to be interrupted unless we call for him."

All four requested that their salads be served with their

meals to avoid being bothered once their discussion began. When the food was delivered, Seilor told the waiter they would like to be left alone, indicating they would call for him if his services were needed.

"OK, what's all the cloak and dagger about, Jim?" Logan asked.

"Well, as I think you both are no doubt aware the Department of Homeland Security issued an *'Elevated Threat'* advisory some days ago suggesting a credible country-wide terrorist threat exists about which the public needs to be aware. Then just before we left our office this evening, we were informed that we could be only hours away from DHS increasing the advisory to an *'Intermediate'* level, with an eye toward a very possible further increase to the ultimate level of *'Imminent'* threat in the not too distant future. This suggests a rather dire scenario for all concerned indeed. Our agency has been placed on full alert, and numerous regional offices around the country—including Chicago—have activated their special, anti-terror task forces to full mobilization on a 24/7 basis."

Cass and Logan looked at each other and nodded. "Yes, I believe we're both aware of the Elevated Threat condition, but none of the other. It's rather scary sounding for sure, but what do these threat levels have to do with us?" Cass asked. "Nothing, I hope. Are you intimating the things we've been working on with regard to the Trotter matter are somehow related?"

"We hope there's no relationship, Cass, but we can't ignore the possibility the threat situation doesn't have something to do with the two of you, Paul Trotter, Nasir, Global United, and so on. Considering our need to cover all bases in a situation like the one we're facing, our District Special Agent, Merritt Daimler, thought it highly advisable the two of us join you here this evening—since we heard you were getting together anyway—and explain our thinking in this regard. Hence, our request to join you."

231

"Okay, so you've got our attention, Jim. I think you already know by now that Cass and I are ready and willing to do what we can. What would you like to discuss?" Logan asked. Both he and Cass appeared visibly concerned.

"Well, from all indications, and as Jim suggested a moment ago, the overall threat situation does seem to be getting increasingly more serious by the day," responded Agent Erickson since Seilor had just filled his mouth with a forkful of salad, "but before we get too far into that, let us preface our discussion by first asking whether either of the two of you has ever heard of the term, hawala?"

There was a moment of pause. Cass slowly shook her head while looking quizzically at Logan. "No, I'm sorry, I haven't. Have you, Logan?"

Logan nodded to the affirmative. "Well, as a matter of fact, I have. I learned a goodly amount about hawala quite a long time ago."

"Really, when, how so?" Erickson asked.

"Well, I first came across the concept quite some years back, during the time just before 9/11, when I was doing some research regarding a large international bank that failed sometime around 1990. I saw the term referred to here and there in articles regarding that situation. I've been curious about it since."

"That's interesting. Might we ask what bank failure it was you were looking into, Logan," questioned Agent Erickson?

"Sure, it was the BCCI failure, Bank for Credit & Commerce International, one of the largest international banking failures in history at the time that it occurred. The situation was a real bag of snakes all around the world financially. The founder of the bank was a guy named Agha Hasan Abedi. Like Global United's Tariq Nasir, he too originated from Pakistan, if I recollect properly. I saw the term mentioned with respect to the way he did business. I tried to research the concept of hawala a little at that time, but there wasn't much one could find about it back then. I looked the subject up online a little more recently, however, and there appears to have developed an abundance of information in the years since 9/11."

"You're right, there has." Agent Erickson said, shaking his head in the affirmative, seemingly impressed with Logan's cogent answer.

"That's funny, here I am a national banking examiner of no few years experience, and I must be the only uninformed person at this table," Cass stated. "I've heard absolutely nothing about this so-called 'Ha-wa-la' business. Did I pronounce it correctly? What exactly is hawala?"

"Well, maybe you've heard it referred to as something else, Cass." Agent Erickson added. "There's a big section of the U.S.A. Patriot Act—or Freedom Act as I believe it's been called over the last few years—that has to do with hawala. In that document, however, the activity is mostly referred to as Money Transmitting or Money Service Businesses. I think the Bank Secrecy Act was changed around the end of 2001 to also encompass MSB transactional activity."

"OK, now you're finally in my ballpark," Cass acknowledged. "I certainly understand what money service businesses are. We monitor what banks do with MSB's a great deal, but I quite frankly still had never heard the term hawala until you mentioned it tonight, or if I did, I don't recollect it. From what I understand, a whole host of financial service providers that do such things as sell travelers checks and money orders, check cashing, currency exchange and other related activities can qualify as MSB's. Western Union, for example, is an MSB, and by definition, even the U.S. Postal Service could qualify as an MSB. So, how does this hawala thing fit in?"

"Everything you just said about MSB's is correct," continued Erickson, "but these guys that practice this business of hawala—hawaladars they're called—although clearly part of the whole host of financial service providers you just described, are rather a breed apart. Their profession principally emanates from places like Asia, South Asia, the Middle East and surrounding areas, and it goes back centuries, predating anything we understand as banking today."

"Who are their clientele?" Cass asked.

"Well, most hawaladars operating in the U.S. today mostly serve various ethnic communities located in many of our larger cities, like Detroit, Chicago, New York, Miami and so forth. Wherever you find diasporas of Asian, South Asian, Asian Indian or Middle Eastern immigrants for example, there you're also going to find one or more hawaladars. Various areas of Europe have for example seen a major expansion in the business of hawala as a result of the significant influx in recent years of immigrants from the areas I've just mentioned. Such businesses are referred to by a myriad of names depending on the ethnic group they serve, but they all basically operate the same."

"What kind of services do they perform?"

"Well, they for the better part transfer sums of money for their clients back and forth between fellow hawaladars around the globe, mostly in third world countries, some of which aren't all that friendly with the U.S. Hawala is a fast system of money transfer that operates at a high level of trust with its clientele thanks in no small part to the extreme confidentiality with which it treats every transaction. But therein also lies the problem.

"How so?" Cass asked. "Don't all MSB's have to register to do business in this country now under the requirements of the Freedom Act?"

"Yes, they do, in this country and many others, but suffice it to say, not all have done so." Agent Erickson continued. "Much of what hawaladars do for their clients is neither illegal nor nefarious for the better part, but not all of their transactions are benign either. That's why the government has decided to require their certification and adherence to essentially the same rules and regulations that all federal and state chartered financial institutions are required to follow when it comes to the handling of cash and transfers of money."

"Well, I certainly would prefer the controls and procedures of the conventional banking system if I were in need of transferring money, but that doesn't really sound all that much of a problem to me," quipped Cass.

"Well, usually it isn't. Normally, most hawala clients are legal immigrants who simply wish to send to or receive money from family and associates in their homelands, but for one reason or another eschew the regular banking system."

"I suppose that's understandable." Cass agreed. "From what I hear, the banking systems in some of the countries you mention aren't all that dependable."

"You got it! So, there's a lot of this hawala-type business that's going on around the world today, many billions of dollars from what I understand. Not all of it, however, is the kind of business you and I would want to see take place. On occasion—and this is what we are most concerned about—hawala clients may just as easily be drug dealers and/or terrorists transacting the kind of business we want and need to stop. By way of example, hawala is how we figure people like al-Qaeda, ISIS and other terrorist crud balls have been moving their money around the world."

"You're kidding!" Cass exclaimed.

"I wish we were, Cass. If you will recollect President George W. Bush used to repeat a lot in many of his speeches after the events of 9/11 that our anti-terrorist forces planned to 'follow the money trail.' Well, an all out investigation of the business of hawala has been part of that promise. Since forever, you traditional bankers have been subject to all sorts of anti-money laundering oversight, while these 'underground bankers' have had no regulation whatsoever. If a bank errs in its handling of such things, the weight of the world comes down on them through people like you, your fellow regulators and us. In the past, however, it hasn't been so with the MSB's or the hawaladars. Hence, the USA Freedom and Bank Secrecy Acts now reach out to cover them as well. A whole new, separate set of even more stringent rules and regulations has been drawn up to cover the activities of all MSB's, whether known as hawala, Western Union, or any other name. They now have to follow essentially the same procedures on cash transaction reporting that all other regulated financial institutions must adhere to. And believe me, most all of what a hawaladar does orients around cash."

"So, once again, what do you figure that has to do with what Cass and I were here to talk about tonight?" Logan asked. "It's not that we don't enjoy your company and all, guys, but it would sound as though you, FinCEN and others have the bases pretty well covered on the MSB front. We bankers have enough troubles of our own to worry about when it comes to cash transaction reporting, preventing money laundering and so forth on our end, without having to worry about the activities of all the hawaladars around the country."

"You're right, Logan, regulating MSB's is the responsibility of the Financial Crimes Enforcement Network and the Treasury Department, and it isn't a banking problem per se. However, we think we may be in the process of looking into something with FinCEN at this time where you folks may be of some assistance to us, and we need to ask for your help in that regard in addition to what you're already doing."

"What might that be?" Logan asked. "You've already stated that we have nothing to do with MSB's other than to follow regulation with respect to how we do business with them. So, how can we be of any assistance to you?"

"In this case, Logan, you may be quite surprised." Agent Erickson looked like a game show host who was about to give a contestant the answer to a million-dollar question they had just missed. "We think Global United may be doing business with a very large, unregistered MSB—in this case actually a very large hawaladar—and may not even know it."

"And just who might that be? We would pursuant to regulation report something like that, I would hope, and I'm not aware that we have," said Logan. "Just who are you talking about?"

Both agents stopped eating, looked at each other and then leaned forward as Agent Erickson responded in a low voice for both of them. "Look, folks, before we answer that, we need to come to a very clear understanding. What we are going to be discussing now are matters that are highly sensitive and of the utmost importance to national security. So, we must insist that everything we discuss here tonight remain highly confidential, or there will be heck to pay if you do not. Can we depend upon your confidence?"

"I think you know you can count on us in that regard or you wouldn't be sitting here talking about this with us. Would you?" Logan answered.

"That's correct, but that needed to be said nonetheless." There was a painful moment of silence as the two FBI agents studied both Logan and Cass' faces before Agent Erickson continued. "Now, both of you may want to hold onto your seats for this one, particularly you, Logan. You see, we think there's a possibility Global United's very own Tariq Nasir may be an extremely large and very successful hawaladar, who has been in the business in the U.S. now for many years." The agents studied both Logan and Cass' faces for a reaction to this information and were slightly taken aback by how little they saw. "As a matter of fact, we even think that Mr. Nasir's entire business empire may have from the very beginning been specifically designed to under-gird the infrastructure of a worldwide network of hawala, the likes of which has seldom been seen before."

"When you say you 'think there's a possibility he may

237

be a hawaladar, Lon, are you saying that Mr. Nasir is in the money service business, and has never registered as such? Is that correct?" Cass asked. "Because if that is the case, then both the FBI and the OCC may be looking at some very big problems."

"That's just our point, Cass," Agent Erickson continued. "We agree with you. If Mr. Nasir is indeed an unregistered hawaladar who does business all around the world—the way we think he might be through his people and companies—then his concurrent ownership of controlling interest in a federally insured U.S. commercial bank is a bit like having the fox in the hen house, so to speak. Aside from breaking federal law by operating an unregistered MSB, he at best would have numerous conflicts of interest in his capacity as Chairman and principal shareholder at Global United."

"You aren't just kidding," Cass responded. "If what you say is true, there would be no way we could allow Mr. Nasir to continue any active involvement—or for that matter ownership—in any federally insured banking institution. How certain are you about all of this? Mr. Nasir is a highly visible community leader, well-known and well-respected, and none of this has been proved yet. Has it?"

"No, you're right, he is, and it hasn't. So, we're moving with caution, but still investigating whether any of this hawala stuff applies to him, any of his companies or any of his people. That being said, I must say though that there is an increasing body of evidence that is leading us to believe just that," said Erickson.

"What sort of evidence are you talking about," asked Logan?

"Well, for the last six months the Financial Action Task Force on Money Laundering—a worldwide, inter-governmental body established some years ago to combat international money laundering, terrorist financing, and so-forth—has been piecing together the organizational structure of a suspected centuries-old hawala network, owned and run by the Nasir family."

"Yeah, I'm familiar with the FATF," said Logan.

"Me too," added Cass.

"Great, well if you are familiar with the FATF, then you should know that they're pretty good at what they do, and they believe that the Nasir family has a money service business that may span multiple continents. They haven't been able as yet to document a North American portion of the operation, but they're working on it, and have involved the FBI in the process."

"And I'm guessing this is where you're about to tell Cass here, and me, that you want us somehow involved in that investigation of yours." Logan injected.

"Well, quite frankly, yes," answered Erickson. "We think you both may be able to help us put together the final pieces of the puzzle as a possible byproduct of what you are currently looking into at Global United. If that is the case, we need that information as quickly as we can get it."

"I will probably be working myself out of a relatively good job position with Global United by helping you with this, but if the bank has a problem of this sort, I want to know about it as much as you. You can, of course, count on me to help in any way possible with your investigation," said Logan, "but I do, however, have a couple of questions I would like to ask before we start down this road together."

"Ask away!" Agent Seilor replied, rejoining the conversation.

"First of all, have you considered or are you considering involving Scott Kruse, the bank's president, in this investigation? And if not, why not?

"We've looked into Mr. Kruse, and considered involving him, but decided against it, in spite of the important position of responsibility he holds within Global United," Seilor responded. "If you are wondering, we haven't found anything of concern about him yet personally, but from everything we can tell, he is quite close to Mr. Nasir, and we just can't depend upon his maintaining the confidence necessary in this situation. Does that answer your question?"

"Yes, it does, and I'm at least relieved in that regard. I'm not all that impressed with Scott's abilities as a banker, but I do think he is basically honest. I was hoping he wouldn't be involved in any inappropriate way with all of this."

"You said you had some more questions though?" Erickson asked.

"Yes, but only one more, and it relates to what I am suspecting you may not have told us about all of this. If most of what the average hawaladar transacts for his clients is simply moving money around the globe for basically honest people who are either culturally averse or nervous about doing business with regular financial institutions, and you have been looking into this matter for many months now, what about the situation makes it so pressing for you?"

"That's unfortunately a fairly insightful question, Logan." Agent Seilor answered. "And we're prepared to answer it, but first let me repeat our earlier reference to the high state of terror alert the DHS has just put the country on. I know I probably don't need to say this again, but we can't tell you enough how important this whole investigation may be to national security."

"We understand quite clearly, Jim," Cass answered. "Would you prefer to go somewhere else to have this discussion?"

"No, this will do fine. Our table is a comfortable distance from anyone else in the restaurant. I'll just speak softly." Seilor paused, looking down at his plate and chewing on the inside of his cheek as he took stock of what he wanted to say next to Logan and Cass. Both could tell Seilor was troubled about what he was going to tell them. "Anyway, hearkening back to our earlier mention of an impending increase in the national threat level, there is a linkage between it and our discussion of hawala."

"In what way?" asked Logan.

"Well, by way of background in that regard, although it may be a big surprise to some people considering the ruggedness of relations between the two countries over the last few years or so, the Russian Federation through its Federal Security Service had a series of back-door chats with our folks at CIA during the last thirty days, in which they passed along some very unsettling information. It seems their sources have recently garnered some very solid intel reporting the possibility that their own Russian Mafiya may have supplied an al-Qaeda-related terrorist organization with a weapon of mass destruction, yet undetermined in exact type, but suspected of being some sort of biological weapon."

"Good grief, let's hope not!" Logan exclaimed. "I think that's the one form of terrorist attack many Americans fear most, me included. Thanks, to the world's recent experience with COVID-19, there are few countries that could endure another pandemic—in particular one of this sort. I understand it's the one nightmare scenario most dreaded by our security people these days. What led the Russians to that conclusion?"

"I understand the Russian government has—just as we do with organized crime here in America—a handful of their law enforcement and intelligence types deep undercover inside the Russian Mafiya. One of those sources has apparently informed the Russian FSB that a recent transaction took place whereby some disenfranchised, female Russian scientist may have many years ago stolen a Bio-WMD, which the Russian mob recently obtained from her. They, in turn, may have sold it to an Islamic terrorist group for a pot load of money."

"That's really scary," Cass said. "Have our people checked out the veracity of this report?"

"As you can imagine, the vetting process on information of this type has been quite extensive," explained

Agent Erickson. "Making the task difficult to begin with, is the official position of the Russian government that any biological weapons of mass destruction that may have been stockpiled by the former Soviet regime, were destroyed after that government fell. So, for them to even unofficially admit that this situation exists leads our people to believe that the threat is real. They claim some experimental pathogens supposedly intended for use in the development of vaccines may have been taken by the lady scientist years before she was let go from government service, and were it not for their undercover source, they might never have found out about the situation. That same source has further informed them the lady was murdered and disposed of to hide the existence of the transaction; and the fact that they haven't been able to find her anywhere since learning of the matter would seem to lend credence to that story."

"If that is all they know, what makes your people think that there may be a threat to the United States?" Logan asked.

"We don't know for certain," said Erickson," but that is exactly why we figure the Russians are so anxious to help with this thing. They don't know for certain either. Their best intelligence indicates that the stuff is headed this way, but they can't be sure. The attack could be headed their way as easily as ours. They've got a pretty serious Jihadist threat coming at them out of places like Chechnya and so forth. So, they're being very atypically cooperative on this, and our people have been on the thing like stink-on-a-stick since we found out about it. Every agency in our anti-terror network is now working on it around the clock. We're involved, the Defense Department, the CIA, all the DHS agencies, Secret Service, ICE, the CDC and so on. They have all pulled out the stops. This one has everybody scared."

"Is everyone's food okay?" The group's waiter had noticed from across the room that the four were eating very little of what he had set before them. In spite of the fact that they had asked not to be disturbed, he thought he should at least check. They thanked him for his attention, told him everything was fine and repeated that they would call him if he was needed. The food was delicious as usual, but none of them really had much appetite for it anymore, thanks to the subject of discussion.

"What information do our people have that might indicate the attack may be headed this way?" Cass asked.

"Well, word has it," continued Agent Erickson, "that the agreement between the terrorists and the Russian mob called for the WMD to be turned over to the terrorists once the mob was in receipt of at least $1 Million, and for another $1 Million to be paid when the weapon supposedly reached the country it was intended for."

"So, how does this tie into hawala? Is that the way they got the money?" Logan asked.

"You're staying a step ahead of me, Logan. That's just what I was about to say. Intelligence sources are also reporting that half of the second $1 Million required for purchase of the pathogens may have already been delivered to the Russian Mafiya located in the Russian city of Saint Petersburg, and the remaining $500,000 may be in the process of delivery as we speak by way of several hawala networks, with the money moving circuitously through a number of major cities around the world to hide the sources.

"Where did you get that information," asked Cass?

"FATF," answered Erickson, "the organization we were discussing a little while ago. Thanks to information from them, we've also been able to determine that some or perhaps most of the money that has been used in this transaction originated from accounts or organizations that are either directly, or at least indirectly, tied to various terrorist organizations."

"Well, how does that tie back to Mr. Nasir and Global United though?" Cass questioned. "Are you suggesting he may be tied to the movement of some of that money involved in the Russian WMD thing? Sounds like a stretch to me if you're unable to confirm whether he is or isn't a hawaladar. What's led you to think that in the first place?"

"Well, it's his family situation, or to be more specific, his father, Mahmoud Nasir. Mahmoud's a fairly wealthy precious metals dealer in Karachi, Pakistan. He's also a substantial shareholder in Tariq Nasir's holding company, AmeriPAK, Inc., to my understanding"

"And you're going to tell us he's a hawaladar," Logan added presumptively.

"Right you are. The elder Mr. Nasir has been for most of his life. It's been a family business for generations from what they tell us. The Nasir family would have everyone believe that their wealth comes from the trading of precious metals, gold, silver, gems, etc., but word has it, the bulk of the family's wealth has over centuries come from their involvement in the business of hawala. The Nasir hawala operation in Pakistan is well-known, well-trusted, and has always been extremely successful. Yet, from all appearances, the Nasir-related hawaladars have hung back on registering various parts of their network. Supposedly, the Pakistani government has been cracking down on such unregistered operations for some time in that country. So, old Mahmoud has registered the Pakistan side of his operation, but he has a lot of political pull and it is our understanding that his business gets very little oversight or pressure relative to required reporting, etc.

Hawala remains the method of choice for moving money around and in and out of that country. Hawaladars are open and ready to do business on just about every other street corner in most bazaars throughout the country—and the Nasir family runs one of the larger operations, albeit far more secretive and international in scope. Putting all the pieces together, our sources feel there is a strong possibility that at least some of the money that made its way to Russia in this situation more than likely passed through the hands of

Mr. Nasir's people."

"I'm sorry, but just exactly how does this hawala thing operate?" Cass asked. "I don't understand. Why can't the Pakistani government or our intelligence people pin down all of this conjecture about these money transfers? Wouldn't there be some audit trail of sorts, like the banking system requires? Some records have to be kept, don't they?"

"No, Cass, that's just it with hawala." Logan became embarrassed that he had interrupted. "Wait a minute, Lon, I'm sorry. Maybe you wanted to respond to that?"

"No, no... go right ahead. You're the banker here. You'll probably explain it much better than me, anyway." Erickson seemed happy to have Logan describe the situation. "I'll stop you if I think you're wandering too far afield with your explanation."

"Well, I'm sorry, anyway. I get a little carried away at times when a subject like this interests me." Everyone grinned. Logan shook his head apologetically before continuing with his explanation. "Anyway, Cass, hawala is, for the better part, a paperless, alternative remittance system where in most cases no money physically moves across any borders. The system consists of a hawaladar receiving cash in one country—no questions of any significance asked— and then arranging for a 'Correspondent' hawaladar in another location or country to deliver a like amount, minus minimal fees and commissions, to an endpoint recipient. The sender provides the recipient with a code word or number, an encrypted message or some other identifier that is then used to retrieve the money on the receiving end. The transaction can occur strictly between a single hawaladar on one end and a single hawaladar on the other; or in some cases, a whole chain of hawala operators around the globe —as I imagine the circumstance to be in this situation Lon and Jim are discussing with us here tonight."

"Well, if no money actually moves, how do these hawaladars settle up," asked Cass?

"The simplicity of it is actually fairly remarkable," answered Logan. "Hawala systems around the world are based on trade of goods and services in most cases, not cash. On some rare occasions, cash may be physically transported to consummate a transaction, but more often than not, cash is given and received on both ends of the transaction, without any funds ever moving between cities or countries to do the deal."

"Well, if there is no wiring or physical movement of funds," asked Cass, "then how do the in-between correspondents get their money?"

"That's the beauty of it. For the better part, amounts of money are carried on the books of one hawaladar as due to or from another with minimal records kept in that regard. It hence becomes an almost untraceable transaction."

"It all sounds rather ingenious," responded Cass, "but what about accountability. How does the remitter know that his or her transaction will take place as intended without regulation and oversight such as exists in the banking system?"

"That too is seldom, if ever, an issue. The word hawala is actually the Hindi word for 'Trust'. Were a hawaladar not to successfully complete a transaction in exactly the manner intended, it might not only result in a disastrous loss of face for which he could be socially reviled, but perhaps as well result in religious excommunication. In some cases it might even result in physical retribution were certain parties—like a terrorist organization—ever wronged. You regulators are tough, Cass, but bankers seldom have that kind of hammer hanging over their head if they are negligent or dishonest."

"You're right about that. Although there are bankers with whom we frequently have to deal who sometimes make me wish we did." Cass rolled her eyes and shook her head as she directed more questions at the FBI agents. They could tell she was half-serious about what she had just said.

246

"I think I understand how this works, gentlemen, but once again, how do Logan and I figure into your investigation? Are you suggesting that Nasir is somehow using Global United in this hawala business?"

"We don't know yet. We don't even know that he or his companies are involved in any way with his father's hawala business, but we want the two of you to help us determine answers to all that. Mr. Nasir and all of his companies do business with Global United, you have access to his financial information, and the OCC has every reason to ensure the rectitude of his relationship with the bank as an insider. All we need for you to do is to continue looking his situation over closely with the thought of hawala in mind and let us know your findings just as quickly as you can as they relate to these concerns."

"Well, let me ask one last question." Cass continued. "Uh, if all MSB's have to be registered in this country and most others, wouldn't any of the AmeriPAK companies involved in any way in that business have to be registered too?

"Yes, that's absolutely correct. Yet, believe it or not, there are still numerous hawala operations around the world who refuse to do that, ignoring the law and operating in utmost secrecy, and we're wondering if that might not be the case with the Nasir operation here in this country. That's why we particularly need your help on this one. If you determine there is something worth looking into and could give us a heads-up in that regard, we would then obtain a federal court order and institute an investigation. Your work could give us a jump on the investigation before Mr. Nasir might cover his tracks if anything is going on, and we really need to know if something is going on. We're looking for any tie whatsoever into this whole Russian thing, and the clock may be ticking on what could be a disastrous situation if some attack is in the making here in the U.S."

"We'll get to it right away gentlemen," Cass promised.

"Interestingly enough, Logan's people and mine may have already done a great deal of work that could help with your investigation into this matter. We were going to discuss the results of some of that effort over dinner here this evening."

"That's great, can you relate some of what you've done to us?" Seilor asked.

"Sure! Well, as you know, Paul Trotter was looking into Mr. Nasir's companies and their relationships with the bank to some degree when he died. Most of his work was stolen along with his briefcase and computer when he was killed. Our people couldn't recollect all that Paul was working on at that time, but they said he was quite animated when he commented several times about Mr. Nasir and his AmeriPAK group. We have, therefore, been looking at the structure of Nasir's loan arrangements, the handling of his deposit accounts and the work that the bank does for him through its international banking department."

"That's great, Cass, just great!" Seilor exclaimed. "That's exactly what we need. We want you to keep working on that, but based upon what we've discussed here tonight, please ratchet up your examination to the extent you can. Look Nasir's situation over with a fine-toothed comb, if you will, and let us know of anything, absolutely anything, you find that might tell us something regarding our investigation. And remember time is of the essence with this. Right, Lon?"

"You've got that right!" Erickson nodded in agreement. "And based on how important this could be, I really feel we need to meet fairly regularly, at least until we see whether this thing with Nasir is going anywhere? The Bureau thinks this is a real serious matter. We need to know if Nasir has a hawala operation like his father, and more importantly if he does, whether that organization has been part of any U.S. link to this Russian WMD matter. Think we could do that?"

"Sure, fine by me." Logan agreed. "How about you, Cass? Neither one of us necessarily has anyone waiting for us at the door when we get home of an evening."

"It's sad to say, but Logan's right," Cass responded. "Count me in. If any of this relates to Paul's death or has anything to do with one of the bank's we oversee, I want to know. It's important to us regardless of the security threat, and even more so with it. Tell me where and when, and we'll be there with all the information we can glean from our examination.'

"You know, it might be wise if we maybe had all future meetings in some more secure location?" Logan suggested.

"No doubt about that," agreed Agent Seilor. "This was probably much too public a place for what we were discussing here tonight, even though I am certain our conversation here was never compromised in any way. What say that until further notice, we meet at the FBI's downtown offices in the Dirksen building on Dearborn, if that works for the two of you. You know where we are, don't you?" Logan and Cass both nodded in agreement. "I would suggest that unless there is some reason that arises where we can't, that we maybe think of getting together in the evenings around 7:00 p.m. when we meet—starting tomorrow night if you're available. And I kid you not, come separately and take care when you come to the meetings to ensure you aren't followed. We don't need anyone finding out about these little tête-à-têtes."

CHAPTER TWENTY

GLOBAL UNITED Bank of Chicago always held the monthly meeting of its board of directors on the fourth Wednesday of every month, set later in the month to accommodate the compilation of the many reports the bank provided its directors. The task of preparing all the varied information each of the directors of Global United received on a monthly basis was far more involved than that of most banks their size, due to the amount of detail the bank's chairman and principal shareholder, Tariq Nasir, insisted the directors receive. Even with the later timing of the meeting each month, however, bank staff was still usually quite pressed to produce all of the necessary information in a timely, accurate manner. The task would probably be almost insurmountable considering the reports demanded by Nasir were it not for the extremely high level of technology utilized by the bank.

Beginning in early 2010, once again in response to the adamant insistence of Tariq Nasir, Global United began expending a great deal of time, money and effort toward automating nearly the entire process of monthly management and board reporting. The eventual result of this effort was that the bank's directors now received all of their monthly board reports electronically, via encrypted e-mail, for review prior to their meetings. A basic prerequisite for a position on Global United's board was accordingly that each individual director be relatively computer literate, and well informed as to the content and purpose of all reports that might be included in each director's monthly packet. To make sure competency levels of all directors remained adequate in this regard, regular training on updates and overall use of the system was made available on-line via what the bank rather creatively called its Directors' University.

As Executive Vice President and Chief Operating Officer of the bank, Logan Hart was not a voting member of Global United's board of directors, but he was expected to regularly attend the monthly meetings. The November meeting would be the second Logan had attended since joining the bank, and he remembered how impressed he had been with the conduct of the first. Global United's board meetings were nothing like anything he had previously experienced, and he had attended many a bank board meeting during his tenure as a bank consultant.

No written reports were used at all for the conduct of a Global United board meeting. All board reports were instead displayed on a large screen on the wall opposite the directors at one end of the boardroom. As Nasir conducted the meeting, he would toggle through the information, highlighting each subject as it was discussed. The directors watched the large screen as the meeting progressed. If a director needed to refer to any information elsewhere in the report other than what was being shown on the screen, located on the table immediately in front of each director was a state-of-the-art laptop computer, synchronized with the information being shown on the larger screen. The reports on each director's computer, however, were fully interactive. So, whenever the need arose a director could, with a couple of simple clicks, move from one report to another on their individual computer to look at any information to which they wished to refer, and make notes to themselves or administration of the bank regarding any questions they might have. Another simple command was all that was needed to return the director's individual computer to a point synchronized with the information being discussed on the larger screen. A small lined pad and pen were placed next to each director's computer for personal written notes if needed, but if anyone used them, it was always the source of some good-natured ridicule. Most all the directors usually instead opted to use a digital note pad provided on their computer where they could easily enter notes to themselves as the meeting progressed. When the meeting ended, these notes were automatically entered into a digital memo that was then e-mailed to the director's office or home computer for later reference. This unprecedented level of technology utilization by Global United impressed banker and bank regulator alike.

The bank's bylaws authorized a total of twelve voting directors, two officers of the bank and ten outside directors. Tariq Nasir as Chairman, and Scott Kruse as President of the bank, occupied the two seats held by officers, and a relatively diverse group of outside shareholders filled the remaining ten board positions. Included among the outside directors were an attorney, an accountant, an educator and seven very well known, successful senior executives from area companies.

As was usually the case, Nasir moved through the November board agenda with efficient dispatch. Minutes of previous meetings, month-end statements of condition, profitability and growth reports along with supporting data were quickly reviewed and dispensed with in an extremely businesslike fashion. Individual chairpersons of standing committees of the board, such as the Loan, Audit, Trust & Private Banking, Asset-Liability Management, etc., then presented their reports as related documentation was concurrently flashed on the overhead and individual computer screens. All the directors usually came well prepared, and Chairman Nasir was quite judicious in his conduct of the meeting when discussion strayed. It was seldom the meeting extended much beyond an hour and one-half, but today a timely adjournment was not to be.

"As you will note from the agenda," intoned Nasir, "our last item of business today is a discussion of the examination currently being conducted at Global United by the Office of the U.S. Comptroller of the Currency, an ordeal that has been ongoing here now for over six weeks.'

"Isn't that somewhat normal, Tariq?" asked director Sulaiman Katai. Katai was owner and CEO of Alliant Group, Inc., a large, fast-growing Chicago insurance agency that catered to the city's Muslim community. He was a close personal friend of Tariq Nasir's and had been a director of Global United since day one of Nasir's ownership of the organization. "I thought the OCC was always in our shop about that length of time."

"No, that's not quite right. An examination for a bank our size by the OCC usually lasts about three to four weeks, and this examination is already in its sixth week. Figuring that some of you may have heard about the situation and might be wondering what is going on, I thought perhaps we could take a few minutes to bring you up to date on the matter before we adjourn the meeting. Scott, would you like to begin?"

"Certainly, Mr. Chairman, I'd be pleased to do so," responded Scott while studying his directors in an effort to gauge how they might receive the information he was about to give. "Well, at the end of last week, gentlemen, our current examination by the OCC appeared to be coming to a close, with the examiners seemingly heading toward an uneventful completion of their review, and a very positive result relative to the bank's *CAMELS* rating." Scott loved using acronyms and buzz words to impress the board, and this one representing the OCC's overall rating as to the adequacy of the bank's Capital, Asset quality, Management, Earnings, Liquidity and oversight of Rate Sensitivity was always an attention getter. "On this past Friday, however, that all came to an abrupt halt. About mid-afternoon of that day, sometime after he left the bank, a Mr. Paul Trotter, the senior person in charge of the OCC team examining Global United, was accosted and murdered about three blocks from here as he was headed home. Police thus far think it may have been a botched robbery, or some such thing. Some of you may have seen or heard about it in the news. There's been quite a hubbub over it."

"I think most of us read about it, Scott," interjected Taylor Parriott, a well-known Chicago attorney and Vice Chairman of the board, who had been a director of the bank since the days when it was still Guarantee Bank, and who was perennially one of the board's more outspoken members. "But what should that have to do with us? Why should that delay completion of the examination?"

"Well, we asked the same question, Taylor, but it's been difficult getting a clear answer out of them about that. To put it bluntly, all hell broke loose when the guy was murdered."

"They can't surely believe his death had anything to do with his work here at Global United, can they," Parriott asked? "That sounds rather sinister."

"Well, he was a senior government regulator—a soon-to-retire deputy comptroller to be exact. Had a lot of connections high up from what I understand." Scott responded. "When he was killed it immediately involved a whole bunch of people other than the OCC—FBI, FDIC and so on. They all roared in here to meet with us. They assured us they had no immediate suspicions that Mr. Trotter's death had anything to do with his work at Global United, but said they would be sticking around a little longer, looking again at areas he had principally concerned himself with while he was here, to ensure that was indeed the case. They're in the midst of doing that now, and they may well be here for some time to come as they reexamine a number of areas within the bank."

"Well, I think I speak for all of us when I say this Mr. Trotter's death was a tragedy, but once again I can't imagine it has anything to do with us?" Parriott reiterated. "When do you think they will finish up their work here? Does the board need to get involved?"

"No, not at this time," answered Scott. "I'm sure they'll let us know if there is sufficient concern about anything that they feel they want to meet with the board before the end of their examination."

There was a great deal of muttering as directors struck up little side conversations on the matter. Disorder at board meetings was not, however, to Nasir's liking. "If I could have your attention, gentlemen!" Nasir waited for the conversation to stop. "I asked Scott to brief all of you on this today, because I thought many of you either had heard, or would soon hear about the extended examination. We feel confident in saying to you that there should be no cause for alarm with this turn of events, but it certainly is an added imposition. We thought we were done with the OCC for this year. We can't imagine they would not be done in plenty sufficient time to enable us to meet with them at our regular December board meeting, but we do not know at this time if it will turn out that way. They may want to meet sooner, and if that is the case, we may need to convene a special meeting. We will keep you informed as to their progress via e-mail, and let you know as well in advance as we can, if we need to do that. Chances are a special meeting will not be necessary, but I at least wanted you to be prepared. You can rest assured that we will extract an official apology from them for all of the additional work, if nothing shows up as a result of their extended examination. Does anyone have any further questions on the matter? If not we can adjourn."

"Mr. Chairman, I just have one more question." Parriott rather liked to hear himself talk, and as a result was infamous for last minute questions that were often incisive. He was not one of Nasir's favorites. "And I would like to direct it to Mr. Hart here, if I might. Logan, from what I recollect, you've dealt with regulators a great deal in your past experience as well. Is this whole extended examination thing something we need to be worried about in your opinion?"

Logan hesitated before answering to consider what he wanted to say. He didn't want to appear to be second-guessing Scott, and it bothered him to have to respond to Parriott's question knowing what he did as a result of the meeting he and Cass had the previous evening with the FBI. He would need to exercise caution in his reply. "Well, admittedly Taylor, this is a situation as new and different for me as it is for all of you. Suffice it to say, I've never had an examiner murdered while he or she was working at any bank I've been involved with. I will tell you this, however. They're leaving no stone unturned in their extended review. If they suspect nothing, they certainly are not acting like it. They are quite serious about this second kick at the dog, so to speak. I am currently the primary bank contact for the examiners, and it is taking almost all of my time and a great deal of added time for many on our staff in responding to their requests. To answer your question, however, if we have followed bank policies and procedures, and have complied with bank regulations as required, we will probably have very little to worry about. The examination was going smoothly before. Hopefully, this added review will go the same way, and it'll all be over soon."

The room was hushed as Nasir tried once again to wind up the meeting. "Logan, as our point man on this, I would like to ask that you keep us all informed as this extended examination progresses. A short, daily progress report via e-mail to all board members might even be in order. Could you see to it that is done?"

"Yes, sir, I can, and I will." Logan quickly typed in a note to himself on the laptop in front of him, acting nonplussed about the whole matter, even though the additional help he was giving Cass and the OCC made him horribly uncomfortable and compromised. Doing things under the table like the FBI had asked him to do the night before was not his style. *I would be history at the bank if anyone in this room were to find out, and perhaps rightly so*, he thought.

"Once again, gentlemen, that completes our agenda." Nasir seemed anxious to end the meeting. "So, unless there are still more questions, I will accept a motion for adjournment."

Logan was a little surprised, but thankful that no questions arose regarding the OCC's interest in all things Nasir-related and their interest in the handling of BSA and AML regulatory requirements at the bank. *Nasir's probably well aware of all that's going on in that regard*, thought Nate. *He's apparently simply made the decision he's better off avoiding the subject with directors right now, and I'm happy with that. That discussion might be a little delicate for me to dance around right now.*

The meeting ended abruptly, with outside directors leaving the boardroom in visiting groups of two or three. Logan figured he could guess the subject of their conversations. The whole discussion regarding the OCC examination had appeared to trouble them all. He also noticed that as soon as the meeting ended, Nasir had corralled Scott and asked to meet with him in Scott's office.

The same thing had occurred after Nate's first board meeting in October, but that meeting had been a whole lot more convivial and upbeat, with Nasir's demeanor mirroring the moment then. This time Logan sensed the meeting between the two was going to be quite different. Nasir seemed quite agitated.

◊◊◊◊

"SCOTT, I am admittedly concerned and a bit disappointed with your handling of this OCC matter thus far." The door of Scott's office had no more than closed when Nasir launched into a tirade. His voice was quiet and controlled, as always, but scathing in its tone nonetheless. "When we hired you here at Global United, what some eighteen months ago or so, one of the attributes you touted, and that impressed both me and the board of directors, was the experience you claimed to have with respect to regulators. I checked with some of my regulatory sources at the time we hired you, and they assured me that all of your previous banks were highly rated and that you perennially fared quite well in dealing with all the regulators. So, why do I get the feeling that you're not quite on top of this situation?"

"That's not the case at all, Tariq. I have been in on nearly every meeting with the examiners."

"That may well be, but from what I understand, between meetings you have delegated all of the responsibility for dealing with the examiners to Mr. Hart. I know he's quite capable, but I am a little uncomfortable that you are not our lead on this situation. Logan Hart is still an unknown. I depend on you to keep me informed on everything going on in situations such as this."

"As you know, Tariq, at your request, I've been very much

involved in negotiations with the bank in Michigan that you're interested in acquiring, and I've been spending a great deal of time with our branch operations people to come to a decision on possible new operations, both domestic and international. I accordingly assigned the day-to-day work of dealing with the examiners to Logan Hart to alleviate some of the pressure I had on my time. I haven't, however, forgotten the conversation we had over at the Federation Club on Monday, and your request that I keep you informed. I've been adamant that Logan keep me informed on a regular basis, and I then in turn will do the same for you. Changing our approach now might send the wrong message to the examiners."

"I suppose that's understandable, but I'm still worried about the OCC'S protracted presence here at the bank. The longer they're here, the greater the possibility they will eventually find something that's unacceptable or a regulatory issue. I expect you, therefore, to either meet with Mr. Hart daily for personal updates, or to at least communicate with him daily by phone, e-mail or any other method necessary to keep both you, and then me, sufficiently informed on everything the examiners are looking into. Is that understood? I want absolutely no surprises out of this situation."

"I understand completely, Tariq. You can accept my assurance that there will be no surprises."

"Good, I knew that I could count on you. Again, I probably don't need to repeat this, but remember the thing with the phones. Use the prepaid cell for anything you consider sensitive whatsoever."

"Yes, yes, I know, I know." Scott's sounded exasperated, but only momentarily so upon noticing Nasir's reaction. "You know I am perfectly willing to do as you ask with the phone, Tariq, but why? I'm confused with all that. People know that I talk to you regularly. Doesn't it look just as strange if no calls show on our bill between my number and yours, what with you being the bank's chairman and all?"

"I didn't tell you to make absolutely no calls to me on the bank phone. As a matter of fact, you should no doubt be making calls to me using your bank phone on a regular basis. You may even discuss the examination with me via your office phone. Just make sure that you discuss nothing of any sensitive or confidential nature relative to me or my businesses via the bank's phone. It isn't secure."

"Secure? You mean you think someone might be listening in?"

"No, I am not saying that, but one can't be too sure. So, whenever in doubt regarding the subject you wish to discuss with me, then use the phone that I have provided, and with that I'll say no more." Nasir turned and left Scott's office without further comment.

◊◊◊◊

THE PRICKLY feeling one gets on the back the neck that accompanies some premonition of impending danger was a regular occurrence for Logan Hart. It had started many years before and served him in good stead while he was a combat commander in Iraq and elsewhere with the military, but the problem was that it never went away after entering civilian life. If anything, it was worse, causing many a sleepless night through the years. Somewhat under control thanks to his wife, Melanie's, continual understanding and some limited medical intervention, the condition—as Melanie preferred to call it—had actually on one occasion been a God-send. While on a hiking vacation in Montana's Glacier Park several years before Melanie's death, one of those ominous feelings had caused Logan to whirl around just in time to fend off what could have been an ugly situation involving an aggressive young Grizzly using a can of pepper spray. Neither he nor Melanie had heard the bear's approach. Now here he was once again experiencing that same sensation on busy Michigan Avenue in downtown Chicago, of all places.

Logan had stayed late at the bank following the monthly board of directors meeting, under the pretext of organizing materials for presentation to OCC examiners at a meeting planned for Friday of that week, the day after Thanksgiving. Most of the bank had emptied out fairly quickly after closing time, in anticipation of the holiday on the day following.

As usual, Myrna Brock had remained late to assist Logan with his work in any way she could. Unbeknown to her was the fact that Logan had an appointment to meet with Cass Price and representatives of the FBI in their downtown offices at 7:00 p.m. The FBI's headquarters was located in the Dirksen Building in the 200 block of South Dearborn, only a few blocks away from Global United's LaSalle Street location. So, Logan had some time to kill. Originally he had figured he could do that by hanging around the office until a little before meeting time, but he knew if he did that, there was little hope of getting Myrna to leave at a reasonable hour. In order to get her to head home, as he felt she should, he decided on another approach.

"Look, Myrna, I think we've worked long enough. Don't you? The business district is kind of decked out in all of its holiday finest right now. So, I think I may catch a later train home this evening, and just stroll around downtown a bit beforehand. I particularly get a kick out of Macy's window displays and all. What say we leave? You can join me, if you wish." The ploy worked, with Logan and Myrna exiting the bank at the same time. They strolled a bit together until they reached Macy's downtown building on State Street, and then the two parted company, with Myrna proceeding on to her downtown condo.

From all appearances, nothing was all that much out of the ordinary for an evening prior to Thanksgiving in downtown Chicago. Crowds of fellow, downtown workers passed Logan on the street either hurrying to appointments or trying to make commuter connections, while a whole host of other early shoppers and tourists joined them milling about the Macy building looking at the holiday window tableaus. The displays were a perennially popular attraction since the building's Marshall Field days. Some, like Logan, were no doubt simply killing time.

That was when the foreboding sensation hit him. He wasn't sure why, but something told him he was being followed. Logan found himself studying the faces behind him that were reflected in the windows to see if he could detect a reason for his apprehension. He was about to chalk the whole thing up to another flash of PTSD paranoia, perhaps brought on by the whole OCC/FBI thing, when he indeed did detect one man a short distance behind that seemed to be studying him intently. *Perhaps it's my imagination.* He thought. *Let's see if the guy follows me into the store.*

Logan turned and nonchalantly sauntered into the Macy building through the portico under the ornate clock at the corner of State and Randolph streets. The store was packed with shoppers, and strategically located on each floor were mirrors of all kinds, both overhead for security purposes and at various locations along the walls and on posts for use by customers. The situation was perfect for checking out whether he was being followed. Once in the building, Logan paused a short distance from the door acting as if he were looking at a display of jewelry, and watched the door in the reflection of a nearby mirror. Within seconds of his entrance, the man he had been watching back out on the street entered the door, gazed about the room, appeared to spot Logan and then began to busy himself nearby. Logan thought this more than coincidental, but figured he would test the situation a little further by taking an elevator to a higher floor and see whether the man followed.

Logan joined the throng waiting to get on the elevators, unaware that the man he thought was following him had hurriedly pushed his way close to Logan in an effort to ensure that he was on the same lift as he. Logan's supposed destination, as with most waiting to get on the elevators, was the eighth floor dining room, where many were hoping to wrangle a table under the giant, two-story Christmas tree that traditionally adorned that floor every holiday season. After a near ten-minute wait for an express elevator, Logan entered and went to the back of the lift. At the last minute, just before the doors closed, the man he had been watching squeezed on.

Located in a rear corner of the elevator, Logan was at an extremely good vantage to study the suspected tail. He estimated the man following him to be around thirty to thirty-five years of age. He was dark-skinned, of medium height, and well dressed. Logan suspected he was of Asian or Middle Eastern extraction. That suspicion was confirmed, when the man responded to some friendly banter from another passenger on the elevator. His responses were brief, but he said enough to confirm Logan's suspicions. His accent sounded very much like some of the customers and staff of Global United.

When the elevator door opened, the man was forced to exit first ahead of the crowd, pushing him out into the dining room. Logan acted as though he too planned to exit the elevator, standing back and allowing those headed back to the first floor to shove their way onto the elevator. Just before the car was full and the doors closed, however, Logan quickly jumped back on. As the doors closed, Logan could see the man struggling to no avail to get back through the crowd and onto the elevator as well. When the elevator reached the first floor, Logan exited immediately, went to the men's department nearby, grabbed a pair of trousers from a table and as quickly as possible entered one of the dressing rooms situated in such a location that he could study those that exited the elevator through a crack in the dressing room door. Logan had no sooner closed the door, when one of the elevators opened with the man who had been following him rudely shoving his way past the other customers. Logan watched as he frantically ran about the store for nearly ten minutes. *Looks like a little boy who's lost his mommy,* thought Logan, as he watched the man disgustedly shove a stack of gloves off of a display table and onto the floor before exiting the building the way he had come in.

Logan looked at his watch. He had thirty minutes until his meeting with the FBI over at the Dirksen Building. He figured he would wait another ten minutes or so in the dressing room, and then leave the building by way of the exit on Wabash. It was opposite the direction that the man who had been following him had left the building, and there was always a line of taxis waiting for fares there under the nearby elevated rail line. He could quickly grab one of those and make it to his meeting in plenty of time. *They warned us about the possibility of this. I wonder what agents Seilor and Erickson will have to say about this little incident,* Logan asked himself as he left the dressing room and threw the unworn trousers back on the table.

CHAPTER TWENTY-ONE

"HERE HE is!" Agent Seilor seemed relieved when he saw Logan walk into the main lobby at FBI headquarters in the Dirksen Building. He and Agent Erickson were waiting there with Cass when Logan arrived. Seilor shook Logan's hand as he pulled him toward an elevator. "You and Cass are both right on time, and that's excellent. We've already got several people waiting for us in our third-floor conference room, and we've got a lot to cover. Let's scoot, shall we!"

The agents ushered Logan and Cass onto a waiting elevator and hit the button for the third floor. Logan felt Seilor and Erickson looked even more serious than they had the evening before, it that was possible. When the elevator reached the third floor, they were taken to a large glass-enclosed conference room in which Logan and Cass could see there were no less than six more people sitting around a conference table, all deeply involved in conversation and seemingly awaiting their arrival. As they entered the room, everyone rose to greet them. Logan quickly recognized the silver-haired, taller gentleman smiling at him from the head of the table as Merritt Daimler, Special Agent in Charge of the FBI's Chicago office, and a long-time personal friend. Daimler reached out to shake Logan's hand.

"Logan, my friend, good to see you after all this time. What's it been, maybe two, three years?"

"At least that, good to see you again too, Merritt." The two shook hands as Logan motioned Cass forward. "Merritt, may I introduce Cass Price of the OCC?"

"You could indeed if that was necessary," replied Special Agent Daimler as he smiled and held out his hand to Cass. "But Cass and I have already met. A few days ago, right Cass? Nice to see you again."

"And you, Mr. Daimler." Cass shook the Special Agent's hand.

Oh, and by the way, Logan," continued Daimler in a much lower voice as he put his arm around Logan's shoulder and guided him just a few steps away from the group, "we sent flowers and a card last year when we heard, but this is the first time I've seen you since Sally and I were moved to Chicago, and I would be horribly remiss if I didn't tell you how sorry she and I were to hear of Melanie's passing last year."

"Thanks, Merritt, I really do appreciate that. It means a lot, and give my best to Sally as well. She's a great gal."

"I will, I will," responded Daimler, as he and Logan turned back to the larger group. It was a private moment between Logan and Daimler, but Cass had been close enough to hear what had been said. Daimler looked at her and smiled. "Oh, and like I said the other evening, Cass, call me Merritt if you would. Misters make me feel a lot older than I care to."

Special Agent Daimler then led Logan and Cass around the long conference table, introducing them to all of those present for the meeting: the first, and only other woman in the room, was introduced as an additional agent of the FBI; two men were agents of the Secret Service; another gentleman was said to be an agent for Immigration and Customs Enforcement Service—or ICE as Daimler called it; and the last person at the table was a young, cocky-looking, curly red-haired fellow in a pinstriped Brooks Brothers suit that Daimler simply introduced as "Raleigh Sutphen, a representative from Department of Homeland Security." Logan had him pegged as maybe CIA until they were told otherwise. Once all the introductions were completed, Agent Daimler asked everyone to take their seats.

"Logan and Cass," began Daimler, "first let me begin by apologizing a bit for throwing such a large group of people at you here this evening, but if you can believe it or not, it could have been worse. This group doesn't include absolutely everyone that is on the Joint Task Force that has been organized for this situation. There are numerous others included who are busy working elsewhere on the matter as we speak. Those who are not with us this evening will nevertheless be kept abreast of all that transpires here. That being said, as I think you know by now, we've had some sobering matters on our plate these days. A handful of incidents have occurred as of late that have attracted our attention and are collectively of grave concern. Taken separately, they might not even be a blip on our radar screen, but when looked at in total all sorts of alarms have started to go off for us, both nationally and here in Chicago. And since I'm not much one for beating around the bush, I have to say we think there's a possibility that the two of you may without knowing it be sitting right in the middle of it all."

Logan and Cass shot a questioning glance at each other and then studied the expressions of those around the table. Everybody had intense, serious looks on their faces. "Agents Seilor and Erickson filled us in last evening on some of what is apparently prompting all of this investigative activity," said Cass. "Have you confirmed some of their horrifying suspicions. Is that what has caused you folks to pull together so many worried looking people here this evening?"

"Worried? Well, you're right there. Let me fill you in on the pieces. As I think Jim and Lon have already told you, about two weeks ago Russian intelligence approached our people at the CIA with some information that they have come across which leads them to believe a terrorist attack of some sort may be imminent in either their country or ours.

They're saying they've recently found out that a small amount of dangerous, weaponized biological pathogens may have been stolen from a strategic stockpile they were certain was entirely destroyed some years ago. To date they've been unable to trace them or the lady scientist they think may have stolen them. Their intelligence sources also feel that the missing pathogens found their way into the hands of the Russian Mafiya, who in turn may have sold them, at least in part, to some Islamic Jihad terrorist group that has smuggled them out of the country through the city of Saint Petersburg, Russia. From there on, however, information is scant."

"Yeah, Jim and Lon told both Cass and I about that last evening, Merritt. I'm not sure about Cass, but I hardly slept at all last night. Considering it's recent experience, I'm not sure the world—or more to the point, this country—could handle another pandemic. COVID-19 would pale by comparison to a smallpox outbreak. It's indeed scary, but what is there about the situation that makes you feel it necessary to bring us into the loop?" asked Logan. "This has got to be highly sensitive information. What more haven't you told us, as it relates to our involvement, that we don't already know?"

"Well, you're right there. This is very sensitive information, and we wouldn't even think of bringing the two of you into the situation if we didn't feel it necessary, and weren't confident that both of you can and will maintain security on the matter." Daimler took a deep breath before continuing. "With respect to other information, however—and remember now, we're still trying to see if the pieces of this puzzle fit together in any way—yesterday a dead man was found floating in the Chicago River, the obvious victim of a homicide. That in and of itself would not normally be anything out of the ordinary for this city. Say's a lot for the City of Chicago I suppose, but we find numerous bodies in that river in any given year. However, there were a couple of things about this one body that caught our attention. First of all, he was a man of Middle Eastern background. We found no form of identification on him, but we did run a fingerprint check on him and we were lucky enough to come up with a match on a set of arrest records for a misdemeanor offense in Cicero, where the guy was picked up in a prostitution pandering sting about four months ago. His name was Imad Fayiz Mufassa. He was a short haul, independent trucker—and get this—the big rig he drove is rented from an outfit called Aurora Transportation Company. Name ring any bells?"

Logan and Cass gave each other shocked looks again. "You've got to be kidding! That's one of Nasir's companies, isn't it, Logan?" Cass asked, looking incredulously at her banking confederate.

"Yes, it is," Logan answered quietly.

"We're aware of that." Agent Daimler responded. "Now that part of the situation may be purely coincidental. I guess Aurora is a pretty big company with a leasing operation that has big rigs leased out all over the city, but we're still looking into the matter with great interest. Then finally, the guy didn't just fall in and drown. It instead looks like a professional job. He was garroted."

"Garroted?" asked Cass. "What does that mean."

"Well, it means he was choked to death with a wire or cord of some type. You don't typically find many people garroted when they're killed on the streets of Chicago. Not many gang-bangers or hoods use the technique. Garroting is more of a military or professional assassin's way of taking somebody out. Too messy for your average Chicago hit man. They prefer a couple of well-placed bullets behind the ear."

"I'm sorry I asked." Cass looked a little like she might be sick.

"The Chicago police brought us in on the situation when they found out the guy was of Middle Eastern extraction with no identifying papers," continued Daimler, "and we became even more interested when we later found that he may have been in this country illegally. The Cicero police hadn't checked him out all that closely when they had him in their possession, and his visa expired between then and now. Between the Chicago police department and us, we've been trying to retrace all of Mr. Mufassa's steps over the last couple of weeks. From what we can tell, he was hauling freight from the docks at Calumet Harbor to various locations around the city during this past week. We're not sure, but that makes us nervous too."

"The way you put it, it does me too!" Logan responded. "First you talk about WMD's being brought into the country, and then in the same breath, you talk about some poor sap that gets himself murdered and thrown in the Chicago River. How do you figure your dead guy is related to that situation? Kind of pushing it a little to link the two at this point. Wouldn't you think? Or is there something else you haven't told us?"

"You're right. It's perhaps still a stretch to link the two at this point, but we can't afford to take a chance considering the threat the Russians are intimating may be out there. The national Joint Terrorism Task Force, of which we are all a part, is looking at any similar situations across the country as we speak. We can't afford not to look into every possible lead."

"Can't say that I blame you," said Logan.

"Well, that's not all, pal. Wait just a minute, the plot gets a little thicker. In checking international ship registers and manifest databases for the last month—one of the things we're doing by way of follow up on our Russian tip— we've determined that no less than two ocean-going cargo freighters recently set sail from Saint Petersburg, Russia, carrying a great deal of freight bound for Calumet Harbor as one of their destinations. Those ships both docked here in Chicago during the last two weeks, and Mr. Mufassa picked up and delivered several loads from both of those ships a couple of days ago before we figure he was killed. On top of that, one of the ships, the Aurora Crescent, is also owned by."

"Oh, no, dear Lord, don't tell us!" Cass gasped.

"Yeah, you got it. The Aurora Crescent is also owned by your Mr. Nasir's Aurora Transportation Company—their shipping division. Add all of this together with the terrorist chatter that we've been picking up during the last month or so indicating some unknown group of Jihadis were about to mount a horrific attack on this country somewhere, and you've got yourself the current heightened terrorist alert this country's now under."

"OK, Merritt, I think I can see where you're headed with all this. You apparently have suspicions regarding Mr. Nasir. Where does that leave us? What do you want from us?" Logan asked.

"Well, just as Jim and Lon told you last evening, we need like crazy for the two of you, and the people you both trust under you, to either help prove or disprove at your earliest opportunity that Mr. Trotter's death had nothing to do with any of this. Further, if at all possible, we need your assistance in helping us find out as much as you can about Tariq Nasir."

"What do you want to know about him?" Asked Logan.

"Well, in a nutshell, we'd like to know whether your Mr. Nasir is somehow in the business of hawala—which we think in all likelihood he is. His family is big-time into the business back in Pakistan and in other places around the world. More importantly, however, we also need to know whether he or any of his people are even in the slightest way involved in any plot we think may be in the offing. His name and that of his companies just seem to be popping up far more than we feel can reasonably be called coincidental. If there is a remote possibility that scrutiny of his dealings with the bank may give us some answers—and we are increasingly of the opinion that we think they are—then we need those answers fast, guys. It's our gut feeling all of these things are related, and that something big is about to come down. We've got to know if Mr. Nasir is involved, whether knowingly or unknowingly. If he is, he might provide just the leads we need to prevent something awful from happening."

There was an uncomfortable period of silence as Logan and Cass tried to take in everything Special Agent Daimler had been telling them. "We'll do the best we can." Cass finally responded.

Logan said nothing, and Daimler could tell something was bothering him. "You're rather quiet, Logan, something bothering you about all of this? Do you have a problem with what we're asking you to do, or do you think you're going to have some trouble getting the answers we need?"

"No, no, that's not it at all, Merritt. I too am willing to help in whatever way I can, no matter how things fall at the bank or with Mr. Nasir. I was just sitting here thinking about something that happened to me no more than about an hour ago, in light of all that you've just told us."

"Why, what happened?" Daimler asked.

"Well, on my way here I am pretty certain that I was being followed." Logan immediately had the room's attention.

"If you'll remember, I told you last evening to be careful about that." Seilor acted alarmed. "What happened? This person surely didn't follow you here did he?"

"No, I'm pretty sure not. I was trying to take a little breather this evening before our meeting. So, I strolled through the downtown looking at the lights, Christmas decorations and so forth. Somewhere around Marshall Field's—or I guess I should say Macy's, on State Street—I decided I was being followed by some guy that I am fairly certain may also have been of South Asian or Middle Eastern origin."

"Are you certain he was following you?" Seilor asked.

"I wasn't sure at first. I was looking at the window displays and repeatedly saw the guy's reflection behind me

272

in the window. It looked like he was watching me more than the displays. So, I ducked into Macy's and ran him around the building a bit. That's when I became quite certain that he was following me. I managed to ditch him and took a cab over here right away. Kind of an uncomfortable feeling."

The group all looked at each other. "That's it, ladies and gentlemen," said Agent Daimler. "We can't go on meeting like this. If someone was indeed trying to follow Logan, they will no doubt try to do so again, and he may not be able to give the guy the slip the next time. That pretty well dashes our getting together here or anywhere else for that matter without running the risk of letting people know Logan and Cass are involved with us. Anyone have any ideas on the problem?"

"Yes, I have one," injected Raleigh Sutphen, the gentleman from the DHS who had been a silent participant in the meeting until now. "We can provide Mr. Hart and Ms. Price here with wireless capable specialized laptop computers and other necessary equipment sufficient to provide them with secure videoconferencing capabilities. We can then simply meet online as the need arises. They can join us here from the comfort of their homes, or just about any good hot spot in the city for that matter. No one will be the wiser."

Everyone looked at each other with the same blank look that said, "and why didn't I think of that?"

"That's a great idea, Raleigh, but we want to keep things moving here. How soon can we get them the equipment?" asked Daimler.

"We'll have the computers delivered to their homes via a yet unidentified courier sometime within the next few days, but certainly no later than Saturday morning."

"Even if it's Thanksgiving?" Logan asked.

"Even if it's Thanksgiving!" Daimler answered. "The major delivery services are all over the place and working extended hours now that the Christmas season is upon us.

So, nothing will look strange about that. However, at this juncture I'm thinking it will more than likely be Friday or Saturday. We'll give you some instructions on usage, passwords and such the like tonight before you head home, so you'll know exactly what to do when you get the computers; but just in case, the delivery guy will be ours. They'll be IT-qualified and also there to help you initially if you have any questions. Just make sure you're home at the right time to receive them when they arrive. We'll call you in advance to arrange the times. Just as soon as you get the equipment, sign on, give us a call, and a qualified someone will be here to answer any questions you may have and get you started. If everything goes well, we should be able to meet in that way as often as we like thereafter, and no one will need to worry about who is maybe following whom."

◊◊◊◊

AL-SAHABA was no stranger to technology. Its young operatives all far exceeded simple computer literacy, with many possessing knowledge and capabilities at expert levels, using the Internet in new and innovative ways to organize and direct activities wherever cells were located around the globe. To avoid potentially compromising situations were hard drives ever to fall into the wrong hands, only cell leaders typically had their own computers, very sparingly using them for communications with other terrorist organizations, planning, organization, command, and control with underlings. Seldom, if ever, did they connect to the Internet via their own ISP. All operatives, whatever the rank, stayed connected when it came to anything related to group matters by utilizing the facilities of cyber cafés, coffee houses or even the free services of public libraries—wherever free public access was available. Such establishments were ideal for al-Sahaba's purposes even though they were quickly becoming a thing of the past.

Particularly favored hangouts for al-Sahaba members were the CyberWorld Internet Cafés, a nationwide chain of coffee houses with multiple franchises located in literally every city where al-Sahaba had cells. One by one, many CyberWorld operations around the country were going out of business, thanks to technological advancements and a glut of coffee houses nationwide. A sufficient number still remained in the cities where al-Sahaba cells were located, however, as to yet make them a very important element of the organization's communication system. At almost any time of the day, a CyberWorld Café was open in one of those cities. If a person knew where and when to look, they could nearly always find an al-Sahaba operative sitting in a CyberWorld Café, staring into a monitor while sipping a cup of coffee or espresso. Using free, Internet-based, e-mail addresses under assigned aliases, members of al-Sahaba would surf the net for hours on end, using coded messages to avoid detection as they plotted and planned with terrorist associates all over the world.

The evening prior to Thanksgiving was an ideal time for al-Sahaba leadership around the United States to meet via the Internet. CyberWorld Cafés in all the cities where al-Sahaba cells were situated would be open for business until their normal midnight closing time, but would no doubt be relatively devoid of patrons for much of the evening as the entire country prepared for the holiday following. As a result, Ahmed Khalid decided to call an online planning meeting for that evening at 6:30 p.m. central time. A message announcing the time and place of the Internet get-together had gone out the day before in a coded e-mail to the addresses of all cell leaders nationwide. Each was instructed to gather at the appointed hour in a free, temporary chat room Khalid had creatively dubbed Birdwatchers VII, in an effort to avoid unwarranted attention. Social media threads had nearly all but replaced online chat rooms as a medium of like-minded exchange on the Internet. Yet, several such services still remained available on the web for the few Internet troglodytes still clinging to the past, or individuals—

like the al-Sahaba—whose agendas were better served by the little online conclaves.

By 6:31 p.m., all seven al-Sahaba cell leaders expected to attend the online meeting had entered the chat room using online monikers designed to tell Khalid that the cell leader—and only the cell leader—was present, and that he and his sleeper team were prepared to follow Khalid's bidding. The code words consisted of the name of a bird designating the city in which the sleeper cell was located, followed immediately by one of two four digit numerical codes that changed daily, and were known only to Khalid and the cell leader. One numerical suffix was used if everything was a go and there were no problems for the sleeper team in that city, and another where security had been breeched or the cell leader suspected he or his cell was being watched. It was their procedure to wait for Khalid to address them after they had all entered the chat room:

PIGEON (New York) 2447: HAS ENTERED THE ROOM.

EAGLE (Washington) 8884: HAS ENTERED THE ROOM

KESTREL (Detroit) 4891: HAS ENTERED THE ROOM.

ALBATROSS (Miami) 3232: HAS ENTERED THE ROOM

ROAD RUNNER (Dallas) 3768: HAS ENTERED THE ROOM

SWALLOW (Los Angeles) 4954: HAS ENTERED THE ROOM

SPOTTED OWL (Seattle) 5332: HAS ENTERED THE ROOM

Once Khalid had determined that all the cell leaders were present in the chat room without problem, his signal to them that everything was okay on his end was "Al-*Qiyamah* —or our Day of Judgment—is at hand for this rookery my friends!" The chat would then begin.

CARDINAL (Chicago) 7777: "*Assalamu Alaikum*! May the blessings of Allah, the merciful and compassionate one, be granted to you and all you hold dear." Ahmed Khalid furiously typed in. "The time has finally arrived when this repugnant nation of apostates shall feel the wrath of Allah. A full quiver of arrows shall be shot into the heart of the Great Satan, and al-Sahaba has been chosen above all others among the *al-Haraka al-Islamiya*, to draw the bow. Never has there been an occasion of greater importance or pride for any of us, my brothers. These modern crusaders shall at long last be visited with divine retribution equivalent to the evils they have perpetrated upon the Ummah for generation upon generation. They shall regret their transgressions amongst our brothers in places around the world where they blaspheme the name of Allah by their very presence. Are you all prepared?"

Each of the cell leaders responded with long glowing tributes to Allah, declaring their dedication and preparedness to enter Paradise as martyrs to the cause:

SPOTTED OWL 5332: "Our team is prepared to strike. When do we obtain the 'arrows' with which to deliver this fateful blow?"

CARDINAL 7777: "May Allah grant you untold rewards in paradise, my brother. The misery that shall be visited upon this land shall be more than it has seen in all its days. We shall soon deliver a blow far greater than that delivered at the hands of our brothers on 9/11. I am humbled to have been chosen as one who will lead you in an effort to ensure that Islam becomes the only path for mankind."

PIGEON 2447: "I believe I speak for all of us in saying, sir, that we are both honored and prepared to give everything in the name of Allah. When will we know the details of what will be required of us in that regard?"

CARDINAL 7777: "The time has come for all of you to know! I am requesting that each of you make preparations to join me here at our prearranged place of meeting one week from now on the last Friday of the month. We shall all, as usual, first join each other for Friday prayers at the Masjid where we have met so many times before during past months. When the Khutbah is finished, however, we will not as before gather at our usual meeting place. We will instead leave separately and regroup at 1:30 p.m. at the special location each of you was shown many months ago. Does anyone have any questions?"

KESTREL 4891: "None, Cardinal! I shall be there."

SPOTTED OWL 5332: "And I, my friend."

ROAD RUNNER 3768: "I too shall be there."

PIGEON 2447: "You can depend upon me."

EAGLE 8884: "And upon me! May Allah, the merciful and omnipotent one, bless us in all we shall soon undertake!"

ALBATROSS 3232: "I will follow your instructions as always."

SWALLOW 4954: "And I shall make the group complete."

CARDINAL 7777: "Thank you, fellow birders. Allahu akbar!"

CHAPTER TWENTY-TWO

"MR. HART, Mr. Haifa is out at my desk, and would like to see you again if you have a few minutes." As much as Logan had tried purposely to shield Myrna Brock from all that was going on with the OCC's extended examination, and everything else that Logan was embroiled in relative to the government's investigation into Paul Trotter's death and Tariq Nasir, it had been difficult to do so. She was way too perceptive an individual. The traditional, disciplined approach she took to her position as his administrative assistant kept her from asking too many questions, but with Myrna, it wasn't what she asked. It was what she didn't. Her actions and the all-knowing tone of her voice told him she suspected something rather serious was afoot.

"Thanks, Myrna, send him right in."

As Raj entered his office shutting the door behind him, Logan could tell that he had a troubled young man on his hands. Almost always friendly and outgoing by nature, Raj usually had a ready smile on his face and something cheery to say to everyone. That was not the case today, however. "Mr. Hart, I'm sorry to keep bothering you, and I'm sure you're busy what with it being the day after a holiday and all, but we need to talk, sir."

"Come in, Raj, no need to apologize. I told you I would make myself available any time. We both have a lot to deal with these days until we get through all that's going on around here right now. I hope you had a nice holiday yesterday, by the way."

"Absolutely, the best! Thank you, for asking."

" Great, what can I do for you, Raj?"

"Well, do you remember the listing of international banking customers the examiners had asked for? I gave you an early, incomplete draft copy a couple of days ago."

"Yes, I do. I've been studying it quite a bit since you gave it to me. Have you provided them a final copy of it yet?"

"Well, no, not just yet. I've been adding a few of our newer clients over the last couple of days, and I'm now finally ready to give them the report. Here's an amended copy for you to peruse and to get your thoughts before I give them their copies," Raj reached across Logan's desk and handed him what appeared to be a quarter-inch thick, letter-sized, stapled report "It's been updated, adding all new and pending clients."

"Great, got any insights?"

"Yeah, well, I nearly know most of our department's customer list by heart. There are few that I haven't had at least some minor personal dealings with. So, there were no great surprises on it. During the last few days, however, I've been looking at the list with a slightly different mindset, and have admittedly found some things that are perhaps generating a few questions this time around, questions that I haven't asked before."

"Oh, yeah, like what?"

"Well, let me begin first by telling you a few things about my background that you may not be aware of, and I think you ought to know before I get into my concerns about our customers."

"OK, shoot!" Logan crossed his legs and relaxed in his chair, still listening intently to what the young executive had to say as he began to leaf through the report.

"Well, as I think you may know, I was born and raised here in Chicago. I attended Northwestern University for my undergraduate work, and then I did a few years in the

Marines before I returned to this city to finish my education and start my career. My dad's a medical doctor and professor at Northwestern University's Feinberg School of Medicine."

"Yes, I hear he's about to retire soon," Logan said, looking up at the young head of international banking.

"Yeah, he is, after nearly forty years."

"That's fantastic! Go ahead, Raj, sorry I interrupted."

"No problem... so, he prevailed upon some of his contacts there and was able to get me into the MBA program at the Kellogg School of Management, where I picked up my graduate degree while working in the international banking department of one of the large regional banks here in Chicago. After spending about three to four years with that bank, I happened to be visiting with my father about the lack of opportunity I thought I had there, and he suggested that I meet with Tariq Nasir here at Global United. He had gotten to know Mr. Nasir by sitting on the board of an Islamic Charity with him here in Chicago. He put in a good word for me with Mr. Nasir. I interviewed with him a short while later, and the rest is history."

"I was aware of most of that, Raj. I've read your resume, and of course we've both commiserated about our mutual military experiences. But what is this all leading to?"

"Well, first of all, I want you to know that I would never discuss anything that is going on inside the bank with people on the outside, and I haven't. Nevertheless, since we were in the process of looking over Mr. Nasir's business here at the bank, I thought I would at least bring the subject of Nasir up with my father when we were together yesterday for the holiday, not anything about his businesses or banking relationships and such, but about him personally. I knew they were still serving on the board of that charity together, and I wanted to know what he still thought of him as an individual."

"What did you ask, and what did he have to say?"

"I simply asked him if he still ran into Mr. Nasir from

time to time, and if so, whether he had had much opportunity to visit with him as of late. He told me that he had coincidentally seen Mr. Nasir in the last few days. Apparently, they both attended a meeting of the foundation board on which they serve together just this past Tuesday afternoon. He started out saying they had a nice conversation before the meeting, but then after pausing to think about it a moment, he got all serious, mumbled something about the meeting and started to clam up. My father's pretty private about such things, but I could tell he was troubled, so I pushed him some. He finally started to open up about what was bothering him."

"What'd he tell you?"

"Well, I had to push him a little about this mind you, but I guess he's been increasingly concerned as of late about some grants that the foundation he works with has been approving. At their monthly meeting a few days ago, an Imam that's on the board brought in a request for a rather large grant to some Muslim group in Europe, a group my father said neither he nor several other members of the board had ever heard of before. He didn't say how much it was, but from what I gather, it was quite a large sum. I tried to push him some further, but he really clammed up then. He wouldn't tell me what took place in that regard, but whatever it was, it must have really bothered him."

"What's that name of this foundation, anyway?"

"It's called the Worldwide Islamic Charities Foundation. It's been around for several years here in Chicago. When my dad first went on the board, the organization was called the Islamic Foundation of Chicago. They were originally set up to primarily assist Islamic immigrants who were newly arrived to the U.S. get established in the Chicago area. Mr. Nasir, like my father, was one of the original trustees. After about two years of quiet membership on the board—and making some of the largest contributions made to the foundation to date—Nasir and the Imam that I mentioned were, I guess, instrumental in convincing most of the board that the thrust of the organization ought to be more global. They eventually talked the trustees into changing the name to Worldwide Islamic Charities a few years back, and they've been making grants all over the world ever since."

"Sounds innocent enough, other than all the stories one hears from time-to-time regarding some of these so-called Islamic charities around the country, and what they sometimes do with their money—no offense intended, Raj."

"None taken, I know exactly what you mean, and that's just it. From what my father says, over the last couple of years the makeup of the board at Worldwide has changed a great deal too, and in his opinion, not for the better. I guess during that time several board positions have come up for reelection, and instead of those trustees being reappointed, people recommended by Nasir, who are, shall we say, a little more fundamental, sometimes even radical in their beliefs, have replaced them. As if this weren't enough concern for my father and the few others like him on the board, he says grant requests have been arriving with increasing regularity in the last couple of years from so-called needy causes overseas that seemed to always take immediate precedence over local requests. With little or no due diligence as to the legitimacy of the requesting organizations, many of the foreign requests have been rather liberally funded. Like you say, during the years since 9/11 a lot of Islamic charities across the U.S. have come under a great deal of scrutiny as possible funding sources for terrorist activities and so forth. Based upon what he's told me of late, I have been very apprehensive about my dad's continued involvement in the organization."

"I'm sure you have been. Does he plan to stay on the board?"

"Well, my father is a very loyal American, Mr. Hart, and he has apparently been quite concerned about all of this. He feels Worldwide Islamic Charities is no longer the kind of organization he helped found years ago. If funds from the foundation are now being used in ways that are even the slightest bit unseemly—and he says he isn't really sure in that regard—then he wants nothing to do with it. His board seat comes up at the end of this year, and he claims he will not stand for reelection again. He says that he doubts, however, that Mr. Nasir and the rest of Worldwide's board will be very upset about that. My dad's been one of the more vocal dissenters to a number of these questionable grants."

"If he is in any way correct in his suspicions, I can certainly see where your father might definitely want to separate himself from that organization at his earliest opportunity. I would agree if I were in his shoes. Did he say anything else that concerned you?"

"Yes, he did, and it really worries me."

"How so?"

"Well, like I said, he wasn't going to tell me any more about this recent meeting of the foundation that had him so upset, but I really pushed him further on the situation."

"Did you get anymore out of him?"

"Yeah, I finally did, and that's really what I wanted to tell you about. I guess during the board's discussion regarding this large grant, there were apparently some on the board, my father included, who questioned the advisability of transferring large sums of money around the world during these times, with no more due diligence than was being exercised. Their questions of concern, however, apparently fell on deaf ears. My father said that those opposed in this way were summarily dismissed as having 'lost sight of the foundation's mission, and the need of all Muslims to assist fellow believers in their hour of need, in the manner of az-Zakat,' one of the five pillars of our religion that requires we Muslims to set aside a portion of our wealth to help others in need financially. But what apparently happened next was what disturbed my father most."

"And what was that?"

"Oh, he said that after the comments regarding government scrutiny of large money transfers came up, Mr. Nasir had rather flippantly dismissed such concerns suggesting that 'there are a number of ways around all of that' if there was a need to avoid scrutiny from time-to-time. My father didn't say how Mr. Nasir indicated he was apparently going to accomplish that, but whatever it was, he didn't much like the idea of skirting government oversight in any way. My father said he was all but shouted down when he told the board, 'If this grant is something we are concerned about in any way, then I question our reasons for and advisability of doing it.' My father is quite concerned, Mr. Hart. His final comment to me was, 'You know Mairaj, I believe I have finally seen a side of Tariq Nasir that I am not all that comfortable with. You be careful. If Mr. Nasir is as cavalier about banking regulations as he is about Worldwide Charities matters that could spell trouble for all of you.' My father seemed sincerely worried, Mr. Hart."

"Well, if what your father says is true, then I can certainly understand his concern, Raj." Logan could see Global United's young head of international banking was distressed, and he understood why. American Muslims were under a microscope in recent years, sometimes even loyal Americans like Raj Haifa and his father. "For that matter, if Tariq Nasir were ever to involve himself in any subterfuge of that sort,--which I hesitate to believe he would—there might be cause for all of us to be concerned. The last thing Global United would need is to have its Chairman and principal shareholder involved in some international incident of the sort that what you describe could become."

"I know, I was awake all night last night thinking about this."

"Look, Raj, your father sounds like a very honorable man. I hope I am privileged to meet him one of these days. However, if he is that uncomfortable about his involvement in this foundation, then he may want to follow through with his plans to resign now and be shed of the worry.right away. If something duplicitous is done like he suggested to you might happen, he could be swept right up in any resulting legal problems."

"I know, I couldn't agree more. I have already urged him not to wait."

"Great, I'm glad to hear you did that. From what you've described, I would even say the sooner, the better, with respect to any resignation, before any grants like that are even funded if you can get him to do it."

"Well, he said he didn't know what the final decision was about funding the grant request that had him so disturbed. I guess he was upset and left the meeting early."

"I'm sure it did upset him. Look, it is really none of my business, but I as I said, I really think you should push him on maybe resigning right away if that is something you can do. Is there any way I might be of help with any of this?"

"No, I can take it from here. I just needed to visit with someone else I felt I could trust about this. I appreciate your advice. I'll be doing as you say."

. "Fine, but let me know if there is any other way I can help with the situation. You have something else for me?" There was a momentary lack of response. Raj seemed completely distracted. "Uh, Raj, you got something else there for me?"

"Oh, yes, yes! Please excuse me, yes, I do." Raj stammered in response. "It's about that information I just gave you on our customers. There's something on it that I think it's important I bring to your attention in light of what we just discussed."

"Oh, and what is that?" Logan asked as he started scanning the pages.

"Yes, well, if I could draw your attention to the third to the last page of the report, you will see that I have highlighted one customer that I think you may find interesting, considering all that we have been discussing these last few minutes."

Logan thumbed through the document. There in the middle of the third to the last page, highlighted with a yellow marker, were the words Worldwide Islamic Charities Foundation of Chicago, IL. Listed below the name were several bank certificates of deposit and a checking account totaling $3.6 Million in amount. "Hmm, Worldwide Charities appears to be a fairly good Global United depositor. Find anything more of interest?"

"Yes, several items. Just as I indicated would be the case, both Mr. Nasir's name and all of his companies appear on the list, but in addition to that—and I have marked all of them with a highlighter—you will find every member of the board of directors for Worldwide Islamic Charities Foundation, except my father, has an account with Global United's International Banking department."

"Are you looking into the transactional history for all of those accounts?"

"Yes. We maintain histories for every account in all of our international offices. Those records go back over four years. I'm still putting the report together, but I hope to have that information for both senior management and the examiners by no later than the first of next week. It's going to be somewhat voluminous. I hope they're prepared to do a little work if they plan to thoroughly review the information." Raj handed Logan another quarter inch thick sheaf of papers. "Here's a little advance information along those lines, however, for the transactions in Mr. Nasir's personal account and those of his companies. I pulled full transactional information together separately on his and AmeriPAK's accounts thinking you might want to see what it had to offer in advance of all the other information I am putting together."

"Thanks, Raj, I was just going to ask whether that might not be something you could do for me." Logan started thumbing through the report. "Did you have an opportunity to glance through this yet? And if so, did you find anything interesting here?"

"Yes, as a matter of fact, I did. As you'll notice, Mr. Nasir's personal activity is pretty standard stuff, mostly international wire transfers, etc. The transactions for his companies are also fairly standard, letters of credit, bankers' acceptances, etc. The only thing that may perhaps look a little different to the examiners, would possibly be the regular transfers a couple of Mr. Nasir's companies appear to make to offshore accounts in such places as the Caymans, Bermuda, Panama, Luxembourg, Switzerland and so forth. I'm not really sure how those relate to normal business. There's certainly nothing illegal about making such transfers, it just may tweak the examiners' interest a bit. Those places are all secret account havens."

"This is great work, Raj. Have you shown this to anyone else yet?"

"No, you are the only person thus far whose seen any of this information I've just shown you. Like I said, I should have the rest of the report together within the next day or so. Do you think I need to visit with Mr. Kruse about all of this, or will you take care of that?"

"No, I'll eventually take care of bringing Mr. Kruse up to date. As we have agreed previously, if he or anyone asks you about any of this, defer to me indicating that you've provided me with any information you have put together to date and that they should see me"

"Yes, I understand, sir." Raj always sounded like a reporting military subordinate whenever he and Logan visited. "I'll do that. I should have all the information the examiners asked for pulled together by the first of next week, anyway. So, that shouldn't be an issue for very long."

"Fine, between now and then stay in touch if you find anything else of particular interest as you look over the other information you're putting together. In the meantime, see to it that Ms. Price and her examiners get all of this information you've put together thus far right away, and I'll plan to visit with her on the matter at my earliest opportunity."

"I certainly will, and if you could perhaps use the information I mentioned to you about my father and Mr. Nasir with great care, I would appreciate that."

"Don't' worry, Raj. I thank you for confiding in me, and I'll be most careful in how I use the information we discussed. Keep me posted on what your dad decides to do about his position on the foundation board if you would. And again, let me know if I can help in any way there. I'm very interested."

◊◊◊◊

YUSSEF IBRAHIM, President and CEO of Crescent Jewelers, winced when he saw the young man he had gotten to know over the last several weeks as Ismail Hamadi come into Crescent's store on State Street in downtown Chicago. To be sure, the Nasir hawala operation had made a decent amount of money handling numerous large currency transactions since young Hamadi had first come into their store, but this was Black Friday, the day following Thanksgiving, and it was always one of the busiest shopping times of the year for Crescent Jewelers. *Our young friend's timing couldn't be worse*, thought Ibrahim.

"Good morning, Mr. Hamadi, how nice to see you again." Ibrahim's broad smile belied his aching feet, made sore already waiting on one customer after another—and there was a lot of the day left. "Please, allow me just a few moments to finish with this nice lady, and I'll be right with you."

"That's perfectly fine, Mr. Ibrahim. I'll simply admire some of your merchandise as I wait." Ibrahim waved off two aggressive young salesmen that had immediately headed

Khalid's way, and Khalid busied himself looking at the store's display of expensive Rolex, Tag Heuer and Patek Philippe watches, while Ibrahim finished with his customer.

Ibrahim quickly dispensed with the lady customer he had already sized up as someone simply shopping for bargains and turned his attention immediately back to Khalid. Ibrahim wasn't exactly sure what this Ismail Hamadi's business was exactly—he wasn't even sure that was his name—but whatever his business was, it utilized tremendous amounts of cash. Ibrahim would like to know more about this regular hawala client, but time-honored dictates of the profession forbade questions beyond those related to the transaction. Khalid was instead met with an embrace and enthusiastic hello. "Assalamu alaikum, my young friend. We are pleased to see you once again."

"Wa alaikum as-aslaam! It is also good to see you doing so well, Mr. Ibrahim, and that your business thrives. Allah blesses you?"

"He does indeed, my friend. Hopefully, you are here to ensure that we do even better. Come, we will, as usual, utilize my office upstairs to discuss your business. I am sure the staff can do without me for now." Ibrahim signaled for one of the young salesmen that had been rushing to serve Hamadi only moments before. "Mr. Malik, would you be so kind as to manage floor activities while I see to some important matters? I will be in my office taking care of our friend, Mr. Hamadi here."

Ibrahim led Khalid to his mezzanine office overlooking the main floor of the jewelry store, where they had transacted business so many times before, and then closed the door and blinds for privacy. Transactions of the size that Ibrahim had come to expect from Khalid were usually rather large. If money needed to change hands, it should be done away from prying eyes.

"I have received no instructions for any incoming transfers for you today, Mr. Hamadi, but I can see you are carrying a large briefcase. Am I to assume by that that you may have money going the other way this time?" To date, the Nasir hawala organization had handled no less than eleven incoming transfers for Khalid—or Ismail Hamadi, as he was known to Ibrahim and his people—and none of those transactions had ever been less than the mid-to-high five figures in U.S. dollars. The total received to date for all of those transfers aggregated in excess of $750,000, providing a tidy five figure profit for the Nasir organization thus far. Something about this young Muslim scared Ibrahim more than just a little, but he couldn't let that bother him. His business was bringing in some excellent fees. They would be happy to handle any transfers Mr. Hamadi was interested in doing with them, whether incoming or outgoing.

"You're quite intuitive, Mr. Ibrahim. I do indeed finally need to send money out this time"

"How much are we talking, and where do you wish to send the money, Mr. Hamadi?"

"Well, depending upon how you look at things, Mr. Ibrahim, I have both good and bad news in that regard. The good news is that all the recipients are located in the continental United States. The bad news is that there are no less than seven recipients in that many separate cities around the country, and I need the money in each of their hands by no later than twenty-four hours from now. Can you handle that for me?"

"I am certain we can accommodate you. What cities are we talking about, Mr. Hamadi?"

"I should have more than enough cash here, and would like to transfer at least $50,000 each to recipients located in: New York; Detroit, Michigan; Washington, D.C; Miami, Florida; Dallas, Texas; Seattle, Washington; and Los Angeles, California." Khalid squinted at Ibrahim as he opened the flaps on two duffles he was carrying. They were stacked full of bundled one-hundred-dollar bills

It appears this young man has been hoarding a great

deal of the money that he has received over these past many months he has been doing business with us, Ibrahim surmised, recognizing some of the currency bands that had been on the money they had given Hamadi before. "That is a great deal of cash to move in a relatively short time, my friend, but we have associates in every one of the cities you mention. So, there should be no problem whatsoever in handling your needs. You should be pleased to know that since there is no foreign exchange involved, there are only transfer fees to worry about. Considering the size of your transaction this time, I think we can keep all fees quite reasonable as well. There would normally be a fee of 2% for a transaction of this sort, but today we will charge you only 1.5%. Our fees will, therefore, come to $5,250. Do you wish to pay the fee here on this end, or have it deducted from each of the transfers? Your recipients would each end up netting $49,250. What would you prefer?"

"No, I'll pay all fees up front here. I believe I have enough cash with me. I want all recipients to receive the full $50,000." Khalid thought all hawaladars a disgusting bunch of leeches, but they were an essential part of the task at hand. He needed to get the money in the hands of each of his operatives in the cities mentioned, and to do it with dispatch. They would need it for travel money and expenses related to the plan that was to be executed by each cell over the next few weeks. Khalid would have paid the fees with minimal fuss had they been twice as much at this stage of the game. "Let's just get on with this, Mr. Ibrahim, I have little time this evening, and this is a great deal of money. The sooner we complete our transaction, the happier I will be."

"Very well, then," answered Ibrahim. Moving with celerity, he squeezed the sides of each bundle, curled the bills, slipped the bands off of each and inserted the bills into a currency machine, counting them with blinding speed. As the stacks were finished, he squeezed the bills on the sides again, curling them in a way that enabled him to easily reinsert the money into the same currency bands that had held the stacks together before. When he was done counting out exactly $355,250 he placed the rather large stack of bills in the vault he had in his office and then removed seven one-dollar bills from his pocket.

"May I suggest as we have so often done before, use the serial numbers on each of these one-dollar bills as the identifiers for the recipients to whom you are sending these transfers. I will write down the name and addresses of our associates in the each of the cities you have designated, where your recipients can go to pick up their money no later than noon tomorrow. I am writing the respective serial number next to each, and in addition, will give you one-half of each of these bills with the city written on them in pencil as additional clarification." Tearing the bills in half after writing the end-point locations on each, he handed them to Khalid. "Neither my associates nor I need know the names of your recipients. They need only go to the persons I am writing down here for you, mention that they are there to pick up the money you are sending, and then identify themselves with the serial numbers we are assigning here tonight. Remember now, they must give my associates in each of these cities the exact numbers I am assigning, or they will not be given the money. Do I make myself clear?"

"Yes, Mr. Ibrahim, you do indeed—same as before. I will communicate these identifiers to my business partners in each of these cities right away and remind them of the importance of accuracy."

"One final but very important thing that I need for you then to do once each of your intended recipients has received their transfers, Mr. Hamadi, is to destroy all information related to the transactions. This will help ensure that added level of confidentiality I think we both wish to maintain with this or any future business. Do we agree on that, Mr. Hamadi?

"We do indeed."

"Well, with that, I thank you as always, my friend. May I be of any additional service?" Ibrahim noticed as he closed the briefcase and handed it back to Khalid that there were three or four remaining bundles in the case that was sitting on his desk. *Evidently, young Mr. Hamadi here was expecting to pay more for our services*, thought Ibrahim. *I could have charged more! Ah, well, as Mr. Nasir so often reminds us—one should never be too greedy.*

The whole transaction would be relatively simple. There were no borders other than state lines to contend with on this one. As soon as he left, Ibrahim would e-mail his hawala associates in each of the cities to which Khalid was sending money. The pickup points for all the recipients would be Crescent Jewelry stores in each of the cities where al-Sahaba cells were located, except for Dallas. The hawaladar in that city was only affiliated with the Nasir group by way of the occasional business they transacted from time to time with PAK-West, Inc., the precious metals wholesaler parent of Crescent Jewelers. The payout there would be handled in much the same way, but settlement would be slightly different. Creative adjustments to inventories at the various Crescent shops would account for transactions at those locations, whereas the Dallas transfer would be accomplished by under-invoicing on PAK-West's next shipment of jewelry, precious metals or gems to that unrelated merchant.

Whatever the method of settlement, each of Khalid's operatives would be receiving $50,000 by no later than noon the following day, with no questions asked, and once again no paper trail regarding anything that had taken place.

CHAPTER TWENTY-THREE

AS THEY had indicated might be the case, the Saturday morning following Thanksgiving turned out to be the time most advantageous for the delivery of the laptop computers the FBI said would be provided Logan Hart and Cass Price to facilitate future communications between them and the Bureau. As planned, both Logan and Cass were at home and on hand to meet with the two IT specialists the FBI sent to their respective places of residence with the computers. Disguised as deliverymen, the IT specialists delivered as promised two new, rugged-looking, military-grade laptop computers pre-installed with the FBI's newest teleconferencing apps. Neither of the laptops were of the sort commercially available. In addition, after reviewing the systems already in place at both residences, special satellite receivers, modems and routers were installed, together with all ancillary equipment necessary to establish fully-secure Wi-Fi capability. Logan and Cass had personal computers of their own, but neither was equipped to meet the communications standards necessary for them to participate in the online meetings the two would be involved in with the JTTF over the next few weeks.

Accompanying the computer equipment were messages to both Logan and Cass from FBI Agent Jim Seilor that read... "Logan and Cass, to try out this new system of communications, we thought we would hold a meeting of all parties concerned online this evening at 7:00

p.m. if you both can make yourselves available. Hopefully, the equipment will work okay. Please, input the user names and passwords we gave you when we showed you how to set up and connect this new equipment. The system is quite user friendly, but if things still don't work right for any reason, call the special phone number our people should have provided you— on your cell phones for the sake of security— and we will talk you through it. See you online tonight—Jim."

Thanks to all the detailed instructions that had been previously provided, Logan had little trouble setting up the new equipment. At the appointed time, he booted up the new laptop and tapped a strange-looking icon on the desktop in the form of a mushroom, which he had previously been informed would give him connectivity to the teleconferencing app the FBI had provided. This immediately brought him online with the JTTF's web-conferencing system. Entering his assigned user name and password, his face immediately appeared in a box on the screen next to a second framing an attractive brunette staring directly back at him.

"Good evening, Mr. Hart! I'm Tally Dennison, Special Agent Daimler's administrative assistant. Mr. Daimler said to expect you online right about now, and you're right on time. We're waiting for Ms. Price from the OCC to sign in at any moment. After she has joined us, I'll bring Mr. Daimler and the other people in our meeting room on screen, and you can proceed with your teleconference. It should be very soon if you could bear with us."

"No problem, I'll be waiting."

"Thank you, I'll return in just a moment, I'm sure."

"Good morning, Logan, glad to have you join us. We just received your sign-on." Following a melodic chime, Logan heard Merritt Daimler's familiar voice followed but a split second later by the framed faces of six individuals simultaneously appearing next to his on the screen of the laptop he had been provided. One of those on the screen was Cass Price sitting in what Logan surmised was an attractively decorated home office. It suddenly dawned on Logan that this method of meeting might have its pluses. He could study Cass Price as closely as he wanted during their meeting, and neither she nor the other attendees would be the wiser. He figured he was going to like this. "Cass Price just joined us as well," said Daimler. "So, we can go ahead and get started with this. Good evening, everyone!"

"Good evening, Merritt! Good evening everybody!" Cass answered. "Gee, this is great stuff! Probably will take us another ten years before we'll have anything like this available to us over at the OCC—even though it would probably save us tons of money all around. Can't have that you know! Some of us use Skype and Zoom here and there, but nothing as secure and sophisticated as this."

Logan simply smiled and waved at everyone by way of acknowledgment.

"Okay, folks, if things are working properly for everyone this evening, each of you should be able to both see and hear Logan Hart from Global United Bank and Cass Price with the OCC on your computers, along with me and the team here at the FBI offices. Vince Magnusson over at ICE—whom I don't think you've previously met—and Raleigh Sutphen with Department of Homeland Security should also be showing on your screens. Let me know if any of you are having any problems seeing any of these people. There ought to be six panes besides your own showing on your screen." One by one, all six parties responded to the affirmative. "Great!" continued Daimler. "Hopefully, this will work out as a much easier and more secure way for all of us to communicate regularly. With that, does anyone have any updates for the rest regarding their respective investigations? Logan and Cass, we're particularly interested in anything either of you may have from your work within the bank? That's mostly what we're here for this evening."

"I'll let Logan answer for himself," responded Cass with a grin, "but our examination team has been making some pretty good progress. Last evening, Mr. Haifa that runs the International Banking department at Global United, brought a great deal of information to us regarding his department's customers, along with a large list of transactions handled by the bank for those people over the last couple of years. If you all will recollect, it is our understanding that Paul Trotter may also have been looking at that department some right before his death. We, therefore, thought we ought to take a much closer look at that area of the bank as part of our review of BSA and AML administration. Tariq Nasir, his companies and a number of his acquaintances and affiliate organizations are all among that list of customers. We're naturally keying in on them first, but there is a great deal of information to go through. It'll probably take us a day or two more. Even though it's a Saturday and into the evening, my team is working on that as we speak, and I will be joining them when we are done with this online meeting. I'm hopeful we can complete our work on that sometime early this coming week."

"Have you found anything of interest thus far, Cass?" Asked Raleigh Sutphen from DHS.

"It's a little early to tell, Raleigh. Nasir's companies do a great deal in the way of international wires. Some of those are back and forth between some offshore havens, but once again, we haven't finished going through the information yet. We've set up a database, and we're loading high volume international banking client information into that so we can analyze it. Just as soon as we find anything worthwhile we'll get in touch with everyone and share that information."

"I hate to keep repeating this, Ms. Price, but could you use any special help from others of us here?" Sutphen asked. "You say you have a great deal of work to do, and we certainly have a goodly number of analysts and systems available to us that we could use to assist you if needed."

"No, not at this moment, I don't believe. I appreciate the offer, and perhaps we may need some help like that before this is all over, but why don't you let us see what we're dealing with before we involve you folks. We'll certainly keep you abreast of where we're at as we move along with our examination, though."

"Fine, we'll defer to you in that regard for the moment, but remember we are on a short string with all of this, and we've got a number of people who could be a big help to you. So, please, don't be afraid to ask for an assist. We're here if you need us."

"Thanks, Raleigh, we will. Rest assured, we'll keep your offer in mind if things heat up for us."

"How about you, Mr. Hart?" Sutphen continued. "How are you coming with your part of all this?"

"Well, I would say, I'm doing all I can to push things along within the bank in support of the OCC's investigations, and my personal project for this weekend is to finish internally reviewing all the Nasir-related deposit and loan account relationships." Sutphen was the one person involved in all of this that made Logan uncomfortable. He still had him pegged for CIA, and what little he had had to do with them through the years had never been all that pleasant an experience. "I completed some of that last evening, but just like Cass and her crew, I still have a little work yet to do. I'll probably have those results done on Monday."

"Well, the sooner the better, Mr. Hart. Like I said to Ms. Price, we need to know as early as possible whether you folks are going to find anything worthwhile. Yesterday wouldn't be any too soon for anything you can get for us. Our country—and most of the world for that matter— really can't afford the effects of another pandemic. The last one was crippling to say the least."

"Well, the primary purpose of our meeting this morning," interrupted Daimler in an attempt to shut off Sutphen's alarm-ism and regain control of the meeting, "was really to test out this technology and see if this form of online meeting was going to work for us; and if everyone agrees, it certainly appears to be the answer to our needs relative to staying in touch and keeping it private. What think you all?"

"Well, I think it's fantastic. It's much easier, and way more secure than personal meetings," Cass exclaimed. "Sometime in the future, I am going to recommend to our people that we look into something like this to communicate between our offices around the country. I would think it could save us tons of money by eliminating a lot of very bothersome meetings our people still run to around the country much of the time. The encrypted aspect of the system is also amazing—something we could really use. By the way, can we use this system to communicate with each other from time to time outside of the meeting setting, such as say Mr. Hart and I as we compare notes on the work he is doing for us?"

Logan liked the sound of that.

"Sure, Cass, feel free," Daimler answered. "But please be aware that the FBI is the service provider on this. So, the system will be monitored, and there will be recordings and a log of all the calls you make on it. You can use the system whenever you need, but you probably should make sure your communications relate in some way to our ongoing investigation. Big brother may be watching, you know! With that, does anyone else have anything further at this time? If not, we can end this for now and get to work on our various investigations."

No one responded. Logan thought for a brief moment about perhaps bringing up the matter of Worldwide Islamic Charities and the related information Raj Haifa had mentioned to him the day before but decided against doing so for the moment. *Better hold on that*, he figured. *I'd like to look that situation over some myself through Raj before stirring a stink that has the potential of ruining lives. I could see such a revelation perhaps having a tremendously negative effect on Raj's father. Might easily become a matter of guilt by association.*

"When are we going to get together again?" Sutphen asked.

"Good question!" Daimler answered. "Let me suggest that we let Logan and Cass have the rest of today and tomorrow to see if they can make some progress on their investigations, and then tentatively plan to get together online again say Monday evening at around this same time, unless they come up with something that requires meeting sooner. Can everyone make that?"

Again, there was silence.

"Fine, hearing no objection, I'll take everyone's silence to be universal assent. Monday evening it is then. We'll let everyone know the exact time earlier Monday via phone call. If you find any time in the interim that you have a conflict, call me on my cell to let me know. We'll know then not to expect you. Logan, Cass, find something here for us if you can. As Raleigh said earlier, we truly need to find out whether any of this investigation into Global United or Mr. Nasir has legs or not."

◊◊◊◊

WHEN HE was home on weekends, which was seldom the case considering the demands of managing a company with varied international business interests, Tariq Nasir liked to save Saturday afternoons for relaxation and time with his sons, eighteen-year-old Faoud and seventeen-year-old Hassan. Melissa, their mother, seldom joined Nasir and the boys on any of these outings. Even though she was extremely close to her sons, the relationship between her and Nasir was far too strained anymore. About the only times the two were together with their sons were at public events, family gatherings, and at special situations related to the boys, such as school functions, sporting events, and birthdays. On such occasions, both went out of their way to put a good face on a bad situation.

Had the Nasirs been anything like the typical American couple, they would no doubt have been divorced years before, but there was nothing typical at all about their marriage. As a Muslim, divorce was, in Tariq's view, his exclusive call to make, and at the present, he was not so inclined. It simply did not fit his current needs or plans. And fortunate for him, divorce was simply out of the question for a staunch Catholic like Melissa. The marriage thus continued as a matter of convenience for one, and for the other, a burden borne out of devotion to God and family.

The Saturday following Thanksgiving had become one of those rare weekend days during the year when Nasir was home alone, with neither his sons nor Melissa present. She and the boys were away on a holiday skiing trip to Sun Valley, Idaho with members of her family. It had become traditional for the Hardesty clan to gather at that time of year for a month of fun on the slopes. Melissa's family—mother, sisters, uncles, aunts, and cousins—always rented out the better part of a condo complex there called Mystic Mountain, beginning the day after Thanksgiving. They had been doing something like this nearly every year since Melissa and her sisters were little girls.

Nasir had no desire to attend the annual outing. Things weren't all that good between him and most members of his wife's family. The annual outing was, however, one thing that Melissa did with their sons that Nasir allowed. Skiing was a sport he heartily encouraged for his sons. A lot of business took place on the slopes, and Nasir figured skiing was a skill that both Faoud and Hassan might one day find useful socially.

Tariq and Melissa Nasir had officially called a 6,000 square foot house on a 20-acre tree-lined estate in the affluent northwest suburban community of River Forest, IL home since 1995. Nasir traveled a great deal, however, and usually wanted to be close to the office. So, most weeknights were spent in his downtown Michigan Avenue condo, or in the private apartment immediately adjacent to his office when business matters were pressing. When he wasn't traveling, weekends at home with his sons were a high priority, with strolls along a picturesque trail next to the Des Plaines River being one of Nasir's favorite things to do with his sons. With the boys away this particular weekend it wouldn't be quite as enjoyable, but Nasir decided to take the walk anyway. He could use the exercise and needed some time to think.

"With your sons absent this morning, Mr. Nasir, would you like me to walk along with you for the purpose of conversation?" Abdul Hasib, Nasir's chauffeur, was also a bodyguard, and whenever he drove Nasir and his sons to the river walk, he always accompanied them on their excursions, hanging back at a discreet distance. When the boys were gone Nasir usually still enjoyed Abdul's company, but today was a little different.

"Thank you for the offer, Abdul, but not today, if you don't mind. If you could give me just a little distance, there are a few things I need to mull over, and could use some relative privacy." He could see Hasib was disappointed. "But I do appreciate the offer."

Nasir had walked only a short distance when he saw the young man ahead of him. He was seated on one of the benches that lined the path, the hood of his sweatshirt pulled up over his head all but concealing his face, hands in his pockets as if to shield them against the cold, with feet outstretched and crossed in front of him as if he were simply relaxing and enjoying the coming of winter. The closer the young man came into view, the more evident it was to Nasir that he might ironically be someone who also hailed from somewhere in Asia or the Middle East. His presence there, however, appeared out of place to Nasir. *Young, looks Egyptian*, he thought, *also looks familiar. Perhaps he's a student over at Concordia College?*

When Nasir came alongside, the young man spoke. "Good afternoon, Mr. Nasir."

"You look familiar. Do I know you, young sir?" asked Nasir, surprised that the young man had addressed him by name.

"Well, we do sometimes attend the same Masjid in downtown Chicago. I see you there often on the occasion of Friday prayers. We did, however, meet and have a couple of very lengthy visits a few years ago. Do you perhaps remember now?"

"No, I am sorry, but I do not."

"Well, that may be understandable. It was not even in this country. We met in Mecca, sir. We were both on Hajj. Does that now ring any bells?"

"Ah, yes, that's it. It's now coming back to me. You were that nice, but intense, young man that I had tea with at the Intercontinental Hotel on a couple of occasions." Nasir shook his head in disbelief. "You have a better memory than I though, Mr... uh?"

"Hamadi, Mr. Nasir, Ismail Hamadi." Khalid used his alias. It was obvious that Nasir hadn't remembered the name he used when they had met and visited on Hajj in 2014, and it was the name he needed to go by for now. "But never mind whether you remember me. I know and remember you, and that is all that matters. May I walk with you a bit, sir? I have been waiting on you. We need to talk."

"Waiting for me? What would you and I have to talk about? I don't really know you, sir!" Nasir was becoming uncomfortable and looked to his rear for Hasib, who was apparently hanging back far enough to the rear that he was obscured by a bend in the path. Nasir was now a bit chagrined that he had asked the bodyguard to stay well behind.

"I realize that sir, but you would do well to listen to me. Please, I mean you no harm. As a matter of fact, my intentions are just the opposite. I want only to offer you some

304

information."

"Information? What information would you have for me? You and I have nothing to discuss." The confrontation was making Nasir nervous. This young Mr. Hamadi's intensity was jogging his memory. He was beginning now to recollect his conversations with a young man in Mecca who was proselytizing for a fledgling group of young Islamic fundamentalists bent on changing the world. He remembered the young man in Mecca made him nervous then, and he was doing it again now. He started to walk away, but the young man rose immediately to walk along with him.

"We haven't but a moment to talk, Mr. Nasir, so please listen, and listen carefully. There are those in my circle of acquaintances who would question my judgment for telling you what I am going to say, but you and your associates have been of great service to us before, and I fear we may need your services again in the future. I accordingly feel compelled to warn you that—how should I put this—we are living in perilous times, times when you and your organization may need alliances with people and organizations of the sort that I and my associates are familiar with. We have much need of a close association with someone of your background and capabilities, and there may come a day soon when you may well need the same from us. The right alliances have been important to you in the past and will be for you and all those you hold dear in the future. I can assure you."

"You're talking in riddles, Mr. Hamadi. What are you trying to say? Are you threatening me in some way?"

"No, no, absolutely not, Mr. Nasir, far be it from such. Please, listen to me though. I have only a moment to say this," said the young man, now looking down the path himself. "There are those, as you know, who are dedicated to the spread of Islam throughout the world, and to that end, by divine providence a day of reckoning is fast approaching for this nation of apostates. May Allah, the most merciful and compassionate one, be praised."

"I share your dream my young friend, but I admit to being confused as to how any of this concerns me or my family?" The stranger was beginning to make Nasir quite uncomfortable.

"Well, it is a matter in which you are very much involved, whether you know it or not, kind sir."

"Come again—as they say?"

"Let me put it this way, Mr. Nasir. I represent an organization dedicated to the spread of Islam to all corners of the world, which is a goal I know you share."

"As I said a moment ago, my friend, that no doubt is a goal we both share, but I'm not all that certain we may perhaps share the same idea as to how we will someday accomplish that."

"Oh, I am convinced we do, Mr. Nasir, and if not now, then we will someday soon. Which is why I am here to offer you words of friendly warning—a warning so that you, your children and your children's children can live to serve the cause of Islam for generations to come. Your family's service has been very much appreciated in the past, and will still be much needed in the future."

"Now you're really confusing me, my young friend? You've said something like that twice now. First, how have I been of service to you in the past, and in what way do you expect me to so again in the future? Further, of what peril do you refer?"

"Please, Mr. Nasir, I don't have time to play games. Whether you've known it or not, you and your hawala network have been of service to us many times, and we will definitely have need of your help again. Therefore, I will tell you this one time. Ensure that you and all that you hold dear are prepared against every pestilence known to man and ensure that it is done immediately. I cannot and will not tell you any more. Just pay heed to what I have said, and pay

306

heed to it literally. Do I make myself clear?"

"No, you do not. I don't understand what you mean. What do you mean when you say, 'prepared against every pestilence known to man', my friend?"

"I have probably told you more than I should have already, Mr. Nasir. You should take from that what you will. I can say no more. Just heed my words!"

"I'm sorry, sir, but what you're telling me is confusing. I don't believe I understand any of this."

"Oh, I think you will after giving it some thought Mr. Nasir. You are certainly no idiot." The young man looked Nasir straight in the eye. "Allow me to say this one last thing. This is a wicked land, full of wicked people, and they will soon reap the whirlwind for all the evil they have wrought upon the Ummah across the ages. They will soon consider 9/11 but a light slap on the hand, compared to the blow that is soon to come. In the words of Sheik bin Laden—may Allah now hold him against his bosom—'Pan Islam will never be peacefully established worldwide. It will take pen and gun, word and bullet, tongue and teeth.' You would do well to both heed that admonition and say nothing about what I have just told you. Do I make myself clear."

"You do, but I do not like being threatened."

"Nothing I have said was meant by way of threat, Mr. Nasir, but quite the opposite. You are a friend whether you know it or not, and we intend nothing but the best for you and your family. That is why I am here."

"I appreciate that."

"Good, my friend. That is important to me and those I represent. I know we will have need of you and your associates in the future. And with that, I have nothing more about which to speak." The young man pulled the hood of his sweatshirt further down over his head, his face now almost fully obscured. Looking one last time at Nasir, the young man touched his arm and spoke softly before turning to jog away down the path. "Allahu akbar, my friend!"

307

"Yes, yes, God is Great!" Nasir mumbled in mock appreciation as the young man disappeared down the path. He wasn't sure what to think. *Was this the ranting of a lunatic, or something about which it would be wise to take heed*, he wondered?

◊◊◊◊

ON THE Sunday morning following Thanksgiving, Logan was surprised to receive an e-mail message from Scott Kruse on his home computer. He checked for e-mail two or three times per day when he was at home, saving on his hard drive most messages that were neither sensitive in nature nor SPAM. To the best of his recollection, this was the only time that Scott had ever e-mailed him at home.

FROM: skruse@globalunited.com
TO: lhart@gmail.com
Logan,
I am sure you are as concerned as I am about all the extra work and business interruption this extended OCC examination is causing for the bank. I appreciate your keeping me informed about the situation this past week via e-mail, but I would like to meet with you personally first thing tomorrow to find out when you think the examiners might be finished. If I don't like what I hear, I may then ask Ms. Price to meet with us and explain when she thinks the OCC will be done with all of this. If they haven't found anything much to substantiate a link between Trotter's death and his work at the bank—which I doubt they ever will—I want them to wrap things up. They have already taken way too much of our time with this so-called extended examination. By their own admission, they were essentially done with their work before this thing happened to Trotter. We have a bank to run!! I hope you agree with me on that. What say we have a cup of coffee in my office at 7:00 a.m. tomorrow morning before everyone starts arriving, examiners

included. Then, if it looks like we need to, it will be
early enough in the day to arrange a meeting with Ms.
Price on Monday after we discuss the matter. Let me
know if you can make it—Scott

Logan had sensed toward the end of the previous week that Scott was getting edgy about the OCC's extended presence at the bank. It showed on his face, in the tone of his voice and in his actions increasingly by the day. This e-mail message confirmed his suspicions in that regard. Logan fired back a response to Scott confirming he would attend the meeting first thing Monday morning, and attached an up-to-date status summary on the examination—minus, of course, any reference to the extracurricular work he was doing for the OCC and JTTF.

As chief liaison between Global United and the OCC on the examination, Logan had promised to keep Scott informed as to progress with the examiners, and he had been making a sincere attempt to generally do just that by trying to make the reports as complete as possible. There was, however, simply no way he could at this time divulge the full extent to which he was assisting both the regulators and other federal investigators. Scott would, first of all, have come unglued. Secondly, Logan also knew Scott was in continuous contact with Nasir about everything that was taking place, and Nasir didn't need to know any more than necessary at this time considering the extent to which the regulators were looking into his involvement at the bank and beyond. Logan had been wording all of his written reports carefully and would be equally careful about what he said to Scott when they met the following morning.

CHAPTER TWENTY-FOUR

SCOTT KRUSE had fresh bagels and coffee waiting in his office on Monday morning when Logan arrived for the 7:00 a.m. meeting Scott had requested. As Logan walked by Mariette Fowler, Scott's thirty-something showpiece secretary, she mumbled sleepily. "Good morning, Mr. Hart. Go right on in, he's waiting for you." Then lowering her voice a bit to avoid Scott hearing her, she added, "And good luck, he appears to be in a bit of a mood this morning." Logan smiled understandingly and entered the office, shutting the door behind him.

Scott whirled with a start when he heard the door close. He had been staring out his second-floor window, deep in thought, when Logan entered. He looked troubled, and it was evident from the footprint pattern on the freshly vacuumed office carpet that he had been pacing about. "Good morning Logan. I appreciate your coming in this early. I realize these early morning meetings require you to hit the road fairly early, what with your having to commute from Palatine and all, but I'm afraid it couldn't be helped."

"No sweat, I'm usually in early, anyway."

"Well, I'm glad you got my message. I felt we ought to talk. First, help yourself to a bagel and a cup of coffee, and then we'll have a seat and get into things."

Logan did as Scott suggested and then seated himself while he watched Scott continue to pace about the room. "What's up, Scott?"

Kruse finally came over and took a seat in the overstuffed chair opposite Logan. He slouched in the chair and looked up at the ceiling before responding. "Oh, I don't know, Logan." He let out an exaggerated sigh. "You'll have to forgive me. This whole OCC examination thing has me in a bit of a tizzy, and I can sense some members of the board also getting concerned."

"I know, I know." Logan took a bite of a still warm but unadorned bagel and a sip of coffee as he listened patiently.

"One examination is enough, and this whole thing essentially amounts to two back-to-back. From all you've told me in your memos, the OCC has basically asked for a whole lot of the same information we provided them several weeks ago at the start of their initial examination, and they continue to pore over the books of the bank as though they think we're a bunch of crooks or something. What the heck do you think is going on here? You're our lead guy on this."

"Well, first of all, Scott, they've neither said nor done anything thus far that would lead me to believe that they suspect the bank of any wrongdoing. They continue to insist they are simply looking back through all that Paul Trotter investigated for them during his time here, to not only complete the work he was doing before his life was taken, but to also assure themselves that none of that work here had anything to do with his demise." Logan regretted how untruthful he was having to be with Scott, but he knew there was nothing but downside to informing him of the full extent to which the OCC was looking through things at Global United. Besides, he had no choice. He was sworn to secrecy with the OCC and JTTF on the matter. "It's only been a little over a week since they began this extended examination, Scott. With all the information they had their first time around and the promptness with which we have provided the second set of information they requested, I would certainly think they would not be too much longer in wrapping up what they need to do here."

"Well, I would certainly hope so. In my opinion, this whole thing is horse dookie, anyway. There's no way this bank had anything to do with Mr. Trotter's death. He was just in the wrong place at the wrong time. They need to end all of this. Like I said in my message to you this weekend, what do you think of me asking for a meeting with this Price lady from the OCC today? Maybe I need to light a fire under her to wrap this up."

"Look, Scott, in my opinion, I think we need to go easy with this. I feel we'll be much farther ahead simply to cooperate with the OCC in every way possible to help them through their examination. Ms. Price is one tough cookie. If we start to put up a stink about wanting them out of here, then she and her crew are going to think we have something to hide and really dig in their heels. Let's at least give it say until the end of this week. Could be they might wrap things up before we have to start pushing them as to when they're going to be finished. I would think they'd have some idea by then. I'll stay right with them on this and ensure that nothing happens from our end that would give them a reason for delay. As before, I'll keep you fully apprised as to progress."

Scott got up and walked back over to stare out of his window for a moment, sighing again rather audibly before answering. "Alright, Logan, I'll take your advice for the moment and back off pushing the OCC very much at this time, but please understand, if this thing goes much beyond this week, I am going to make a stink all the way up to the Comptroller of the Currency himself if I have to. This is a busy time of the year for our staff in most cases anyway, and I have a lot on my plate trying to negotiate this possible Michigan bank acquisition thing for Mr. Nasir. Like I said, I... uh, should I say... we don't need this right now."

"I understand, Scott. Once again, I assure you that I will stay heavily involved with Ms. Price and her examiners, and push this thing along as much as I can. You can inform Mr. Nasir of that if you would like." As he said that, Logan was thinking to himself, *if the guy only knew!*

◊◊◊◊

"CAN MS. Price come in now, Mr. Hart? She says that you called her and asked to meet?" Myrna Brock enjoyed watching the chemistry she thought was developing between the two.

"Yeah, thanks, Myrna, show her right in." Logan got up from behind his desk and walked to the door to meet his increasingly favorite regulator. "Good morning, Cass. I appreciate your making some time for me." Logan shook hands with Cass as she entered the room. Her hand was slender and quite feminine, but her handshake firm. He held it just a smidgen longer than was perhaps appropriate.

"No problem. We probably needed to meet, anyway." Cass didn't appear at all put off by the frequent interaction the situation at Global United had foisted upon the two.

Seated across from each other at Logan's conference table, both studied each other for a brief moment before he broke the silence. "You know, Cass, I had a meeting with Scott Kruse earlier this morning, and you should have been there. It was a somewhat testy time."

"Oh, really, I can readily imagine."

"Yes, we spent the better part of an hour discussing the OCC's protracted examination here at the bank. Scott was expressing increasing exasperation with the length of time you folks have been in the bank. He was nearly apoplectic. I felt rather sorry for the guy. I'm dead certain he's getting pressure from Nasir, and perhaps even some of the board."

313

Cass seemed nonplussed. "I'm sure they're all edgy. I suppose I would feel the same way if I were in their shoes, having to put up with a bunch of regulators to the extent we've had to be here. It remains to be seen, but you and I both know there may turn out to be a lot of good reasons for us having to go through all of this again."

"That's true, but I couldn't really communicate any of that to Scott this morning. The whole situation is getting rather untenable. I tried to be as truthful as possible while still skirting the issue to the extent I could by telling him I wasn't really aware that you folks had found anything yet. That is basically true but was hardly sufficient disclosure to help the situation. Scott was frustrated enough that he wanted to meet with you right now, but I talked him into waiting until at least the end of this week or first of next week before plowing into any situation with you folks."

Cass smiled and shook her head before answering. "Well, I suppose we could have a progress meeting if Scott were to insist, but as you're painfully aware, Logan, I can't really tell them very much right now either. We have quite a bit of work left to do before we can be sure whether there is any basis for concern for either the OCC, or the JTTF you and I are trying to assist. I would hope we could be done by the end of this week, but I can't say that right now with any certainty. Perhaps I could give Scott and the board a report of sorts that would settle them down for the present, but really little more.

"Maybe you could put it to him just that way for now. Scott asked what the areas were that the OCC was looking closest at, and I tried to be as candid as possible with him without giving away any of what we've been discussing with the JTTF and so on."

"Well, again, as you can well appreciate, Logan, I'm not all that certain how comforting any meeting of the sort he wants would be for senior management and the board here at Global United. If I were to offer even a hint of disclosure regarding some of what we're finding thus far as a result of the very necessary extra work we've been doing here since Paul Trotter's death, I doubt it would be comforting to either Mr. Kruse or the board. They'll be particularly unnerved if we get into any of our findings or suspicions relative to Mr. Nasir and that AmeriPAK outfit of his."

"Why? I rather doubt I'll be much surprised, but what things are you finding? Anything we haven't already discussed before with the JTTF, etc?"

"No, I guess I would have to say the things we've been increasingly delving into would not generally be anything far afield from most of what we've previously discussed with the FBI and so on. It's just that we're digging a lot deeper and looking the things we're finding over a great deal more carefully this time. You know, Logan, even though we've discussed this before, both you and we have continued to question the significant levels of cash and cash-related transactions that show up on the books of nearly all of Mr. Nasir's companies, a circumstance very atypical for the types of business some of them are involved in. Then to make that all further perplexing, those same companies constitute a large part of the bank's international wire transfer business. You know, I have to say, now that we're beginning to understand the Money Service Business industry a little better and look at things from that vantage in our review of the AmeriPAK companies, one begins to see a pattern of business that just might support the FBI and DHS's supposition that Mr. Nasir and his associates may be making this hawala thing an integral part of most of the business they all do."

"It's interesting you would say that. I was waiting until our online meeting tomorrow evening to tell the criminal investigators and the DHS about this, but did want to tell you in advance that I am regretfully finding much the same thing in my analysis. I spent a lot of time over the weekend studying recent credit reviews and financial information on all of Mr. Nasir's companies, and it would seem that their balance sheets support exactly what you say — actually glaringly so. There are a great deal of inter-company transactions, and nearly all the companies appear to have tremendous amounts of cash for operations of their type. If someone was going to use a network of conventional businesses as the underpinning for the business of hawala, as it has been described to us by the FBI and others, I agree it would seem that Nasir's organization is one that has been designed and operated to do just that."

"I suspected you might be headed to a determination of that sort," Cass replied, "but what I'm most worried about —if any of our mutual suspicions are correct that Mr. Nasir and his associates may indeed be hawaladars—is the possibility that he might be in the process of making Global United Bank an integral part of such an operation. Or, worse yet, that he already has in some way!"

"Well, I have a little more work to do yet on this, Cass, but we may have an interesting online meeting tomorrow night. We're going to have to report all of this to the investigators."

"You're right. There'll be much to discuss, I think. In the meantime, if you want to try to assuage your board a bit to buy us some time, you could maybe tell Mr. Nasir and Mr. Kruse that I'd be happy to meet with them sometime toward the end of this week to bring them up to date on where we are with all of this. This, of course, can't be part of any conversation you might have with them, but I really want to get past our meeting with the FBI and DHS before we meet with any Global United people; and I also need to bring all the people I answer to in the OCC current on where we are thus far before any such meeting."

"Fine, I'll see what I can do to keep everyone patient by passing that along to the board and Mr. Kruse, but Mr. Nasir is apparently going out of the country for a few days, and wanted to meet with you folks before he left. I'm anticipating he'll be upset we aren't going to be able to do that before he goes."

"Do the best you can, Logan. I really don't want to meet with Mr. Nasir and Mr. Kruse until we have a real case about this put together, and I can't see us doing that in less than a few days at the very least. I've got to tell you, if the FBI agrees with us pursuing the questions I have, I doubt whether any meeting we have with your people is going to be all that pleasant a session. If Nasir is indeed a hawaladar, he's not going to be that happy with all the questions I think we're going to have to ask." Cass studied Logan for a moment. "That being said, let me ask you a personal question if I could. How are you yourself going to be with all this if our suspicions about Nasir turn out to be true? Things could really blow up around here if they do."

"Look, I've already come to the conclusion that I may have made a bad choice in accepting Global United's offer for this position, but I am committed to seeing all of this through. There are some really good people around here, and I'm not sure that the institution of Global United has been compromised too much just yet. Maybe I can be an instrument of good in all of this and help some people out in the process."

"I appreciate your answer, Logan. It's reassuring. Tell me one other thing though. Where do you think Scott Kruse is going to shake out in all of this? If Mr. Nasir is involved in hawala, do you think Mr. Kruse is aware of that, or even worse directly involved?"

"You know, Cass, I may be proved grossly in error with this, but somehow I don't really believe that Scott knows whether Mr. Nasir is or is not involved in the business of hawala. Why, I'd be surprised if he even knew what the term meant."

"Well, you've mentioned several times how close the two are."

"Yes, I know, but I still doubt he would know anything

about any hawala operation Nasir might have going. Scott's highly paid, has a number of great perks and likes the prestige of his position, so he panders to Nasir like you wouldn't believe. Nasir certainly has Scott in his hip pocket, so to speak, but I don't think he has convinced Scott to do anything worse thus far than to be his eyes and ears relative to all that is going on here. Let me put it this way, Scott may be Nasir's toady, but I don't think he's on the wrong side of the law, at least not yet."

"I hope you're correct. I would have to say I'm inclined to agree with your assessment thus far in that regard, but I guess we'll just have to wait and see." Cass closed the portfolio into which she had been entering notes. "Well, we've probably taken up too much of each other's time already. Anything else you feel you need to talk with me about this morning?"

"No, no, that's all I really wanted for now. I'll talk with Scott and Nasir and try to arrange a time for a meeting ostensibly when Nasir returns from Europe and gets back to you. In the meantime, I'll put some finishing touches on my review of the Nasir companies, and plan to see you next during our little online session with the JTTF tomorrow evening—providing I don't bump into you around here sometime before."

Cass stood to leave. "Fine, if we don't cross paths before then, I'll see you online tomorrow evening. It should be an interesting one." As she was going out the door, Cass turned and smiled at Logan. He could tell she was hesitating a bit. "Uh, maybe when this is all said and done, perhaps we could try out some place other than that little Italian restaurant of yours, and have dinner together sometime when we don't have to discuss all these serious banking matters."

"You know, I'd enjoy that very much. We'll have to make sure we make that happen when this is all over." Logan watched Cass walk away. His wife, Melanie, had been gone for a year now, and he still missed her horribly. It might not be going anywhere, but somehow he had the feeling Melanie would approve of the feelings he seemed to be developing for this attractive bank regulator.

◊◊◊◊

CASS PRICE wasn't exactly sure what it was about Sammy al-Dajani that bothered her, but somehow he did. She figured it might be a cultural thing, but she really couldn't be certain in that regard. The bank had quite a few Muslim staff members, but al-Dajani was the only one that affected her the way that he did, and she wasn't alone in that regard amongst her team of examiners. Al-Dajani had a supercilious, condescending way of responding to Cass and other female examiners when he had to deal with them. She found it quite irritating. When she asked one of the Muslim lady tellers about it, the woman just rolled her eyes and said, "Mr. al-Dajani is of the old school. He's that way with all women. We Muslim women on staff understand, but most of the non-Muslim female employees under him do not. There have been complaints, but no one seems to want to do anything about it."

"This is America!" One of Cass' exasperated female examiners commented sarcastically. "The guy should either get with it or go back to wherever he came from!" Cass could tell by the set in the young lady's jaw, and the looks on the faces of her other female examiners that Sammy had made no friends on her team, and that did not bode well for either he or the bank. Her lady examiners were making his areas of responsibility matters of particularly close scrutiny. *He may come to rue the day he offended this bunch*, thought Cass. She had to admit, however, it was difficult to muster much by

319

way of sympathy.

One of Sammy's areas of responsibility that Cass' young team of examiners continued to look at in great detail was the bank's handling of cash transactions, and the information gleaned through their close review thus far was going to be prompting some interesting questions by the OCC in their next meeting with bank management. Of continuing interest to Cass and her team was Global United's list of businesses exempt from regular CTR reporting. The list seemed rather large in comparison to other banks of similar size, and exempted many businesses by type that most other banks would never have typically included. Chief among these were many of Nasir's AmeriPAK group of companies.

In this regard, it was conceivable that a company like AmeriPAK's Aurora Vending, Inc., which had coin and currency-operated vending and arcade machines all over the Chicago area, might with some regularity generate large amounts of cash for deposit, but certain aspects of that company's business specifically excluded it from exemption. With some stretch PAK-West, Inc.'s Crescent Jewelry store operations, which claimed to have a large ethnic clientele it said dealt heavily with cash, might qualify under certain circumstances for exemption, but examiners did not feel that anything like that could be said for Nasir's other companies. Yet, most of them were included on the bank's list. This made Global United's past determinations regarding exempt accounts an area of concern that required further investigation.

CHAPTER TWENTY-FIVE

THE DIRECTORS' Loan Committee at Global United met twice per month, normally at 8:00 a.m. on the first and third Tuesdays. Logan Hart had been perfectly aware of this when he had visited with Cass Price the day before about the possibility of she and her OCC examination team giving a progress briefing to members of Global United's board of directors, but it had slipped his mind at the time. After a later look at his calendar jogged his memory regarding the meeting, Logan quickly called Cass back and asked that she consider using the occasion of the bank's first December meeting as an opportunity to bring at least some of the board members up to date as to progress of the OCC's work at Global United.

Cass was hesitant at first, but after some deliberation admitted that subject to careful planning such a meeting might be a good way keep the momentum of the examination going in the long run. "I'll need to pass this by Merritt Daimler and the JTTF to agree on what we would plan to cover were we to meet with your directors," said Cass, "but absent their disapproval, I can't see why we couldn't move things up a bit and meet with your board tomorrow. I'll give Merritt a call right away."

"Fine, I'll also give Scott Kruse a call and let him know you've expressed a willingness to meet with he and board members tomorrow at the end of the loan meeting to bring them up-to-date on the examination. I'd appreciate your letting me know just as soon as you can affirm your attendance."

"I'll do the best I can, Logan."

Tariq Nasir was an appointed member of Global United's loan committee, but he rarely attended. In spite of an expressed desire to be there to hear what the OCC had to say as to their progress, and extreme frustration that the meeting would be held without him, it appeared as though his record of poor attendance was hardly going to be improved by December's participation. Some very important business matters in Luxembourg and Brussels, Belgium were going to require Nasir's presence there for a couple of days beyond the first December loan committee meeting.

As Executive Vice President and Senior Lender of the bank, Logan was the only voting member of the loan committee who was not a director. Scott Kruse was the chairman of the committee, but more often than not due to absences necessitated by one supposed conflict or another, Logan had been standing in for him in that capacity in nearly every meeting of the committee since his arrival. That would not be the case for the first meeting in December, however. When he heard that Cass and some of her team were going to be present to give committee members a progress update regarding their work at the bank, Tariq Nasir had insisted that Scott be there to run the meeting and be prepared to brief him on what had occurred via a long-distance conference just as soon as the meeting was adjourned. Scott assured Nasir he would do just that.

The typical Directors' Loan Committee meeting always followed the same agenda. The committee would first review reports on past due loans, loans classified by the bank or regulators as those that were of sufficiently poor quality that they either needed more regular scrutiny or were in the midst of a workout or collection. Then the committee would also review and sign off on formal applications for loans or lines of credit to any customer in excess of $1 Million—a trigger limit set by policy—and loans of any amount to any officer or director of the bank. The last part of the meeting was always reserved for discussion of any regulatory compliance issues that might be facing the lending division of the bank at any given time. For this first meeting in December, committee members had been forewarned they should reserve at least an additional hour out of their schedules to "discuss regulatory issues."

As it turned out, however, at the last minute Cass Price sent word to Logan and Scott Kruse that the OCC would require no time on the agenda for that morning. Cass stated that unexplained circumstances beyond the regulatory team's control were going to preclude any report of update from the OCC regarding the examination.

This naturally greatly frustrated and embarrassed Scott. He had made a special effort to be present at the first December meeting thinking regulators would be there, and Tariq Nasir was expecting a long-distance report just as soon as the meeting was complete. Perplexed at this turn of events and knowing that committee members were expecting at least some discussion regarding the prolonged examination, Scott asked Logan to instead provide a slightly more abbreviated report.

"Gentlemen, you all have my most profound apology regarding the OCC's last minute cancellation of their progress report to us on finalizing their examination here at the bank." Scott's voice quivered with exasperation. "I am totally unaware as to what may have happened, but I certainly intend to find out. In the meantime, our primary liaison between the bank and OCC relative to their examination here at Global United has been Logan Hart here. This is due to my heavy involvement as of late with our pending acquisition of Celebris Financial in Dearborn, Michigan or I would be acting in this capacity myself. I would like to, therefore, call on him to give us an update to the best of his ability on the OCC's yet ongoing efforts here. Let me preface his comments by saying that Logan has been keeping me informed regarding the matter with daily memos and frequent meetings, and has been doing a very good job in working with the regulators. Logan, the floor is yours."

"Thank you, Scott! Well, gentlemen, I know you were all made aware at your regular monthly meeting last week regarding the extent to which the Office of the Comptroller of the Currency has been examining our bank since the death of one of their regulators about ten days ago. As we told you then, when their examiner, Paul Trotter, was murdered the OCC was near completion of their examination, and we seemed to be faring quite well in that review. The examination was just about over. Mr. Trotter's death, however, prompted them to take a new look at our bank. As they put it, they wanted to 'confirm that his death had nothing to do with his work at Global United.' Since then, it has become quite apparent that they're leaving no stone unturned in their effort to make that determination."

"I think we've all been through the whys and wherefores of this before, Logan, and as you say, we discussed it at some length at our most recent meeting of the board," interrupted committee member and successful downtown attorney, Taylor Parriott. "Yet, the time they're taking does make one wonder. If you can, just tell us what, if anything, the examiners have found thus far that may be new, and when you think they will be done?"

Logan smiled weakly and nodded as if he understood and sympathized. It did seem like this was about the fiftieth time he had gone through all of this. "Soon, I hope, Taylor. They really haven't spent a great deal of time in the lending area this go-around. They must have satisfied themselves before Mr. Trotter's death that Global United was in pretty good shape in that regard—something this committee can take some comfort in, I would think. Lest we become too self-assured, however, they instead appear to be expending far more effort in the area of operations, administration, policies, controls and procedures, and departments of the bank such as Trust, Private and International Banking. They've really been looking those areas over quite closely."

"Can you tell us where the examiners are in the process, Logan, and would you have any idea whether they've found anything of concern that we should know about?" Parriott asked. "Scott and I had a few moments to visit before our meeting here, and he says we've been quite open and cooperative in providing them with everything they have requested. In addition, he says we've given them whatever staff support was necessary to help them complete their review. It would almost seem that enough is enough! I'm told they have now been here over six weeks. Don't you feel they perhaps owe us some explanation as to where they are in this process? It would be good to know what, if anything, they have found and when they maybe think they will be finished. You all have a bank to run, and their continued involvement here has to be increasingly debilitating."

Scott was nodding in agreement. Logan had seen Scott and Parriott with their heads together before the meeting and suspected the two had no doubt been commiserating about the examination. Parriott's comments had sounded very much like some that Scott had made to Logan the day before. "Well, I am not all that certain they haven't perhaps developed some concerns with bank operations and our International and Private Banking departments," Logan answered. "They've certainly been spending a goodly amount of time in those areas. In particular, they've been looking very closely at our compliance with the Bank Secrecy Act, our money laundering controls and procedures, and international banking transactions. It may not turn out to be much of anything, but they have asked for a great deal of information from all those areas."

"We can hardly afford to have problems in any of

those areas of the bank. I think everyone is aware that we have experienced a great deal of growth in both International and Private banking, and we've invested a lot of money expanding our international branch network." Scott was almost shouting, uncharacteristically slamming an open hand on the table for emphasis. "I think they owe us a meeting to update us on their progress, and so does Tariq Nasir for that matter. I can't believe Ms. Price had the gall to blow us off the way she did here this morning. I'm becoming a bit concerned, and so is Tariq. I am told that word has finally leaked out that the examiners are spending a lot of extra time poking around the bank, and it has caused a great deal of speculation amongst our customers."

"Look, I'm not really sure why Ms. Price and her crew had to cancel their briefing here this morning," answered Logan, "but I'll do my best to find out and try to reschedule a session with them as soon as we can. I had been assured by Ms. Price that she was willing to meet with us. Once we're done here this morning, I'll see if I can't chase her down for an explanation, and then I'll let you know, Scott."

"Be sure you do," said Scott in what appeared to be another one of his efforts to show who was in charge.

◊◊◊◊

A YELLOW cab was waiting for Sammy when he left for lunch at noon. His staff was accustomed to him taking an extended lunch hour on most Tuesdays. "Assalamu Alaikum, Mr. Hamadi," Sammy greeted his driver with familiarity as he climbed into the cab. "Have you been waiting long?"

"No, my brother, I only arrived moments ago. It is good to see you as always. What news do you have for me this week?"

"It is good that you should ask. I have been anxiously anticipating this meeting, Mr. Hamadi. It was becoming imperative that we talk. The regulatory examination that I have been telling you about for weeks continues in full force as we speak, and the examiners are now expending even greater effort than before looking into all the same areas that bothersome old fool, Trotter was reviewing before he was eliminated. In spite of how intrusive his investigations may have been, I fear we may have, however, opened the proverbial Pandora's box by taking the steps you took with respect to him. We now have numerous additional federal investigators crawling all over us, and that whore from the OCC who replaced him is a real tiger. She seems committed to finding violations of bank regulation in my areas of responsibility, and I am fearful that she and her cohorts may succeed. She has had a fairly large team of examiners assigned to the effort almost from the moment she arrived, and as much as it perturbs me to say so, she is disgustingly capable and incisive in nature. Can't wait until we are shed of her."

"As you know, Mr. al-Dajani, the most important thing we were trying to accomplish when we silenced that old man for you was to buy time. We took the steps we did based upon information you provided to us that the old bureaucrat might be closing in on transactions that could ultimately lead him to our hawaladar of choice, and in doing so perhaps then to our activities before it was time for us to move ahead with the operations we have been planning."

"Yes, but I fear we bought ourselves very little time by taking out the old regulator. If you will recollect, I was very much against such a move. I felt his investigations ultimately held little threat to any al-Sahaba activities or planning."

"Yes, but as I told you then, that wasn't your decision to make, Mr. Al-Dajani. It was mine."

"I know, but to what avail, Mr. Hamadi?" Sammy had always considered al-Sahaba's U.S.-based leader someone who was just slightly unstable. There was good reason to be hesitant in differing with him on much of anything. "Look, I'll say no more regarding the efficacy of your decision relative to the OCC's Mr. Trotter. I instead just repeat my concern that some of the enabling I helped facilitate through the bank for certain of the Nasir-related companies was indeed ultimately used to disguise some of our financial activities. The situation may yet bring much unwanted scrutiny—and perhaps very soon."

"Calm yourself, my friend. The time purchased by our having impeded that old bureaucrat's investigations has been of great benefit. All we need now are just a couple more weeks. Once we reach the Christian holiday season, it will be too late to stop the day of reckoning we have planned for these devils. None of your concerns will matter much then."

"I don't know! I just don't know! How can we be certain this is the time in which we should be making our move, my brother?"

Khalid looked at Sammy in the rear view mirror. The young banker's reticence and perpetual nervousness had always bothered the al-Sahaba commander. "It is no longer a matter of choice, Mr. al-Dajani. This operation has progressed far too much in its execution to stop it at this point. Much planning has gone into its timing, and any decision as to its execution was of neither your purview nor mine. We are answerable to others, and they have decided the when, where and how."

"Most of us know so little about 'the operation' to which you keep referring. So, it is difficult to understand what you mean. What is more important about this time than any other?

"Can you not see it, brother?" Khalid's frustration with al-Dajani's increasing uncertainties was beginning to show. "It has been many years now since the events of 9/11, and the Ummah is beginning to reassert itself with respect to the spread of Islam throughout the world. There is an invigorated leadership within al-Qaeda and its various affiliates—such as we in al-Sahaba—and a renewed commitment to doing something big. The people of this country are all becoming complacent and overconfident again. As decadent and materialistic as Americans are, they forget easily.

In addition, their current president is also a far more bellicose and unpredictable commander-in-chief than the country has seen in some time. Years of feckless leadership prior to his election allowed for many opportunities to advance the cause of Islam, but much of that has now changed. In just a few years, for example, most of the gains made by the Islamic State across the Levant have nearly all but been erased. Their supposed new caliphate has been decimated. It is time for us to strike back—and strike back we will. This country of reprobates has not changed. They are inherently weak and uncommitted. The country's younger generations have never felt true deprivation. Never has there been a group more entitled. Hit them hard enough, and it is felt they will fold this time. They must once again feel Allah's sting of condemnation and rebuke."

"But you must admit, Mr. Hamadi, this country and others like it around the world have instituted a lot of changes specifically designed to thwart the kinds of things people like us may have planned for them. I see them every day in the heavy government oversight with which we must contend at the bank where I work. It has, for instance, become nearly impossible to move funds anywhere in the world without some sort of governmental oversight. Were it not for certain hawaladars of this world, like the Nasir family, financing for any operation we wished to undertake would perhaps be completely choked off. I apologize for my uncertainty, but it seems to me detection of our efforts could come from almost any corner."

"Calm yourself and take heart, my friend. We are on a mission blessed by Allah—may his name soon be praised by all. The successes these non-believing dogs have claimed they've accomplished over the years with all their heightened

329

security will soon be known to Muslims worldwide as an ineffectual canard. They've used their military might to establish puppet regimes—which they call democracies—all round the world, in places sacred to all true Muslims, and in so doing have convinced many within this ignorant mass of unbelievers that these temporary victories have blunted the Sword of the Prophet. It is time they find out how far that is from the truth. The attack we are planning will shake their fragile resilience like nothing they have experienced before."

So, the time we have been preparing so long for has finally arrived, has it?" Sammy's question had a tinge of sarcasm and seemed to lack enthusiasm. At thirty-nine years of age, he had been in the U.S. for nearly eighteen years until recently a deep al-Qaeda sleeper, having trained as a recruit for that organization for two years prior to his arrival in the states. It seemed as though he had been waiting a lifetime for notification he was being called into service. As he awaited such activation, Sammy had managed to parlay an undergraduate degree in systems and technology, and an MBA from a prestigious American university into his current position as Senior Vice President in charge of Bank Operations at Global United. Although he knew from the beginning that a call to arms by his al-Qaeda overseers was inevitable, with enough passage of time and all the positive things that had happened in between, Sammy couldn't avoid the feeling of upset on the day he was finally notified by al-Qaeda high command that he was being activated and transferred to the operational control of al-Sahaba—and the brashness and harsh command of its senior U.S.-based operative, Ahmed Khalid, hadn't made it any easier. It was not a good day. Known only to Sammy and other subordinates by his alias Ismail Hamadi, Khalid was not Sammy's kind of person. "Once and for all, you're sure of this?" Sammy asked.

"Yes, the time for which we all have been waiting has indeed finally arrived, my banker friend." Khalid smiled confidently as he wound his yellow cab through downtown traffic. "The American people have this unbelievable capacity to forget with the passage of time. In spite of the damage done to them by our al-Qaeda brothers on 9/11 and the most recent pandemic, they still think they are relatively safe behind this thing they call their Homeland Security. Even as we speak, befuddled appeasers amongst them weaken their resolve. They do not have the stomach for protracted conflict. They think they once again hold the followers of Islam under their thumb, starting the day they deposed that Iraqi pig, Saddam. They have since done their best to set up puppet governments in that country and Afghanistan; have hunted down and murdered Sheik bin Laden, and later his son Hamza. More recently they have assassinated the likes of Abu Bakr al-Baghdadi, General Soleimani and a host of their underlings. The Islamic State has been all but erased. These trespasses cannot go unanswered. They must be taught that the conflict is far from over. The Ummah are now rising up in a multitude of locations around the world, and we of the al-Sahaba are those who have been chosen to once again bring the war to the infidels here in their homeland. This attack is certain to shake their confidence to its foundation. They will learn to praise Allah, or die!"

"All that being said, Mr. Hamadi, when, where and how will I be needed in this operation of yours? I am prepared to give all for the cause if called upon to do so, but what part do you have planned for me to play?" Sammy found his so-called leader tiresome. Hamadi was a jihadist zealot of the first order. To be in his company at any time meant being repeatedly subjected to the same diatribes again and again. "Look, I mean no disrespect, but I've heard such things before. I am at the point after all these years of needing details to convince me something big is coming down that I am to be a part of. I for example have been asked, or should I say required, to do a number of things for al-Sahaba that I feel are quite debasing and much below me, but I have done

331

so without question. I just feel it is time that I know more."

"Look, it's up to you whether you wish to believe me or not, Mr. Al-Dajani, but we are indeed quite near the time when you will know, my friend. I can understand and appreciate your consternation and questions, but I cannot answer you with specifics at this moment. I would instead ask that you attend a meeting of cell commanders that I have called for later this week, immediately following Friday Prayers. I am confident I will be able to answer all of your questions at that time."

"Where are we meeting?"

"The Dominion Janitorial Supply warehouse again on West Ontario. This meeting is extremely important, and your attendance essential. We will be discussing full details of our plan at that time. Take great care that you are not followed, however. We can ill afford to compromise the operation at this late date."

"Well, as I hope you would know by now, Mr. Hamadi, you can count on me, but there is one thing about which I must say I greatly disagree with you on."

"And just what is that, Mr. al-Dajani?" Kahlid hissed while glowering at Sammy in his rear view mirror.

"The degree of resolve with which this country's youngest generation may respond when they are attacked as you say we are preparing to do. I think you may be greatly underestimating the ultimate strength of their character. As Japan's Admiral Yamamoto said following his country's attack on the U.S. base at Pearl Harbor generations ago, such a move by us may only serve to *awaken a sleeping giant and fill him with a terrible resolve.'* With that, I suppose I've said enough. Pull over at this next corner if you would, Mr. Hamadi. We are only three blocks from the bank. I will walk back from here."

There was a long, uncomfortable period of silence as Kahlid pulled the yellow cab to the curb, weaving through traffic and skidding his tires as he did so. "Yes, Ma'a Salama,

Mr. al-Dajani!"

"Allah yisullmak, Mr. Hamadi. See you on Friday!"

CHAPTER TWENTY-SIX

THIS ONLINE conferencing approach beats butt-in-the-chair meetings all to heck, thought Logan again as the JTTF convened its second online meeting with he and Cass Price on the first Tuesday evening in December. The purpose was to again get updates on their respective investigations into matters related to the examination of Global United and possible conflicts arising from Tariq Nasir's controlling ownership in the bank. Both Logan and Cass continued to be impressed with the clarity and speed of the audio and visual capabilities of the government's videoconferencing system. On more than one occasion since being provided connectivity via the special equipment provided by the FBI, both had remarked to each other how vastly superior the system seemed to be in comparison to other commercial systems available in the marketplace. Both bemoaned the inevitability of disconnection from such a system once their work with the JTTF was complete.

Those from the JTTF participating in the video-conference were the same as before. Logan was one of five participants including Merritt Daimler, Jim Seilor and Lon Erickson of the FBI and the DHS's Raleigh Sutphen to sign on within seconds of each other. A couple of minutes later Vince Magnusson of the Customs Service and Cass joined the group. Logan wondered if all the other men taking part in the meeting looked forward as much to seeing Cass' face appear on the screen as he did. *They would have to be blind if they didn't,* he mused. *In spite of being in a relative position of 'power' herself, it's a good thing she doesn't know what most of us are probably thinking. The way things are these days, we'd no doubt all be in hot water.*

"Alright folks, it appears everyone has signed on now. What say we get down to business?" Daimler had early on assumed a leadership role over the investigation being conducted by the JTTF and hence had also been serving as moderator for their little online meetings. "To begin, I'd like to repeat for everyone's benefit that we're really starting to come under pressure to determine whether anything our group is looking into here in Chicago has any legs with respect to what the DHS thinks may be about to take place here in this country. There are similar investigations going on in many locations around the U.S., but our work here in Chicago has thus far shown the most promise. We've got to make some progress if we can. This one has everybody running scared. Doesn't it, Raleigh?"

"That's the understatement of the year," Sutphen exclaimed! "Several agencies under the aegis of DHS have been monitoring increasing chatter between various terror groups that leads us to believe an attack is imminent somewhere in the U.S., and the increased vulnerability of the holiday season we are entering has everyone on edge."

"Is that really anything new?" Logan asked. "The news has been reporting the concern of the DHS for some time now."

"I suppose that's right to a degree," Sutphen replied. "From about late July through to this year's anniversary of 9/11 pervasive Internet chatter led to increasing fear that terrorists might try to mount some sort of commemorative attack. Then along comes this recent intel provided by our dubious 'friends' at the Russian FSB, and you might begin to appreciate the extremely heightened level of anxiety of the DHS at this time."

"Raleigh's right," added Daimler, "The consensus isn't

if, but when, something may happen, and this intel we're getting about a possible biological WMD being smuggled into the country is hardly doing anything to alleviate those worries."

"And you now think the holidays are the time about which to worry?" Logan asked.

"Yes, we do! No doubt about it, we're way more vulnerable than usual this time of the year. It's peak travel time for people running hither and yon. Exponentially increases the difficulty of monitoring the threat situation. We need any leads we can get." Logan could see the concern on his old friend's face. "That being said, Logan and Cass, we hate to keep pushing you folks for what we're after from you, but do either of you have anything for us yet with this Global United thing that could prove useful? I know we've been saying that every time we've met, but we really mean it this time. It's our thinking we need to be able to move on anything you might have that's worthwhile sometime this week."

"Well, perhaps we may have some worthwhile information," Cass responded first. "Logan and I had an opportunity to visit over the last couple of days at the bank, and we think there's a possibility we could jointly be looking at evidence that our Mr. Nasir may indeed have some sort of hawala-type business going on within his organization. The resources and the business pattern of the AmeriPAK companies are certainly such that it could lead one to believe that might be the case."

"I can't say any of us would be surprised with such a conclusion, but how so?" Daimler asked.

"Well, to begin, we've determined through an in depth investigation into Global United's cash transaction and money laundering control systems that Mr. Nasir's companies are heavy into the use of cash, and most of his companies are not of the sort where a situation like that is normal. Additionally, a few of his companies have been mistakenly exempted from nearly all reporting required by the BSA and Freedom Acts. The bank may well have some significant violations in that regard."

"Anything else?" Asked Sutphen

"Yes, nearly all of Nasir's companies do a significant amount of international business, mostly wire transfers. As a result, the bank has a fair amount of information gathering and reporting required by regulation, but it would appear they've been keeping only the bare minimum of records with respect to those transactions. Their reporting along those lines appears woefully inadequate. The transfers may be for perfectly legitimate purposes, but their lack of required record-keeping is making it difficult to get a handle on that.

"Is that it?"

"Yes, that's all I have for now, but I think Logan may have found some things of interest too. Logan, do you want to comment on your findings?"

"Certainly," Logan answered, "as I told you all in our last visit, I've been reviewing in some depth the credit arrangements and related financial condition of the AmeriPAK companies, and as I told Cass when we visited yesterday, the companies are in excellent financial shape, but there are certain aspects of how they're run that I'm not sure we perhaps know enough about."

"What things?" asked Sutphen.

"Well, as I said, Nasir's companies appear to be pretty strong financially, but there are certain aspects regarding their financial statements that really do give rise to questions, the answers to which might well support some of the suspicions Cass just expressed regarding the supposed 'other business' Mr. Nasir could be running."

"And those are?"

"Well, for one thing, just as Cass indicated, all the AmeriPAK companies appear to be awash in cash, levels of cash quite atypical for companies of the sort they are."

"You mean they seem to be keeping a lot of cash on

hand they don't need?"

"Yes, that's basically correct. And in addition, there are myriad inter-company liabilities that look equally strange. It's like the companies are trading money, or if you will this cash, back and forth for seemingly no good business reason."

"That does admittedly sound strange," Daimler interjected. "Wouldn't seem like a very profitable way to run a business to me."

"Well, I would say it isn't unless there is something the AmeriPAK folks know about corporate efficiencies that we don't. Nothing illegal about it from a technical standpoint I would suppose, but it's something AmeriPAK really needs to explain to us at some opportunity. Not much investment return for AmeriPAK on cash traded between its sister companies." Logan smiled and shook his head disapprovingly. "Add all of that to certain other information recently brought to my attention regarding Mr. Nasir and some of his involvements, and it does make one wonder."

"What other information," asked Daimler.

"Well, in a recent conversation with young Mairaj Haifa, the gentleman who runs our International Banking department, he related a rather strange story to me regarding Mr. Nasir and some of his outside involvement with a certain Islamic charity that has really given me pause for thought."

"You've got our attention, Logan." Raleigh Sutphen snapped, expressing the heightened interest of the group. "Anytime someone mentions something regarding an Islamic charity around the DHS these days, it seldom fails to raise eyebrows. What, pray tell, did he have to say in that regard?"

"Well, Raj explained to me that his father, Faris Haifa, a really nice, older professor out at Northwestern, for some years has been involved with an organization here in Chicago called Worldwide Islamic Charities. I guess he's been on that organization's board of directors with Nasir since nearly its inception."

"Yes, we're aware of Worldwide Islamic Charities," Daimler commented. "They've been on a watch list of ours for some time. Nasir chairs the organization, doesn't he?"

"Yes, that's what Raj said. He also told me, however, that his father has been becoming increasingly concerned about some of the activities of the organization for quite a while. Raj told me the details in confidence, but in light of everything we're seeing here, I immediately knew I needed to pass it along to you all."

"I would hope so." Raleigh Sutphen snapped sarcastically. Things went quiet for a second as everyone studied Sutphen's face on their screen. Logan wasn't alone in his dislike of the DHS agent's supercilious personality.

"What'd the young man tell you, Logan," asked Daimler in a much more conciliatory tone than that of the DHS operative?

"Well, Raj told me his father has apparently for some time been quite concerned that this Worldwide Charities foundation has been authorizing a number of recent grants to supposed charitable groups around the world that he felt had not been adequately vetted with respect to their origination and purpose."

"Around the world you say?"

"Yes, from what Raj indicated mostly to Islamic organizations in areas like the Middle East, South and Southeast Asia. Raj told me Worldwide used to be primarily oriented toward domestic efforts, giving a helping hand to recent Muslim immigrants, and such the like. In the last couple of years, however, they changed their name 'to reflect a more Global outreach,' as he says some put it, and then they began to rather liberally grant monies to groups and/or individuals outside the U.S. who claimed to be in need. He says his father has become increasingly disenchanted with the way Worldwide has been doing things. He either already has or is going to resign from the board to my understanding."

"And how are they doing things," asked Daimler?

"Apparently very loosely, with respect to the kind of due-diligence the organization should be conducting relative to the many recipients of grants they're making around the world."

"I don't know about the rest of you, but I for one find this one of the more interesting things I've heard to date about Nasir," Daimler exclaimed. "Worldwide Islamic Charities Foundation has been an organization of interest to us for quite a while. It's time we stepped up the investigation into their activities. Uh, anything further your young banker friend may have told you that might be of interest to us, Logan?"

"Well, yes, there was one thing more that Raj told me about that I have to admit could perhaps add to our suspicions regarding hawala activity and such the like."

"And just what was that," asked Daimler?

"Well, before he finished, Raj informed me that there must have been some discussion at this meeting prompted by comments raised by his father and a couple of other members of Worldwide's board regarding the advisability of making large grants and transferring large sums of money these days, considering the high level of scrutiny given such things by banks and government authorities."

"And what was their response to that?"

"Well, according to Raj, his father and the other dissenters were somewhat ridiculed for not possessing the kind of charity required of their faith, and then were apparently further informed by Nasir that the board didn't need to worry about all the government oversight of such things. Nasir apparently claimed he knew of ways of enabling grants and ultimately getting the money to their intended recipients without the government being any the wiser about it."

"Do you think you can trust this Mairaj Haifa fellow, Logan?" Daimler asked. "Because if you can, this is some of the best information we may have received thus far on our Mr. Nasir."

"Yes, I really think we can. He's a native-born American, a former Marine officer, and straight as an arrow in my book. He seemed legitimately concerned about his father's involvement with this Worldwide Charities organization. Apparently his father is a good, reputable senior Muslim. I don't think he could have raised as fine a man as Raj and not be. When they visited about this Raj really pushed him to resign from the organization's board of trustees, and got the impression the old man either already had or would soon be doing so. I am confident we can trust him all the way on most all of this. From what he says, Raj really doesn't appear to be much of a Nasir fan either, even though he was brought into Global United by Nasir and ultimately works for him."

"Well, I can see we're going to have to dig more into this Worldwide Charities group," injected the FBI's Daimler. "Let's bring the elder Mr. Haifa in and see what he maybe has to offer us, Jim," Daimler instructed Agent Seilor. "Sounds as though he may have some really good information for us. Anything else you might be able to tell us about this charity, Logan, that could give us a leg up in that regard?"

"Yeah, perhaps one other thing that could be a big help. When Raj told me about all this, he also informed me that Worldwide Islamic Charities has apparently been a fairly significant depositor at Global United."

"I was about to ask that," said Cass. "I was sitting here thinking I had seen that name somewhere in the information the bank has provided us. We can jump right into looking them over."

"Yes, apparently not only Worldwide Islamic Charities but most of their board of trustees as well. Raj told me that just about all of them have personal and business accounts at Global United, and that many of them are also

341

international banking clients."

"This could really be helpful to our investigation folks. We should start looking at this organization forthwith." Raleigh Sutphen seemed almost ecstatic with this newfound information. "And you're sure we can trust this Haifa fellow?"

"Yes, that's what I believe I've said a couple of times already," Logan answered just a little sarcastically this time. "I would bet my bottom dollar on it!"

"And I would be inclined to agree with Logan on that," Cass added. "Mr. al-Dajani has not been all that forthcoming with the information we have requested, or all that easy to work with on this examination. He is typically arrogant, rude, and uncooperative, but not Mr. Haifa. He's been easy to work with and quick to respond with nearly every request we've made of him—and he's a perfect gentleman."

"So, you think we might be able to work with this Mr. Haifa, Logan?" Daimler asked.

"Yes, I would say so. He's a stickler for propriety, he's seemingly no fan of Nasir's, and I think someone we could trust to keep any investigation confidential. If there's anyone in the organization that might be involved with Mr. Nasir and others with respect to all of this, it's more than likely Sammy al-Dajani. He has access and perhaps motive."

"What do you mean motive?" Raleigh Sutphen asked.

"Maybe that isn't the best choice of words, but one aspect of Sammy that's not difficult to pick up over time, is his hard line, fundamentalist approach to his Islamic beliefs. Not so much with customers, he's quite careful there. However, when it comes to fellow staff members, it takes little provocation to have him launch into some Jihadi-type diatribe. His attitude is kind of a turnoff to a lot of his fellow workers, and most assuredly to his subordinates. We've had numerous people under him resign because of the situation."

"Why hasn't the bank done anything about it?" Daimler questioned.

"I've asked that myself. I think it is a wholly

inappropriate situation and I've expressed my opinion in that regard to the bank's President, Scott Kruse, and a few others on a couple of occasions, but I'm new to the organization and it would seem as though Mr. al-Dajani has a champion or two in the bank that would have a great deal to say about whether he were to be let go or not, not the least of which I think is Tariq Nasir. Nasir and Sammy are quite thick, and if Nasir is high on you, then it's an automatic pass from Scott, so to speak. Whenever Mr. Nasir is in the bank, there are few if any more solicitous of him than both Sammy and Scott. So, there you have it."

"Perhaps we should also begin checking out this Mr. al-Dajani at the same time," Daimler commented. "What more can you tell us about him?"

"Well, by way of information, and I may be repeating myself on this," answered Logan. "He's single, in his mid-to-late thirties, well educated and quite sharp. According to his resume, he's of Saudi origin. He's been in this country for going on twenty years, I think. Got his citizenship some years back, I believe. He got a lot of his higher education in this country, U of I and Harvard to my recollection. That's about all that I know. He certainly is capable at what he does, but difficult for many within the bank to work with. I am ostensibly the number-two person within the organization, and he isn't a great deal more respectful of me than he is of any others within the Global United organization. He and I have had only one confrontation, and I doubt there will be another. Nevertheless, he's pretty full of himself."

"I can readily agree with that," Cass added. "He's been the one most difficult to work with in the bank. Condescending as all get out toward women."

"Well, finally we have something to work with here," Daimler responded. "Cass and Logan, if you both could put together copies of all the background documentation you have for the things you have mentioned here this evening, and have it available perhaps to e-mail to us by say first thing tomorrow morning, that would be most helpful. I think we ought to bring in this al-Dajani fellow for a little conversation and step up our investigations into Worldwide Islamic Charities, et al." Turning toward fellow agents Seilor and Erickson, Daimler snapped. "Jim, Lon, I want to put a tail on this al-Dajani guy ASAP, and let's check into a tap on both his office and home phones, if we can get them. We need to know more about that young man as quickly as possible."

"I'll talk to your guys in DOJ, and work with them to see if we can speed up authorization for the taps via the Foreign Intelligence Surveillance Court on all the players here, Merritt." Sutphen offered.

"Fine, we'd appreciate that, Raleigh. That's probably enough for now. Whew, looks like we're finally starting to get somewhere. I'd really like to stay in fairly good touch going forward. We can meet any time there is a need, but things will go a lot faster, I think, if we regularly communicate online whenever you find even the slightest item of interest. Unless there's a need to do so sooner—which I hope there may be —let's at minimum plan on all getting together like this again same time Thursday, day after tomorrow, if that works for everyone. I'm encouraged somewhat this evening and think we're making progress, but I would stress again that we're really under pressure here to find whatever information we can, no matter what quarter it comes from. If any of this that's going on here in Chicago has anything to do with this potential WMD thing, we've got to find it out. I sense we're really in a race with the clock on this."

"Amen to that!" Sutphen added somberly.

◊◊◊◊

"LOGAN, CASS Price here again." She sounded extremely apologetic. "So, sorry I have to be the first person you hear from every morning. I'm sure getting a daily dose of the

OCC with your morning coffee isn't what you signed on for around this place."

"No, no, that's perfectly alright Cass." Logan laughed. "I've actually come to expect your calls. Any time, any time!"

"Well, you're one of the more gracious liars I know." Cass' own mirthful response embarrassed her more than just a little. "Nevertheless, after that bomb you dropped on all of us last evening, I thought I ought to get to you first thing this morning."

"Yeah, sorry I wasn't able to visit with you about some of that before I brought it to the whole group."

"Oh, no, that's no problem. I was just thinking, however, that considering all you had to say, and the fact he's been clamoring for it anyway, maybe it's indeed time for us to get together with Mr. Kruse and start filling him in on some of the concerns we've been developing and where we are with respect to this extended examination. Think he'll be willing to meet with me after us blowing him and your loan committee off the other day?"

"I have no doubt about it. He was beside himself the other day when you didn't show up at the loan committee meeting. Left him imagining all sorts of reasons why you would have begged off. I'm sure, therefore, that he'd probably drop whatever he's doing to get together with you."

"Think you could set that up for us?"

"Dead certain of it. He isn't in today, but I'm pretty sure he'll be in tomorrow. Here, wait just a minute, I'll pull up his schedule on my computer and see if he has some time available. Pretty much all of the staff share each other's schedules on a hierarchical basis. So, he and I can look at each other's schedules. Let me check as we speak." Logan activated the bank's scheduling and collaboration software on his computer screen, clicked on Scott's calendar and saw that he was indeed free for a meeting between 9:00 and 11:00 a.m. the following day, the first Friday in December. He quickly inserted the meeting on Scott's schedule. "Yeah, looks as though he has most of the morning open, and I'm taking the liberty of right now entering up to a two hour meeting with you and your crew beginning at 9:00 a.m., just so he doesn't schedule something before I'm able to get hold of him directly about it. I'll also mention it to his secretary and try to reach him on his cell phone as soon as we hang up. Any other people you want to be present for this little con-flab?"

"No, let's just leave it at Mr. Kruse and you for this moment. Depending on how the conversation goes, we may end up needing to have Mr. al-Dajani join us later if the FBI doesn't find a need to corral him first. But for now let's just make it Scott Kruse. Our primary focus for this meeting is really to see how much he knows about Mr. Nasir's bank-related business and determine whether he's going to be a help or a hindrance if we decide there are any serious regulatory issues we're going to have to pursue with Mr. Nasir. And as you know that is looking very likely."

"Fine, I'll see that he's there."

"Logan, for obvious reasons, we're going to approach our conversation with you and Mr. Kruse tomorrow as though you and I have only had general discussions regarding any of these matters to-date. I think it will be better for all concerned if we handle it that way. I'll go out of my way to conceal the extracurricular work you've been doing for us and the JTTF. I don't want to compromise your situation in any way."

"Sounds fine, that's the way I had hoped we could approach this meeting whenever we had it. Can you give me a heads up as to how far you plan to take the conversation, considering all that I had to say last evening? Not too much for now I would hope."

"You're right. Like I said before, I plan to only get into concerns we've developed thus far regarding the bank's handling of BSA, cash transaction reporting, international transactions and so forth, as such relate to Mr. Nasir's companies. Anything concerning the JTTF's investigations into Nasir's possible hawala activities and such the like will remain a matter to be brought up later in conjunction with the task force's investigations. Our concerns are plenty without getting into any of that. Not our place anyway. I just want to feel out Scott Kruse a little better by seeing how he reacts to just what we have, considering how close he's been with Mr. Nasir since his arrival at the bank."

"Does Merritt Daimler know that you're planning to involve Kruse to that extent now, Cass?"

"Yes, he does. I spoke with him about it this morning, just before I called you. I told him that unless he had some strong objection, we had our own regulatory agenda that we needed to pursue on a timely basis, if for no other reason than to avoid suspicions here at the bank. He said he understood that, and agreed that we might also try to determine what kind of problems, if any, we were going to have with Mr. Kruse before he and his people perhaps head your way with subpoenas and such the like, something I think they are apparently working on as we speak."

"Fine, Cass, unless you hear something different from me in the meantime, Scott and I'll see you tomorrow."

◊◊◊◊

SCOTT CALLED Logan within minutes of him hanging up from his conversation with Cass Price. He had called in to his secretary to check for messages, and she had informed him of the "Meeting with Examiners" posting on his calendar. "It's about time," was his reply to Logan. "They're going to be there this time aren't they?"

"Yes, Ms. Price swears they'll be there. Apologized all over the place for them being unable to meet last Tuesday."

"Good, see to it she is, Logan. We need to get a handle on when this is all going to get wrapped up. I was about to ask you what progress you had made in arranging a makeup meeting with them anyway. I'll be back in town tomorrow. So, I'll be there. Just you and me, or did they ask for anyone else to be in attendance?"

"No, just the two of us right now, from what I understood." Logan expected Scott to be apprehensive but didn't detect that in his response.

"That's just fine. I want to get into it a bit with them on where they're going with all of this and why it has taken so long. There's no reason to have anyone else besides you and I in on that. See you in my office tomorrow at 9:00 a.m. then."

CHAPTER TWENTY-SEVEN

"I APPRECIATE you meeting with Latisha and me this morning, Mr. Kruse, and allowing us some private time to visit with just you and Mr. Hart here regarding some issues that have come up as part of the expanded examination we've been conducting here at Global United since Paul Trotter's death." Cass Price lost no time getting directly into the 9:00 a.m. Thursday morning meeting that had been scheduled with Logan and Scott. Personal greetings at the outset had been minimal. The tension was palpable.

"What issues?" Scott asked, immediately assuming a defensive posture. "You aren't suggesting you've found something here at the bank that you think is linked to Mr. Trotter's death, are you? Like I've said all along, I can't for the life of me believe that would ever be the case!"

"No, we haven't found anything yet that we feel is related to Paul's death. Thank God! Hopefully, this is all just pretty much standard compliance stuff, but that in and of itself is of goodly concern to us, nonetheless. You see, in reviewing for the second time some of the areas that we know Paul was examining before he died, we have indeed developed a goodly list of questions regarding certain aspects of bank administration that we thought we ought to discuss with you and management before we go any further. That's the reason we've asked for some time with you and Mr. Hart this morning."

"What areas of bank administration?"

"Well, we've mentioned this to you before, but specifically, we find ourselves definitely needing to discuss once again the bank's policies and procedures relating to compliance with the Bank Secrecy Act, cash transaction reporting and so forth."

"Oh, you're still on that, are you? Look, as I've told you before, Ms. Price, I've always been given to understand that our policies and procedures in that area of compliance were quite adequate and that our staff rigidly adheres to all the controls we've implemented along those lines. Why, I want to even recollect that our own compliance officer looked rather closely at our performance under BSA regs not long ago, and we got a rather positive report from her." Scott was reacting in his usual defensive manner, turning and looking at Logan as if searching for words of support as to what he was saying. Scott didn't handle regulatory criticism well. "Logan, help me here! Didn't the board receive a report on the bank's compliance with BSA, the Freedom Act, AML, and all that stuff just last month from Colleen Murphy, the head of our Audit and Compliance division?"

"Yes, that's correct," Logan answered.

"Well, there you have it." Scott continued in his defense to Cass. "Didn't our audit staff give you a copy of that report?"

"Yes, Mr. Kruse, they did, and we've read it," responded Cass. "And as you say, that report purportedly shows that the bank has made every effort to ensure adequate compliance with all cash transaction reporting requirements, and ostensibly that is the case if you accept therein Global United's reading of the law as it relates to those who the bank would be required to file reports for under the act. It is, however, the bank's interpretation in that regard about which we have questions."

"You don't say," Scott responded incredulously. "The Bank Secrecy Act is fairly straightforward. Good policies, good procedures, stay on the mark with those, and I'd say you've got it covered. Don't you? I can't imagine that we're reporting on anyone we aren't supposed to. Do you have some examples for us?"

Well, yes I do." Cass' response had an air of increasing defiance. "But that's where things get a little dicey, Mr. Kruse. The questions that we have with respect to BSA, cash transaction reporting and certain areas of your international banking operations aren't about your bank reporting on accounts or people unnecessarily, but instead it's the bank's failing to report on certain situations where you really should be doing so. To be specific—and we're certain from past conversations that you will probably be none too pleased with this—many of the issues we feel are necessary to raise deal once again with Global United's relationships with the companies owned by your chairman, Tariq Nasir."

"You've got to be kidding me!" Scott almost shrieked in response, as he got up, poured fresh coffee into his cup from the carafe on his credenza and began to pace the office. Cass and her fellow examiner, Latisha Caldwell, both noticed Scott's cup was nearly full, to begin with. Latisha rolled her eyes at Cass. It was evident they had hit the proverbial nerve with Scott. They could tell he was trying to think of a response to what they had just laid on him. "I can't believe this. We've always gone out of our way to be particularly certain that all of Mr. Nasir's personal business, and that of his companies, was circumspect and in agreement with every regulation applicable to any business the bank does with him. He's been insistent about that." Scott sighed rather audibly. "OK, what have you got? I want to clear this up before it ever gets to Tariq if we can at all avoid it. He would hit the roof."

"Certainly, we'll try to do that. Hopefully, you'll have all the answers we need. Latisha, why don't you show Mr. Kruse and Mr. Hart here what we've been looking at and tell them the questions we have."

Latisha Caldwell was one of Cass' favorite examiners.

351

She had "street smarts," as Paul Trotter used to put it. Born in Chicago and raised by a firm but loving single mother in the Cabrini-Green tenement district, previously one of the toughest neighborhoods on the city's near northwest side before the Chicago Housing Authority began to tear it all down beginning in the late 90's, in an attempt to rebuild the area. Working extra jobs to pay for tuition, special clothing, and travel expense for the 45 minute ride one-way, Latisha's mother managed to see to it that her daughter attended all four years of high school at St. Ignatius College Preparatory School, where she graduated top of her class. Such performance at the prestigious Catholic high school led to a full scholarship for undergraduate study at Notre Dame University, where Latisha once again graduated with honors. Slender, petite and extremely attractive, she wore one of those super-short hairstyles that only served to accentuate classic ebony features.

Being the ladies man that he was, Scott Kruse would normally have reveled in meetings like this with Cass and Latisha. Had it not been for the tenseness of the moment, he would no doubt have been at his patronizing best. "Two of the prettiest regulators I believe I've ever come across," had been a loathsome, misogynistic previous comment to Logan. For reasons that were becoming increasingly obvious, however, neither of them was looking very attractive to Scott at present.

"Thanks, Cass. Gentlemen, what we have here is a report that lists numerous pages of transactions over the last four years that we think warrant scrutiny, and some sort of explanation, if you will, on the part of bank management—perhaps including where needed management of Mr. Nasir's various companies." Handing both Logan and Scott a fairly thick set of spreadsheets, Latisha continued with her comments. "In our review of Global United's handling of cash transaction reporting, one of the things that we did was review in depth cash transactions for all the companies and/or individuals the bank has determined, for one reason or another, they wanted to exempt from such reporting on a regular basis. Some of Mr. Nasir's companies were included on that list. For purposes of discussion, those companies are the following subsidiaries of Mr. Nasir's holding company AmeriPAK, Inc: Aurora Development Company; PAK-West, Inc., Mr. Nasir's precious metals company that also runs a near nation-wide chain of jewelry stores called Crescent Jewelers; Aurora Tech, his computer hardware and software company; and Aurora Net, Inc., a regional Internet service provider operation. In what would appear to be some slight effort at holding to bank regulations on the matter, AmeriPAK subsidiaries, Aurora Transportation, Inc and Aurora Vending —both business types specifically listed as ineligible by regulation—were omitted from the list. The holding company itself, AmeriPAK, Inc., carries no direct deposit accounts and conducts no corporate transfer business that we have found thus far on the books of Global United."

"What's so strange about those designations?" Scott asked, defensively interrupting Latisha's comments. "To my understanding, Tariq's companies you just mentioned were exempted because they regularly generate significant amounts of cash as an integral part of their business. If I recollect, that's one of the tests for excluding depositors such as they from regular reporting. Further, I haven't personally reviewed our files on this subject, but I want to recollect hearing that as required by law for dealers in precious metals and gems, etc., that PAK-West and Crescent Jewelers has a CTR reporting program of their own. So, I would think we're reasonably well covered there. Wouldn't we be?"

"Well, I don't recollect seeing any documentation covering that matter, and am not certain that would exempt PAK-West and Crescent Jewelers if they did have a program of their own," responded Latisha, "but if you have any information regarding those entities, and would care to include it in any new information provided, we would greatly appreciate having the opportunity of reviewing it."

Logan cringed at Scott's defensive demeanor and obvious lack of understanding as to how BSA and cash transaction reporting worked. *Is Scott really this uniformed*, he wondered, *or is he responding this way simply because the bank and Nasir may be in a tight here? Either way*, he thought, *this is no way to handle regulatory criticism.*

"Now, Mr. Kruse, if I may continue with respect to exemptions overall." Latisha Caldwell was a tenacious little gal, an endearing quality in Cass' eyes. It was what made her an effective examiner in situations of this sort. "You're correct, that being a regular user of large amounts of cash as a 'part' of a depositor's business is indeed one of the tests for an exemption that must be passed, but it is not the only one. A bank needs to determine not just that the companies or individuals they're exempting generate a goodly number of large cash transactions on a regular basis, but additionally whether those transactions are 'typical' or 'standard' for a business of that sort. Why would companies such as Mr. Nasir's development or computer hardware companies, for example, be generating large, regular cash transactions—as they often do? Cash isn't typically used in the conduct of those types of businesses. Perhaps we could envision Mr. Nasir's vending company generating large amounts of currency, or maybe, just maybe, his jewelry operation, but not in our opinion his other companies. I guess, therefore, we would like for you to explain to us what logic was used, and what due diligence the bank underwent in determining those of his companies that would be exempt from reporting. At best, we're looking at a naive, cavalier interpretation of the law by Global United that totally discounts the spirit and intent of BSA, and we would have a big problem with that."

"Well, as I said before, I haven't personally reviewed any of the documentation to which you refer. So, I don't have an immediate answer for you regarding our determinations as to who would be exempt and who would not, but I am sure I can get one for you." Scott's increasing nervousness was obvious. "Er, uh… one thing I can tell you is that Mr. Nasir's companies all deal with a goodly number of people and businesses from his ethnic community, and as you know, many of them utilize cash in a lot of their business dealings."

"That is perhaps true, Mr. Kruse, and we thought of that as we were reviewing all of this, but we're not sure that premise holds much water. Our study is of course not complete, but we took the liberty of looking at your credit department's analyses of Mr. Nasir's various companies, and in that information we found fairly comprehensive listings of accounts receivable and accounts payable for each. Looking those over, I would have to say to you that although there are indeed customers on those lists that would appear to be of the sort that you describe, they don't really represent but a small portion of his business. Further, one would have to assume that they themselves don't all do business in cash. So, we would like a better explanation of this from both the bank and Mr. Nasir's companies, vis-à-vis any documentation either can provide with respect to the matter. We may be looking at perfectly understandable anomalies here, but until the situation is explained to our satisfaction, we feel compelled to tell you that we may be looking at potentially blatant violations of both BSA and perhaps the U.S.A. Freedom Act, for which we may have to cite the bank if we can't be provided satisfactory answers to our concerns. It is a matter we consider quite serious."

The room was quiet for a painful length of time until Scott finally broke the silence with a cryptic response. "Fine, I'll visit with Mr. Nasir right away about this, but I'm sure we can explain everything. He's out of the country at this time, but I'll get with him on the matter just as soon as I can reach him. Now, what other problems do you think you see along these lines?"

"Well, Mr. Kruse, as you may or may not be aware,

when the OCC finds areas of question involving a bank's handling of BSA, we automatically look at other areas of bank administration that have to do with that institution's anti-money laundering activities, and we…"

"Money laundering, you've got to be kidding me. Where in the devil is this going? Are you folks digging around in all of this simply because Mr. Nasir is of the ethnic and religious persuasion that he is?"

"Now, just a minute, Mr. Kruse," injected Cass, "Let's not even go there. We would have these same questions of Mr. Nasir were he a German Lutheran. We have not said anywhere yet that we suspect Mr. Nasir or the bank of wrongdoing. We only want to get to a reasonable explanation for the bank's exemption of Mr. Nasir's companies and the kind of transactions, if you will, that prompt so much of the activity that we see flowing through his accounts. Mr. Nasir is not just your typical customer. He is your bank's Chairman and its largest shareholder. That all puts him in a position of much greater accountability when it comes to compliance with BSA, or any other regulation the bank is subject to for that matter. We are only here this morning to apprise you of what we've found to date, to provide you with some questions that we need answered, and then to give you and Mr. Nasir the opportunity of doing so. So, please don't get too defensive with what we need to do here, or we'll call this meeting to a halt, let the next one be with your entire board, and the chips fall where they may."

Scott sipped his coffee and stared straight at Cass as she spoke, studied the floor for a moment and then looked disgustedly at Logan before answering. "I think you're going to find that there is no problem whatsoever in this. I repeat, I have the utmost confidence in the way that Tariq Nasir handles his businesses, and the effort he's made to comply with all aspects of bank regulation. I just hate to have to drag him through all of this. Pardon my upset, and please, go ahead with your comments."

The two lady examiners glanced at each other, and Cass nodded at Latisha to continue. "Well, Mr. Kruse, what I was starting to say, was that as a result of these questions regarding the heavy number of cash transactions by Mr. Nasir's companies—that may or may not have needed to be reported—we decided to look at the significant amount of international wire activity his companies were also involved in." Scott sighed and looked at the ceiling in exasperation as Latisha continued. "There once again, we have some questions."

"What kind, Ms. Caldwell? Mr. Nasir's companies do business all over the world."

"We realize that Mr. Kruse, but a couple of them—like say his vending and development companies—really don't have all that much in the way of international clients. Yet, they too have a fairly sizable number of international transactions that draw our attention. Once again, please bear in mind, Mr. Nasir's companies may have perfectly good explanations for all of this, but we do want to have some discourse with the bank, Mr. Nasir, and his people regarding all of these transactions."

"What about the international transfers gives rise to question, Latisha?" Logan finally injected, in an effort to give she and Cass the opportunity for greater elaboration, and perhaps take some of the tension out of the meeting.

"Well, for one thing, Mr. Hart, a goodly number of the international wires from some of Mr. Nasir's companies not only go to some fairly well-recognized international tax haven countries where offshore banks have secret numbered accounts, but in some cases, they also end up in certain countries where our government has concerns relating to both the banking systems and political situation."

"Can you give us some examples?" Asked Logan.

"Yes, sir, I can. If I could draw your attention to the report that I have given you this morning, take a look at page number thirty-four. That is where we begin to list by company the international wires that Mr. Nasir's various entities have generated over the last couple of years. If you will note, many of these wires are to and from countries such as Panama, the Cayman Islands, Netherlands Antilles, Montserrat, Liechtenstein and so forth, destined for numbered accounts or foreign companies that appear—from notes we gleaned in Mr. Nasir's financial information—to be owned by him. The banks on the other end more often than not also appear to us to be of questionable repute as far as financial institutions go. Once again, this all may be explainable, but we are still interested in gaining further information as to the substance and purpose of all this transactional activity."

Scott nodded as he studied the floor in contemplation. The room grew silent again as Cass gave Logan a furtive glance and a weak smile—the latter of which didn't go unnoticed by Latisha. The thought had crossed Latisha's mind a couple of times that there might be something cooking between the two, but she dismissed it as highly unlikely. *Cass is far too straight a regulator.* She thought. *If she won't take up with all the good-looking young guys around our shop that have come on to her, then she surely isn't going to go for some banker she oversees. But then,* she mused, *this Hart guy doesn't look too bad for his age. Enough of this*, she warned herself as she waited for Scott's response, *Cass would probably chew my tail if she knew what I was thinking.*

"Alright, may we keep these reports to work from in doing our investigation of all this?" Scott asked, breaking another long silence.

"Certainly, that's why we brought them this morning," answered Cass. "Please know, Mr. Kruse, that we are not yet accusing anyone of anything. We simply want some explanation for these matters we're questioning, because so far this all quite concerns us."

"Fine, I'll uh...contact Mr. Nasir's people right away,

and get going on all of this. As I said, Mr. Nasir will be out of the country for a few days. So, maybe I can visit with the heads of some of his companies in his absence, and then we can have some of this answered by the time he returns. I'm sure his people will be able to provide you with many of the answers you'll need." Scott paused to contemplate the situation before continuing. "Now, if we can answer these questions satisfactorily, can you tell me when we might expect your examination to be finished? It is my understanding that you were about done with us before Mr. Trotter's death. Hopefully, you've not found anything about the bank that anything to do with his demise or you would have surely informed us by now. I would think you ought to be done soon."

"I would indeed hope that we'll be wrapping things up soon," answered Cass, "but I can give you no guarantees on that. We haven't found anything yet that would lead us to believe Mr. Trotter's death had anything to do with his work here, but we aren't completely finished with our added review yet either. As demonstrated by the fact that Mr. Trotter had asked you and your management group to meet with him on the Monday following his death last month, on matters specifically related to some of these same items we have discussed with you here this morning, it is only natural for us to have similar concerns. What we've given you this morning may well have been some of what he wanted to visit with you about then. Our examiners say he had been looking into some of this same information at the time of his death. We may never know if he had arrived at the same questions we have asked about this morning, but we certainly plan to do our best to follow up where he left off if that is the case. Can you understand that?"

"Yes, I can," answered Scott. "I am simply concerned that we get this all over with as soon as possible. We have a lot on our plates these days here at Global United."

"I'm sure you do," responded Cass. "And the sooner

we get your responses to these and any other concerns we have, the sooner we can get out of your hair. Can you tell me when we might expect your response on all of this?"

"I'm not perfectly sure. I'm uncertain of Mr. Nasir's availability or that of his key people, but if they're readily available, I would hope we could respond to you in the next few days."

"Fine, Mr. Kruse, we'll leave it in your hands. If you need anything further from us in the interim, any clarification of the regs or any of our questions, simply get in touch with either Latisha or me, and we'll get right on it for you. With that, we appreciate the time you gentlemen took from your busy schedules, and we'll get out of your hair for now."

◊◊◊◊

"TARIQ, YOU and I have to talk!"

"What about this time, Scott?" Nasir sounded impatient. "I would hope you're chasing me down all the way over here in Luxembourg to tell me that the OCC has finished all of their business at Global United and is about to leave, but I sense from the pathetic sound of your voice that may not possibly be the case."

"That's unfortunately correct, Tariq." Scott had a way of losing the confidence in his voice when he was troubled, and Nasir could always detect it. "Not only is the OCC not finished, but I think they're dredging up some questions that could give the bank and you and your people some real headaches."

"And just what might that be, Mr. Kruse?" Nasir always addressed people formally when he was perturbed with them. "Everyone in our organization, particularly me, is quite busy these days. So, we really don't have a tremendous amount of time for distractions."

"I'm sure that's the case, Tariq, but the examiners are

360

stirring around this time in some areas where you and we could have some real headaches if we can't come up with the right answers to their questions."

"Well, get on with it! I asked what might that be?" Nasir sounded more than just a little perturbed.

"Well, similar to what we've discussed before, they're looking over everything regarding the bank's compliance with the Bank Secrecy Act, and all of our anti-money laundering policies and procedures. As a result, they've zeroed in, of all things, on all the transactions of your companies that may be related to that area of activity."

"BSA, BSA, BSA... A bit of a cracked record, Scott." There was a long, audible sigh on Nasir's end of the phone. "I doubt it's good news, but go ahead and give me the latest I suppose. This is not a new subject between you and I."

"Believe me, Tariq, I really do wish I had something better to report with respect to what's still going on here relative to the OCC's continuing investigations, but I really don't. They're still questioning our past exemption of certain of your AmeriPAK subsidiary accounts as it relates to cash transaction reporting and so forth. Mr. al-Dajani has repeatedly explained that the exemptions that have been granted result from the historically high frequency of large cash transactions experienced by many of your companies, but they still take issue with that. They say they feel the cash transactions your companies engage in aren't commonplace for business concerns such as those within the AmeriPAK group. They're also starting to dig into all the international transactions your companies generate, asking us for backup detail on all of that as well." This time it was Nasir who chose to remain silent. "Tariq, are you still there? What do you want to do about all this?"

"Scott, do you have details on all the information they want?"

"Yes, sir, I believe we do."

"Well, then why don't you put it all together and

contact my administrative assistant, Falanna Kristoff. Have her put together a meeting between you and the heads of any of my companies embroiled in this thing—hopefully as soon as this afternoon your time. She'll let me know when it's scheduled for, and perhaps I can plug in and attend the thing online as some of my people often do when they're out of town and we have any such meetings. You bring copies of everything you have to date on all of this, along with a list of the kind of information we might be able to provide you that could perhaps mitigate some of the damage we're experiencing. Bring it and yourself to my office late this afternoon, and we'll go over the situation?

"Great, great, sounds fine to me. I'll get right on it." Scott responded.

"Oh, and perhaps it might be advisable for you to bring along Mr. al-Dajani to the meeting whenever you get it arranged. It is my understanding he oversees all the BSA and anti-money laundering programs at the bank. It is obvious we're going to have to ultimately involve him if we have any expectations of getting through all this scrutiny by the regulators even partially unscathed." Nasir gave Scott no indication he had already been in touch with Sammy a number of times about the whole BSA/AML matter.

"Certainly, Tariq, I'll make sure he's there."

"Something tells me, Scott, that this OCC crew of yours is making a special project out of my companies and me. Don't really know why, but that's what I suspect, at least."

"You're right, and we may have some damage control to do here."

"Well, if that's the case, Scott, my people and I are going to lean heavily on you to ensure that we get through all of this without any problems. This is where you earn your money, my friend. I hate to repeat this so much, but again remember you said you could handle regulators when we hired you. Now we shall see if that is indeed the case."

"No, sweat, I can handle it!"

"Good, I'll expect you to do just that. See you and young Mr. al-Dajani online whenever you and Falanna get all of my people together for a meeting—preferably this afternoon as I previously said. Make our response to this situation top priority, Scott. Regulatory matters of this sort aren't like fine wine—they don't get better with age."

◊◊◊◊

SAMMY AL-DAJANI left the bank late Friday morning, as it was his weekly habit to do, to attend midday prayers at the Islamic Institute of Greater Chicago. He informed his staff that he also had a couple of customer calls to make on the way back afterward and indicated he might not return until sometime late in the afternoon.

The masjid was quite full of worshipers when Sammy arrived. For some reason, attendance was always good on the last Friday of the month. Surveying the congregation for familiar faces, he recognized a number of acquaintances. Mr. Nasir was usually in attendance, but he had heard Nasir was out of town. Sammy always made an effort to greet Nasir sometime before he left following the Imam's khutbah. The Imam was sure to be enthusiastic in his delivery today considering the size of the audience that appeared to be gathering.

Looking around the room, Sammy also noticed that his friendly cab-driving al-Sahaba commander, Ismail Hamadi, was in attendance as he had said he would be a few days before. Sammy's stomach had been doing continuous flip-flops since Hamadi had informed him of the meeting to follow today's services. After waiting so many years to hear of it, knowledge of an impending operation had him all keyed up. Sammy still wanted to be an instrument of change in the furtherance of the pan-Islamic cause, but doubts were creeping in as to whether he would be as capable of making the sacrifices as readily today as he had been years before when he first aligned himself with al-Qaeda—not to mention the devastation he was sure would accompany such an operation.

Immediately following the sermon, Sammy walked a few blocks south on North Michigan Avenue, and quickly ducked into a couple of large, busy stores in an effort to shake anyone who might be following. Reasonably assured that no one was tailing him, he then found a passing cab and asked to be taken to the location of his first "customer call" of the day. "1600 block of West Ontario, please." Sammy had done everything in his power to avoid being followed, but if he was somehow unsuccessful in that regard, he could always claim that his visit to the warehouse occupied by Dominion Janitorial Supply was a customer-related call. Dominion Janitorial was indeed a depositing customer of the bank. To make the ruse even more believable, Sammy had a second call on another legitimate customer planned for after his meeting at Dominion.

Sammy was met at the front door of Dominion by an intense looking, dark young man, who recognized him right away and greeted him in Farsi. He was then led to a meeting room on the second floor of the warehouse. In the middle of one large, open 5,000 square foot storage room, surrounded by chairs, were four six-foot-long rectangular folding tables, put together to accommodate conferencing a large group of people. Around that table sat nine men, a couple with whom Sammy was vaguely familiar, but most were strangers. All appeared to be of either South Asian or Middle Eastern background.

"Allahu akbar, my friends, and praise be to Allah! May his blessings be showered on all that we are about to undertake in his name!" Ahmed Khalid, or Ismail Hamadi as everyone around the room knew him, was standing, jabbing both fists into the air as he yelled his greeting.

Almost acting as one, all the young men rose to return the greeting. "Allahu akbar! Allahu akbar!" They shouted again and again as they jammed their fists into the air. Sammy's participation in the response was somewhat muted.

Motioning for silence and the men to take their seats, Khalid continued. "Gentlemen, thank you all for coming. I appreciate your time, and I will try to keep this meeting short for all of you. Nevertheless, the time has now arrived for al-Sahaba to strike all enemies of Islam in the name of Allah, may that name be praised. As we have been called upon to do by the blessed prophet, Muhammad, peace be upon him, we shall now undertake that which is necessary to further the cause of Islam throughout the world."

"Tell us, Mr. Hamadi," asked Nagif Fadallah, Saudi born head of the Seattle, Washington-based cell of al-Sahaba, "what pray tell is the plan and schedule of our attack? Many of us have trained and waited years for this moment, and we all have driven far—some around the clock —to attend this meeting. We are anxious to strike a blow against the infidels in the name of Allah. When shall we know that which has been predestined by Allah for all us to do?"

"I realize that many of you have driven great distances to be here today, and I thank you for your indulgence in that regard. It was essential that we meet, but I could not afford to have any of you flying at this time. You will see the reason for that before our meeting is over." Khalid was standing now with the knuckles of both fists planted firmly on the table in front of him, slowly scanning the eyes of everyone around the table. "The time has finally arrived when each of you shall understand the purpose behind all that you have been asked to do over the last couple years of planning and preparation."

Khalid studied the expressions of the young terrorists in attendance. None was beyond his forties. All had confused but expectant looks on their faces. They had been loyal players in a grand scheme for a very long time—some for years now—without knowing why they were doing what they were being requested to do, and it had been a difficult life for some. They were anxious for what might lay ahead, and Khalid was finally relieved to be able to tell them about what was soon to unfold.

"Let me begin by explaining some of the things we have asked all of you to do over the past couple of years," began Khalid. "As you are well aware, Dominion Janitorial Supplies here has always been a front for the operation we have been planning. The company has existed solely to facilitate the eventual attack we had in store. We have operated the company as a legitimate business, but its real purpose has been to function as both a cover and an instrument for what we were actually planning to do. As requested, all of you have established branch offices of Dominion Janitorial in your respective areas of operation: Seattle; Los Angeles; Dallas; Detroit; Washington, DC; New York; and Miami. Under my instructions, you have also over the course of the last two years developed businesses selling janitorial supplies to both private and public sector clients in your areas of operation, sometimes 'buying' that business, so to speak, by often selling some products in your catalogs below cost to some of your clients. Hopefully, you will soon understand the method to our madness in this regard. Additionally, under my instructions, each of you over time has managed to install many of your operatives in janitorial positions with major building maintenance organizations, but not just any organization. By design, our people have specifically managed to be hired by the various services that clean and maintain the major airports in each of your cities. In Chicago for example, we have three people who mop floors and clean bathrooms for Chicago Airport Services, the organization that maintains our O'Hare Airport terminal. In each of your respective cities, you have done the same with similar organizations."

"Indeed we have, my brother, but not without significant complaint among our followers." Muktar El-Amir, head of the Dallas, Texas based cell of al-Sahaba lamented. "Asking our people to debase themselves in the ways they often have has been difficult to explain.

"Yes, I am sure that is correct. I am no doubt certain that all of you have had to field questions from our brothers as to why it is that they needed to lower themselves to cleaning the filth of others while awaiting their call to action in the cause of Islam. I certainly have from my people here, and it has been difficult not to be able to answer them fully. Most all of our operatives are extremely capable and well educated, and what they have had to endure during the past couple of years has been completely and utterly beneath them. There is, however, a reason for it all, and you and they shall now understand why."

Al-Sahaba cell leaders sat in rapt attention at what Khalid was now finally disclosing to them. It had indeed been horribly difficult to come up with logical explanations for their operatives as to why they had to stoop so low and perform tasks they nearly all considered vile, in order to further the cause of al-Sahaba. Khalid continued. "Before each of you, my brothers, is a case of one of the products that we have above all others attempted to make a market for in each of the cities where Dominion Janitorial has sold materials for the building maintenance industry. As you can see, it is a case of our room deodorizer aerosol replacement canisters for use in many of the automatic dispensers that are hanging on the walls and hidden above ceilings of bathrooms all over the cities in which we do business. If you were to go into any of the bathrooms around the O'Hare terminals here in Chicago, for example, you would find this very room deodorizer being automatically dispensed from timed units twenty-four hours a day. There is, however, something vastly different about the canisters each of you has before you today, and those all of you have sold and installed again and again over the past two years."

"The boxes look the same to me, Mr. Hamadi," said Allaidan Hussain Alwan, Egyptian head of the Washington, D.C. cell of al-Sahaba. "How are they different? I myself clean the bathrooms at Reagan International three days a week, and this looks exactly like the replacement canisters I have installed in the dispensers there many, many times before. What is so special about these?" Alwan asked as he started to open the box.

"Just one moment my friend. I would ask that all of you refrain from opening the boxes in front of you at this time. Each of you will be taking these cases, along with several others like them and other janitorial supplies, back with you when you return to your home cities. And all of it needs to remain unopened for purposes of transportation."

"Why is that, Mr. Hamadi?" Alwan asked, looking around the room, knowing that he was asking the question on everyone's mind. They all looked confused.

"OK, gentlemen, here it is!" Khalid paused and took a deep breath. "The canisters in the cases before each of you are not only filled with room deodorizer as those that you all have sold and installed so many times before do. These canisters also contain a weaponized form of what scientists refer to as Variola Major."

Gasps could be heard from some of the meeting participants, and one cell leader pushed his chair back immediately. "Smallpox, Smallpox pathogens?" Barzan Ibrahim Hassan, the Sudanese born cell leader from Miami, was a degreed biochemist, as was al-Sahaba leader Khalid. "Surely, you jest, Mr. Hamadi?"

The room was silent as Khalid stared coldly at Hassan. "I never jest about such things, Mr. Hassan. See here, my brothers, there is nothing to fear here. All of these canisters were sealed in a controlled environment, sterilized on the exterior, and brought into this country during the past few weeks under very careful supervision—right under the noses of American customs, I would have you know. It cost a great deal of money, but we were able to convince a customs insider to alter computerized records of the ship's manifest to reflect a shipment far different than the one actually received. To be specific, with but a few key strokes what was once described as a shipment of room deodorizer is now a large pallet of prophylactics delivered to a non-existent health services supplier in Peoria, IL."

Recounting this subterfuge caused the room to erupt in laughter, the loudest of which was none other than Khalid himself. Sammy found it difficult to join in.

"If you were unaware of what I have just told you," continued Khalid, "and you were to open the cases before you and look at the canisters, you would see nothing different from that which you have seen many times before. You would expect nothing. The only way to tell these canisters containing the bio-weapon from others you will be taking back with you and already have in your storerooms, is by way of a small red 'X' on the bottom of the boxes and canisters containing the weapons. In all other respects, they resemble the canisters of room deodorizer you and your people currently have in your warehouses and have for sometime been inserting into dispensers in bathrooms all over the cities in which you operate. They even smell the same. Only you will know the difference."

"Mr. Hamadi, are we and our people looking at death in what we are about to do here? Should we be preparing for martyrdom, for shahid?" Assem Rafiq, an Egyptian born New York immigrant and head of the al-Sahaba cell in that city sounded nervous. "The world's recent experience with COVID-19 was a true nightmare, but the release of this pestilence on the world would yet be something else. From what I understand, death by way of Smallpox is a horrible, horrible way to die."

"I must be honest, my brothers. I cannot guarantee

what may occur for any of us in that regard. It is my understanding that what you have before you is a particularly virulent form of weaponized Smallpox pathogen. Yet, if I am not mistaken, each of us, and all of our operatives, have at sometime during the last eighteen months been vaccinated for the Smallpox virus. By all accounts, we should be protected against infection. The outcome for all of us should be vastly different from that of our al-Qaeda brothers who died for the cause of Islam while executing the attacks of 9/11. If all goes well, each of us to the contrary should live to fight another day."

All of the al-Sahaba cell leaders were well-informed, well-trained terrorists. One by one, each was beginning to visualize the attack that was about to take place. "I believe that all of us are beginning to get the picture as to what form this attack will take," said Rafiq, "but tell us more of the details, please. How, when and where do we plan to use these weapons?"

"Fellow *mujahideen*," answered Khalid, "beginning at 1300 hours Eastern Time this coming December 24th—the Christian crusaders' Christmas Eve—our attack will begin. You and your operatives will start that day, as you have so many times before over the last year to eighteen months, by simply going to work cleaning the bathrooms of the airports in the cities where your cells are located. While doing so, however, you will replace the canisters in the room deodorizer dispensers of both the men's and women's bathrooms nearest the busiest domestic terminals in your respective airports, with those that are contained in the boxes in front of you. That day, those dispensers will be releasing more than just sweet smelling perfumes. They will in addition be spreading death and destruction in a way these wicked ones have never seen or felt before. Within hours, before anyone realizes what is taking place, we will have exposed thousands of people, headed in all directions throughout this evil land, to a plague that will exceed even the worst fears of this country's tragically inept Department of Homeland Security. Befitting the dogs that they are, the devastation throughout the country will be exponential. The COVID-19 epidemic and post 9/11 upsets will both pale by comparison."

"What will be the outcome of this attack?" Asked Nagif Fadallah, the Saudi who led the al-Sahaba cell in Seattle. "When you say 'devastating', just how devastating can we anticipate such an attack to be?"

"To be exposed, my friends, a non-immunized human being need only inhale or touch a sub-microscopic infected droplet, such as those that will be released into the air by the canisters we will install on December 24th. Usually, within one to two weeks, those exposed will begin showing symptoms of the disease—a fever, headache, backache, vomiting and a rash similar to the measles. If the victim is wise enough to seek medical attention, then their infection may be diagnosed and word would go out across this country like wildfire that a Smallpox outbreak has occurred. That alert would more than likely not be given, however, before that victim had typically infected at least ten or more other people on average, and each of those a similar number, and so on and so forth until it is projected through studies done by the United States' own Centers for Disease Control that within seven weeks of detection of the outbreak, as many as three million people could be infected and another one million dead. The scenario by the CDC in this projection, however, presumed only a handful of localized outbreaks, and that will not be the case with what we are about to unleash. With the potency of the pathogens that you gentlemen now have in your hands, and the overall disbursement of the disease that we can accomplish throughout this country by way of planeloads of infected travelers departing and arriving eight of its largest airports, I feel this projection may be woefully short of what may actually occur once we strike."

"Haven't most Americans, and really others around the world, been vaccinated against infection by Smallpox, Mr. Hamadi? Won't most of the infidels have an immunity against this disease?" Nagif Fadallah further asked.

"Interestingly enough, by the late 1970's, the World Health Organization had declared the disease eradicated throughout the world. Americans quit vaccinating their children against the disease. And for those who were vaccinated prior to that, immunity begins to wane ten years after inoculation. Experts feel that most of the country is now at risk if exposed. The government has vaccinated a goodly number of their military and first-responders, but not the bulk of their populace. Many people can become seriously ill from just the vaccinations. They have been fearful of panic."

"Please, Mr. Hamadi, I mean no disrespect in asking these questions, but what about detection?" Fadallah continued to press for information. "I have read that the Americans are greatly fearful of an attack of this sort— particularly after the Coronavirus outbreak. I have heard airport staff in Seattle discussing some sort of 'air sampling' system that has apparently been installed at SeaTac which supposedly tests the air continuously for airborne pathogens, etc. Wouldn't it be the same at all our respective airports? What if the attack is immediately detected? Word could go out grounding all aircraft, and those exposed could be vaccinated before the disease progresses too far. I understand there is a three to four day window when vaccination can greatly reduce impact of exposure to Smallpox. Such a situation could significantly limit the effects of our attack."

"You are well informed, Mr. Fadallah. We too are aware of the air sampling systems that have been installed in major cities around the U.S., actually in most of the cities where our cells are located. It's called BioWatch, a DHS program that has been in place for years and now receiving great emphasis in the wake of the COVID-19 pandemic. It does air sampling in such public places as major airports, shopping centers, skyscrapers, sports arenas and so on around the country. As well thought out and fully implemented as it may be, however, we nevertheless estimate that the program will still be too little too late for what we are planning to do."

"How do you figure?" asked Fadallah.

"Well, most of these operations utilize a system of specialized screens that continuously collect airborne particulates for testing. Those screens are then periodically removed—typically about every four to five hours or so—and the samples are then taken to separate laboratories for DNA testing. A false alarm with respect to the results can be so disruptive that the confirmation process relative to any positive test for pathogens on the CDC's category 'A' list must be as deliberate as possible. So, there could easily be a four to six hour window of exposure before confirmation if an attack took place right after a screen change. This creates a situation that is particularly problematic for major airports where people are hurriedly coming and going with regularity, but a tactical opportunity for us, The damage inflicted could be significant by the time action is taken and aircraft are grounded. In spite of the country's recent experience with Coronavirus and so forth, these American dogs are still relatively unprepared for what lies ahead with an attack of this sort."

Sammy sat in stunned silence. Beyond joining the exuberance of the group at the start of the meeting, he had said nothing throughout the discussion. Devout in his beliefs, he had always been an early, enthusiastic supporter of Osama bin Laden and his near worldwide consortium of terrorist organizations he called the International Islamic Front for Jihad—al-Qaeda or the Base for short—but things were different from the heady days following 9/11. Sheik bin Laden was now dead, killed in the attack by Navy Seals some several years before. Sammy had been a U.S.-based, al-Qaeda sleeper for many years now, and his devotion to the cause had been tempered by many things. He had developed relationships with, and affinities for, people difficult to dismiss from his mind as he listened to Khalid unfold the group's plan of attack. Visualizing any of his many friends and associates infected with such a horrible disease sickened him, in spite of his commitment to jiihad.

This man known to him as Ismail Hamadi, had scared Sammy from the day that he first met him some many months before, when Khalid picked him up in his cab and identified himself as a leader of al-Sahaba, delivering a message to Sammy from al-Qaeda that he was now "activated" as a member of the smaller organization. Thereafter, Khalid insisted on weekly meetings with Sammy in his yellow cab, and seldom did they meet that Khalid did not remind Sammy he might soon be called upon to offer up his life in the service of Allah.

When Sammy had dutifully informed Khalid about the OCC's examination at the bank in early November, and about how close the examiner, Paul Trotter, might be to figuring out that Tariq Nasir was involved in the business of hawala, Trotter was dead not quite twenty-four hours later. "We can ill-afford any interruption in the flow of funds so essential to our operations that come to us by way of Mr. Nasir's hawala operation at this late stage of the game," had been Khalid's explanation to Sammy. In spite of Sammy's admonition regarding the potential ramifications of such a move, Khalid unilaterally decided that Trotter's immediate death would buy just enough time for the execution of al-Sahaba's impending attack. Sammy had found it hard to sleep after Trotter's murder, and now knowing the specific date of this attack, that would not get any better.

CHAPTER TWENTY-EIGHT

COMPARTMENTALIZING HAD always been the secret behind Sammy's ability to lead the double life that had been his for the last several years since he had become a part of the international Jihad, but recent events were making it increasingly difficult to strike a balance in that regard. While the OCC was still scrutinizing everything at Global United—with a particular interest in his management of such sensitive matters as the bank's anti-money laundering policies and procedures—Sammy had to respond adequately while doing his best to reconcile his complicity in al-Sahaba's impending attack, now only a few weeks away.

With the examiners suggesting that Global United might be cited for regulatory violation under the Bank Secrecy Act and related anti-money laundering requirements, Sammy knew in his gut that he would have great difficulty explaining why he had instructed that certain things be done. Those same criticisms had been developing when the old regulator, Paul Trotter, was previously examining Sammy's areas of responsibility. Sammy had hoped as long as Hamadi was insisting on it that Trotter's demise might steer the OCC in other directions, but that hadn't turned out to be the case. Trotter's death served to only slightly delay, and then eventually heighten the OCC's efforts. To make matters worse, most of the questions the OCC now had were also focusing on Tariq Nasir's deposit account relationships and international business. Sammy knew this too could be disastrous in a number of ways. *What if they make me the fall guy?* He worried as he lay awake at night. *Worse yet*, he wondered, *what if they somehow link me to the old regulator's death and begin to question me in that regard? I could become a threat to the success of al-Sahaba's coming operation.* Sammy knew what it might mean for him personally were Mr. Hamadi or any of his cohorts to come to that same conclusion.

When Sammy began to realize how much Trotter was beginning to close in on perceived problems in the cash transaction reporting areas of Global United before his death, Sammy had confidentially informed Nasir of the situation. Each time that Sammy brought the subject up, Nasir had simply responded. "Make the situation go away, Mr. al-Dajani. I don't care how you do it. Just make it go away. I have supported you in every way imaginable since your arrival at Global United. Now it is time that you return the favor. My colleagues and I cannot afford problems of this sort right now. I have appreciated the discreet manner in which you have from time-to-time handled the often unique service requirements of both my companies and me, but if push comes to shove, I can ill afford problems with the regulators. It is regrettable, but I would have to take the position that I was completely unaware that you were handling our transactions in any special manner. Do I make myself clear?" Sammy understood all too well what Nasir was intimating. If things went wrong for Nasir at the bank relative to the handling of his accounts, Sammy would be the fall guy, perhaps in more ways than one.

Sammy was the al-Sahaba sleeper with the longest time in the U.S., and although he could never admit it to his terrorist counterparts, he had somewhat come to enjoy the lifestyle he, by and large, enjoyed as a successful Chicago banker. That would all soon be history, however. His involvement in the forthcoming attack by al-Sahaba would see to that. He found those prospects disquieting and was beginning to develop second thoughts about the whole affair now that he knew more details. There was nevertheless no way out for him now. If any of his fellow al-Sahaba had even the slightest hint that his conviction was dwindling, his life would be forfeit.

Although it was always thought to be operational backup, one way in which Sammy might ultimately be involved in the attack to come was really quite ironic when he thought about it. Here he was, a responsible, respected member of the management team at a relatively successful Chicago bank, who had been—unbeknown to banking associates, friends and other acquaintances over the previous six months—moonlighting on a part-time basis as a janitor for Chicago Airport Systems, the contractor that handled part of the day-to-day cleaning of that city's monstrous O'Hare Airport. Doffing his banker's pin-striped suit, wearing Airport Systems coveralls and using an assumed name and fake IDs, Sammy could on numerous occasions be found cleaning toilets and urinals, and scrubbing floors in many of the bathrooms used by O'Hare passengers. It was an odious task that Sammy despised. He had inquired once why someone of his stature was being asked to belittle himself in such a manner, but was told it was not something he should be questioning. The only explanation he received was that the charade was a necessity to establish his cover and that of his terrorist comrades if he was needed for the attack that was being planned for the future. He decided it was probably best he left it there.

Most of the time, when Sammy was involved in these clandestine activities, Ismail Hamadi and other al-Sahaba operatives would be working right alongside him. Sammy worried little about the fact that any of his cohorts might be recognized while cleaning a bunch of urinals. Their day-to-day "covers" made their involvement in the activity believable. Not so, however, for Sammy. He was stressed every minute when he was working as a janitor that someone would see him. What would he say? What reason could he give that he, a successful banking executive, was working nights and weekends scrubbing toilets? Tell them it was a second job to pay for vacation?

On one occasion Sammy's worst fears along these lines were nearly realized when Leland Tucker, Global United's head of Trust Banking, and his wife went through O'Hare on their way to a short vacation in the Bahamas. As Sammy was washing toilets, Leland was standing in front of a urinal not more than ten feet away from him, studying the bricks on the wall. Leland had looked right at Sammy, but blithely went about his business and exited the men's room expressing not even the slightest hint of recognition. *I guess pushing a mop around a bunch of toilets in a busy airport is a good way to go unnoticed*, thought Sammy at the time. It had been a close one though.

SAMMY HAD just returned from his earlier meeting with fellow al-Sahaba operatives and was in the midst of a teleconference with a number of his branch managers when Scott called him and asked that he immediately drop what he was doing to accompany him to a supposed meeting with Nasir in his offices over at AmeriPAK. Scott seemed upset. "Whew, glad you're finally back, Sammy. Tried you on your phone but couldn't reach you. I'll need to visit with you about that when we have some time. For now, however, we've got to leave right away for a meeting over at AmeriPAK. Tariq Nasir is going to be there via a video-conference link, and we need to be there by 4:00 p.m. this afternoon." Scott seemed particularly anxious.

"Do I need to bring anything," asked Sammy?

"No, I've got all that we need, and I will bring you a copy. Looks like the examiners have zeroed in on some things in your area of responsibility—namely BSA and AML problems—that could cause Mr. Nasir some real headaches, and I need you along to explain to him exactly how the situation may have come about, and what we're going to do to correct it, if we can. Where were you, by the way?"

"Oh, had to make a couple of customer calls." Sammy cringed. He knew what Scott was talking about. This was exactly what he had spoken to Nasir about numerous times already. The examiners had been banging away at him with all sorts of questions on the bank's cash transaction reporting, wire transfers and such the like throughout their whole examination. *That has to be what this is all about*, he thought. *Nasir will go ballistic, and I'll be the scapegoat, just as he forewarned sometime ago. As if all of that matters, I suppose. That will soon be the least of my problems, considering everything else that is about to come down.*

Tariq Nasir's offices were an approximate ten-minute ride from Global United by automobile. Scott went there often, and usually always took a taxi as opposed to driving himself. It allowed him time to get mentally prepared for his discussions with Nasir. He figured he could use those few minutes today to acquaint Sammy with the problems at hand.

"Here, Sammy, is a copy of a report I was given by the examiners in a meeting that Logan Hart and I had with them only few hours ago." After Scott and Sammy had climbed into one of the cabs that were typically parked outside Global United's LaSalle Street offices, and he had told the driver where they wanted to go, Scott had launched into what he thought was a very necessary, quick update on what he thought was to take place in the video conference that would happen soon in Nasir's AmeriPAK offices. He seemed fully unaware of Sammy's previous involvement with Nasir on the matter. "Some of this may look familiar to you since I would imagine you were the OCC's primary source for this data. Nevertheless, it looks like they're homing in on our lack of reporting on a multitude of cash transactions by Mr. Nasir's

379

companies. Someone, perhaps you I would assume, Sammy, must have exempted many of his companies from reporting, and they aren't buying it. They're threatening to write us up for violations along those lines and are now also wanting to get a bunch of information on a great deal of International wire traffic that was generated by the AmeriPAK group. Looks like the proverbial 'excrement is going to hit the fan,' if you know what I mean."

Sammy didn't have to look at the information. None of it was a surprise, and he told Scott so. "I was expecting this, Scott. The examiners have been beating on me about this for several days. I visited some with Mr. Hart, and I think he may have forewarned you we might have some problems with BSA, etc."

"Why would you exempt all of these AmeriPAK companies, Sammy? Most of them aren't the types of businesses that use a lot of cash. That's the part that may get sticky. The OCC is making a big deal out of that. If we don't have some good answers for them on this, they could really come down on the bank. I took a new look at an Executive Summary regarding the high points of BSA and the Freedom Act, etc., and there are some big criminal and monetary fines associated with anything ruled as a wrongdoing on the part of the bank or bank management. That's the last thing we need. I hope you have some good answers."

Sammy shook his head as he perused the information. He had never cared much for his boss. In his opinion Scott was just another money hungry toady hanging on to Nasir's coattails that Sammy would have gotten rid of long ago had he been in Nasir's place. "If you don't mind, Mr. Kruse. Let me glance over this information while we ride, and then I will do my best to answer all of your questions and those of Mr. Nasir's when we get to his office. This all looks similar to what I provided to the examiners, but I see they've highlighted a number of items. I would like to familiarize

myself with some of this before we get to Mr. Nasir's office."
Sammy simply wanted some time to think about what he was
going to say when they were online soon with Mr. Nasir. This
was all really the same as what he had previously discussed
with Nasir before the Paul Trotter affair took place, but
Sammy didn't know how well Scott was informed about that.
So, he needed to get his wits about himself before the three
of them were together.

◊◊◊◊

TARIQ NASIR'S corner office on the fourth floor at
AmeriPAK's headquarters on Grand Avenue was, to put it
bluntly, spectacularly opulent. Nasir had used the best of
everything throughout the building when it was decorated,
but the most outstanding area within the building was his
personal suite of offices. Occupying over two thousand
square feet of space, the office was really far more like an
apartment than an office. The nine hundred square foot work
area, rivaled that of any Fortune 500 executive in the city,
replete with turn-of-the century, traditional American office
furniture of hand-carved mahogany, and a whole raft of
Western American artwork, to include several original
Remington bronze sculptures. This area was where Nasir
did most of his office work and typically received all business
associates and guests. It never failed to impress most
visitors. It was, however, the remaining eleven hundred
square feet of Nasir's suite that would have boggled their
minds, had they been privy to viewing it.

Built into the wall next to a bookcase immediately
behind Nasir's desk, was a floor-to-ceiling mahogany panel
which hid a door leading to a living quarters that Nasir now
used far more than he had ever imagined he would, due to
the difficult situation that existed between him and his wife in
recent years. Nasir had a luxury condominium in a new

North Michigan Avenue development that he could also use whenever he wanted to stay downtown overnight for business or entertainment purposes, but more often than not he eschewed that in favor of the private living area behind his office. It was more conducive for work. Complete with a bedroom, bathroom, kitchen area and sitting room, the apartment was decorated even more extravagantly than the executive office nearby. It was Nasir's sanctuary when he really wanted to be alone, but still be close to work and the nerve center of his increasingly international operations. Small intimate discussions with customers and associates were often held in the seating area of Nasir's outer office, but meetings of six or more people were always held in the AmeriPAK board meeting room located adjacent to his office suite.

When Scott and Sammy arrived at Nasir's office for their 4:00 p.m. meeting, Nasir's extremely attractive, auburn-haired administrative assistant, Falanna Kristoff, immediately ushered both men into the AmeriPAK board room. Asking the bankers to have a seat and apologizing for the delay, she explained that they would soon be joined by what supposedly would be the CEOs of all AmeriPAK subsidiaries, after which Tariq Nasir would be addressing them via Internet connection from Brussels, Belgium, where he was standing by waiting to be informed of everyone's arrival.

Falanna Kristoff had been with Nasir for more than a decade. Some said the relationship was far more than a working one, but that was purely unfounded rumor. There was no concrete proof that such a relationship existed, but had more people known about the living quarters adjacent to Nasir's office, the rumor would no doubt have been far more rampant. Falanna assisted Nasir in most of his personal and corporate business and doubled as a receptionist. Her desk was located at the end of a long carpeted hallway leading past the AmeriPAK boardroom and large corporate worship area that Nasir had built adjacent to his suite of offices for he and his many Islamic staff members. Nasir's office had no windows or signage telling any visitors it was there, and to gain access one had to pass by Falanna, who restricted entry like a Marine embassy guard.

Within ten minutes of Scott and Sammy's arrival, all but one of the heads of the AmeriPAK companies arrived and immediately signed into AmeriPAK's state-of-the-art videoconferencing system. Once it was determined that everyone who had informed Falanna they would be able to make the meeting had arrived, the CEO of the AmeriPAK, Inc. holding company, Abu al-Madi, contacted Nasir in Belgium via the videoconferencing system to kick off the meeting. He explained that Scott and Sammy were present in Chicago along with the CEOs for all AmeriPAK companies except for Assem Rafiq, President of Aurora Tech. Rafiq was attending a computer gaming trade show in Las Vegas, but would be participating via Internet connection from there.

When Internet linkup was made with Nasir in Belgium, he was just wrapping up a telephone conversation that he appeared to want to finish before doing anything more than acknowledge everyone on the Chicago with a raised-fingered wave at the camera. Scott and Sammy could hear Nasir making comments about "foreign currencies, exchange rates, and adequate fees," but didn't hear enough of the conversation to understand what type of business might be taking place. All the AmeriPAK CEOs seemed totally nonplussed at the delay and completely disinterested in what Nasir was saying in his conversation. They all simply waited patiently until he was finished, to start the discussion. After dispensing with whomever was on the other end, Nasir clicked off the phone and started the meeting out right away. His expression was grim.

"Good afternoon, gentlemen," said Nasir. "Let me start this little meeting off if I could by first thanking Scott Kruse and Saud al-Dajani, President and head of operations for

Global United Bank of Chicago for taking time out of their busy schedules to join us here at AmeriPAK to bring everyone up to date on some unsettling things currently happening at Global United that I think could have some impact on our little group of companies. Scott and Sammy, do you need introductions to any of us gathered here today, or does everyone know everyone else reflected on our screens?"

"No, I think Sammy and I are both pretty well acquainted with all the company CEOs present here today, Tariq. Isn't that right, Sammy?"

"Yes, that's correct," answered Sammy, looking around the room at each of the AmeriPAK CEOs as he did so.

"Fine, well, let's get on with this then. Gentlemen, I asked Scott and Sammy to meet with we AmeriPAK folks here today to bring us up-to-date regarding the rather lengthy examination of the bank that has been going on now for nearly two months by the Office of the Comptroller of the Currency, the U.S. agency I have told you about before that regulates national banks in the U.S. like Global United. In that regard, I have been informed by Scott, Sammy, and others at the bank that a great deal of the OCC's emphasis in their review has centered around compliance with regulations governing the bank's policies, procedures and handling of all things relative to the Bank Secrecy Act, U.S.A. Freedom Act and all things relating to anti-money laundering monitoring. In particular, I have been further informed that in so doing, the OCC has been looking at all of our AmeriPAK-related accounts with great interest. Am I correct with all of that, Scott?"

"Yes, that's pretty much correct, Tariq. As a matter of fact, if anything the intensity of the OCC's investigations into the areas you just mentioned, along with all AmeriPAK accounts, has intensified since the death of the old OCC examiner a couple of weeks ago."

"Well, as I am sure you can well appreciate, Scott,

nothing about that news pleases any of us." Nasir paused a moment, appearing to gather his thoughts before continuing. "So, from what you're saying, if none of these problems we've been discussing with respect to this OCC examination appear to be going away, then perhaps we AmeriPAK people need to address the situation pro-actively. Just where would you say we are with our examiner friends? Things sounded rather ominous during our phone conversation. I thought we ought to game-play the situation."

"You may have a point there, Tariq. The situation with the OCC certainly hasn't been getting any better. I would say there's little downside to your suggestion we become, as you say, more 'proactive' in our approach."

"Give us more details," said Nasir. "Might help determine an appropriate approach in that regard."

"Be glad to," answered Scott, "but first though let me say that matters regarding any examination by bank regulators such as the OCC are, by and large, confidential with respect to anyone other than the bank's board of directors and select bank personnel with a need-to-know. You of course have every right to be privy to much of this as Global United's chairman, Tariq, but not the rest of you gentlemen assembled here. There could be real legal problems involved for all of us were it to get out that I discussed these matters writ large with you all today. That being said, I am willing to tell this group what I know within limits, but must be assured that my having done so remains in the strictest of confidence. I hope I can depend upon you all in that regard," said Scott, glancing around the room at the various AmeriPAK CEO's.

Sammy remained silent. He knew Scott had just crossed a line he shouldn't have.

"You have our word for that, Scott. We all are quite sensitive when it comes to a need for confidentiality in certain situations. Now what can you tell us?" Nasir asked.

"Well, Tariq, as I told you this morning over the phone,

and you said just a moment ago," answered Scott, "the examiners have been looking into the bank's management of its anti-money laundering policies and procedures, and they have come up with a whole raft of questions relating to our handling of your accounts in that regard."

"In what way, Scott? How are they questioning your handling of our accounts?"

"Well, to begin with, some of the AmeriPAK companies are exempted from regular reporting on large cash transactions in excess of $10,000, and they are questioning that."

"And why would they question that?" asked Nasir. "Our companies do a great deal of business in cash. What is so strange about that?"

"Nothing apparently if, per their indication, the size, frequency, and type of those transactions is typical for that type of business, but that is one of the problems they say they are having. Their contention is that such a significant use of cash is not typical for firms such as yours that we have exempted, and they would like a clearer understanding of that. And then that's not all. As a result of their questions regarding the exemption of your companies from cash transaction reporting and the level of cash used by your companies, they've also been looking over all the international business Global United has done for both you personally and your businesses during the last couple of years. They're questioning all of that too."

Nasir's face first drained of color, and then gradually turned red in anger. It was evident this news upset him. "This is disturbing to hear, gentlemen." Nasir's eyes were closed, and he was slowly rubbing the center of his forehead with his fingers as he pondered what Scott had just told he and the AmeriPAk crew. He very audibly sighed before continuing. "As I said to you earlier on the phone this morning, Scott. I have expected you and your staff to keep our companies and me away from such controversy. What's gone wrong here? This is your area, isn't it, Mr. al-Dajani. Explain to me how we've gotten into this situation, and how we're going to get out of it. And if you can't, Mr. al-Dajani, then I expect you to do so, Scott."

The room grew quiet for a moment. The AmeriPAK CEO's were used to Nasir pushing, but on this occasion, he sounded extremely distraught. Neither Scott nor Sammy quite knew how to answer him either. Sammy figured that any comments Nasir directed at him were more than likely part of a simple ruse to cover the fact that he had more knowledge of what Sammy had done for him in the past than he wanted to let on—but he wasn't sure. *Could be Nasir's getting ready to dump the blame for exempting most of the AmeriPAK accounts from cash transaction reporting on me,* he thought. He wasn't sure why Nasir was claiming to know nothing of the situation, but figured he was expecting Sammy to play along for the moment. *What the heck*, he mused. *Things are probably going to be in enough turmoil for me soon enough that it won't really matter if I defend myself or not.*

"How about it, Mr. al-Dajani? What can you tell us on this?" Nasir asked, continuing to perpetuate the charade.

"Well, sir, as Scott said, and I think you know, in keeping with requirements of the Bank Secrecy Act and the beefed up requirements under the U.S.A. Freedom Act, the bank has to report regularly on all cash transactions over $10,000 that take place within the bank unless they are originated by various customers that the bank has exempted. Those companies and individuals..."

"Look, Mr. al-Dajani, don't waste my time and yours. As you say, I am quite familiar with the requirements of BSA, the Patriot—or should I say—Freedom Act and the bank's need to regularly report so-called suspicious transactions to, what is it they call it, the Financial Crimes Enforcement Network, FinCEN or something like that; and most of my CEOs here are well aware of many of the details as well. I believe you told us last month at our meeting of the Audit Committee of the board that you report twice a month to this FinCEN via the Internet or some such thing. So, you've apparently not been reporting any cash transactions to them on us—or at least most of us?"

"Yes, that's pretty much correct."

"I don't remember the bank's auditor, Ms. Murphy, making any issue of this last month. Why not, if the examiners are so concerned?"

"Well, I just think Colleen Murphy reported on exceptions, and since the AmeriPAK companies were exempted and have been for some time, their cash transactions weren't thought to be a problem by she and her auditors."

"Well, gentlemen, I plan to take the position that I was completely unaware that our companies had been exempted. I will meet with the examiners myself if necessary. Uh, as a matter of fact, I want you both to go back to them and tell them that; and when you do, indicate to them that I have requested you immediately place our companies back on the list."

"Well, that is but one side of the problem, Tariq." Scott interrupted. "What about the cash transactions themselves? I am not exactly sure what the examiners will want us to do with respect to remedying the omissions, but it would seem highly likely that they will want us to submit reports on all the cash transactions your companies have generated in the past and for which the bank hasn't reported. Are your people here going to be able to give us all the background information we need relative to the purpose of those transactions and so on if we have to do that after the fact? Then further, from what I understand, if the OCC finds that we have flagrantly violated BSA requirements with all of this, there will be all sorts of reports to FinCEN and others that they will have to file, and there could be some hefty fines that the bank may be facing."

"I'm most unhappy with this, Mr. al-Dajani," snapped Nasir. "What sort of penalties or fines might we be facing if something like this goes south for us?"

"Well, I glanced at the regs, and from what I've read we could be facing fines something like twice the unreported amounts, up to well in excess of $1 Million." There was a great deal of murmuring amongst the AmeriPAK CEOs. Scott continued. "And then, and I hate to bring it up, there are all the questions about your companies' international transactions that the examiners have also dredged up as a result of their apparent suspicions about all of this other."

Nasir got up and began to pace a rather palatial-looking office he was transmitting from in Belgium. "We've somehow got to squelch all of this gentlemen. We really don't need the government poking around in all of our international business. Give me a day or two to think through all of this—and I would appreciate all the rest of you doing the same. Then perhaps I should meet with the examiners just as soon as I return stateside." Nasir tapped on his computer keyboard, looking at his schedule. "Hmm, today is Friday, and I am supposed to be back in the U.S. by Thursday of next week. What say, Scott or Sammy, we try to set a meeting with the OCC examination representatives immediately after my return—perhaps a week from today, if you can arrange it. In the meantime, I need for you AmeriPAK people to visit with Scott and Sammy, get as much detail as you can get on some of the things the examiners appear to have found and are asking questions about, and then get busy documenting whatever you can to mitigate some of the criticisms brought up by the regulators on these matters. Remember to provide only the minimum amount of information necessary to get the job done. I'll get a few other people—legal, accounting, etc—together and we'll begin to put some kind of face on all of this that will hopefully be palatable to the examiners. It would seem we have everything we need on our end already, Scott, but let

Falanna make sure we have full copies of all the information you brought along with you this afternoon for reference, and we will get busy looking up the whys and wherefores of all of this business. We haven't much time, but maybe we can do some damage control here. Think they will wait until say after the middle of next week if they have to, gentlemen? You, uh, can tell them I would meet sooner, but that I have meetings here in Brussels and Luxembourg that I just can't reschedule."

"I am not sure, Tariq, but I would think they would allow us at least a couple of days for a response. They know that this kind of information takes time to put together," answered Scott.

"What about these international transactions you have listed here, Scott?" Nasir further questioned. "Do you think it would be helpful for us to pull in young Mairaj Haifa, the head of that department? Perhaps he could work with our people in putting a good face on all that we do there."

"I'll speak with him, Tariq. I'm not sure how much he can help, but at a minimum, as head of that department, he should certainly be involved in whatever response we put together. It's just an observation, but I think he and Logan Hart have developed a pretty good rapport with the examiners. Maybe that will help us some. Need to look for whatever angles we can."

"Is Mr. Hart fully aware of all that is going on here, Scott?" asked Nasir. "I really don't want any more people involved than necessary while we try to straighten this out."

"Yes, sir, he is. He's been our key liaison with the OCC throughout this entire examination, and he sat in on the meeting with the examiners this morning when they went over all of this. He's pretty knowledgeable. Maybe he'll also have some suggestions as to how we might mitigate some of these issues."

"Fine, but just keep this whole thing confidential within a select group of people with the need-to-know you mentioned earlier, until we get through all of this. We don't want an uproar going through the whole bank." The three stared at each other with looks of resignation as Nasir pressed a buzzer summoning his assistant, Falanna for a long-distance talk. "And with that gentlemen, I think we all know what we have to do. I have another long-distance meeting in just a few minutes that Falanna also arranged for me, and you both need to return to the bank and begin throwing water on this fire. As always, keep me posted. Now, if you will excuse me."

Nasir was deeply concerned. The Nasir hawala network and a great deal of its business were an integral part of all of this that the bank examiners were looking at right now. Since it was not registered with the government as an Informal Value Transfer System, as was required by the Freedom Act, everything possible needed to be done to shield its activities. The select clientele with whom the Nasir family had so exclusively dealt for so many generations relied heavily on the confidentiality accorded them in the way the generations old organization did business, and Nasir's U.S. network of hawaladars had purposely broken the law to maintain their way of doing business. It would be a tremendous family disaster if any of this problem at the bank led back to any disclosure regarding the "shadow portion" of Nasir's business empire.

CHAPTER TWENTY-NINE

THE FIRST Friday in December was a long day for Logan. The morning had begun with several protracted conversations between OCC examiners and the heads of the various divisions within Global United, sandwiched around a very involved commercial loan closing that had required his direct involvement. Rounding out the day had been a late afternoon meeting with regulators, the purpose of which was a follow-up discussion of certain loans determined as substandard during the examination. At issue with respect to these loans of lesser quality was the resulting adequacy of the bank's Allowance for Loan and Lease Loss Reserve to cover any losses that might occur as a result of such problems. All of this had necessitated Logan's involvement as the bank's senior lender.

Once these discussions were complete, the examiners then took up what little was left of the day asking Logan and the head of the bank's new Islamic Banking Services Division a litany of questions regarding Global United's nascent entry into the provision of Sharia-compliant banking services for its growing base of Muslim clientele. Thus far the bank's offering of this type of service had been limited to assisting in the purchase of residential real estate properties, but the bank was in the process of expanding its outreach in numerous other areas of religiously compliant financial services—both retail and commercial. The offering of Islamic banking services was a new phenomenon within the U.S. banking system, thus far limited to participation by but a few of the larger banking organizations in the country. Banking regulators were still trying to determine appropriate regulations and struggling to aggregate the necessary tools and examiners adequately trained to oversee such new and foreign concepts within the industry.

Holland & Associates, Logan's previous firm, had several years before his departure taken note of a growing Islamic population across the country and the resulting interest of many major banks in offering services to this new market that fit the dictates of their religious beliefs. Seeing potential in offering consulting services to the industry along these lines, and taking note of Logan's previous exposure to the cultures of Asia and the Middle East while in the military, the firm had asked him to sharpen his expertise on the matter and put together a team of Islamic banking experts to service those organizations interested in entering that market.

Suffice it to say, the number of bank closings during the decade following the most immediate past recession, and the degree of troubled institutions yet remaining amongst those escaping closure, had left regulators fairly uncomfortable with banks entering new markets. In particular, there was great concern regarding institutions the size of Global United entering new fields of offering, like Islamic banking, where oversight capabilities were still limited at best.

When grilled by examiners on those matters, Logan and Global United's Islamic banking people proved to be extremely knowledgeable and well-versed on nuances of the subject as they related to concerns of regulators, but the OCC still evidenced a goodly amount of hesitation. Of particular concern to the examiners was the bank's ability to maintain adequate separation of its traditional financial service offerings from those within the new line of products it was beginning to offer its growing base of Muslim customers.

The meeting went reasonably well, and Logan had done his best to be as upbeat as possible when responding to regulators' questions, but more than once during their conversation he had needed to choose his words carefully to avoid exposing the ancillary work he was doing for Cass Price and the JTTF. The whole situation was beginning to make him increasingly uneasy, and uncertain as to what the future really might hold. He had already begun to reconcile himself to the fact that his days at Global United might well be numbered. Even if the governance, management and regulatory issues that beset the bank weren't enough to make him want to resign of his own accord, once the OCC examination was finally completed, it might not be a voluntary matter. He anticipated the bank's board of directors might not look favorably on how much he had been cooperating with the examiners and outside investigators without their knowledge—and perhaps understandably so.

Logan was looking forward to the weekend, however. Providing things at the bank and his ongoing assistance to the OCC and JTTF didn't reach out to usurp too much of his time during the next couple of days, he planned to take care of the minor amount of Christmas shopping that was on his list to do. Logan had no children of his own, but he did have some nieces and nephews back in North Carolina, and if circumstances at the bank didn't keep him from it, he planned to spend the holidays with family back there. Right now, however, with the bank situation becoming increasingly tense, things looked a little iffy in that regard.

On the train ride home to Palatine that night, Logan read through the Sun-Times and a few articles in the Wall Street Journal that he hadn't found time to look at earlier in the day. Reading helped him relax. When he got to Palatine, he grabbed a quick bite at a pub near the commuter station, figuring that would save him some much needed time when he got home. The FBI and DHS folks had contacted everyone who was working with them on the Trotter matter and confirmed an online meeting for 8:00 p.m. which Logan was supposed to take part in again.

Based on the frequency of these online meetings, Logan sensed that the law enforcement and intelligence members of the task force were becoming increasingly on edge. Biological WMD's were scary stuff. If they were out there, they had to be found. No source of information could be overlooked, and the holidays were fast approaching. As Raleigh Sutphen from DHS had put it in their last discussion. "With all the business and personal activity, travel and such, there is no other time when we are more vulnerable. If terrorists are truly able to unleash some deadly disease on an unsuspecting public at this very busy time of the year, the results could be disastrous."

In spite of the seriousness of the meetings, Logan had come to look forward to them on a personal level. It was a somewhat voyeuristic opportunity to be with Cass Price via computer and observe her in a personal setting. Logan thought about her as he wolfed down a burger and a cold bottle of Lienenkuegel's Red. She was serious about her work and capable, but at the same time extremely personable and attractive. Again, she reminded him of his Melanie. *Industry, brains and good looks, a great combination,* he thought. *There's no wonder she's advancing so quickly at the OCC. I'll bet she doesn't, however, have much more of a life outside of work than me,* he mused sympathetically. *Perhaps when this is all over?* He paused in the middle of what he was thinking. *Nah, I know she alluded to something like that recently, but I rather doubt it has a snowball's chance of happening. Examiners and bankers are social oil and water, and when all is said and done, she appears to be all business. Legal and professional ethics would no doubt put the kibosh on any real date with her after all of this is over. Just my luck,* he figured, *finally find someone that I think even Melanie would approve of me seeing socially, and she turns out to be some untouchable regulatory muckety-muck sitting across the table from me.*

The Internet get-togethers were nevertheless proving effective. A fairly large group of individuals in several locations could visit in relative privacy, and never leave the comfort and security of their home or office, and the four bedroom, English Tudor in Palatine that Logan had shared so many years with his wife was certainly one place where he felt comfortable. Everywhere he looked in their home he saw her in so many ways: photographs both taken by and of her; her artwork; her birdhouse and wooden tree collections; and on and on. He had thought of selling the forty-year-old, 4,200 square foot executive residence when she passed away, but he couldn't bring himself to do it. He felt close to her there. The place even still smelled like her here and there.

Logan got home in just enough time to change into something casual, feed Melanie's old parrot—that he hoped would keep its mouth shut during the meeting—and brew some coffee before time to go online. At precisely 7:55 p.m., he went into his home office/library, pulled the blinds shut on the windows behind his desk, sat down, connected to the Internet and signed on at 8:00 p.m. sharp, as directed by the amiable message from his old friend, Merritt Daimler of the FBI, earlier that day.

Logan wasn't sure why he felt compelled to close the blinds. The windows faced a large fenced in backyard that was surrounded by trees, but since that evening before Thanksgiving when he was certain he was being followed, Logan still somehow felt like there was somebody dogging his tail. He had not seen anyone, but he still sensed he was being followed. It made him uneasy. He had even purchased a box of shells for the M9 Beretta he had purchased as a keepsake when he was still in the service. It lay on his desk now next to his computer. *This is all getting bizarre,* he thought. Although he was an expert in the use of nearly every small arm in the U.S. Army's arsenal back when he was on active duty with the military, he hadn't fired any weapon other than his 30.06 deer rifle on but a few occasions since his return from Iraq in 1992. *May need to do something about that*, he mused.

◊◊◊◊

"GOOD EVENING everyone! Once again, we appreciate your making the effort to get together like this. We have some urgent things to discuss." FBI Special Agent, Merritt Daimler, seemed anxious to begin the JTTF update. "It looks like we have everybody present and on time, and that's good. Raleigh, you said earlier today in a conversation with me that you had some important information for everyone this evening. Why don't you start?"

"Fine, thank you, Merritt, I will, and good evening everyone," replied the DHS's Raleigh Sutphen. "Well, as you all have no doubt seen or heard in the news, the Department of Homeland Security has been maintaining an Intermediate condition of threat advisory under our National Terrorism Advisory System for the last few weeks, but as a result of certain additional information recently received from Russian intelligence—if you can believe that—there is consideration of perhaps moving the advisory to the more severe level of Imminent."

"Are you at liberty to give us any specifics on what is prompting that, Raleigh?" asked Vincent Magnusson of U.S. Customs Service.

"Well, I'll do the best I can, but let me first remind you all once again of how sensitive everything we are discussing here is relative to national security. It is imperative that what we're discussing here this evening be kept in the strictest of confidence. Even a small leak might precipitate national or even international panic."

"Goes without saying," Magnusson responded.

"Well, I've been instructed to repeat it again," snapped Sutphen. "That being said, however, the Russians recently provided us with additional information that would seem to corroborate their earlier suspicion that a terrorist organization has managed to smuggle some sort of biological weapon from their country into the United States, and may be planning to use it soon. Additionally, we are intercepting more and more traffic on the Internet and through other communications media—chatter as it's often called—that would seem to indicate something big is about to come down. As Merritt said a few minutes ago, we feel particularly vulnerable at this time of the year. "

"Thanks, Raleigh, we all needed that now that we've arrived at that time of day when we maybe would like to get a restful night's sleep," Cass nervously injected. "How though —as I've also said before—do you expect we banking-related types can be of any help with that?"

"Well, from what I understand from our people, the information the Russians are providing continues to come via undercover sources who are part of some ongoing investigations into their Mafiya. I believe that was mentioned to you all some time ago. If you'll recollect, word was that organized crime elements over there were the original sources of the bio-weapons we're looking for. These Mafiya sources informed them that delivery was made and that a bio-weapon was shipped out, likely headed for this country. Word further has been that the terrorist organization who had purchased the stuff was apparently paying the Russian Mafiya in installments if you will. Well, just lately, the Russians determined how the money was coming into the country and confirmed that a so-called 'last installment' had been received."

"What does that mean exactly?" asked Logan. "Does that necessarily indicate use of the weapon may be imminent?"

"Yes, Russian intelligence sources appear to be

saying just that." Sutphen's online image wasn't perfectly clear for some reason, but as he continued the strain on his face was still discernible. "Supposedly, their informants— whom they claim are quite credible — told them a final payment in the amount of $500,000 was to be made when the shipment 'reached its destination,' and that apparently took place."

"Well, once again, that is sobering to all of us, but where do you figure that fits into what we are looking into for this group if that is how far things have progressed?" Cass repeated.

"I'm getting to that. The last and final thing the Russians told us was that apparently all of these payments made their way to their Mafiya by way of a Saint Petersburg-based hawala network. Apparently, their informant was someone who regularly did business with the resident hawaladar, and as a result was asked to help with the transaction. Thanks, to information he provided, Russian authorities were able to scarf up everyone who was involved in the transaction on their end, and although it apparently took no small amount of questioning and encouragement— something we are well aware the Russians are quite adept at doing—they managed to eke out enough information to follow the money trail back along its route of delivery and determine that most of the money originated here in Chicago, IL. Now you can perhaps see where we are headed with this."

"Yes, you're intimating this hawala transaction may have something to do with Global United Bank of Chicago and/or Tariq Nasir." Cass made the comment before Logan had the chance to do so. "Is that what you're saying?"

"You're right. We feel there's a strong possibility that could be the case, particularly considering all the info Logan gave us a few days ago." Merritt Daimler answered. "Look, Cass, while you, your team of examiners and Logan have been looking over all of Mr. Nasir's ownership in and business with Global United, we've been doing some investigations of our own about him. It has been difficult to ferret out, but we were recently able to co-opt an individual that managed to work a hawala transaction through some people at one of his Crescent jewelry stores here in Chicago. It was a sham transaction from Afghanistan that some folks in their intelligence service were able to help us with. The money went through a couple of countries before it got here from Afghanistan, but get this folks, it originated via money originally delivered to a hawala operation in Kabul that is apparently run by folks working for a company called PAK Metals, Ltd, and PAK Metals is owned by none other than Mr. Nasir's father, Mahmoud Nasir."

"Yes, and PAK Metals is one of Nasir's companies that is also a customer of Global United," injected Cass.

"And the corporate owner of the Crescent Jewelry chain," added Logan.

"That makes none of this look very good for Mr. Nasir," said Logan, shaking his head. "As involved and informed as he is relative to all of his businesses, including the bank, there is no way anyone in his organization could be involved in the business of hawala, and him not know it," said Logan.

"That's correct, Logan. We couldn't agree more," said Daimler, "and that's why we're so actively looking into everything about Mr. Nasir, his businesses, and his people. So, it's imperative you, anyone you can conscript at Global United, and Cass' OCC team find out everything you can for us. One thing for sure, if he and his companies are involved in the business of hawala, none of them have properly registered as money service businesses. If that's the case, there's no doubt he and his people are in deep guano."

"Great, next thing you'll perhaps be telling us, Merritt, is that I'm working for a terrorist?" Logan shook his head as he leaned back in his chair, crossed his arms and looked at the faces of everyone on his screen. Studying Cass' expression particularly close, he could see she was deep in thought.

"Yeah, well, if all of what you say is true," Cass finally injected, "then Mr. Nasir's ownership of and involvement in any financial institution insured and regulated by the U.S. Federal government may become a matter of history."

"Well, Cass, no matter what your position and that of the OCC's may be in that regard," Daimler was quick to add, "we would have to ask that you take no immediate steps of your own relative to Mr. Nasir until we've had our opportunity to work our wonders with he and his crew first as it relates to all of this."

"I can fully understand that Merritt," Cass responded, "and we would absolutely work with the JTTF in whatever way you wish relative to any regulatory action we might take. I'm also certain everyone up top in the OCC will agree in that regard, including the Comptroller himself, once he and other key officials within our organization have been basically filled in on the situation."

"And we appreciate that," said Daimler. "If it will ease your mind any at present, Cass and Logan, we think it safe to say we rather doubt Mr. Nasir or any of his AmeriPAK associates to be directly involved in any impending terrorist operation, outside being unwitting facilitators via the international hawala operation we suspect he and his family are running. That won't be any excuse for he and his colleagues in the long run. Proven to be involved even to that extent will make them equal conspirators. However, we don't think you need to be concerned any of them may be directly involved in any violence."

"Well, I still hate to think about what effect the disclosure of any of this is ultimately going to have on Global United should it turn out to be true and becomes public," said Logan.

"We couldn't sympathize more, Logan, but I know you, and I'm rather certain you would want us to be as truthful with you as we can. It's just that our experience with these hawala operations is that they sometimes are not all that selective about who they do business with. We're not sure how much it might be the case with the Nasir family, but often an element of fear can come into play relative to any hawaladar doing business with a bunch of terrorists, should they know that to be the case. The Nasir's are international, and fast becoming big business aside from any hawala operation they may be running. That renders them not less, but probably more vulnerable when it comes to threat. Business—in particular the business of hawala—can at times make for some strange bedfellows. Our understanding to date is that we're dealing with a supposed al-Qaeda-linked, pan-Islamic terrorist organization in this situation that we are trying to chase down. Even though the Nasir organization may be only indirectly involved, I would bet you dollars to donuts they have people within their organization who would be willing to be more directly involved were they called upon to do so. From what we've been told, more than a few of Nasir's senior management-types have made statements in the past, both verbally and in writing, that would suggest they harbor Jihadist sympathies. At a minimum there would be a strong inclination to look the other way and ask no questions when dealing with the sort of people we're looking for."

"I guess you'd have to say this is all a big puzzle, and we're still trying to put together all the pieces." Sutphen explained. "That's where we're hoping you and Cass can continue to greatly assist us by finding out as much information as you can before we put the squeeze on this guy and all the surrounding people—something we plan to do real soon here. If this Nasir or any of his associates can lead us to anything that might help us ferret out the perpetrators of this plot before something potentially catastrophic happens, we want to move soon. And we won't be fully prepared to do that without the information we're expecting you may be able to provide us. So, at the risk of sounding like a cracked record, how soon do you both think you'll be done? Yesterday, maybe?"

"I would say quite soon," answered Cass. "We're really about there now. We've basically finished our review of most aspects of the bank, and have narrowed down our investigation to that which we've discussed before—the bank's anti-money laundering policies, programs and procedures, and the extent to which Mr. Nasir's companies are involved therein. I'm sure our investigation is moving right along the path that you would want us to be following. We're waiting on some responses to a number of final questions bank management is working on right now, and when we get them, we're going to try to arrange a meeting with bank management and the board of directors, if need be. What do you think, Logan? When can we expect to hear from the bank's people regarding our questions?"

"I would say we ought to have all responses in the OCC's hands by Tuesday or Wednesday of next week," Logan answered. "Before I left the bank today, I e-mailed Sammy al-Dajani with that same question, and he told me that he thought they would have have everything done within that time frame."

"Let's try to make sure that happens, if you can, Logan." Daimler injected. "As Raleigh said, we need this thing to move ahead as quickly as possible. And while we're discussing your Mr. al-Dajani, I suppose I ought to tell you that we think he and the bank's president, Mr. Kruse, are sufficiently tight enough with Tariq Nasir that they warrant closer scrutiny. Since our last meeting, we've been following both men's coming and going, as I think we said we were going to do. Not but a few hours earlier today, Lon Erickson here and another of our agents tailed both al-Dajani and Mr. Kruse to Nasir's offices, where they attended a meeting there for some time. We're not sure what it may have been about, but it lasted for about an hour or so. Considering the timing so soon after yours and Kruse's meeting with the

OCC, Logan, and the fact that he would choose to take your Mr. al-Dajani to the AmeriPAK offices with him for a meeting suggests to us that the meeting was very likely related to all that's going on at the bank with the OCC's examination."

"That's strange," said Logan. "You say the meeting took place this afternoon at the AmeriPAK offices?"

"Yeah, something strange about that to you?" Daimler asked.

"Well, it's my understanding that Mr. Nasir is in Europe on business," said Logan, "Belgium I understand. So, they would have to have met with him by phone or some such thing if he were to be part of any meeting."

"You're right there, pal. He is indeed in Europe," said Daimler. "So, we too were wondering how he might be involved in any meeting with Kruse and al-Dajani, but Lon here has some information that might shine a little light on that. Lon, you want to fill us in with your take on that?"

"Sure thing," answered Agent Erickson. "Well, as Merritt indicated, we followed both Kruse and al-Dajani to Mr. Nasir's AmeriPAK offices around 3:30 p.m. this afternoon, where they were joined shortly after their arrival by a number of men we know to be CEOs of some AmeriPAK companies. We have no eyes nor ears in their place just yet and knew that Nasir was out of the country. So, we are unsure what the exact purpose of any meeting there might have been, but we have since found out that AmeriPAK apparently has some state-of-the-art kind of online videoconferencing communication system— something similar to how we're all communicating right now, I guess. They apparently can and do use it to maintain contact with Mr. Nasir when he is away. So, we're thinking the purpose of Mr. Kruse and Mr. al-Dajani going there was still probably to fill Nasir and all his people in on progress with the OCC at Global United inasmuch as they would be able to do that."

"That's interesting." Logan interrupted. "If his meeting

over at AmeriPAK was related to the OCC's work at the bank, Scott really didn't waste much time after Cass and her assistant, Ms. Caldwell, met with both he and I on the Nasir situation. The packet they provided us with is the one constituting the final interrogatory Cass just referred to, which included queries regarding cash and international wire transactions related to Nasir and his companies that the OCC wants answers on. Scott got a copy of all that. So, I guess that might well have been part of what he wanted to discuss with them."

"Cass, can we get a copy of the questionnaire you gave Logan and Mr. Kruse this morning?" Daimler asked. "Could be enlightening, and we might want to add some requests for information of our own."

"You certainly may. I'll email a copy over to you just as soon as I can. I should also inform you that we used the Patriot Act Communication or PACS system to forward some of this same info to FinCEN early this morning. They will be analyzing our request for information against their database of SAR's and CTR's formerly submitted to them by Global United, checking for reporting deficiencies that we can use in visiting with the bank on this situation. Whenever we get any reply from them to that request, I'll plan to also send a copy of that along to you. Oh, and might I add, if Kruse and al-Dajani did indeed have a meeting with any outside people other than Nasir to discuss matters involved in any regulatory examination, such as ours, they've broken a whole other set of laws. That's a separate matter that is certainly minor in the scheme of things here at present, but you can be assured its something that will have to be addressed somewhere down the road." Logan and the rest of the JTTF could tell Cass was becoming incensed. No one chose to pursue her latter comment.

"Say, Cass, as long as it isn't breaking any laws, and if it isn't too much bother to include us, we wouldn't mind perusing copies of all the information you're referring to as well." Raleigh Sutphen interjected. "Think we could do that?"

"Certainly, no problem with any of the parties here, we'll be glad to copy you with everything we've gotten thus far, and anything else we receive as we get it," Cass answered. "We'll send it to everyone here in the form of a PDF," Cass answered.

"Well, I would appreciate everyone else's opinion on this," said Merritt Daimler, "but I think that it's about time we push this situation at the bank forward. Who is it that you plan to visit with at the bank when you meet with them regarding your determinations, Cass?"

"Just as soon as we've heard back from FinCEN— which I rather think should be a fairly quick turnaround—I was planning to ask for a meeting with senior management and perhaps either the full board or audit committee of the bank."

"Would Nasir normally be included in that group?" Daimler asked.

"Yes, he would normally," injected Logan. "He's the chairman of both groups. If either was asked to convene, he would normally be part of that meeting, but as we've discussed, he's out of the country right now. So, he wouldn't be part of any meeting planned during the next few days."

"Uh-huh, as we've said, we are well aware of that," Daimler stated. "He doesn't know it, but when he flew to Belgium a day or so ago, a couple of our guys were traveling with him. Will his absence keep you from having such a meeting, Cass?

"No," Cass answered, "we will probably go ahead and still have a meeting after we've pulled everything together. We're thinking it would probably even be better were Mr. Nasir not there. It'll give us a chance to really open up with the bank board members. They'll probably be getting an ear full."

"Sounds perfect, Cass! You know as I think about it, however, it might be a good idea if we folks from the FBI also attended that meeting— might even be part of such a contingent myself. Time they maybe heard from us too. What would you think of that?"

"Be great with us, if that's what you want, Merritt. You're most welcome," answered Cass.

"Good, we'll do just that then," said Daimler. "We may significantly compound their discomfort with what we'll probably have to say on top of the OCC's comments, but it's probably time that senior management and the directors of Global United Bank finds out about some of our concerns. Let us know whenever you have an exact time and place on that, Cass. We'll remain flexible on our end until we hear from you."

"I will. Not sure exactly how soon FinCEN's going to get back to us, but I'll call them again and push them as much as I can," said Cass.

"Maybe we can help move things along some at FinCEN." Daimler offered. "We're in pretty regular contact with them in this office, and we know a few people over there. I'll get in touch with the powers that be and let them know how urgent this is. Maybe we can get a quick answer for you. We really need to move this situation along, Cass. What if we can get the necessary info together by Monday morning? Would you be able to convene Global United's board members by then?"

"Don't know," Cass answered. "Your opinion on that, Logan?"

"I would suppose that's possible," answered Logan, "but remember we're dealing with some outside directors here, each with schedules of their own. We might not get everyone, but spur-of-the-moment meetings do happen from time-to-time. We could give it a try. Maybe we could even start on that over the weekend with an e-mail notification that we may need to have a special meeting. That's been done before, to my understanding."

"Well, let's do that if we can," said Daimler. "This is

really urgent overall. If things lead the way we think they will with this, we're going to want to pull in Mr. Nasir when he returns from Europe next week, and I'm thinking Mr. al-Dajani for questioning. Not sure about Kruse yet, but we'll make a decision on that after our meeting with your audit committee first of the week. In the meantime, we've got to find out whatever we can that will help us shed some light on our hunt for these bad guys. We feel the clock is ticking on an attack and truly suspect there may be some tie here. So, do what you can to pull that group of bank directors in, if you can, Logan."

CHAPTER THIRTY

THE AUDIT and Compliance Committee of Global United Bank of Chicago's Board of Directors usually met once a month on the afternoon of the second Tuesday, with Tariq Nasir chairing when he was in town; and as opposed to other committees of which he was a member, it was one committee meeting that Nasir seldom missed.

"Mr. Nasir's out of the country on business until Thursday, Logan," was Scott's Kruse's reply when Logan called him at home on the first Sunday in December to inform him that the OCC had requested a special meeting with either the Audit Committee—or full Board of Directors if the bank so chose—the following Monday morning at 8:00 a.m., a day earlier than normal. "I'm absolutely certain," said Scott, "that he would want to be here for any meeting with examiners. The OCC's taken long enough to get to this point. What's the big deal with them waiting until he returns later in the week? Don't you think they could at least do that?"

"No, Scott, the OCC says they would like to meet as early as possible tomorrow with at least the Audit and Compliance Committee and as many other members of the board as might be present. And as for Mr. Nasir's not being there, well, perhaps this is one he won't mind being absent from."

"Oh, yeah, why is that?"

"Well, I think some of the matters the examiners are

planning to discuss relate to certain concerns they have with personal and business relationships Mr. Nasir and his AmeriPAK group of companies have with Global United. Mr. Nasir might well decline to attend anyway if he knew that."

Scott knew better. There was no way that Nasir would not want to be there to defend himself and AmeriPAK. Yet, Scott also couldn't afford to let Logan know how keenly aware Nasir already was of all the scrutiny his companies were receiving from regulators. To do so might put both he and Nasir in an awkward position. So, perhaps Nasir's absence at this meeting with examiners might be for the good of all concerned. Knowing Nasir wouldn't be returning until the following Thursday, Scott would just have to convince him his absence was maybe best this time around. He wanted to do as he was instructed by the bank's Chairman and principal shareholder, but was worried it might look suspicious to the examiners were he to insist they delay until Nasir's return. "I'll see what I can do about getting the committee and any other directors as might be available together for that time if I can, Logan, and get back to you."

"Oh, and in that regard, Scott, judging from what Ms. Price had to say and the way she said it, I don't believe there is any chance she and her crew are going to want delay their requested time of meeting. I may have spoken out of turn, but I told her I thought we could e-mail all of the directors over the weekend requesting their attendance, and she really jumped on that. I think she's expecting us to do it."

"I wish you wouldn't have done that, Logan, but if that is what they're expecting, I guess we'll have to meet their demands. Mr. Nasir's going to be livid, but I'll do what I can to intercede with him. See you and the examiners tomorrow at 8:00 a.m., I guess."

◊◊◊◊

SCOTT WAS on the phone to Nasir within fifteen minutes

after his discussion with Logan, chasing him down at his favorite hotel in Luxembourg to inform him of what was coming down with respect to the OCC and their requested meeting with bank directors,. "Scott, I absolutely can't get back for this by either tomorrow or Tuesday morning. Isn't there any way you can delay the meeting until Thursday. I will be back in town at that time, and I would definitely like to sit in if I can."

"You know, Tariq, it looks as though the examiners are insisting on holding the meeting just as soon as they receive some last minute information they are waiting for. They claim they're trying to stay on a schedule to exit the bank, and you know we certainly want them to do that just as soon as possible."

"Yes, but not if it leaves the bank and my organization in an uproar in the process."

"Well, as I said, the way they're acting it would seem as though they may want to wrap things up soon, and if this meeting with the board members will make that happen, then I wouldn't want to do anything whatsoever to stand in their way. Wouldn't you agree?"

"I would think you would know my answer on that one, Scott, if that is indeed what they're intending to do. So, let's hope that is the case. If things blow up with these people back there in Chicago, and I think it was something that could have been avoided by my having been there, I plan to hold you accountable for that, Scott." There was an uncomfortable moment of silence as Scott tried to gather his wits to respond. "Scott, are you still there?"

"Uh, yes, I'm still here Tariq, and I guess I would have to say that I think it would be better were we to go ahead with the meeting. I want that OCC bunch out of here as quickly as possible. I promise that I'll be on the phone with a report immediately after we adjourn with them."

"OK, you go ahead and have the meeting without me, but as you've promised, I want a call from you telling me what took place just as soon as the meeting is over, and if there is much criticism of me and/or my businesses as a result of what is said, then I want you to arrange another meeting between me and the examiners immediately upon my return next Thursday. Is that clear?"

"Yes, yes, it is, Tariq. Hopefully, this will all be perfunctory in nature. They've been poking around here for some time, and have said little to me to date. Let's just hope whatever violations, if any, they've found are minor in nature, and that they give us some time to correct those mistakes and leave it go at that. I'll stay in touch with you."

"See that you do," snapped Nasir.

◊◊◊◊

AS ANNOUNCED via a weekend email, a special meeting of Global United's Audit Committee was convened at 8:00 a.m. on the first Monday in December—a day ahead of its normal time— with Scott Kruse chairing in Tariq Nasir's absence; and although it was seldom the case, all members of the committee other than Nasir were present. Outside directors: Taylor Parriott, senior partner of the downtown law firm, Callihan, Murphy and Parriott; Kenneth Townsend, president and CEO of Quantum Pharmaceutical; Clarence L. Kariokos, owner and CEO of Olympic Food Distributors, a large purveyor of food and related supplies to Chicago area restaurants; and Jonas T. Latham, President of Triton College, a four-year liberal arts school in the Northwest part of the city, were the outside directors that made up the committee. All of these gentlemen were long-term members of the bank's board of directors, with Parriott having served for thirty straight years, and the other three an aggregate of over forty years between them. Each was well respected within their individual fields of endeavor.

When all the members of the committee arrived for the

meeting, the boardroom was already full of a number of serious-looking folks with whom Scott was only partially acquainted. This immediately worried him. He recognized Cass Price, the lead OCC examiner, and he was familiar with most of her young cohorts who were present. Also in attendance and known to him were FBI agents, Seilor and Erickson, who appeared to be accompanied this time by a third rather distinguished, steely-eyed individual whom he had not met before. "Why the FBI again, Logan, and who the heck is the officious guy who looks like he's accompanying Seilor and Erickson?" Scott whispered under his breath to Logan Hart as they entered the room. "Don't really like the looks of this, Mr. Hart. OCC, FBI, and heaven knows who else. Also appears as though Ms. Price has dragged in most of the Chicago office of the OCC with her this morning. Do you know what the heck's going on here?"

"No, Scott," Logan answered, lying through his teeth. Prevarications of any sort weren't part of his nature. "but I would imagine we're soon going to find out."

Scott's comments to begin the meeting were brief. After reintroducing himself, members of staff and each of the outside directors present for the meeting, he immediately turned its conduct over to Cass. "I believe we have everyone from the bank that you requested here this morning, Ms Price, and except for Mr. Nasir, who's in Europe on business until Thursday, everyone from the bank's Audit and Compliance Committee is here. I see there are a couple of new faces in your group this morning, Ms. Price. So, I'll let you take things from here. You called this meeting today, and we're here to listen and respond. Why don't you introduce your people to us and lay out what you want to discuss?"

"Thank you, Mr. Kruse, and thanks to all of you from Global United for coming in to meet with us on such short notice this morning, in particular, you gentlemen that are outside members of the board." Cass began. "We appreciate Mr. Kruse and Mr. Hart putting this meeting together, and we thank each of you for changing your schedules to attend. We know that this meeting would not normally take place until tomorrow, but we felt it imperative that we get together with your committee right away. We have come across some matters of great concern in our examination that we felt we needed to discuss with all of you at our earliest opportunity."

The tenseness in the room was palpable. Finding such a large regulatory contingent was quite unexpected, not to mention representatives of federal law enforcement. The entire room was doing its best to appear relaxed and convivial, chatting it up and sipping at their cups of coffee, but most everyone was uptight. Questioning glances flitted between staff members and directors as all listened to Cass' foreboding opening.

"Before we get into what we wish to discuss this morning, let me begin by introducing the members of our regulatory group present this morning. As most of you except for outside directors know by now, I'm Cassandra Price— Cass to most of my friends—Deputy Assistant Comptroller with the OCC here in Chicago. Present from the OCC with me this morning are some of my assistant examiners who've been with me on this rather lengthy engagement here at Global United, Latisha Caldwell, Craig Garrett, Barbara Howell, Nell Parker and LouAnne Blaine. Also here with us this morning—and we will get to the reason for their presence in due time—are Mr. Merritt Daimler, Special Agent in Charge of the Chicago field office of the FBI, and his agents Mr. James Seilor and Lon Erickson."

With the latter introductions, one could have heard a pin drop in the room. Scott's stomach began to tighten and he could feel his pulse pounding. He was uncharacteristically silent, and everyone else connected with the bank followed suit, preferring to let the examiners explain themselves.

"As I think most of you know, and I realize this backgrounding may be a repeat for some of you," continued Cass, "our examination of Global United Bank of Chicago was nearly complete last month, just prior to Thanksgiving. To my understanding, we had at that time essentially looked over most everything involved in determining the safety and soundness of an institution this size, having spent more than six weeks with over twenty examiners involved in the process. As of that date, our determinations were, to be quite truthful, heading toward a final grade for the bank that was to the best of my knowledge going to end up providing the bank with an overall CAMELS rating of '2', a determination that would have been largely satisfactory. Our decision in that regard was very suddenly and very necessarily delayed, however, when our dear friend and colleague, Mr. Paul Trotter, a long-time senior regulator who was involved in the examination here at Global United, was slain only blocks from here in what to this day is still considered being a tragic incident of street crime. Paul's death very much remains a situation of federal and local criminal investigation as we speak."

"Ms. Price," interjected Jonas Latham, the president of Triton College, "if you would excuse my interruption, I think I speak for the entire board of directors here at the bank in saying we were as upset with that tragic event as anyone, but I hope you aren't going to say in bringing that up, and with the presence of the FBI here this morning that you think anyone or anything at the bank was involved in that."

"Well, Mr. Latham, at this point, I would have to say that we do not, but I would be less than honest were I to say that we were certain it will remain that way." Latham chose to say no more. "The only reason that I brought all of that up was by way of backgrounding for you board members only. All of the bank staff has heard our comments on Paul's situation ad infinitum. When he died, there were things he was working on here at the bank that were left incomplete, and as we have repeatedly told bank staff, a great deal of his paperwork and his computer were lost in the incident that took his life. We, therefore, felt compelled as a result to conduct an extensive follow-up examination of Global United. We have now finished most of our work in that regard, and wanted to discuss some of our findings with you —some findings about which we are more than pleased, and others where we are not."

"What areas would you 'not be pleased' with?" Scott asked, wanting to appear a man-in-charge in front of his board.

"Well, I would prefer to comment on those areas that we were perfectly satisfied with first, and then I will get to the problems. In so doing, I'll follow the various parts of our CAMELS rating we assign to banks as part of our evaluation. I believe you all are quite familiar with that regulatory acronym. First of all, in the area of bank Capitalization, we find the bank's capital levels with a ratio of tangible capital at 7.86% of total assets, to be quite satisfactory for a bank this size. That situation places the bank in the upper tier of banks within its peer group in that regard. In the area of Asset Quality, we also have found little about which to be concerned there. The quality of your loan portfolio is generally excellent overall, with problem loans very manageable and loan loss reserves at a very sound level. All of the bank's policies and procedures related to the lending functions of the bank appear to be more than adequate. They are well designed and fairly strictly adhered to. Then as to the area of Earnings…"

"Wait a minute, Cass, what about bank Management?" Scott interrupted again. "As you can imagine, as President and CEO of Global United, I'm fairly concerned about our grading by you in that area."

"Well, I would like to get to that later, if I could, Scott. I always like to save that part for last after we've made comments on the other areas of assessment, and further, some questions we have to discuss here this morning should really be a part of that discussion."

"Fine, I'm sorry to have interrupted you." Scott

apologized. "Please continue. I'll not say anything more until you've finished."

"No, that is quite alright. That was a natural question, and I will get to our assessment of management in just a little while. As I was saying, however, we found in our review of bank earnings that Global United is making money at a rate unmatched by many in its peer group during these days of some remaining industry stress, rather amazing really. In spite of its tremendous expansion over the last few years, with numerous new domestic and foreign offices being opened, the establishment of the bank's new international banking operation, and introduction of certain new product lines such as Global United's Islamic banking services, the bank is still earning money at a rate that should well maintain capital levels where they need to be to match growth for the foreseeable future. At a 1.36% return on average earning assets, we think the bank is doing quite well with its earnings for a bank this size."

"You know, Ms. Price, all you've said thus far this morning would sound quite encouraging" injected Taylor Parriott, the only attorney on the board, "were it not for all of these big guns from law enforcement that have accompanied you here this morning. I don't know about everyone else, but this is the first time to my recollection that we've had three people from the FBI sit in on an Audit Committee meeting, particularly when you've had nothing but good to say thus far. Why do I get the strong sense there's a shoe about to fall?"

A couple of directors chuckled nervously as Cass remained quite serious looking and continued with her comments. "I'm sure it looks that way, Mr. Parriott, but let me first comment on the last two areas of assessment we make in the bank before we get to my comments on management and the possible downside to what we need to discuss here this morning."

"Sure go ahead, Ms. Price. As important as I know is,

some of what you're relating is a bit mundane, but we'll try to remain quiet."

"I know, I know, Mr. Parriott, but all of these things are equally important, and procedure requires that I cover each and every aspect of our examination," Cass responded. "So, just let me continue by saying that we also found the bank's Liquidity to be in excellent condition, with plenty of cash flow and liquid assets available to meet a substantial demand, and additionally found the bank's management of Rate Sensitivity to be quite satisfactory—something that concerns us a great deal these days when both assets and liabilities of most banks are quite sensitive to movement in market rates, etc. In our review of Asset/Liability Management here at Global United, we find both the policies and procedures being used by the bank to be quite adequate, and the bank's approach to management of that aspect of bank operations to be much the same. The bank's Asset/Liability Management Committee meets regularly, monitors market and rate trends and plays an active role in the setting of rates on both sides of the balance sheet. Regular analysis of the bank's rate situation seems to indicate that the bank is well balanced to withstand any significant rate swings one way or the other. All in all, we think the bank is fairly well prepared for any major market changes. Are there any questions thus far?"

"Thus far this is pretty encouraging, Cass," Scott responded. "But since this group is only that portion of our board of directors saddled with the responsibility of monitoring bank audit and compliance, will you be sharing all of these very satisfactory findings with the bank's full board of directors at some future time?"

"Yes, we'll set a time at some future date for a meeting with your entire board, perhaps to be convened at a time of mutual convenience when we have concluded our examination. Hopefully, timing will allow us to have that meeting in conjunction with one of your regular board meetings, but if that is too far out, it may need to be another special meeting. We'll let you know sometime soon in that regard. That being said, as good as everything I've told you sounds up to this moment, I do have some concerns that we need to discuss which may or may not—depending on how the bank is able to respond—greatly overshadow some of these other very satisfactory findings during our exam."

"Please, Ms. Price, why don't you get to these special concerns, if you would." Clarence Kariokos said, making his first comment of the morning. "You have us all sufficiently on pins and needles. Tell us what it is that apparently has you folks so concerned."

"Well, ladies and gentlemen, from the start this examination was strictly meant to primarily assess the bank's safety and soundness." Cass continued. "Our review of the regulatory compliance in a bank this size is usually reserved for a separate engagement intended to look strictly at that aspect of bank management. We glance here and there at the bank's compliance with various regulations as we move throughout the bank in a safety and soundness review, but we usually reserve our compliance exam for another time. In this instance, however, perhaps due to the unusual circumstance of Paul Trotter's death during the examination, we did choose to take a rather thorough look at the few areas of regulatory compliance he was making a cursory review of while he was here. For example, since he was looking at the bank's handling of cash transaction reporting and adherence to such areas of regulation as the Bank Secrecy Act and the most recently enacted U.S.A Freedom Act at the time of his death, we felt it imperative that those areas be closely looked at again during our extended review."

There was quite a pause, and the room remained silent again. All of the bank representatives had serious looks on their faces. To a person, they all knew how much of a hot button BSA and the Freedom Act were to the regulators and people in charge of national security. It had been discussed a great deal at both management and board levels.

"Cass, if I might," Scott interrupted, "I would like to have us dismiss everyone on our management crew but Mr. Hart at this time before we go into your comments on this. We will make sure to fill them all in later about what you had to say in their absence, but for reasons of my own, right now I would like us to keep this discussion strictly at senior management and board level due to the delicate nature of some of what you may wish to bring up. Would you mind if we did that?"

"No, Scott, that would be fine," answered Cass, "but who are you suggesting remain?"

"Well, at this time, I would suggest we have everyone step out but our directors, of course, and say Logan Hart here and myself."

"OK, I think we could agree with dismissing everyone except two people that I would like to keep, due to their involvement in these areas of the bank. If we find ourselves hung up on any subject that requires an answer from anyone else who is not present, however, we would like to have your agreement that we could call them back in."

"That's not fully what I would prefer, but you're calling the shots here," said Scott, his face was becoming increasingly flushed. "Who do you want to remain?"

"Well, if you don't mind, we would like to have Mr. al-Dajani here, head of bank operations, and Mr. Haifa, your head of the bank's International Banking department, remain in the meeting." Cass and her FBI counterparts studied the expressions on the faces of both those bank officers. Sammy's face drained of color, while Raj Haifa's countenance remained relaxed and confident. It told them a great deal.

"Fine, thank you." Scott turned to his management staff and dismissed all of those present except Logan,

Sammy, and Raj. The discussion stopped until everyone had exited the room. "Alright, now that we've taken care of that, Ms. Price, please feel free to continue."

"Fine, thank you, I'll do just that. As I was saying before, we again looked very closely at the bank's handling of the requirements of BSA and the Freedom Act, and other anti-money laundering activities of the bank. By and large, the bank's policies and procedures are in keeping with the dictates of both of those regulations, and we were satisfied to that extent. Beyond that point, however, we found the bank's day-to-day management of those areas of the bank to be sadly lacking. So much so, gentlemen, that we may be in the position where we may have to cite the bank for significant violations in those areas of compliance. Further, as we have looked over the specifics of our concerns, we have found questionable activities that have caused our associates here from the FBI to ask that they be included in this discussion."

"What kind of exceptions are those?" An exasperated and embarrassed Scott blurted out. "As I've told you in previous discussions, we here at Global United have always gone out of our way to adhere to the requirements of BSA and the Patriot Act or Freedom Act or whatever the heck you want to call it." Scott was totally flustered. "You just got through saying that our policies and procedures were good, and our internal audits have disclosed no concerns." Scott looked nervously around the room. He was concerned about what his directors were thinking at this juncture.

Logan had chosen to say very little to this point and figured he would continue to do so until his input was asked for. He, Cass and the FBI had agreed beforehand that he would take this approach during the meeting. Cass had even avoided looking at him much since the meeting started, but he had caught a raised eyebrow or two from his old Army buddy, Merritt Daimler.

"Well, generally speaking, Scott, Global United's

adherence to the requirements of most major regulations is right on target, but that's not the case when it comes to its compliance with BSA and related regs. In those areas, the bank has been cavalier at best in its interpretation, almost appearing at times to having gone out of its way to circumvent very essential reporting of questionable transactions for some accounts as required by the law."

"What you're saying is upsetting. I can assure you, we all take these matters seriously" Taylor Parriott appeared to speak for the now rather subdued committee. "Can you give us the specifics as to what the bank may or may not have done that is contrary to law and regulation, Ms. Price?"

"Yes, Mr. Parriott, I can, but you may find the details a bit unsettling," Cass answered. "You see, many of the accounts and transactions about which we have questions— and we had previously discussed our concerns about this with bank management before this meeting—unfortunately have to do with business transacted over the last couple of years by none other than the companies owned and operated by the bank's Chairman and principal shareholder, Tariq Nasir."

"Is that the reason Tariq is not here with us today?" Jonas Latham asked excitedly, looking at Scott

"No, absolutely not!" Scott quickly retorted. "Mr. Nasir knows nothing about this as yet." Scott felt a queasiness in his denial. He had just lied to the Audit Committee. If the board ever found out how much Nasir was aware of the situation, it could mean the end of a promising situation with Global United. "Mr. Nasir was aware there were some questions that the examiners had regarding our BSA compliance and so forth, but he is unaware that there were any questions regarding his companies and their transactions. He really and truly is in Brussels and Luxembourg on business. He would have been here, but the business he needs to conduct there is quite important, I understand. As a matter of fact, he was rather upset this meeting couldn't be delayed until he returned toward the end of this week. I spoke with him this morning, and he asked that I express his regrets that he could not be here."

"Well, what about this then," asked Taylor Parriott again. "What exactly are we talking about by way of questionable transactions?"

"Cass, may I make some comments in response to some of this please?" Merritt Daimler asked, finally weighing in on the matter."

"Yes, absolutely, go right ahead Agent Daimler."

"Well, gentlemen, let me start by telling you first of all why the FBI is actually sitting in on this meeting at all this morning."

"Please do, Mr. Daimler, that's one question that has no doubt been on the minds of everyone affiliated with the bank since we all walked in here this morning," Parrlott responded.

"I am sure it has, sir. So, let me give your board some background in that regard." Daimler explained. "To date, the FBI's involvement here at Global United has principally been due to the tragic murder of Paul Trotter. Normally, a murder on the streets of Chicago would be investigated solely by the Chicago Police Department, but when a high ranking official of the federal government is taken out in the violent way that Mr. Trotter was, the FBI usually gets involved. As part of that process, we interviewed a number of key individuals here at the bank and sat in on a couple of the early meetings the OCC had with bank management, to discuss the work Mr. Trotter was involved in here at Global United just prior to his death. Since Mr. Trotter's computer and most of the material resulting from his later work here were lost at the time of his death, the OCC decided to reexamine a number of those areas. When Ms. Price and her OCC team began to find they had some serious questions regarding certain areas of bank operations that Mr. Trotter may have been looking into prior to his death, we asked to be kept informed to determine

423

whether there might be any link therein to other aspects of our investigation. And that, sir, brings us to our meeting this morning."

"Good Lord, that all sounds rather ominous and foreboding, Agent Daimler." Kenneth Townsend, the pharmaceuticals executive, seldom spoke at board-related meetings unless he was really concerned about the subject being discussed. Yet, when he did, his words were chosen carefully and people most often listened. "I think I speak for us all in saying I can't in my wildest imagination believe anyone here at the bank, in particular someone of the character and reputation of a Tariq Nasir, could ever be involved in something so insidious as murder to cover up simple business transactions hardly within his day-to-day purview. What on earth could someone need to hide that would justify such a dastardly thing? I'm sickened to think about it."

"I can certainly understand your feelings in that regard, Mr. Townsend," Daimler responded somewhat sympathetically, "and your loyalty is certainly admirable. Yet, these abnormalities, whether honest mistakes or misinterpretations of the law or not, have occurred in areas of the bank Paul Trotter was investigating prior to his death, They may indeed have nothing to do with the situation involving Mr. Trotter, but they nevertheless look questionable to the examiners under current laws and regulations, and we agree. So we need answers to whatever questions we have about them as quickly as possible."

"All of us here at the bank have been cooperative from the start with every bit of this, Mr. Daimler, and you can rest assured we will remain so until both you and the OCC are finished with your work here and are satisfied that neither Global United, nor for that matter, Tariq Nasir, has done anything for which we could be criticized under the law," Scott stated emphatically. "We want to get to the bottom of this as quickly as you do. These are busy, important times for everyone here at the bank, and we need this all behind us"

"Well, it's good to hear you say that, Mr. Kruse, since it really is in the bank's best interest to do just that. I hate to be the one to say this, since it probably should come from Cass and her friends here with the OCC, but I hope I don't need to remind all of you as directors of both your overall and individual responsibility for the bank's adherence to every law or regulation that governs this bank. Ignorance of what management may or may not be doing does not alleviate any of that responsibility. Your cooperation is imperative."

"Well, again, as I believe someone asked early on in this meeting, Agent Daimler, can you give us some specifics regarding those questions?" Townsend repeated.

"Certainly, Mr. Townsend, but I think the bulk of that answer might best come from Ms. Price," answered Daimler. "Cass, would you like to handle Mr. Townsend's question?".

"Certainly, I would be most pleased to do so, Special Agent Daimler," Cass responded. "Uh, as I begin my comments I've asked Latisha Caldwell, head of our examination team since Paul's death, to pass out some information for all of you to review here this morning. Bank management may keep three copies for future reference in responding to our interrogatories, but I would like to ask that the outside directors please give their copies back to me at the end of our meeting here this morning. What you will be looking at is basically a copy of that portion of our draft Report of Examination relating to our review of Global United in those areas of concern that Special Agent Daimler was referring to in his comments a few moments ago." Latisha got up and began passing out the excerpt that Cass was referencing. As it was received, each of the directors began to read it intently.

Cass continued. "Inasmuch as all of you have either been directors or involved in bank management for many years, I am sure you are well aware that any information like this that we might share with you here this morning is strictly confidential and must be treated as such. That being said, before each of you here this morning are packets of detailed information relating to the findings in our examination regarding many of the shortcomings we've detected regarding Global United's requirements under the Bank Secrecy Act and its overall administration of Anti-Money Laundering activities. One chief area of concern, among many I'm sorry to say, is the bank's handling of Cash Transaction Reporting as it is required under BSA. In that regard, the bank has a fairly substantial list of customers that have been regularly exempted from Cash Transaction reporting, which we think have inappropriately been authorized that designation. To the extent we are correct in that regard, certain of those accounts would have generated numerous cash transactions, both large and small, that would have mistakenly gone unreported when they occurred. Part of what's before you here this morning is a pretty thorough list of customer accounts and related transactions for the last three years for those relationships that we feel fall within this category. With regrets, as you will no doubt readily see, at the top of this list are all the accounts for the bank's Chairman, Mr. Tariq Nasir, his AmeriPAK, Inc. holding company, and all but two of its subsidiaries."

"Well, as we have already suggested relative to this matter," Scott asked in an attempt to lessen the impact of Cass' comments, "wouldn't at least some of Mr. Nasir's companies indeed qualify for such an exemption?"

"Yes, perhaps that is correct, but bank management was unable to document anything beyond very basic due diligence in that regard—something that might in and of itself be considered a violation. There again, to the extent we were able to find such documentation, the analyses provided were stretches at best in making a case for exemption. We think this represents a reckless disregard for what is required of the bank under the regs—and to make matters worse, it is insider-related."

"What about some of the specific transactions themselves, Cass?" Daimler asked in an attempt to lead the discussion in a direction of FBI concern.

"Yes, I was just about to get to that, Merritt. As Special Agent Daimler indicates, gentlemen, the transactions themselves also need to be explained, and there are two types about which we need a great deal of justification if we are to avoid some very severe sanctions of the bank."

"And what are those?" director Kariokos asked, beginning to show real concern.

"They're numerous, large cash transactions and related wire transfers occurring in the bank's International Banking department over the last couple of years for Mr. Nasir and his companies," Cass responded.

"I'm sorry, perhaps I don't understand. What's so strange about international transfers?" Kariokos asked. "I have relatives in Greece, and I make wire transfers to people over there quite frequently. Mr. Nasir is from South Asia. He has family and business interests there and quite frankly all over the Middle East, Southeast Asia, the Pacific Rim and so on. So, what would be so strange about those?"

"Well, it is not the transactions themselves that are of primary concern—although we do question what they may be for—but instead the bank's propensity not to report them. Mr. Nasir's companies also regularly transfer substantial sums of money to numerous offshore tax havens, and to a number of banks and companies that we believe are questionable themselves. Then they also regularly send money to countries that are on the OFAC list of questionable destinations."

"OFAC list?"

"Office of Foreign Assets Control, Mr. Kariokos, they're an agency of the U.S. Treasury Department that administers and enforces economic and trade sanctions in support of national security. OFAC maintains lists of all the governments, companies, individuals, and so forth, who are considered to be a threat to our national security. Entities from around the world, who are of concern to the government with respect to the sort of business we're discussing here this morning."

"Oh, okay, thank you," said Kariokos rather sheepishly.

"In short, we feel that the bank has conveniently ignored the spirit and intent of the BSA and other anti-money laundering-related requirements in its handling of such matters. So, as we've said, considering his serious insider status, the bank needs to very quickly work with Mr. Nasir and his associates to provide satisfactory information regarding all of these transactions that we list for you here this morning by way of question."

"My goodness, Scott, it would seem both the bank and Tariq—and perhaps us from what Mr. Daimler said just a bit ago—may be in one heck of a pickle if we can't quickly provide correct answers for all of this," Kenneth Townsend snapped at Scott while shaking his head. "And what about all of this from your point of view, Mr. al-Dajani and Mr. Haifa? You, gentlemen, are responsible for properly monitoring this sort of thing, aren't you?"

"Yes, we are, Mr. Townsend," answered Sammy "and I admit that much of this may be my fault. It was my recommendation, and mine alone, to exempt those of Mr. Nasir's companies listed here from suspicious activity reporting and so forth. I am deeply regretful that I may have opened Mr. Nasir up to criticism and sanction as a result."

Logan and Cass glanced at each other out of the corners of their eyes. Both were amazed at how quickly Sammy was willing to "fall on the sword", so to speak. It was completely out of character for him.

"What about you, Mr. Haifa, how about all of these international transfers that were supposedly unreported," Townsend asked of Raj Haifa.

"Well, here too, I may be at great fault. However, when

I first arrived at the bank a few years ago, I started out by reporting many of the transfers you have questioned. Sometime shortly afterward, both Mr. Nasir and our president at the time prior to Mr. Kruse's arrival, told me they felt it wasn't necessary to report all of these transactions. They said that it brought unwarranted scrutiny on Mr. Nasir's operations, based upon the frequency of that kind of business for he and his companies. I differed with them on that and said so in a memorandum to the board of directors wherein I quoted all pertinent regulations as best I interpreted them. I was later told by the president of the bank that the board had duly noted my warning, but that they agreed I should cease reporting most all of Mr. Nasir's transactions. I did so from that time forward until Mr. Kruse arrived. I then again repeated those concerns to he and our audit department. To this date, I have received no replies to my concerns." All of the directors glared at Scott in obvious consternation.

"That's interesting to hear, Mr. Haifa." Cass looked quite surprised. "I would have to say to you and everyone else here this morning that I and my team have reviewed the minutes of the bank's monthly board meetings in great detail for the past four or five years, and I don't believe we saw any mention of any such memo or any discussion of such a matter anywhere in those minutes. This is additionally concerning. I would have to say that we're also going to need an explanation of what transpired relative to Mr. Haifa's memo. If there is any documentation relative to the matter, we're going to need to look at that."

"I saved dated copies of all correspondence and documentation I was involved in relative to the matter if they might be of interest, Ms. Price," Raj responded.

"That's fantastic, let's you and I visit about that immediately following this meeting, and I would like to have you join us on that if you don't mind Mr. Hart," Cass answered.

"Certainly, I'd be happy to do that," Logan replied.

The room was again painfully quiet for what seemed to be an interminable amount of time following this little exchange. The directors present appeared highly frustrated, and Scott looked like he was about to explode. Director Parriott finally broke the silence. "Scott, this is serious stuff. I think we're all well aware of how important this BSA and Freedom Act thing is anymore, and what we as banks are expected to do in these days of threat to our nation's security and all. I think I speak for all of us when I say to our government overseers here, that we do not take any of this lightly, and will make it a top priority to get to the bottom of this at our earliest opportunity."

"We appreciate that Mr. Parriott, but I should tell you in the meantime that at least the way it looks right now, the bank is going to be written up in rather strong language for egregious violations in the areas of BSA and Freedom Act compliance. Depending on what the bank's response is— and it may be that nothing at this time will keep this from happening—there will no doubt at a minimum be a Memorandum of Understanding requested from the bank's board of directors, outlining what is going to be done by the bank to correct these deficiencies. Does everyone understand the implications of that as far as the bank and the board is concerned?"

All around the table nodded in assent. They realized how serious the matter was in the eyes of the regulators, and the presence of all of the FBI agents served only to put an exclamation point on the matter.

"Let me make a final comment, gentlemen." Merritt Daimler added. "Perfunctory administrative response may be enough for the OCC right now—no offense intended, Cass— but as for us, we will not be done with our investigations into this situation until we have a number of additional questions answered. In the meantime, we are going to ask that no one in this room speak with Mr. Nasir about any of what has been said here, other than in generalities, until he returns to Chicago later this week. We plan to meet with him then in a similar fashion to the way we have met with you all here this morning. Further, Mr. al-Dajani, we would like to have you meet with my agents and me perhaps first thing tomorrow morning, if you would, to discuss this matter at greater length. We think there may be more you might be able to tell us regarding a lot of this that could speed things along in this investigation. We can do that here or at our office, whichever you would prefer."

Sammy's face drained of color. "I, uh... certainly, I can do that, and I'd be happy to meet wherever it is easiest for you, Special Agent Daimler."

"Fine, then maybe it would be best for all concerned, if we had that conversation over at our offices, say at about 10:00 a.m. tomorrow morning. Our offices are located on Dearborn. Do you know where that is?"

"Yes, sir, I think I do. I'll have no problem finding it." Sammy felt like he was going to throw up. Thoughts of what Ismail Hamadi and his al-Sahaba brothers might say, or worse yet do, if they heard any of this were running through his mind.

"Now, before all we FBI guys depart this meeting this morning, are there any more questions any of you from the bank have of us?" Daimler glanced around the room, but there was no response. Most everyone looked like they just wanted the meeting to be over.

Trying to end the meeting on a positive note, Taylor Parriott finally spoke up. "If I could presume to speak for our Audit Committee, I believe we all want to thank you folks from the OCC and the FBI for meeting with us here today. It's rather evident that we here at the bank have a great deal to do, and do quickly, in response to all of this. To begin that process immediately, I would like to suggest, Scott, that bank management perhaps leave the room for a short while to allow we outside members of the board to discuss all of this a bit. When we're done, we'll let you know, and then maybe you and Logan can rejoin us to discuss where we go next with all of this."

CHAPTER THIRTY-ONE

BY THE morning of the second Tuesday in December, FBI
Agents Seilor and Erickson had by themselves accumulated
a multitude of extra man-days investigating Tariq Nasir, and
the evidence thus far garnered by them and numerous other
agents within the Chicago field office had convinced the FBI
and JTTF that the apprehension and interrogation of Mr.
Nasir immediately upon his return to the United States was
imperative. The plan currently called for taking Nasir into
custody for questioning at Chicago's O'Hare Airport later that
week on Thursday, when he was due back in Chicago from
Luxembourg, where agents of the FBI confirmed him to have
been on business for most of the week preceding. In
preparation for that event, the FBI and other JTTF member
agencies were utilizing wire taps, monitoring Internet traffic,
scouring public and private informational databases,
executing sting operations and expending a great deal of
time of the gumshoe variety, in an effort to piece together as
much information as they could before they confronted him
and his attorneys.

   High on the list of tasks for Seilor and Erickson this
day was to visit with the Nasir's sisters-in-law, Margaret and
Maureen Hardesty, in an effort to fill in some blanks relative
to Nasir's domestic situation prior to his return. Interviews
with numerous social acquaintances of the Nasir's had
disclosed a wide-spread impression that Nasir and his wife,
Melissa, had been having marital difficulties for some time,

and the FBI felt there might be some useful information in an investigation of that situation. An appointment had been set up for 10:30 a.m. to visit with Maureen Hardesty at her apartment in the trendy Wrigleyville area on Chicago's north side. She had indicated to Seilor and Erickson that she would also have her older sister, Margaret, a catholic nun who lived with her, join them. When Agent Seilor talked with Maureen by phone the day before, she had seemed more than willing to assist in any way. There appeared to be no love loss between her and her brother-in-law. Her comment to him had been, "Why, what's the creep done now? It's about time someone looked into what that guy's all about."

Seilor did his best to convince Maureen that the FBI's questioning was simply part of a routine investigation, but he could tell by her reaction that she suspected otherwise. He elicited a promise from her that she and her sister say nothing to anyone about their appointment with them, asking in particular that they not mention the matter to Nasir's wife, Melissa. Maureen agreed, repeating that she was anxious to help. It was obvious she didn't care much for Nasir.

Agents Seilor and Erickson showed up at the Hardesty sisters' downtown apartment at precisely the appointed time. The agents didn't want to mess up on this one. There appeared to be excellent potential for enlightening information.

"Thank you, ladies, for taking time out of your busy days to visit with us," said Seilor. When they arrived, the two agents had been seated at the sisters' kitchen table and were being served hot coffee and scones that Sister Margaret Hardesty was insistent they partake of. She looked and acted every bit the proverbial Catholic nun. A request sounded much like an order. Seilor continued. "We're sure this is a slight inconvenience for both of you, but we appreciate it. Thank you, for treating this visit as a matter of confidence. For reasons we would prefer not to explain at this time, this discussion must be kept private."

"We understand fully, Agent Seilor. We will be more than pleased to help both of you gentlemen in whatever way we can." Maureen Hardesty seemed almost anxious to assist. The love-loss between her and Nasir was increasingly evident.

"Maureen, honey, we talked about this before Agents Seilor and Erickson arrived this morning. Didn't we?" Margaret Hardesty admonished her sister with a raised eyebrow as she refreshed the agents' coffee. "Gentlemen, I am sorry for my sister's exuberance about all of this. As you can tell she has a thing about our brother-in-law, and she promised me that she would try to be as objective as possible when you visited this morning." Sister Margaret again looked disapprovingly at Maureen. "Whatever the reason may be why these gentlemen are here Maureen, we want to be fair with Tariq. So, please!"

"Oh, alright, Margaret, I'll try, but just for the record, let it be known I think the guy is a louse. Now with that, gentlemen, drink your coffee, eat your scones and ask your questions."

Erickson grinned knowingly at his partner and started the questioning as Seilor took a drink of his coffee and an obligatory bite out of the hot blueberry scone lying on the plate in front of him. "Thank you, ladies, we'll try to take as little of your time as possible. As I believe Jim here mentioned to you yesterday by telephone, we're doing some routine background investigation into your brother-in-law, Tariq Nasir, and in that regard, we're interested in obtaining a reasonable assessment of his personal situation. Other sources have indicated to us that there may be some stress in your sister's marriage to Mr. Nasir, and it is our thinking that this could be an important piece of information as it relates to what we are investigating Mr. Nasir for. Would you be able to shed any light on that situation? Oh, and feel free as you do so to make any other comments you wish about Mr. Nasir's personal or business situations that you think might be of interest to us."

"Great, I've been waiting for an opportunity like this!" Maureen looked defiantly at her sister. "How much time have you got?"

"Maureen, remember what we said!" Margaret cautioned again.

"Yeah, sis, I know, I know. Look, guys, things have not been good between our sister and Tariq for some years now. When they first got married, he was supposedly God's gift or some such thing. He seemed loving and attentive to her, and always kind and solicitous to our folks and us. You might say, he was the perfect son or brother-in-law, and our sister was head-over-heels in love with him. He's extremely good-looking. I'll give him that. And he can be very likable if he has a mind to. So, he was a welcome addition to the family during the first few years of our sister's marriage."

"What happened to change that?" Agent Erickson asked.

"To be truthful," continued Maureen, "we're not really all that sure. I personally wonder how much was ever genuine when he first joined our family, but again that's just me, and perhaps it's neither here nor there in all of this. However, a number of years back, our father died in a hit-and-run accident downtown that was never solved. Shortly after that, Tariq, who was already involved in my father's development company, bought whatever he didn't already own of the company out of my father's estate, and the rest is history. He changed the name of the company to that AmeriPAK thing that is now his corporate end-all-to-be-all, and he was off to the races. I detest the guy, but I will have to admit he does have a Midas touch when it comes to business."

"So, are you saying that your sister's marital problems started when he took over your father's business?" Erickson asked, continuing to delve into Nasir's personal situation.

"No, not exactly at that time. I think the business thing

was certainly part of their problems, but not all of it."
Maureen sighed. "Their marriage really began to fall apart
after my sister's sons were born. Wouldn't you say,
Margaret?"

Sister Margaret nodded in agreement, adding
comment for the first time. "Yes, I would have to agree, and I
really don't know why that would be. You would think the
advent of those boys would have just brought Melissa and
Tariq closer together. Faoud and Hassan are absolutely
fabulous young men. Maureen and I love them dearly. I am
saddened somewhat that they are being raised Muslim, but I
am praying about and working on that." Sister Margaret
closed her eyes for a second before continuing. "You see
after the boys were born, Tariq began to rigidly control their
upbringing. They were sent to special Islamic schools here in
Chicago, and Melissa has always had to have Tariq's
permission regarding nearly everything they do. Our sister
loves those boys, and they adore her, but she is allowed little
say on much of anything in their lives. They are allowed, for
example, to do very little with our side of the family. They just
got back from an annual skiing trip out West over
Thanksgiving with our family that Tariq for some reason or
another does allow them to go on each year, and they're
planning to go back sometime after Christmas for a few
days, but beyond that, they're not allowed to do very much
with we Hardestys."

"So, what you're saying is the situation with your
nephews may be the primary source of discord in your
sister's marriage?" Agent Seilor asked, figuring he would
give his partner a chance to drink his coffee before it went
cold.

"Yes, the situation with the boys is probably the main
source of the problem, but it's certainly not the only one."

"Hmm, what other problems have you observed?"

"Well, please don't get this wrong, me being a nun and
all, but I would have to say that the religious differences

between my sister and brother-in-law have not really helped things in their marriage."

"In what way?" Seilor asked.

"Well, Melissa was, just like us, raised a strict Catholic, and she remains so to this day. There is hardly a day she doesn't head over to the church to pray. In the case of Tariq, it is much the same way for him in his religion. When they first got married, he wasn't really all that strict a Muslim, but after the boys were born, he began to more rigidly adhere to the rather structured tenets of his faith, pulling the boys right along with him. Then slowly but surely, he really went somewhat off the deep end with it."

"How's that?" Erickson questioned.

"Well, over the course of the last several years he has become quite defensive about his faith, and all. Melissa said that he would rant and rave about devious, conniving Christians whenever any TV or newspaper article criticized Muslims in any way, claiming people in this country were nothing better than modern-day 'Crusaders', hearkening I guess back to a not so pretty a time in the history of our church. He's also become extremely devout in his faith, things like praying five times a day and all that. He's even built this really opulent worship room in the building at his place of business. We haven't seen it, but I guess it is really something. He is also very involved with a number of Muslim groups and in a lot of activities at that big mosque downtown. What's it called, Maureen? Islamic Institute of Chicago or something like that. He's really like two people. He has this public persona that works for him when he's dealing with the business or public sectors; and then he has this private, Muslim side to him that he uses when he's dealing with people within his faith and so on; and it's not all that pleasant, at least not in our way of looking at it."

"Would you say he has become fanatical in his religious activities?" Agent Seilor questioned.

"No, no, I wouldn't say fanatic. I would describe it

more as overly devout, perhaps. His religion has simply become one of the prime motivators in his life. Take, for instance, that Hajj thing, the annual pilgrimage that Muslims are apparently required to make to Mecca at least once during their lives. For the past four years, Tariq has gone every time. This year he plans to go again and take the boys with him. We're scared to death about that. You know there are literally millions of Muslims that go to that thing, and it isn't rare that people even die when they're there, due I understand to problems with the crowds and all."

"Yes, we're both familiar with the Hajj, Sister," Seilor commented. "Please, continue."

"Well, I guess we're just afraid for the boys. And then there's some of the really strange things Tariq does from time-to-time."

"What things?" Asked Erickson.

"Tell them, Margaret, tell them about the shots Tariq had the boys get yesterday." Maureen urged her sister. "Tell me that isn't strange if you don't mind."

"What's she talking about, Sister?"

"Oh, Melissa just told us this morning that before he left for Europe this past weekend on business, Tariq instructed her to take the boys to his doctor yesterday for an appointment he had apparently made for them. I guess he wanted the boys to get a bunch of vaccinations against every imaginable disease under the sun. He said they needed it for when they accompany him on trips around the world, such as this Hajj thing. Well, Melissa dutifully did what he asked, and she says they've been really under the weather since, a reaction to some of the shots she suspects. We just think that kind of thing is strange."

"Do you know what may have prompted him to do this?"

"We have no idea whatsoever. Why, even if they go with him on that Hajj thing, Saudi Arabia is hardly the kind of Third World country where the boys would get all sorts of diseases and so forth. Why their hotels and restaurants over there rival the best of anything you would find here in Chicago, and that brother-in-law of ours won't be staying in any hut. We're more worried about some nutty suicide bomber or a bunch of kidnappers."

Seilor and Erickson gave each other a sideways glance before continuing the conversation. "That is perhaps a little different. Would you know, for example, what this doctor vaccinated them for?" Seilor asked.

"Well, not really everything, but Melissa did mention a couple of things that the doctor gave them shots for that certainly seemed strange to us." Sister Margaret answered.

"What were those?" Seilor questioned.

"Well, for example, one thing was Smallpox," answered Sister Margaret. "I thought nobody was vaccinated for that anymore. They quit doing that when we were young girls to my recollection. I was reading an article on that sometime back. Hasn't that basically been eradicated around the world? Have you people heard of any outbreaks of that anywhere?"

"No, you're correct, we haven't," answered Erickson.

"Well, we haven't either, and we rather doubt the boys would encounter such a thing in Saudi Arabia, much less anywhere else in the world. The boys have been really sick. Melissa told us they both stayed at home this morning, high fevers and all. She may be taking them back to the doctor. Says she thinks it's perhaps a reaction to the shots they received."

"Now if you ask us, that whole thing is strange. Wouldn't you two agree?" Maureen asked. "Can't you see why we think the guy's a weirdo?"

"You said that. I didn't, Maureen." Sister Margaret remained apologetic.

"Well, I'm sorry, Margaret, I think the guy's weird. What really gets me too, is that our sister seems powerless anymore to stand up to Tariq. Whatever he asks or instructs,

440

she does"

"Maureen, go easy here. You know that Melissa tries to go along to get along for the boys and all." Sister Margaret patted her sister's arm in an effort to calm her down.

"Yeah, I know," Maureen responded. "But that's just because I think she's afraid that Tariq will try to take the boys away from her. He treats her like dirt anymore. Kind of like you hear those Muslim guys treat their women, and all."

"Come on, Maureen, you know not all Muslim men are like that with their wives. Many, I am sure, are very loving."

"Perhaps, but I guess I would have to say my experience with Muslim men, if Tariq is any example, isn't all that reassuring in that regard. Next thing you know, he'll be insisting she wear one of those hijab thingies on her head."

"Oh, Maureen!" The thoroughly exasperated nun smiled and shook her head in an effort to break the tension as she nervously refilled the agents' coffee mugs a third time. "Well, gentlemen, there you have it. You probably got more of an earful than you really wanted from us, but suffice it to say, things aren't all that easy for our sister in her marriage. Our brother-in-law, Tariq, is a brilliant, successful businessman, but he is apparently very difficult for our sister to live with. I realize there are two sides to everything, but she has, we think, tried very hard to make a go of things with him. I pray for her daily."

"Well, we certainly do thank you for both your time and candor, Sister," said Agent Erickson, speaking for both he and his partner. "Look, you ladies have been most helpful. I think you've given us a fairly good picture of how things are in Mr. Nasir's personal life, and we thank you for that. I think we have enough for now. If we could perhaps reserve the right to visit with you both sometime again if we feel the need to do so, we will get out of your hair for now and let you both go on with your day."

"Can you tell us what this is all about before you go?" Maureen queried the agents. "I would like to know what that brother-in-law of ours has done if you don't mind."

"Well, I am sorry, but I'm afraid we can't comment on that. We'll just say that it's a routine matter, and once again, we would prefer that you keep this conversation strictly between you and us at this time, in particular where your sister is concerned. If any of this were to get back to her husband, it would be, shall we say, less than constructive. Would it be possible you could give us some assurances in that regard?" Erickson asked.

"Absolutely, Agent Erickson, you have our word on that. Don't they, Maureen?" Sister Margaret said, cocking her head in the direction of her sister.

"Yes," sighed Maureen Hardesty. "Yes, they do!"

Seilor and Erickson were in a rush to leave. Melissa Nasir's two sisters had given them much more usable information than they had anticipated. *One never knows what you are going to find, and from where*, thought Erickson as he dialed his cell phone to report their findings to their boss, Merritt Daimler. *That thing about the vaccinations for Nasir's sons is eerily foreboding considering what we're working on. It's possible Nasir is either involved in this situation we're chasing all over the country now, or at least may have some information.* Seilor hurriedly wove the car through downtown traffic in an effort to get he and Erickson back to FBI headquarters as quickly as possible. What they had just gotten by way of information from the two ladies was potentially hot stuff.

◊◊◊◊

IT HAD been a long night for Sammy. It was now 12:00 noon on Wednesday, the day prior to Tariq Nasir's return, and he had been undergoing continuous questioning at the Chicago field office of the FBI since 10:00 a.m. the previous day. He had gone there of his own volition to ostensibly meet with FBI agents for the purpose of discussing anti-money laundering activities and other related matters at Global United. The meeting had been agreed to the day before following a meeting at the bank with OCC examiners. In spite of horrible misgivings Sammy had concluded a voluntary sit-down would demonstrate good faith and cooperation. He had calculated any reluctance to do so might engender suspicions that could be ill-afforded at this very inopportune time. Too much was afoot relative to impending operations of the al-Sahaba brotherhood.

When Sammy arrived at FBI headquarters in the Dirksen Building the day before, he was met at the door by three serious looking agents—none of whom he had previously met. He was then immediately taken to a stark-looking, dimly lit, soundproof room somewhere within the bowels of the facility. It didn't take much more than about fifteen minutes of questioning for it to dawn on Sammy that he might well be realizing his worst nightmare, considering the double life he had been leading for many years now as both a banking professional and a terrorist operative. This was no discussion. It was an interrogation.

Sammy had been trained to handle such a grilling if it ever occurred, but that training had been many years previous, long before he had come to the United States. He had always told himself that he could handle such a situation if it came to be, but now he wasn't so sure. Sammy had grown soft in his intervening years as a banker, having become accustomed to the easy living in this country that he and his fellow Jihadists so regularly derided.

In the beginning, no less than nine people were participating in the questioning. Augmenting the group and taking the lead in the questioning were five representatives from the FBI's High Value Detainee Interrogation Group. Formed in 2009, the HIG was an organization specially trained and deployed in situations where detainees were identified as possibly having access to information with the greatest potential of preventing terrorist attacks against the United States and its allies. Utilizing a rapport-building, information-gathering approach, the group possessed an extremely high success rate in gathering useful intelligence in situations such as the one currently facing the FBI's Chicago District Office.

Based upon what was being asked and how they were going about it, Sammy suspected his questioners weren't all with the FBI. Some of those present handled themselves differently and hadn't identified themselves as part of the FBI contingent. After about only ten minutes or so of feigned pleasantries at the start of the ordeal, the interrogation began to increase in intensity. Once the agents really got into it, heated questions were directed at Sammy by first one agent and then another in an ever-increasing crescendo. "Why would he have exempted Tariq Nasir's companies from suspicious activity reporting when the type of business they were transacting was completely unusual for operations of that sort? What did he know about the use of all of that cash by AmeriPAK, Inc., and all of its subsidiaries? What did he know about Nasir's organization, his people and his use of offshore accounts? How close was he to Tariq Nasir? What did he know about the Islamic Institute of Chicago where they knew he attended, or Worldwide Islamic Charities? Did he know this person or that person, mostly men with either Asian or Middle Eastern names?" The questions were rapid fire and non-stop, and there was never any less than four to five agents in the room at all times, with participants rotating every couple of hours. The agents fed him when he asked for it, and frequently offered him coffee or soft drinks, but the questioning was relentless and rapid-fire. Sammy was becoming extremely tired.

As truth would have it, Sammy had for some time now been having serious second thoughts about his terrorist involvements, and the meeting he had attended of al-Sahaba cell leaders at the Janitorial Supply warehouse some days before this ordeal had done nothing to help. When the man he knew as Ismail Hamadi had described for the group in graphic detail what would happen to those who would be exposed to the deadly Smallpox virus the group was planning to soon release, it had sickened Sammy greatly. He hadn't been able to sleep throughout the night since.

Generally, Sammy had a great deal of disdain for Americans, and for that matter, most of their allies around the world. Their so-called War on Terror stood in the way of global Islamic dominance, the ultimate goal of Sammy and all of his brothers. Yet, in spite of how much he tried to avoid it, some of these people had become his friends. It was hard to envision any of them dying the horrible death that Sammy knew could befall any one of them, were they one of the many potentially unlucky people who happened to contract the insidious disease about to be loosed upon their country and beyond. And then there were the children and the infirm. A similar fate to the innocent and the helpless was ghastly to think about. His ability to compartmentalize in the name of Jihad would be tested to the extreme.

For several hours Sammy held his ground with the interrogators. After it appeared they had asked him all of the questions they could think of more times than he could count regarding Tariq Nasir, Nasir's companies and associates, and his own involvement at Global United, Sammy tried out of desperation to go on the offensive. He demanded to know why he was being held and questioned so. "I know my rights!" He claimed. "If there is something illegal you think I have done, then charge me. Otherwise, let me go, or let me have an attorney. I am done with this. I am an American citizen, and I have my rights!"

When that outbreak occurred, the interrogation came to a temporary halt. All of the interrogators departed the room, leaving Sammy alone for several long, blissfully quiet minutes. Thinking that he had actually accomplished something toward ending the ordeal, he laid his head in his arms on the table in front of him and tried to rest his eyes. This respite was short lived, however. He had no sooner closed his eyes, than the room again filled with agents.

"Good afternoon, Mr. al-Dajani, how goes it in here with all of these wonderful people?" Sammy looked up to see Merritt Daimler, the tall, rangy, silver-haired gentleman who had invited him to this inquisition the day before, enter the room. This was actually the first time Sammy had seen Daimler since he arrived at the offices of the FBI. Daimler was followed into the room by the whole pack of agents that had taken turns bedeviling Sammy for the last some eighteen to twenty hours. "I understand, Mr. al-Dajani that you have complained about the need for an attorney. Is that correct?"

""Yes, it is Mr. Daimler, numerous times to be exact. If you were in my shoes, you would want an attorney too. I don't know why I am being treated this way. I came here in good faith, based upon our agreement yesterday at the bank, and since I arrived, I have been grilled like a criminal or terrorist or some such thing. I am done with all this. I want an attorney."

"Well, perhaps we may eventually be able to accommodate you in that regard, but first you and I need to talk a bit.'

"About what, sir?" Sammy asked defiantly. "I have told your people all that I know about Mr. Nasir and his relationship with Global United. I now painfully realize that some of my management and decision-making at the bank with respect to Mr. Nasir's personal and business accounts may have been misguided, and I further know that I will have to answer for that with both Global United management and banking regulators. Yet, as I have said again and again for far too many hours now, that does not rise to the level of the treatment I have been receiving here over the last near twenty-four hours. Either charge me with something or turn me loose. I know nothing more."

"Perhaps that may be, but let me tell what we know, Mr. al-Dajani, and then we will go from there," Daimler spoke authoritatively as he removed his coat and sat down across the table from Sammy. "The first thing I know is that under the U.S.A Freedom Act of 2015 and the National Defense Authorization Act, if the Attorney General of the United States, for whom I work, suspects that you as even a citizen of this country are involved in terrorist activities or might in any way be a potential threat to the security of this country, we have the ability to detain you without charges for up to seven days. If during that time we make a positive determination along any of those lines, I can extend that time to six months with possibility for further extensions beyond that if need be. In a nutshell, please understand there would be no Writ of Habeas Corpus that would apply in such a situation."

In truth, FBI and HIG interrogators were concerned about questioning Sammy beyond a seventy-two hour window of time without allowing him the protection of Miranda. Daimler was to some degree running a bluff. They would need to make headway with Sammy sometime soon.

Sammy felt his stomach sink. He had read the stories about how individuals suspected of terrorist activities were being held for months and even years on end by the U.S. military without formal charges being brought against them or any provision of legal counsel. Secretly, he doubted his ability to withstand prolonged questioning at the hands of these American agents. He had much to tell if they were successful. He was scared. It hadn't even been twenty-four hours since he arrived at FBI headquarters, and he was already having difficulty contending with the questioning. *What will it be like if this is kept up for days on end?* he asked himself. *How long can I take this? Worse yet, what if I say nothing and Ismail Hamadi and my brothers in al-Sahaba find out about me being taken into custody, detained and questioned for a prolonged period? Will they even believe that I've said nothing?* Sammy knew there was too much at stake relative to the attack that was being planned.

He had seen Hamadi and his cohorts operate. When it came to the mission at hand, anyone was considered expendable if they were even the slightest threat to the security of the plan. What about Imad Fayiz Mufassa or old man Trotter? They represented only a modicum of perceived threat to the plan, and yet Hamadi ordered their elimination without even the slightest bit of hesitation. That thought kept running through Sammy's mind as he listened to Daimler. *Am I already at the point of no return?*

"Then further, there is our concern regarding your personal involvement with your boss, Mr. Nasir." Daimler continued. "We are still investigating the matter yet, but we are fast developing the opinion, based upon information we have gleaned thus far, that Mr. Nasir may well be involved in a multitude of financial activities, both domestic and international, that could be both highly illegal and perhaps a threat in many respects to the security of the United States of America. In that regard, we suspect in looking closely at your handling of his personal and business relationships within the bank—a bank I might add, where he owns controlling interest—that you may have knowingly enabled these activities for he and his people. As you may or may not be aware, our nation is currently on high alert regarding certain imminent threats of terrorist attack, and we wonder whether there might not be some connection between those threats and some of Mr. Nasir's business activities. If we turn out to be wrong about either you or Mr. Nasir, you both will have our profound apologies for any difficulties we put you through, but we cannot afford to take a chance. We think we are facing some serious threats. In summary, young man, I would suggest you relax. You're going to be with us for a while."

◊◊◊◊

"MR. HART, it's a Mr. Daimler calling with the FBI here in Chicago. He's on line one. Do you want to take the call?"

"Sure, Myrna put him through. Merritt and I are old

friends. I was expecting his call." Logan wasn't being completely truthful with Myrna. He hadn't been expecting Daimler's call, but he didn't want her to know that. She was a pretty perceptive individual, however, and was aware that there was a lot still going on at the bank with the OCC and FBI. He knew she might surmise the call was related but had felt it better to tell her Daimler was an old friend. It was a true statement, and there was no need for her to know any more than that.

"Hi, Merritt, how'd the meeting with Sammy al-Dajani go yesterday? Must have been fairly taxing on him. I understand the guy didn't show up for work this morning."

"That's exactly why I'm calling, pal," Daimler answered. "It was indeed a little rough on him, and I guess you might say it remains so. We've still got the guy here."

"The heck you say!" Logan sounded surprised. "Whew, what's going on with Sammy?"

"I can't go into a lot of detail at this time, fella, but perhaps I'll be able to fill you in soon. In the meantime, however, we need some more of your help on this."

"What kind of help?"

"Well, we're going to be holding your Mr. al-Dajani for a while. We think he knows a lot more than he has told us, and we need more time on that without alarming anyone. That's where you come in, guy."

"What do you want me to do?"

"Well, we need for you to run some interference for us. We don't need any of this investigation, or the fact that we're holding al-Dajani to get out yet. Is there any way you might cover for us with your people at the bank in some way? Uh, maybe tell them that al-Dajani was called away or something? We need some time."

"I suppose I could. I guess I could call some of his staff and people in HR, and tell them that he contacted me and was called away suddenly on family business, or some such thing. Has he done something, Merritt? Is he in trouble?"

"Well, like I said, I really can't say much right now, Logan, but suffice it to say, we think your Mr. al-Dajani has at minimum been involved in some activities with Mr. Nasir that demand some explanation. We're going to keep him until we know more. Maybe we can visit about the situation sometime later. We'll probably have one of our online meetings in the next couple of days. In the meantime, thanks for helping us out on this, old friend. I know we're really putting you in the middle of some strange goings-on here."

"Yeah, if nothing comes of your interrogation of al-Dajani, and he returns to work and debunks the trumped-up story I'm about to tell, there'll be the dickens to pay. No problem though, with all you say may be about to take place, my personal situation seems of little importance. In for a penny—in for a pound! I'm perfectly willing to help."

CHAPTER THIRTY-TWO

WHEN SAMMY al-Dajani failed to show up for his weekly, noon yellow cab meeting with Ahmed Khalid on the second Wednesday in December, Khalid began to worry. *This isn't at all like al-Dajani*, thought Khalid. *He's too nervous and apprehensive about everything that's about to take place to miss his meetings with me.*

After waiting twenty-four hours, and hearing nothing from Sammy and placing numerous calls to his personal number, Khalid decided to violate one of his own strict rules of staying away from either an operative's place of business or home, by telephoning Global United and asking for him. Yet, it was imperative to find out whatever he could about Sammy's whereabouts.

When Sammy's staff reported him as being away from the bank for a few days on family business, Khalid's stomach sunk. He was fully aware that Sammy had no family in the United States, and at this stage in the execution of al-Sahaba's plan of attack, Khalid knew there was no way that he would have taken the chance at being gone, particularly without letting Khalid know. Something had to be wrong.

"Would there be anyone, please, that might be able to tell me where I could reach Mr. al-Dajani? It is imperative that I get in touch with him." Khalid was talking with Theresa Maynard, assistant vice president of operations, to whom his call had first been referred.

"No, sir, I am afraid I don't know where Mr. al-Dajani

can be reached." Ms. Maynard replied. "Perhaps Mr. Hart, the bank's Executive Vice President might know. I believe it was he that sent the memo around informing all of us that Mr. al-Dajani was going to be out of the bank for a while. Apparently, Mr. al-Dajani contacted him when he called in on the matter. I was quite frankly surprised Mr. al-Dajani didn't call me too, but then that is sometimes how he is. Oh, and as I think of it, one other person who might have some information on Mr. al-Dajani's whereabouts could be Mr. Haifa in the bank's International Department. He might know something. He and Mr. al-Dajani are fairly good friends, I think."

"Thank you, could you perhaps transfer me to this Mr. Haifa first?"

"Yes, sir, I'll try to do just that right now. If I should lose your call for any reason, and you need to call back, Mr. Haifa's extension is 4378."

Khalid figured he would start first with this Mr. Haifa the lady was referring to. Haifa's name suggested that they might have something in common. "Assalamu Alaikum, Mr. Haifa. My name is Tammam Basharra, a close friend, and customer of Mr. Saud al-Dajani's." Khalid was always careful to use a second alias other than Hamadi whenever he was on any fishing expeditions like the one that prompted this call. "I phoned the bank this afternoon, looking for him regarding some important business he was trying to help me with, and they informed me that he is gone and will be out for a few days. I have an urgent need to talk with him. Is there any possibility that you might be able to help me with his whereabouts?"

"And peace be upon you as well, Mr. Basharra. No, sir, regretfully I know very little about the purpose of Mr. al-Dajani's absence, or where he may be right now. I guess when he called in to tell us here at the bank that he would be out, he must have spoken directly with Mr. Hart, the bank's Executive Vice President. Mr. Hart is the person that sent

around the memo regarding Mr. al-Dajani's absence. I
believe the memo mentioned a family emergency of some
kind, but beyond that, I know very little. I am sorry I can't
help you more. If your situation is some kind of emergency,
and you don't mind telling me what it is, perhaps I could help
with the matter or get you to someone else that can."

The name Logan Hart was not new to Khalid. Early on
after the death of the old bank regulator, Paul Trotter,
Sammy had informed him that he felt this Mr. Hart might be
working with the OCC to establish a connection between the
old bureaucrat's death and the work he was doing at the
bank. Khalid had assigned one of his operatives to follow the
banker for a time but had called him off when the effort failed
to be productive.

"No, Mr. Haifa, I am afraid that Mr. al-Dajani is really
the only person that can help me with this situation. What
about this Mr. Hart? Could you perhaps transfer me to him? I
really need to get in contact with Mr. al-Dajani if at all
possible."

"Certainly, I'll transfer your call to his assistant, Ms.
Brock. I am sure she can get you in touch with Mr. Hart. He
should be here now. His extension is 4301 for your
reference."

◊◊◊◊

"MR. HART'S office, Myrna Brock speaking. How may I help
you?"

"Myrna, this is Raj Haifa over in International Banking
speaking. I have a guy by the name of Basharra, a Mr.
Tammam Basharra, that apparently had some very important
business pending with Sammy al-Dajani, and he's quite
anxious to get hold of him. He claims it's something that
can't wait until Sammy gets back. He apparently asked to be
transferred to me, but I told him that I was in a totally

453

different area of the bank and had no information regarding Sammy's whereabouts. I thought perhaps Mr. Hart might be able to help him since it was he who sent around the memo about Sammy's absence. Would Mr. Hart be available to speak with this Mr. Basharra at this time? I have him on hold right now."

"Certainly, put him through, Mr. Haifa." Myrna was becoming concerned. There were a lot of strange things going on within the bank in recent days. The OCC now seemed to be almost permanently ensconced at the bank, the FBI was trotting in and out supposedly still investigating the Trotter murder, special meetings of directors were being convened, and now people were absent from the bank with little explanation. Myrna liked working, but not in the midst of turmoil. She made a mental note to speak confidentially with Mr. Hart when she had the chance. If she didn't like the answers she got to her questions, then perhaps it might be time to accelerate her already much-delayed retirement. At her age, she didn't need all of the excitement.

"Mr. Hart, I have a Mr. Basharra on line one, he is apparently trying to get in touch with Mr. al-Dajani, and Mr. Haifa directed him to you. May I put him through?"

"Yes, Myrna, go right ahead. I don't know much about Mr. al-Dajani's absence, but I will try to do what I can to help." Logan wondered just how long it might be before the FBI released Sammy, if at all. There would be some explaining to do within the bank when that occurred. He guessed he would just have to handle that in the best way he knew how when that time arrived. "Logan Hart speaking. How may I help you?"

"Mr. Hart, my name is Tammam Basharra. I have been talking with a number of people now at your bank in an effort to get in touch with Mr. Saud a-Dajani. Mr. al-Dajani was working on some very important financial matters for me last week, and I hadn't heard back from him about it. So, I called your bank trying to reach him. Your staff told me that you might be able to help me get in touch with him."

"Well, I'm very sorry, Mr. Basharra, but I really don't believe I can. Mr. al-Dajani wasn't forthcoming with much information when I talked with him. He just simply said that he was going to be away from the bank for a while to take care of some emergency in his family. I simply circulated a memo to the staff to let them know that he was going to be gone. Is this something that I could perhaps help you with, sir?"

"No, Mr. Hart, this matter is something very personal, having to do with some family matters of my own in Egypt. Because of the sensitivity of the situation, Mr. al-Dajani as a Muslim was uniquely qualified to help me, and I really don't want to involve anyone else at this time. It is imperative that I get in touch with him. Do you think he might be calling in?"

"That's possible, sir." Something about this Basharra seemed strange. Logan thought he would lead him on a bit. "You know, Mr. Basharra, we do have a number of other very capable Muslim staff members here at the bank—some who even work for Mr. Al-Dajani—who might be able to help you, even Mr. Haifa you spoke with earlier. He's the head of our International Banking area, as he may have told you. He's particularly well backgrounded in matters such as yours. Any possibility you could perhaps speak with either him again or one of Mr. al-Dajani's subordinates in his absence?"

"No, no Mr. Hart, Mr. al-Dajani was specially equipped to handle my particular situation, and I would also prefer not having to start all over again on the matter if I can avoid it."

"As you wish, Mr. Basharra. Once again, I really don't know if Mr. al-Dajani will be calling in or not, but if he does, do you want to give me a number where you can be reached, perhaps a cell phone number or something? We could have him get in touch with you if he calls in."

"No, Mr. Hart, I don't have a cell phone, and I will be in and out of the city during the next few days. So, he won't be able to reach me. I will have to call back. Might I take the liberty of calling you again later to see if you have heard anything from him?"

"You certainly may. I'm sorry I can't be of more help to you at this time."

"Me too, this is rather urgent. Thank you, for your time, however."

Both men sensed something not quite right with the conversation they had just had with each other. Each made mental notes to follow up on the matter in different ways. Logan made a call to Merritt Daimler and informed him about the situation immediately after he hung up from Khalid, and Khalid made a decision of his own to find out more about this banker named Hart. Nothing this Hart said sounded anything like what al-Dajani would have done at this very sensitive time. Something was wrong, and Khalid had to find out what it was. There was too much at stake. If there was any chance that the plan was going to be compromised in any way, al-Sahaba would need to move quickly. The attack date of December 24th would need to be moved up if there was a problem.

◊◊◊◊

THE MEETING that Raleigh Sutphen from Homeland Security asked for that same Wednesday in the Chicago offices of the FBI was the manifestation of one of his worst nightmares since being assigned to the Information Analysis and Infrastructure Protection division at DHS. It was the IAIP's responsibility within DHS to identify and assess a broad range of intelligence information concerning threats to the homeland, to issue timely warnings, and to take appropriate preventive and protective action in case of an impending attack. As the IAIP's lead investigator in Chicago, it was Sutphen's opinion that indications of a potential bio-weapon attack in that city were strong enough now, that it was time for some serious contingency planning.

Attending the session at Sutphen's request were representatives of numerous agencies of the government. Present were qualified response team members from the FBI and their HIG, the National Security Council to the President, the Center for Disease Control, U.S. Customs, the DHS's Border and Transportation Security division, and State of Illinois and City of Chicago law enforcement and health-related agencies. It wasn't the only time these individuals had been together before, but in previous instances the meetings were part and parcel of pre-response training exercises, which were preceded by plenty of advance notice to all participants. This was the first time that this high-powered bunch of first responders had been asked to drop what they were doing and come immediately to an important meeting. They all knew something serious must be happening.

"I think we have everyone here now, folks. Let me say thank you to all of you for dropping all of the very important things I am sure each of you was involved in to make this meeting. This get-together is of the utmost importance to national security, or I can assure you we would have given all of you much more advance notice. Let me begin by first saying that no information regarding anything we are going to discuss here this morning can leave this room except through official channels as determined by individuals at the highest levels of DHS. This goes for everyone in the room. From this moment on, any breach of this restriction could hold devastating results for the entire country. Am I clearly understood in that regard? If there are any questions about that, please ask them now."

No one responded, and looking around the room, Sutphen saw no questioning looks on anyone's face. Waiting for what seemed an interminable length of time for a response, he continued. "Fine, with that I am deeply troubled to have to inform you all that our intelligence and law enforcement sources are in possession of extremely credible evidence that this country, and more specifically this City, may be the intended target of an attack with a biological weapon of mass destruction. And let me assure you folks, this situation is not a training exercise. Intelligence suggests this attack is imminent."

The room sat in stunned silence, until Dr. Marian Elliott, head of the Chicago office of the CDC spoke. "Do you have any specifics at all as to what kind of biological weapon may be intended for use?"

"Yes, I do Marian, and it scares me even answering." He paused again for a moment, sighing. He could see the entire room was collectively holding its breath. "However, our intelligence sources tell us that it looks extremely likely some terrorist group—perhaps loosely affiliated with al-Qaeda—may have gotten hold of a supply of weapons-grade Variola Major, Smallpox if you will, folks."

Faces drained of color. "Holy crap! Are you absolutely sure of this, Raleigh?" asked Newton Lewis, the young NSC representative hurriedly sent to Chicago for the meeting. "Your office had informed us sometime ago that there was potential this situation existed, but it hadn't yet been confirmed. Are you now telling us it has been confirmed?"

"No, I didn't say 'confirmed', I said it was 'extremely likely', but whatever the case, we're going to treat it like it has been confirmed. We are in possession of very credible evidence that this city, this country, may be the intended target of an attack with a biological WMD, and those indications are strong enough that we think it warrants contingency planning, planning that is going on right at this moment, not just here but in several places around the country as we speak," Sutphen answered.

"Where did you get this information?" asked Lewis.

"Well, you haven't been part of our previous discussions on these matters, Newton, but from the Russians."

"You don't say! I wouldn't think they're particularly high on our list of dependable intelligence sources. Do we think we can trust the information they've provided us on this? Knowing all of the nonsense we've been going through regarding them over the last few years, I wouldn't put it past them to be trying to put one over on us. Slime-balls!"

"Look, I understand your reaction, Newton, but in this particular situation, we are inclined to trust them. Quite frankly, we really have no choice. Can you imagine what would happen if we were to blow them off, and they turned out to be correct."

"Yes, but still, based on experience with those yard birds, you know."

"Well, in this case, they are admitting the pathogens to their knowledge originated from there, and there is no way they would admit that if there wasn't a verifiable threat. They actually feel very strongly they may also be a target. In their case a Chechen-related threat. So, they apparently felt it was in their best interest to cooperate on this, and we're taking them up on it."

"And what are their sources," asked Lewis?

"Well, they claim to have irrefutable evidence the Russian Mafiya was in possession of some weapons grade Variola pathogens, and that they sold those materials to an Islamic terrorist organization. Word has it, this yet unknown terrorist organization—believed to be an offshoot of al-Qaeda—was supposed to make progress payments at different stages along the route these materials took to their destination, and sources within the Russian mob report that all of that money has been received."

"Meaning in other words that the pathogens have reached their destination?" Lewis asked for clarification.

"Yes, that would seem to be correct, and the Russians claim that these materials were shipped via ocean vessel to the United States sometime during the last sixty days. Perhaps you might want to comment on that, Vince? Folks, for anyone who doesn't know him, let me introduce Vincent Magnusson of the U.S. Customs Service here in Chicago."

"Sure, Raleigh! I certainly wish I knew more, but I'm glad to at least comment on what I do know. When we received information regarding this situation from our intelligence sources around the end of last month, we ratcheted up our scrutiny of all vessels coming into our ports out of Russia during the period cited, Chicago was one of those locations. Using every technology at our disposal, we have looked as closely as we could at all shipments, but thus far we have come up with nothing, I am sorry to say. Something of this type could be inside just about any type or size container. Thus far, we're at a loss."

"Well, that's just great!" Lewis of the NSC sounded exasperated. "With no more information than that, what makes you think that the U.S., or for that matter Chicago, may be the destination of this weapon?"

"That's where we hope some of the other pieces of information we've been able to gather may help us. Lacking any success in trying to interdict the shipment itself, we have concentrated since we heard about this, on what many like to refer to as the Money Trail." Sutphen responded. "Teams of bankers and people from several agencies of the government, Departments of Justice and Treasury, etc., have been working feverishly since Russian intelligence contacted us to determine where those monies may have originated from and traveled to with respect to this situation. In so doing, they have informed us that some sort of alternative remittance system was the source of the money received by the Russian Mafiya for this weapon, and their best estimate to date is that at least some of this money may have originated here in the Chicago area with respect to the transaction. Hence, our feeling that Chicago might be one of the targets."

"And again, you say there have been Russian ships and other means of transportation and shipping coming or going in the Chicago area during this time, where this weapon could have been on board?" Lewis asked.

"Yes, indeed there have," Magnusson answered.

"And?" Lewis pressed with a tone of sarcasm.

"Well, and, that's about all we have to report about that at this time, but in total all of this information has been enough to prompt convening regional JTTF response planning meetings similar to this one here in Chicago and in major cities all over the country today—but a lot of emphasis is being placed on this one. We think Chicago might easily be the epicenter of any attack that might take place." Sutphen could see he had everyone's rapt attention.

"What about our preparedness, Dr. Elliott?" Magnusson asked. "How ready are the CDC and all of our health responders in this area for a situation like this?"

"Oh, great day, first let's all pray this turns out to be a false alarm," responded the CDC representative, "but if it is not, I do think the CDC is as prepared as we can be. Since 9/11, preparing for a bio-chemical weapons attack has been a top priority for our agency, but the recent COVID-19 pandemic was a real wakeup call. That was admittedly a natural disaster, but it caused us to game-play various scenarios ad infinitum clear across the country, involving every essential health agency and first responder group necessary to react to an attack of this sort; and believe me, an attack using Smallpox pathogens as a weapon has been front and center. If anything like this had occurred plus/minus twenty years ago, say right after 9/11, it would have been a nightmare. Now, however, we're a lot better prepared than we were then."

"In what ways?" Lewis asked.

"Well, for one thing, right after 9/11, we had only a limited number of dosages of Smallpox Vaccine," answered Dr. Elliott, "but now after a concentrated effort to increase supplies during the years intervening, we literally have enough to vaccinate everyone in the country against the disease, if need be. Targeted vaccinations within the 'ring of exposure' to each identified case of an outbreak would be the highest and best preference, but circumstances of exposure may not allow for that. More indiscriminate, wholesale inoculation of the general public may be necessitated. This could exacerbate the occurrence of post-vaccination complications amongst certain groups of the public at greater risk. If that is the case, then we now also have a couple of newly developed products, such as Vaccinia Immune Globulin available for use in sufficient quantities. A number of years ago, VIG was somewhat experimental, and supplies were limited. That has since been remedied."

"Wouldn't there be a goodly portion of the public that would still be immune from childhood vaccinations, etc.?" FBI Special Agent Merritt Daimler asked, finally weighing in on the matter. "There are a number of people here in this room, me for one, who had vaccinations when we were kids. When the government had that program recently to vaccinate first responders, I opted out because of that."

"You should have read the materials you received on that program a little more clearly at the time, Merritt. I really don't think that will be of much help to a lot of people like you anymore." Dr. Elliott answered.

"And why not?"

"Well, as many of the health industry types in this room will tell you, most people in this country under the age of say about forty-five or so probably were never vaccinated. Sometime around the early 70's, the World Health Organization declared Smallpox a disease that had been officially eradicated as a threat worldwide. We stopped giving children vaccinations in this country sometime in the early 70's, and then to further complicate matters, it is also pretty much the consensus that any immunities you or I would have had as a result of vaccinations we might have received when we were children, would have gone by the way a number of years ago. You should go get your vaccination just as soon as you can, Merritt. We don't need first-responders like you laid up in a situation like this. By the time symptoms are identified, it's often too late for the vaccine in most cases."

"We'd lose control that fast?"

"Yes, real fast. Smallpox has a typical mortality rate of thirty percent or more, and with the strength of the stuff the Soviets probably developed and may have lost into the hands of these terrorists, it will no doubt be much, much higher."

"With that folks, we've got a lot of sharp people gathered in this room today. I hope everyone came prepared to take notes and offer ideas." Sutphen admonished the group. "Like I said, there are groups just like ours meeting all over the country today, and planning for the worst. Dr. Elliott, I am going to give you the floor so that we can get this session going. If we are unable to locate these monsters before they strike, we're going to have to know what to do when. Doctor?"

CHAPTER THIRTY-THREE

ABDULLAH AMAR and Bashir Sharif were Syrian born veterans of several terrorist operations throughout the Middle East and Europe by the time they were in their mid-twenties. Minimally educated in Damascus Madrassas, where they were thoroughly indoctrinated in Wahhabi dogma by a series of zealous mullahs, both men were ideal al-Sahaba foot soldiers. They would eagerly give their lives in support of the Pan-Islamic movement, were they asked to do so. In their minds, there could be no higher calling than to be shahid, or martyred in the service of Allah.

When there was dirty work to be done, Amar and Sharif were the operatives to whom Ahmed Khalid turned most often. It was these two who had taken care of the snooping old bank regulator, Paul Trotter, who was dead within twenty-four hours of the time he was identified for them by al-Sahaba's operative inside the bank he was examining. It was Amar and Sharif who also disposed of the body of Imad Fayiz Mufassa, the al-Sahaba comrade who had threatened the security of that organization's plans through his loose talk. It would now also be them to whom Khalid would assign the task of searching out the banker, Logan Hart, and determining what he did or did not know regarding the whereabouts of their brother, Saud al-Dajani, and whether Mr. al-Dajani's absence foreshadowed any threat to the operational plans of al-Sahaba.

A stickler for detail, Khalid had insisted that each of his

operatives provide him, to the extent they could, the names, telephone numbers and home addresses of all the key people with whom they worked in their day jobs. He had a mania for maintaining that depth of information on his operatives. He remembered that it had been very easy for Saud al-Dajani to meet the requirement. Apparently, all he had to do was print out a list from a database maintained on Global United Bank's computer. Khalid transferred such information from all of his people to his own laptop. It was, as a result, a simple thing for him to provide Amar and Sharif with Logan Hart's home address in Palatine, Illinois. Khalid was certain that this Mr. Hart's story was a sham when he had talked with him by telephone. Al-Sahaba would soon find out what had happened to their brother, Saud.

The plan called for Amar to follow Logan on foot and then accompany him on his nightly commuter ride to his home in Palatine. Amar was the only al-Sahaba operative personally familiar with Logan, having followed him some through downtown Chicago a couple of weeks before around the holiday the Americans called their Thanksgiving. Sharif, in turn, was to drive a car to the city of Palatine, where the two would link up via cell phone. The car would be needed later to aid in their getaway after they completed what they had planned for the banker.

The information al-Sahaba possessed on Logan indicated he lived alone. The plan was simple. Amar and Sharif would enter Logan's home sometime during the evening hours after he retired for the night, take him captive, extract whatever information he had about the disposition of Saud al-Dajani, and then terminate him and leave. Amar and Sharif were good at what they did. By their calculation, the task would easily be completed before sunrise.

◊◊◊◊

WHEN OTHER responsibilities didn't require Logan to take his automobile into the city on business, he usually rode

METRA's commuter running the UP Northwest line back and forth to his home in Palatine. He could read the newspaper, work, or simply relax for the approximately one hour long ride to and from downtown. On most evenings like that of the second Wednesday in December, if his schedule allowed, Logan tried to ride the train leaving at 5:16 p.m. It was an express that stopped at only one station in Arlington Park between downtown and Logan's Palatine destination, shaving no less than twelve stops and approximately twenty minutes off the ride. That train was usually full of other Palatine commuters who rode it for that very same reason.

It wasn't until Logan disembarked that he saw the dark-complected young man leaving the train with him in Palatine. At first, it was one of those you-know-I've-seen-that-guy-before-type of things. Then after a double-take at the man's reflection in a window of the station house, Logan finally remembered where he had indeed seen him before. He was the one who had followed him into Macy's the evening before Thanksgiving.

Logan hurried to his car in the parking lot at the station, and just sat there in the darkness watching the young man for several minutes before leaving for home. The stranger didn't act at all like he recognized Logan, or that he was following Logan in any way. He instead tarried on the station platform, talking to someone on a cell phone during the whole time that Logan watched him from the car. *Maybe it's not the same man*, thought Logan, *or if it is, perhaps this is simply one of those one-in-a-million coincidences.* Logan nevertheless decided he would again call Merritt Daimler immediately after he arrived home and tell him of the incident.

All the way home from the station, Logan had that same sense of foreboding he used to experience many years before when he was preparing for combat missions in the Middle East. This whole Nasir, hawala, terrorist thing was bringing it all back to him, and it wasn't pleasant. He had been sleeping with one eye open, so to speak, for many nights now, but to some degree that was nothing new. It was a military-related post traumatic circumstance far more in check when his wife, Melanie, was around to help maintain some semblance of equilibrium, but now that she was no longer around nighttime hyper-vigilance was once again becoming the norm. Unlike a lot of homes in Logan's Palatine neighborhood, his house did not have an alarm system. He was a little sorry now that he hadn't installed one before. He would probably be getting more sleep these nights. The M-9 Beretta on the bed stand beside him helped some.

Logan called Merritt Daimler right after he walked in the house to tell him about seeing who he thought was the young man who had previously followed him the month before. "I wouldn't swear to it, Merritt, but I think there's a strong possibility the guy was following me again."

"You may be right, Logan, and I don't want to take a chance in that regard. What say I send a couple of our people to your house for the night, just in case?"

"No, no I wouldn't think that's necessary. He wasn't following me when I left the station. I'm not worried. I don't think you need to bother. I just wanted to let you know what happened."

"Well, I know Aidan Stoessel, the police chief in Palatine, pretty well. So, I think I'll call him and ask that he have his guys do periodic drive-bys during the night, just in case. He runs a fantastic department. You call both them and me if you have the slightest problem, and then we'll check on you first thing in the morning."

"Fine, whatever you think best. It probably doesn't mean a thing. I just thought I ought to let you know."

◊◊◊◊

AL-SAHABA zealots, Amar, and Sharif took great pride in their capabilities as trained operatives. They were good at

467

what they did, whether it was surveillance, intelligence gathering, interrogation or assassination, and they would be doing all of those things during the early morning hours of the second Thursday in December.

It was easy for them to enter Logan Hart's house. Picking the lock was a snap. There were no alarms, and no signs of a dog anywhere to be seen. They entered by way of a single door at the rear of the house that lead into the kitchen. All of the lights in the house were off, but the curtains were open on that side of the building and it was a full moon. The natural light from outside made it relatively easy going. Perhaps they wouldn't have to use the small, red-filtered penlights they had brought along. Moving carefully and quietly, the two men worked their way slowly down a short hallway leading to the den that doubled as Logan's home office. They could see that room connected to a front foyer and some stairs leading to the second level. All was going extremely well until they were about halfway between the kitchen and den. Both men jumped with a start as Mac, the old Senegal parrot that used to belong to Logan's deceased wife, Melanie, let out a scream, followed by a loud, raspy "Hello!" It only happened once, but Logan was sleeping lightly enough in his upstairs bedroom that he heard it. Mac didn't make that kind of racket unless he saw someone, much less after the lights were out.

Logan slid quietly out of bed and grabbed his loaded and chambered Beretta. Releasing the thumb safety as quietly as possible, he slowly left his bedroom and made his way carefully down the hallway toward the stairs leading to the lower level, hugging the wall in the darkness as he moved. Rounding the corner very carefully at the top of the stairs and looking down toward the lower landing, Logan saw the two intruders only seconds before they did him. All three men were surprised, but Logan's reaction was far more instinctive and immediate. It was as though the years between Logan's days and nights of combat in the Middle

East and this home invasion in Palatine, Illinois had never taken place.

Before either of the two terrorists could raise their weapons, Logan fired twice with surprising accuracy, hitting Bashir Sharif in the chest both times, propelling him backwards into fellow terrorist Abdullah Amar, and causing them both to fall together in a heap at the bottom of the stairs.

"How bad are you hurt, my brother?" Amar asked of Sharif as he pulled his partner of many years behind a table in the entry foyer at the bottom of the stairs.

Sharif gasped and spat blood. "I can't move, Abdullah. I can't move. I don't feel a thing."

Amar figured at least one of the rounds had gone through Sharif's spine. *There's no way my friend is walking away from this*, thought Amar. Shots rang out as Logan pumped two more rounds into the table that protected the two terrorists. One round passed within inches of Amar's head.

Logan had eleven more 9 mm rounds left from what had been a full clip, but the people at the bottom of the stairs don' t know that, he surmised. He decided to save his ammunition and wait to see what the intruders' next move was before firing again. There was a period of brief silence in the foyer below, followed by the sound of voices. Logan could hear one of the men whispering, but it was difficult to understand what he was saying.

"Allahu akbar, my friend, allahu akbar!" Amar spoke softly to his associate as he placed the silenced barrel of his handgun against Sharif's temple and pulled the trigger. Two more muffled shots rang out and plaster exploded away from the corner of the wall next to Logan before he heard the sound of someone running back through the den, into the kitchen and out the door at the rear of the house. As the person once more passed through the hallway between the den and kitchen, he could hear old Mac the parrot say

"Hello" again to whomever it was. He then heard tires squeal as a car pulled out of the drive and sped away.

Waiting for what seemed like several minutes and hearing nothing, Logan stood up, turned on the lights at the top of the stairs and cautiously made his way to the first floor of the house looking over the barrel of his automatic at what appeared to be a lifeless body lying several feet from the bottom of the steps. He could see there was blood everywhere. When he got down to the body, he started to reach to check for a pulse but decided it was futile when he saw that one whole side of the man's head was gone. The young man lying at Logan's feet had a dark complexion like the fellow who had appeared to be following him earlier that evening, but he couldn't tell whether it was the same man. Whoever had been with this man had made sure his partner was dead before he fled the house.

Within five minutes of the incident, there were City of Palatine police officers all over Logan's house. When he called "911", the first squad was just making its way around the corner heading toward Logan's house to do a drive-by, as their department had been requested to do throughout the night by the FBI. Within another twenty minutes, the first agents of the FBI arrived on the scene, and another thirty minutes after that, Daimler himself arrived to take charge of the investigation.

"Good grief, Logan, you're kind of hard on unwelcome guests, aren't you?" Daimler quipped in a morbid effort at lightening the moment. "Did you do this guy's face like this?"

"No, that's the crazy thing. If my aim was good, I only hit him twice in the chest. I think his own partner did that to him."

"Yep, two holes in the chest from what I can tell. Probably knew their plans were botched. He couldn't take his buddy with him. So, he decided to send him along to all of those virgins waiting for him in paradise. Pretty cold, huh! Can you tell at all whether this is the guy you called me about earlier this evening that you saw on the train and so on?"

"No, Merritt, I can't. Same color of hair, same build, and same complexion, but as you can see, his face is mostly gone. I've been standing here trying to remember the clothes the guy at the station was wearing, but I can't be quite sure. I am thinking that it isn't the same guy, but I can't be certain."

"Whatever the case, there won't be much sleep for you tonight. For now, for reasons of our own, we're going to release this situation to the press as a botched home invasion, where one of two perpetrators got his. We'll say that a second party got away and let the Palatine police do the talking to the press. As far as the press is concerned, the FBI was never here."

"What's your thinking, Merritt? Why are you handling it that way?" Logan asked.

"Well, my gut tells me that the al-Dajani situation is somehow related to this. First, you call me earlier today, relating your conversation with the so-called customer that was demanding to know the whereabouts of al-Dajani, and then you call me later about the guy on the train, and now this situation later tonight. I've got to think this is all related to our detention of Mr. al-Dajani, and maybe somehow to Nasir as well."

"You think Nasir is involved in all of this, Merritt? I know there's a lot going on with him, but that sounds far-fetched to me."

"Well, maybe not directly, but I would bet you a month's salary that he, or at least one of his people, are involved in the money part of all that's been happening. Somehow, we have to find out what we can in that regard as quickly as possible."

"Can you tell me, how do you plan to do that?"

"Yes, I can, but once again it has to remain confidential until you supposedly hear about it like everyone else, but we plan to begin an all out investigation of Mr. Nasir later today. He's getting back to the U.S. from Europe in the afternoon, and we're planning to pick him up and bring him in for questioning, just like we have been doing with Mr. al-Dajani for the past couple of days."

"Nasir's pretty high profile, Merritt. When news of that gets out, the press is going to be immediately involved in a big way?"

"Oh, you're no doubt correct. We've been trying to keep this whole thing under wraps, but when we pick him up that could change all that."

"Is there any way your apprehension of Mr. Nasir could be kept on the QT to the extent it doesn't impair or delay your investigation in any way, Merritt?" Logan asked. "I'm merely thinking about the impact the eventual news of Mr. Nasir's being detained is going to have on the bank."

"I can't promise you anything, but I'll do what I can, Logan. You know though what pressure we're under in this situation, and all that is at stake, but we'll do what we can."

"Great, that's all anyone can ask. With that, is there any other way I can be of further help?"

"Well, you've already helped in more ways than you will ever imagine, Logan, and based upon what happened here tonight, I'm rather hesitant to ask you to do much more."

"You haven't heard me complain about it at all, have you?"

"No, I haven't, but I still hesitate to push your involvement too much farther. What I need you to do for us, however, is give it your best effort to go to work tomorrow and make as little out of this as possible—as hard as that might be. If news of this gets out and people you work with get wind of it, treat it with them just as we plan to treat it with the media. I'm pretty sure I can get the Palatine police to go along with the botched burglary story for a while when I clue them in on the sensitivity of all this. Hopefully we can buy just a little more time until we can get hold of Mr. Nasir and his people, and see if that leads us to something about how these terrorists are operating. I don't mind telling you old friend, this is getting scary. I sincerely hope we find something on this WMD thing soon. The whole situation has become the source of nightmares."

CHAPTER THIRTY-FOUR

MERRITT DAIMLER returned immediately to the FBI's downtown headquarters on Dearborn following the incident that occurred at Logan's place in Palatine. On the way in he called Jim Seilor, the agent currently in charge of the intense questioning of Sammy al-Dajani, on his cell phone to tell him everything that had taken place in Palatine. He indicated he was headed back downtown to check up on Sammy's questioning, and to ensure that things were progressing relative to the Nasir investigation. Turning off his phone, Daimler knew it was a near impossibility, but he truly wished everyone on his call list would somehow lose his number for the remainder of his ride back into the city. He needed some time to think, and the return drive to FBI headquarters would be a welcome respite.

Daimler hadn't slept much for the better part of a week. The meeting of the day before with the CDC and other members of the JTTF had been particularly unsettling. He had a wife, three children, and seven grandchildren, and it was hard to imagine any of them being hit with the disease that caused the ghastly disfigured visages in the pictures they had shown at the meeting the day before. Somehow, everyone had to work together to stop this horrible thing from happening if it was indeed in the offing somewhere in the country. *How could anyone unleash something like that on his or her fellow human beings?* Daimler asked himself. *It takes sick, sick people, with no conscience whatsoever!*

474

By the time Daimler started to pull into the FBI's downtown-parking garage in the Dirksen Building, he had reached a difficult decision. He knew full well the restrictions that he and other investigators involved in this whole nightmare had placed upon themselves with respect to how far they could go in the questioning of Sammy, but they were surely running out of time. If sleep deprivation, near round-the-clock questioning and appealing to the man's humanity wasn't enough to convince him to cough up at least some helpful information within the next twelve hours, Daimler had decided that he was going to appeal to other agencies for help, asking them to use whatever other means were available.

Al-Dajani was a naturalized citizen who had lived in the U.S. for over eighteen years, and there were limits to how hard they could push their questioning. Considering the threat at hand, several options were running through Daimler's head, but al-Dajani's citizenship was a major stumbling block to most all. Linking him to a major potential terror threat gave some latitude, but not much. They would need to take care with what was said, and how things were done, but there was much they could threaten by insinuation. There was a part of Daimler that wished they could bring in spook specialists to be a little more coercive, but such a thing just wasn't in the cards. *A little Sodium Pentothal or water-boarding might work wonders,* he mused. Experience told him al-Dajani possessed a good deal of information. *Drastic times often require drastic measures. These people we're up against are animals. Rights be hanged,* Daimler thought for a brief moment—but only a brief moment. He had always been a defender of individual rights, and there was still the chance they could be wrong about Mr. al-Dajani. *This is the United States. We do that, we're no better than the people we're trying to defeat,* he thought. The whole situation was frustrating considering the nightmarish scenario he envisaged.

◊◊◊◊

"HOW GOES the questioning, Seilor?" Daimler was clearly anxious for news of progress when he arrived in the observation room adjacent to where Sammy had been grilled by an increasingly anxious FBI and other intelligence agents for what was now going on three days. Looking through a two-way mirror at al-Dajani, he could see the banker looked tired and beaten. Sammy was still claiming vociferously that he had nothing to do with terrorists, knew nothing about any hawala activities, and wanted to be treated like the citizen he was. Daimler could hear him tearfully imploring the agents.

"For the thousandth time, I know nothing about Mr. Nasir's business activities. My exempting his companies from regular cash transaction reporting was my decision and only my decision. I only wanted to please Mr. Nasir by making things easier for his companies and had no idea that the regulators would make such a big deal of it. All of his companies dealt so much in cash that it really didn't seem as though I was necessarily doing anything that was wholly inappropriate. You've got to believe me! I meant no harm!"

"Have you shown him the pictures yet?" Daimler asked.

"No, we were just about to do that," Seilor answered. "He appears about ready to break. Our plan was to bring in a friendly Muslim military chaplain to help mollify the situation, show al-Dajani pictures of people in the final stages of black Smallpox, tell him what we know or suspect about the bio-weapon attack we think may be in the offing, and then try through the chaplain to appeal to his conscience as a 'peace loving Muslim'. How does that sound?"

"Sounds like as good a plan as any we've got left. Let's get on with it," said Daimler. He and his crew weren't desperate yet, but they were close to it. If Sammy didn't break soon, they weren't exactly sure what their next step might be. "Perhaps if and when we bring in Nasir, maybe we can make sure that al-Dajani sees him being questioned or some such thing," added Daimler. "Maybe that might shake him up a bit. Where do we stand relative to Nasir?"

"We're ready for him," answered Seilor. "Our people in Paris indicate Mr. Nasir departed Luxembourg City sometime last night, linked up with an Air France flight at Orly, and is due to arrive at the International Terminal in O'Hare sometime around 2:25 p.m. our time today. We plan to meet him at the airport and bring him in for questioning."

"What about all of the people around him," asked Daimler. "What are we doing with them?"

"We think we have everything covered, sir. As you instructed, we've worked with the U.S. Attorney's office here in Chicago, and obtained federal subpoenas and warrants to search all of Nasir's offices, confiscate what we need, and bring in all of his company CEO's and their key staffers for questioning. We're planning to serve those at all of the pertinent locations at exactly 10:30 a.m. this morning. We've got a crew of people from our agency, the U.S. Attorney's office and a whole slew of U.S. Marshals to back us up. We plan to hit all of Nasir's offices at once. We've also asked for similar authority to hit the Worldwide Islamic Charities Foundation at the same time, just like you asked."

"Got any logistical backup?"

"Sure do! We expect this is going to be a big chore, so we've requisitioned a whole fleet of panel trucks with a number of bonded movers to haul in records and files. They won't know what hit them, Merritt. We also think Mr. Nasir will be totally unaware of what is taking place until he is on the ground at O'Hare, and in our custody. We're taking steps to ensure that Internet connections are conveniently down on his flight. He shouldn't be much aware of anything that's going on when he hits the ground."

"That's great. Sounds like you're all doing a good job, but one word of caution. This Nasir guy is well connected," Daimler warned. "I suspect all heck is going to break loose when we hit these places and pick him up. We're going to have the press and half of Chicago looking over our shoulders on this one. For reasons of my own that I would prefer not go into at present, I would like to keep Mr. Nasir's apprehension as quiet as possible, but not if it hinders any other aspect of our investigation. If his situation has to go public immediately to avoid investigative problems, then so be it. Whatever the case in that regard, however, we need to play everything by the books with respect to Mr. Nasir—you know, polite and circumspect in all that we do with this. What about Global United Bank? Have we done anything to cover our rears there?"

"Yes, we have similar subpoenas to acquire whatever we need over at Global United, but as you know, we have a leg up through the OCC, Cass Price, and Logan Hart, etc," said Seilor. "They're all working with us. So, we should be able to do everything we need there without making much, if any, public fuss."

"Well, let's not presume anything. If at all possible, we want to make sure we don't give away the fact that we've been working with Logan and Cass at any time prior to this. Let's serve all the papers on the bank's President, Mr. Kruse, and just like everyone else, have the bank ostensibly jump through all the same legal hoops as Nasir and all of his companies. Perhaps we can acknowledge their recent previous work with the OCC, and suggest we might be willing to accept some of their responses in that regard to the extent it can save the bank some time and effort—but see to it they provide us with everything we need nonetheless. Just make sure Logan and Cass aren't in any way outed in the process. Got it?"

"Absolutely, we certainly do," answered Seilor.

"Finally, Jim, I absolutely want nobody but me, or my designee, speaking to the press regarding anything related to any of this until we are prepared as to what we want to say. Do I make myself clear on that?"

"Yes, you do, sir."

"Fine, then I'm going to my office to make some much-needed phone calls, and grab a few minutes of shuteye on the couch there if I can relax enough. It's been a long night. Let me know when you all are ready to head out to AmeriPAK or if we have any breakthroughs with al-Dajani when you show him the pictures and tell him what we know about this terrorist plot. See if that moves him in any way. We've got a lot coming down here. So, keep me posted. Got it?"

"Sure will! But, whoa, wait before you go. How's Logan Hart? We all heard about what went down out at his place in Palatine tonight. Is he okay?"

"Sure is! Logan may, like me, be a little longer in the tooth these days, but he hasn't forgotten everything he learned years ago. Back in Iraq, he was one of the best darned soldiers I knew of, and he's nearly as tough now as he was then. Those goons just picked on the wrong person this time. Rack one up for the good guys, Jim."

◊◊◊◊

AHMED KHALID honked the horn of his yellow cab three times that same Thursday morning in December as he pulled up to the large overhead door in front of the downtown-Chicago warehouse rented by Dominion Janitorial Supply on West Ontario. The door slowly went up just enough to allow him entry and then went immediately down behind him. Pulling the cab further inside, he exited to be met by an ashen-faced Abdullah Amar.

"Please, tell me you have something good to report regarding the whereabouts of our brother, Saud, and that obtaining that information was a painful ordeal for that pig I am certain lied to me yesterday."

"I am most disheartened, Mr. Hamadi, but I cannot."

479

Khalid now noticed the tears rolling down Amar's cheeks. "Last night was an utter fiasco, sir. The man you sent us to question was either expecting us or must have heard the alarm sounded by a large, pet bird we mistakenly aroused. He fired upon us out of the dark, and Bashir was severely wounded. He was semi-conscious, and I could not move him. In the name of all that is sacred, it was I who had to usher him into paradise. He is now with Allah, the most merciful and compassionate one. We were friends since childhood. My heart is indeed heavy."

"Then what you are telling me is that I have lost another operative besides Mr. al-Dajani. I fear that we must change our plans quickly. If we tarry much longer, I will have no one left with which to wage war against these bastard pigs, and they may well be onto our plans. Please, assemble everyone at this location for an emergency meeting by no later than 2:00 p.m. this afternoon, Mr. Amar. I wish to see all five remaining operatives here at that time. Meanwhile, I shall be in the office upstairs."

Amar could see his al-Sahaba commander was furious. Had it not been for the fact that every man was needed, the consequences of Amar's failure of the previous night might well have far exceeded a verbal reproach. Amar could see it in his leader's always unforgiving eyes.

May Allah grant all of our brothers special dispensation, and me uncommon wisdom at this time. Khalid offered up prayers as he slowly climbed the stairs to his warehouse office. *This whole operation could easily come crashing in on us. This is a time for calm decision making. Strengthen me, oh, blessed one!*

Khalid was now certain that Saud al-Dajani had been taken into custody by U.S. authorities. That could be the only reason for his mysterious disappearance. Khalid went immediately to his desk and pulled out his laptop computer. It was time to compose a message to his cell leaders. They must be made aware of the potential breach in security. If al-

Dajani was indeed now in custody, it might only be a matter of time before he said something that compromised al-Sahaba's intended attack. Plans would have to change, and change immediately.

FROM: Chicago7777#@Dominion.biz
TO: Detroit4891x#@Dominion.biz;
Seattle5332x#@Dominion.biz;
   Los Angeles6439x#@Dominion.biz;
Dallas3768x#@Dominion.biz;
   NewYork2447x#@Dominion.biz;
Washington8884x#@Dominion.biz;
   Miami5341x#@Dominion.biz
Gentlemen,
Circumstances beyond our control now make it imperative that we change the date for the introduction of our new and improved bathroom air freshening product at all outlets. Please, deliver an ample supply of this new product to all of our clients in sufficient time that they may be used by no later than tomorrow evening, at 1700 hours EST—as opposed to its release on December 24th, as previously planned. Please, acknowledge your understanding of this directive at your earliest opportunity. Thank you! I.H.

◊◊◊◊

AT EXACTLY 10:30 a.m. on the morning of the first Thursday in December, teams of representatives from the U.S. Attorney's office in Chicago, together with agents of the FBI and various U.S. Federal Marshals showed up at all offices and places of business within Tariq Nasir's AmeriPAK, Inc group of companies. They were armed with subpoenas and warrants as needed to take into custody selected company CEO's and senior management officials for the purpose of questioning for the potential violation of several aspects of the USA Freedom Act, in the handling of company financial matters. The documents served also

481

allowed federal officials to confiscate company records of all kinds, both paper and electronic, along with computer hardware where it was deemed appropriate. Hurried calls were made to AmeriPAK attorneys, who were at the sides of their clients before the authorities had even partially removed the requested materials.

What particularly amazed all of the government officials participating in the raid of the Nasir organization was the completely unruffled reaction of most of the staff within the AmeriPAK group. Even those individuals upon whom warrants were served seemed nonplussed. "What the heck is going on here?" Jim Seilor asked of his fellow FBI agents, as they searched through Tariq Nasir's personal records in an effort to determine those that they wanted to confiscate. "These people seem totally unmoved about all of this. What do they know that we don't know?"

"Where can I find Mr. Daimler, gentlemen?" The agents stopped rifling through Nasir's files and turned to see a tall, blond-haired, well-dressed, distinguished looking man in his approximate late forties with a briefcase under his arm. He was accompanied by what appeared to be two younger aides, a man and a woman, who were also toting large briefcases. Approaching the agents, the man offered his business card.

"I'm Steven Augsberger, gentlemen, Senior Partner in the law firm of Carrier, Augsberger, and Kafir, and these people here are my associates, Phillip Jensen and Cynthia Howard. Our firm represents Mr. Nasir and all of the AmeriPAK companies. We need to speak with either Mr. Daimler or someone from the U.S Attorney's office, which we understand is also here as part of this unwarranted interruption of business for my clients. Could one of you direct me to whoever is in charge please?"

"Yes, sir, I would be pleased to do that," Daimler responded. "I'm Special Agent Daimler, and that gentleman over there is Thomas J. Lauderbach, Assistant U.S. District

Attorney. How can we help you, Mr. Augsberger?"

"Well, to begin with, I would like to review your court orders and any other related documents, if you don't mind. My clients and I want to know what the basis is for this intrusion of privacy and business. This has the makings of a very expensive interruption of business for my clients. AmeriPAK has worldwide operations, and..."

"That may be," interrupted Lauderbach, "but we have reason to believe that AmeriPAK's 'worldwide operations', as you call them, may be part of a secretive, unregistered money transfer and perhaps even money laundering business that has been breaking numerous federal laws and regulations for some time now. We suspect that there may also be links, whether knowingly or unknowingly, to organizations harboring harmful intent toward this country. Do you know how we can reach Mr. Nasir, Mr. Augsberger?" Lauderbach already knew the answer to his question, but he thought *a little subterfuge wouldn't hurt in dealing with this pompous, legal twit.*

"Yes, I do. He is, as best I understand, right now on a flight back to this country from a business trip to Luxembourg, where he's been for the last few days, but then somehow, I think you probably already knew that," Augsberger quipped as he began to peruse the court orders. He had a supercilious air about him that irritated law enforcement types with regularity, and he worked at perfecting it. "Just so you know, gentlemen, we're going to fight this tooth and nail. Neither Mr. Nasir, any of his companies nor any of his staff are guilty of wrongdoing, and that will be made readily apparent to you in short order. This all has the potential for being a rather costly mistake for the government, and I intend to make it a personal goal to see to that. Are these copies that I can keep of the orders, gentlemen?"

"Yes, sir, they are," Lauderbach answered.

"Fine, then I'll leave for now, but we will be seeing

each other very soon. You can bank on that. This is one mistake that I think the U.S. Attorney's office is really going to regret."

CHAPTER THIRTY-FIVE

"LOGAN, CAN you join me in the boardroom right away?" Poking his head into Hart's office, Scott Kruse's voice sounded extremely agitated. "I know you've had a pretty hellacious last several hours with what happened at your home and all last night, but I could use your help."

"How'd you hear about that already?"

"The FBI just informed me, and I guess I'd have to say, I'm surprised you're even here."

"Well, I figured it wouldn't do me any good hanging around home. The police had the situation nearly wrapped up by the time I normally head into work. They were done with me, so I left them a key, told them to lock up when they were done, and headed into work."

"You're a better man than I am, I guess. I'd ask you if you thought your ordeal last evening had anything to do with all that has been going on here relative to the OCC, FBI, that Paul Trotter and Mr. Nasir and all, but I'd be afraid of what your answer might be."

"And your fears might be well-founded, but let's perhaps just not go there for right now. What do you mean by FBI, however? Are they here already this morning?"

"Yeah, they and a batch of lawyers from the U.S. Attorney's office waltzed in here just a bit ago with the OCC in tow—and they have a bunch of subpoenas they're serving the bank on all of Tariq's accounts, those of his companies and basically all the BSA-type information the OCC's been

485

going over during the last week or so. I'm not sure what is going on here, but I could use your help if you don't mind. We'll all be in the boardroom."

"I'll be there right away, Scott." Logan hung up the phone he had been about to dial before Scott had barged in his office, and headed immediately for the boardroom that was located on the same floor but on the other end of the building. He felt for Scott. It had become evident that he didn't handle stressful situations well to begin with, and Logan knew he probably had little idea of the difficulties that no doubt lay ahead for him and his bank. *This is one time when what the bank needs is 'a wartime consigliere,' like the line in the Godfather movie*, thought Logan, *and Scott Kruse is hardly that. He has always instead appeared to be more of an enabler when it comes to Nasir. Things are about to get a little rough for Scott where our situation is concerned here at Global United. He's embroiled in a real mess as a result of his own ignorance, and completely out of his element on this one.*

When Logan arrived at the bank on Thursday morning, no one but Scott acted as though they had heard anything about the break-in and shooting at Logan's home the previous night in Palatine, and for whatever reason it was the FBI who had informed him. At their behest, the Palatine police had been fairly cooperative in holding back news of the incident, even delaying its appearance on the station blotter for several hours. A young intern the Daily Herald regularly sent around to suburban police stations every morning finally hit on the story around midday. So, it failed to make the morning print editions and only showed up in the online editions late Thursday afternoon. Aside from a few of Logan's neighbors that were awakened by all the lights and commotion, there was hardly even anyone from the neighborhood who knew about the break-in before they left for work.

As Logan walked into the boardroom, he recognized

his now confidential investigative partner, Cass Price, agent Lon Erickson, and Scott who was seated at the end of the long conference table, but none of the other four suits in the room looked familiar.

"Morning, Mr. Hart, nice to see you again." Erickson greeted Logan with a handshake, acting as if it had been some time since their last meeting. "Hopefully, you will remember me. I'm FBI Special Agent Lon Erickson."

"Yes, Lon, I remember you well. Nice to see you again." Enjoying Erickson's subterfuge, Logan glanced over and smiled at Cass Price. "Good morning, Cass!"

She smiled back. "Good morning, Logan." That bit of familiarity wasn't lost on Scott, but he was too nervous to make much of it.

"Mr. Hart, as I said to Mr. Kruse a few minutes ago, we appreciate both of you taking the time to meet with us again on such short notice." Erickson was making an extra effort to purport only a passing acquaintance. "Please, before we get started, let me introduce some people that I have with me here this morning. Mr. Kruse has already met them." Four men in suits stood up. Logan played along. "With me here, this morning, are Special Agents Harry Cutter and Irvin Rosenberg from our offices, and these other two gentlemen are Mike Benson and Garrett Palmer from the U.S. Attorney's office here in Chicago." Logan shook hands all around, and everyone took their seats. "Mike, now that Mr. Hart is with us, do you want to explain why we're here?"

"Sure, Lon, I'd be happy to," Benson answered. "Uh, Mr. Hart, as we've already explained to Mr. Kruse, we're here this morning to serve the bank with subpoenas and orders of discovery giving us the right to investigate any and all loan and deposit account information for Mr. Tariq Nasir and all of his companies under the banner of AmeriPAK, Inc. I believe there are about nine different entities here for which we will be requiring information. They're all on the list that Irv is passing out. Included in this order are any and all other bank records that bear any reference whatsoever to Mr. Nasir or his companies, such as minutes of Global United's board of directors and board committee meetings, audit records and so forth. It's rather all encompassing. The way we'll probably approach this will be to have your people pull together the information we're requesting, and then we will make necessary copies."

"Can you tell us at all what this is about, gentlemen?" Scott asked, seemingly emboldened by Logan having joined the meeting. "I wanted to ask that before but thought I would to wait until Logan here arrived. Mr. Nasir, as I think you know, is our largest shareholder in the bank and Chairman of the Board. This is quite disconcerting to us, and I am certain it'll be the same to him. To your knowledge, is he aware that all of this is going on?"

"There's not a lot I can tell you at this time about this investigation beyond that which I've already indicated, and I'm not sure whether Mr. Nasir has any knowledge of these actions yet or not. We understand from his staff that he's been in Europe for a few days and is on an Air France flight coming back as we speak. When was the last time either of you spoke to him?"

"I spoke with him just before he left, and then the other day on a conference call," answered Scott, "but he certainly mentioned nothing that would lead me to believe he was expecting anything like this to take place. He's going to go ballistic."

"We full well expect he will not be pleased. We have people serving similar documents at all of his offices as we speak. This will probably be fairly disruptive for him and his businesses, but I can assure you we feel it is all necessary, and a federal judge has concurred." Benson stood as if to signify they needed to end the meeting. "Now, if you don't mind, gentlemen, if you could steer us to all the appropriate people within your organization to begin putting this information together, we'll get to it."

"Scott, if you would like, I can take over and begin working with these folks to get all of this on the road." Logan rose to leave with the investigators. "I'll get them to the right people and see that they get all the help they need. No need for you to get involved at this point. I'll keep you informed."

"If you don't mind, Logan, perhaps I'll tag along with you and these folks," Cass added as she stood to leave with Logan and the rest. "If I could visit with you gentlemen about what you're asking the bank for, it might well be that some of the information we've garnered through our examination could be of some use to you in this situation. We could perhaps save everyone some time."

Scott didn't move, remaining seated instead at the end of the long boardroom table, looking pale and nauseated. "Thank you, Logan, I would appreciate that. I'm still quite involved in some other matters."

Logan was taken aback that Scott would so readily delegate such a situation to him. *What other matters,* thought Logan, *could in any way be more important than this is right now? If I were in his shoes, there would be no way that I could sit idly by while this was all going on around me.* The look on Scott's face was one that Logan had seen before. It was the vacuous look of someone who was just realizing he might have aligned himself with the wrong parties. As CEO of Global United, seen by most since his arrival as being nearly joined at the hip with the bank's Chairman, Scott was well aware his career at the bank was no doubt inextricably linked to Nasir's demise. It would be a bitter pill. Litigation was still pending with his previous employer after a rancorous departure.

◊◊◊◊

AT EXACTLY 2:25 p.m. on the second Thursday in December, Air France flight 4360 arrived at O'Hare International Terminal 5, with passengers disembarking at

Gate M-12. FBI Special Agent Merritt Daimler, Assistant U.S. Attorney Thomas Lauderbach and a fairly sizable contingent from both of their offices met first class passenger, Tariq Nasir, as he came through customs. By this time, the press had somehow gotten wind of what might be coming down with the well-known Chicago luminary. So, they were on hand, but being held at a discreet distance by Transportation Safety Agency officials. Nasir looked surprised and perplexed as two agents stepped up on both sides, lightly taking him by the arms.

"Mr. Tariq Nasir, I am Assistant U.S. Attorney, Thomas Lauderbach, and I'm here to serve you with these warrants allowing us to take you into custody for questioning regarding your suspected involvement in activities contrary to laws and regulations of the United States of America, laws related to the control of money laundering, racketeering and possible other activities that might be detrimental to the security of this country. If you…"

"Mr. Lauderbach, I would like to see those papers, if you don't mind?" All eyes turned to once again see Nasir's attorney, Steven Augsberger, step forward and snap the court orders out of Lauderbach's hands. "Hopefully, I don't have to reintroduce myself as Mr. Nasir's attorney, gentlemen. Tariq, please, let me take care of this."

"Certainly, Steven, this is the kind of thing I pay you that big retainer for." If Nasir was upset or concerned about what was happening, he was extremely good at hiding it. He seemed completely in control, disdainful of what was taking place, yes, but otherwise completely in control. "These are of course ridiculous accusations, but I am perfectly willing to cooperate with whatever they are investigating. If everything looks in order to you with those documents, Steven, I will very willingly accompany these gentlemen wherever they wish me to go, and do what I can to help. This has all got to be some mistake."

"Fine, Tariq, you go with them for now, and I will follow

along to be with you just as soon as I make some calls. Just where are you taking my client, gentlemen?

"We'll be taking Mr. Nasir to FBI headquarters over at the Dirksen Building on South Dearborn. If you know where that is, Mr. Augsberger?"

"Fine, I do indeed. I want no questions asked of my client, Mr. Nasir, however, until I am there to be with him. Do I make myself clear?"

"Fine, we can wait for you. Can you tell us how long that will be?" Lauderbach asked, finding it hard to hide his frustration with the cocky Augsberger.

"I won't be much more than fifteen to twenty minutes behind you." Augsberger indicated to the investigators as he was walking away. "And remember, gentlemen, I want no questioning of Mr. Nasir until I am there."

◊◊◊◊

"AL-QIYAMAH—Usual place today at 3:00 p.m.," had been the simple text message to all five remaining undercover operatives belonging to the Chicago cell of al-Sahaba. The Arabic word signifying that the Day of Judgment had arrived, was the only message they needed to hear to know that the meeting was one of emergency. It was al-Sahaba's call to arms.

"My brothers," intoned Ahmed Khalid, as he began to address his cell members once everyone had arrived at the downtown offices of Dominion Janitorial Supply on West Ontario Ave, "The time you all have been anticipating has finally arrived. We shall now deliver the crushing blow each that will bring death and destruction to this evil land of apostates. They shall finally see that there is no place to hide from the ever-increasing wrath of Allah, the Exalted and Omnipotent One, who is known by many names, not the least of which is *al-Muntaqim*—the Lord of Retribution, the Avenger! We shall be his arm of justice. By the time the sun sets tomorrow we shall have done our work. Our attack will be underway, and there shall be no going back."

"Brother Hamadi, I do not know if I speak for us all, but I for one am confused." Nayef Hawatmeh, a young, former Syrian refugee and ISIS combatant who had snuck back into the United States by way of the Mexican border only months before, and now labored as a janitor at Chicago's O'Hare International Airport, looked questioningly around the room at his fellow terrorists. "I, like my brothers here, am prepared to die in the name of the Almighty One, but I was under the impression we were not to proceed with our attack until the evening of December 24th. You said the attack was to coincide with the height of the Christian holiday travel season, not tomorrow as you are now indicating. May I ask, what has changed?"

"You may indeed, Mr. Hawatmeh. That is a question everyone here should be asking. As all of you can see here today, our numbers have dwindled. We no longer have Mr. al-Dajani, one of our most experienced operatives, to count among us, as we fear he has been taken into custody by U.S. authorities. Further, last evening, in an effort to find out about his disposition, we mounted an operation in one of the northwest suburbs that went horribly awry, resulting in the death of our brother Bashir Sharif. Mr. al-Dajani is a well-trained, dedicated member of our organization, but if he is in custody I fear that it may only be a matter of time before the American security forces find out something through him that might compromise our operation. I have, therefore, decided to move the attack up to tomorrow at 1700 hours EST. Air travel is already moving at a fast pace with the onset of the Christian holidays, so even though it is early, it is still an opportune time to unleash our weapons. I have already notified our brothers in the seven other cities where we plan coordinated attacks, and they are no doubt at this very minute having similar meetings in their respective locations for attacks there at the same hour tomorrow."

"What, if anything, will be different with the conduct of this earlier operation as opposed to that which was previously planned for December 24th?" Hawatmeh appeared concerned about all the sudden change. "One thing that I worry about is the fact that some of us, Juma Fazani, Fathi Shallah and me are full-time workers on the Chicago Airport Systems cleaning crews. We are there every night, but our other two brothers, Abdullah Amar and Badr Aldin here, are only part-time. We had taken care of making arrangements for Abdullah and Badr to work the evening of the 24th by offering to fill in for a couple of people who wanted the night off in order to start the holiday out early. They're going away, I guess, for the holidays. Two weeks earlier, however, that will not be the case. What shall we do in that regard?"

"That is easy, my friends," Khalid answered almost immediately. "We will simply send your two idiot coworkers, and perhaps a couple more for good measure, on an earlier, more permanent vacation. Brothers Amar and Aldin here will take care of making sure that happens at the appropriate time. They then will be conveniently available to stand in that day for your 'recently departed' coworkers. Once everyone is on the job, the rest is simple. There will then be five of you working the cleaning crews at O'Hare tomorrow, and you will all simply ensure that it is you who cleans the bathrooms in the three main domestic terminals. As you do so, you will exchange the canisters in the automatic room deodorizers for those of ours which contain the pathogens, set them to dispense the medium as per usual, and then depart the terminal as soon as you can do so without drawing attention to yourselves."

"I hate to bring this up, Mr. Hamadi, but what chance is there that one of us won't come down with this dreadful disease as a result of our direct exposure to the vapors from these dispensers?" Abdullah Amar looked concerned. "I am prepared to die for our cause, but I would prefer it not be in the way this disease might make it happen if it can be avoided."

"I can make none of you any guarantees in that regard, my friends. I can only offer you comfort in the knowledge that each of you has at least been vaccinated against the disease in the last couple of years. That will certainly be more protection than the many thousands of people that pass through those restrooms tomorrow night will have." Khalid answered. "But then again, we should all be prepared for shahid if the need arises. To this end, I ask you all to arise early tomorrow and pray. Shave your bodies and bathe in sweet smelling waters. Make peace with Allah, for we know not at all how smoothly the operation will go. Be prepared for the worst, as this is a very delicate mission, but take comfort in knowing that you are doing much to further the cause of Islam around the world. Jazakallahu khairann— may Allah reward you for the good that you do my brothers!'

"In sha' Allah," shouted Amar, "if Allah wills!"

"Allahu akbar, allahu akbar!" The group began to chant. "God is great!"

CHAPTER THIRTY-SIX

WHILE STEVEN Augsberger, Nasir's attorney, was still present with Nasir in the international terminal at O'Hare, Merritt Daimler Mirandized Nasir and then gently handcuffed him for the trip back downtown. What was going to take place over the next several hours with respect to the handling of Nasir had been thoroughly scripted by the FBI, the U.S. Attorney's office and other government agencies that were now involved in this very important investigation. Nasir had a bevy of attorneys with a lot of political influence at his beck and call, and the government was not exactly sure how long it might be able to hold Mr. Nasir. They had to make the best of the time they had him.

The number of people who had been brought in for questioning relative to the Nasir case was sufficiently extensive that it was really stretching the capabilities of the task force that had been mustered to investigate the Nasir matter. Discounting Sammy al-Dajani, who was still being grilled nearly around the clock regarding his involvement in the situation, investigators needed to interrogate fully no less than twenty-five business and other related associates of Tariq Nasir. These included: Mustafa Agha Khan, President and titular CEO of the AmeriPAK holding company; all six CEOs and ten other senior executives of the various AmeriPAK subsidiaries; and all eight business and community leaders listed as trustees of the Worldwide Islamic Charities Foundation. Included among the latter were: Imam Abdul-Hakim, who ran the foundation on a day-to-day basis, and was the congregational leader of the very prestigious downtown mosque, the Islamic Institute of Greater Chicago; and Dr. Faris Haifa, retired Northwestern University MD, and father of Raj Haifa, head of International Banking at Global United Bank. Recognizing how politically volatile such a situation could be where it was necessary to interrogate so many well-known business and other leaders from Chicago's Muslim community, all the investigative agencies involved were attempting in every way they could to handle the questioning with the utmost sensitivity. The American Civil Liberties Union and the Council on American-Islamic Relations had both gotten wind of the arrests and were beginning to ask questions. Much of the press was already demonstrating an inexplicable bias of support for those detained that was somewhat confusing to investigators considering the element of national security that was involved in the situation. In spite of the tremendous fear and sense of urgency involved, with organizations like the ACLU, CAIR, and a sympathetic press stirring around the situation had the potential of becoming very explosive from a political point of view.

The whole group that was assembled for questioning was initially seated in a large glassed in meeting room on the third floor of FBI headquarters, waiting their turns to be grilled by the investigators. When Nasir was brought in, Daimler and Lauderbach made sure that he was paraded past that room in handcuffs, as he was taken to a completely separate area to await the arrival of his attorney, Steven Augsberger. The decision had additionally been made to question him in the proximity of the room where Sammy was currently being interrogated. The plan was to ensure one way or the other that the two saw each other. The investigators had begun to feel that Sammy was about to break in some way, and they thought seeing Nasir might just push him over the edge. Nasir himself showed no reaction whatsoever at seeing either his AmeriPAK execs or al-Dajani in the proximity, but the same couldn't be said for Sammy. Seeing Nasir being led in wearing handcuffs had quite an effect on him.

"Look, it's time we really turn up the heat on this al-Dajani fellow, Jim," Daimler instructed Agent Seilor. "I think the guy's about to break. Did you see the way he reacted when he saw Nasir being brought in next door?"

"Sure did," answered Seilor. "The wind really seemed to go out of his sails,"

"Agreed! Let's all get together and give it one more full-court press to see if he doesn't cave. I think we're about there."

"So do I. It's been nearly three days of on and off interrogation now. We've given him the requisite rests and adequate nourishment, but other than that we've really kept the pressure up on him. He's one tired, rattled puppy."

"Anything else you think we can do?"

"Perhaps, he does seem to be pretty steeped in his religion. Maybe if we brought in a Muslim Chaplain to help us out? I know an Imam in the U.S. Army by the name of Lt. Colonel Kamel Ghadamsi. Guess he's advised the JTTF out here in Chicago some before. Perhaps we could have him start sitting in to see if he might not have some influence on al-Dajani."

"Great, I know Kamel quite well, Jim. He's a Qu'ranic scholar with total command of all the Hadiths and a thorough knowledge of Sharia law. He could be very helpful. He ought to be able to give al-Dajani chapter and verse as to why he should be helping us out if he can at all be appealed to in that fashion. Let's take al-Dajani back downstairs right away for that, Jim. March him by Nasir and all the detainees as you do so and let's do it quickly." Daimler ordered. "Nasir's attorney should arrive any minute to sit in on his questioning, and I would prefer that al-Dajani not see him arrive. Don't want him to think Nasir might have a possible walk on any of this."

After a short bathroom break, Sammy was once more ushered into the interrogation room where he had been spending nearly all of his waking hours under intense questioning during the previous couple of days, he sighed in desperation and collapsed into the straight-backed, wooden chair to which he was led. He was beginning to despair. He ached in every fiber of his being. *Is this never going to end?* He asked himself.

The room was again full of investigators. They all drank cokes and coffee and slouched in the soft chairs located around the room as though they had all the time in the world. If the modus operandi were to remain the same, they would all take turns grilling him while coming and going in and out of the room at their leisure. The whole idea was to suggest their ability to easily outlast al-Dajani in this battle of wits.

"Mr. al-Dajani, don't you think it's about time you helped us out here with what you may know about Mr. Nasir's business practices, or whatever you may be aware of regarding any terrorist activities your personal or business situation may have brought you in contact with. We really need your assistance here. We think someone out there, someone you quite frankly might know, is planning an attack that has the potential of claiming many, many lives. If that happens, Mr. al-Dajani, you really don't want the blood of thousands, perhaps millions, on your hands, do you?" Daimler was using a soft, conciliatory tone as he spoke, contrasting other interrogators, who had been fairly alternately yelling and screaming at Sammy for most of the time he had been in custody. "Mr. al-Dajani, let me introduce you to Imam Kamel Ghadamsi here if I could. He's a member of your faith and a very respected friend of ours. He says he'd like to visit with you some about this whole matter if he could. All of us will leave the room and let him do just that."

Sammy looked up to see a distinguished, grandfatherly looking gentleman enter the room. "*Barakalla*, Mr. al-Dajani, may the blessings of Allah be upon you." The older man spoke softly and in a very caring manner to the dejected Sammy, who gave all the outward appearance of a man nearing wit's end. Older than most of his military peers, Colonel Ghadamsi was a Muslim cleric of Egyptian background who had been part of the U.S. Army Chaplain's Corps now for over ten years. Well-respected by both military and non-military persons alike for his seemingly steadfast patriotism and outreach to all in need of wise counsel, he had on numerous occasions been depended upon to intercede in situations of the sort facing the JTTF with Sammy al-Dajani this day. His usual attire was either a business suit and tie, or Army dress greens, but both were eschewed by him today in favor of the traditional Arab *Thobe*, in this case, an ankle-length, flowing, plain brown robe. On his head was a small black cap called a *Kufi*. Gahadamsi had calculated a traditional appearance might help reassure any devout Muslim subjected to the stress he figured Sammy had been undergoing. "Gentlemen, if Mr. al-Dajani and I could have some time alone," said Ghadamsi, looking sternly at the interrogators, "I believe it would be most helpful."

"Guys, let's do as the Imam says," Daimler responded respectfully, motioning all of the interrogators out of the room. "Let's give Colonel Gahadamsi and Mr. al-Dajani a little quiet time together."

As the door closed behind the FBI contingent, the Imam seated himself across from Sammy and spoke to him in a reassuring voice. "Young man, as Special Agent Daimler told you, I am indeed a Colonel in the U.S. Army's Chaplain Corps, ministering to our fellow Muslim believers within the ranks, but I also from time-to-time lead worship and prayers at many varied Masjids across the Midwestern United States. I have consulted with Special Agent Daimler, the gentleman who just left the room, for many years now in various matters, and he has asked me to visit with you on their behalf."

"I'm not sure we have anything to talk about, Imam, unless you think you have a way you can make all of this come to an end. These people have been unjustly detaining me here for a couple of days now and accusing me of all sorts of suspected vile and seditious acts, simply because I am Muslim and made some perfectly understandable mistakes in how I administered some business at the bank where I work. I have been denied counsel and deprived of satisfactory rest or sustenance. I have done nothing wrong. So, if you say you have helped others like myself in similar situations in the past, can you then intercede for me now?"

"First, Mr. al-Dajani, let's agree about where we are with respect to all that is going on here with you. According to Special Agent Daimler, whom I have always found to be trustworthy and honorable when it comes to matters regarding people of our faith, he is detaining and questioning you regarding not only the discrepancies in which you were involved at your bank, but primarily because of their suspicion that you may be privy to information that might help this country avoid another attack of the sort it experienced on 9/11. If that is indeed the situation that exists, then there is no way whatsoever that they will back off of you until they have settled their minds in that regard."

"I still say I don't know what any of that has to do with me. I am privy to no such a threat."

"Yes, that's what they've told me your story has been. But please understand, Mr. al-Dajani, they are very much afraid. These are apparently serious threats that we face in this matter."

"Yes, I know, that is what they are telling me too, but I assure you I have done nothing to deserve this. I have tried to be a model American since I arrived in this country many years ago, and I am now a citizen of this country. This is most inappropriate and unfair."

"Yes, it's my understanding that you have for all intents and purposes been a contributing member of American society for a number of years, but you have now come under question in matters of national security, and like it or not, the situation is a dire enough threat of terror that these people feel that they must get some answers, and that you are perhaps the repository of at least some related information. Under today's laws, that gives these people involved in Homeland Security the right to detain and question you, as they are doing now, for just about as long as they need if they think you have information for them regarding a possible terrorist attack."

"You do nothing to reassure me that this will all soon be over, Imam. I am tired and still contend that I know nothing that will be of help to them in their investigation. I just want this all to end. Whose side are you on, anyway?"

"On the side of right, according to the dictates of our blessed Prophet as told to him by Almighty Allah, is my hope, Mr. al-Dajani. My purpose in coming here today really wasn't so much to be 'reassuring' to you, as you say. I'm afraid that I'm not in much of a position to do that. What I am here for, however, is to council you as a member of our faith, and to appeal to you to help if there is indeed anything at all you may know that could perhaps help this country avoid some devastating attack." Sammy sat silently, carefully studying and listening to the Imam. "Mr. al-Dajani, if what these people tell me is true, and there are misguided members of our faith out there with plans to unleash a hideous attack on this country, and perhaps even the world, then you and I as true Islamic believers must help. I have received training about some of these weaponized biological weapons, and the devastation that something like one of them might wreak on mankind, were it loosed, would be ghastly. Are you aware that is what they need your help for? If you, therefore, know anything about it, young man, you

501

must in the name of all that is holy, help them."

"I am well aware of what these people want of me, Imam. They have been at it for days now."

"Then if you know something, you must help, Mr. al-Dajani. A disease of the sort they say may be involved here is indiscriminate in nature. It will be no respecter of persons as to whom it will slay in its path. To be sure there will be Jews and Christians alike that will be stricken, but there will also be believers within the Ummah who will also be slain. As with COVID-19, small children, the elderly and infirm will be particularly vulnerable. What I am most importantly here with you for today, is to reinforce how imperative it is that you cooperate with this investigation, if you are able. It is your responsibility as a good Muslim to do what you can to avoid the deaths of any innocents at the hands of people so misguided as to believe that such an act furthers the cause of our faith and the dictates of the Almighty One, may his name forever be praised."

"I am not saying that I am one, Imam, but there are indeed those who believe that violence may be the only way to reconcile the world toward Islam."

"Ah, yes, people such as the followers of Muhammad ibn `Abd al-Wahhab, and others like him. There are many Wahhabi's in this world, but it is my belief that they are misguided in their interpretations of the teachings of the Prophet, Peace be upon Him." Reaching over the table, the old Imam laid his hand gently on Sammy's arm. "Young man, in Surah al-Maa'idah (5), ayah 8, it is written, 'And let not the enmity and hatred of others make you avoid justice. Be just: that is nearer to piety.' Allah, the Most Merciful One, instructs Muslims to act with the utmost mercy, not to kill innocents. If you know something, you must tell. I cannot urge you more. Honorable men do not indulge in wanton destruction."

Sammy sat silently looking at the kind old cleric. He was tired and angry with his inquisitors, but he was also heartsick for the part he was now playing in the vicious, deadly attack that was soon to come. Whichever way this went, he was probably a doomed man. If he were to be released, he would be too much of a threat now to the success of the planned al-Sahaba attack. He would need to be eliminated. If he admitted who and what he was to the American authorities, he would be branded a terrorist and suffer greatly at their hands for many years to come. Yet, if he simply waited and let things unfold with al-Sahaba, as he knew it surely must be proceeding at this very moment, then he could as the Imam so indicated be held accountable as a traitor to his faith. He was, as the Americans put it, between the proverbial rock and a hard place. *I need sleep*, he thought. *If only they would give me some time to rest, to think, perhaps there would be a way.*

"With that," said the Imam, "I will leave you with your thoughts. You look like a good man to me. I am sure you will do the right thing. *Jazakallahu khairan*, my friend—may Allah reward you for doing good."

As Imam Ghadamsi left the room, he stopped to visit with Special Agent Daimler and his men in the room adjacent to the now very much alone Sammy al-Dajani. "My friend, if you and your men here will now allow Mr. al-Dajani a small amount of rest, and then return to your questioning using an approach that emphasizes his responsibilities as a Muslim, I believe he may eventually come around. I know you are in a hurry for news and intelligence, but if this man is who you think he is, he now has to overcome years of misguided indoctrination. It is only conjecture on my part, but I do believe he may be close to breaking. Be persistent if you will, but continue to take the tack that you heard me use. If anything will work that is the only thing that will. Please, keep me posted. I will be more than willing to return at any time of the day or night to assist in whatever way you think I can."

◊◊◊◊

WHEN ATTORNEY Steven Augsburger arrived at FBI headquarters to join his client, Tariq Nasir, he came armed with a federal court order of his own. He had cashed in some of his biggest chips with a former associate now sitting on the bench of the Twelfth U.S. District Court, and had obtained an order limiting the questioning of his client to no more than four hours that day, and no more than eight hours per day for the next thirty days thereafter, at which time the U.S. Attorney had to present himself to plead the case that his investigation of Mr. Nasir should continue. In the interim, Nasir was ordered to relinquish his passport to the U.S. Attorney for safekeeping but otherwise was released on his own recognizance at the end of each questioning session. The DHS, U.S. Attorney's office, and the FBI were livid.

"Mr. Nasir, according to this order, we have you for only three more hours here today, but let me say first of all that we will expect you back here first thing tomorrow morning at 8:00 a.m. with your attorney to resume our questioning." Asst. U.S. Attorney Lauderbach was almost beside himself. *Doesn't this judge understand how important this situation is that we are working on?* Lauderbach wondered. He would make it a point to get to the judge and see if they couldn't better explain the situation.

"I am very busy with things in my company, and I really don't quite know yet what it is you think I and my people may have done that would have anything to do with this money laundering you claim my organization has been involved in. I hope you are aware of how disruptive your so-called investigation is to my business and how damaging it will be financially. I will have no alternative but to seek financial redress of every nature my attorneys deem appropriate when this is all over." Staring down at his hands, Nasir was quiet for a moment as though he was pondering the situation. He then looked up at his interrogators and took a deep breath before continuing. "Nevertheless, if this is as you say some instance of national security, I am anxious to assist in any way. I simply need for you to expedite my involvement to the extent that you can."

"Please understand, Mr. Nasir, we are going to file an appeal regarding this order immediately. We have never quite heard of such a hair-brained ruling. In the interim, however, we plan not to waste one second of the time that has been allotted us. With what is facing us, we have very little of it. There is too much at stake," Lauderbach answered. "Now let me tell you and your attorney by way of short summary what it is we are investigating. First of all, it is our belief that you and/or the people in your organization are involved in the unregistered and thus illegal business of money transfer by way of the various subsidiaries that constitute AmeriPAK, Inc. The business of hawala, I believe it is called. Additionally, we think that you have been working in league with various associates at Global United Bank of Chicago, a bank where you are both Chairman of the Board and principal shareholder, to violate various federal anti-money laundering laws and regulations, in an effort to hide the existence of financial transactions which may well have been illegal. In short, Mr. Nasir, we think you are the principal behind a major illegal money transfer and money laundering business."

"Now see here," interrupted Nasir's attorney Steven Augsberger, "my client resents these accusations, and…"

"No, just a moment, Steven." Nasir blurted out. "I do indeed resent this, but let me respond to some of it anyway, if I could."

"OK, but I will interrupt if I feel you are about to say anything that these people could unjustly use against you, Tariq."

"Fine, Steven! First of all, let me say that I am well aware of what the business of hawala is, and I am sure that you knew that. My father, Mahmoud Nasir, as I am certain you are probably aware, is one of the most successful hawaladars in South Asia, with money transfer facilities in

505

countries all over that part of the world, the Middle East, Southeast Asia and Europe. He comes from a long line of hawaladars going back for centuries in Pakistan. He is quite successful, very respected in the business and I am very, very proud of him. That is, however, where my involvement in the business of hawala ends. When I came to this country, I with his permission departed from the tradition of the family business for other very lucrative endeavors, and I have been quite successful enough without the additional mantle of hawaladar."

"Well, Mr. Nasir, that all makes for an intriguing story, but we think we have evidence that what you say is not quite the truth. What would you say if I were to tell you that we have first hand knowledge—evidence by way of a documented sting operation—that some of your people have been facilitating illegal money transfers through your businesses?"

"I would be furious, Mr. Lauderbach. I have forbidden any of my people to be involved in such activities. I have never wanted the additional legal and regulatory hassles. I have had plenty enough dimension in my businesses and being involved with the bank, without looking to add to that. I could, as you might well imagine, considering my father's history and success, have easily been in the business, but I have chosen not to be. If someone in my organization has been transferring money for others—which I doubt—it has been without my knowledge whatsoever. My involvement in finance has been strictly limited to my ownership and board-related activities at Global United Bank, where believe me everything is well regulated, well documented and accurately accounted for in the time-honored traditions of modern banking. Besides, as I understand it, even if one of my companies were involved in the business of hawala, all I would have to do to be legal in that regard, would be to be registered and comply with all necessary reporting, etc. That is, however, not the case, and I resent you saying

506

otherwise."

"Well, that, sir, may be where you and we will need to greatly differ once again. We have reason to also believe that you, your companies, and your people may well have been party to an orchestrated effort to conceal on a regular basis cash transactions that have not always been for legitimate purposes," Lauderbach responded. "We..."

"I hope you have evidence to prove up the accusations you are making here this morning, Mr. Lauderbach." Augsberger threw his pen on the table. "My client said he resents your accusations, and we will vigorously defend him in that regard."

"Steven, please," corrected Nasir, "let me respond once again to that if you don't mind. Mr. Lauderbach, as Steven has repeated for me, I do take great offense at your accusations. I have at all times tried to adhere to all local, state, federal and international laws in the conduct of my businesses, and have rigidly followed all banking laws and regulations to the best of my knowledge and ability when it has come to my involvement as a shareholder and officer at Global United. I have always admonished and trusted bank management to watch out for my behalf in that regard. Here once again, if there have been any infractions like you describe, they have been unwitting and inadvertent on my part."

"Well, let me assure you, Mr. Nasir, we don't intend to let you off that easy on these very serious matters. We have amassed a very copious and voluminous accounting of everything we describe, an audit trail if you will, that we think demonstrates a concerted pattern of disregard for the laws and regulations that you claim you have so closely adhered to. And what may make matters even worse, we are currently investigating the possibility that these activities may have aided and abetted the causes of international crime and possibly even terrorism."

Nasir sat up straight in his chair and flushed red in the

face, but maintained his storied composure. "Gentlemen, hear and understand me clearly, there is absolutely no way I would have ever knowingly helped any criminal or terrorist organization in any transaction. I am innocent of such a charge, and I will spend my last dime to defend myself against such accusations. Show me this evidence you claim to possess."

"You got it, sir!" The frustrated Lauderbach responded. For the next two hours remaining available to them, he, his assistants and the FBI began to lay out the trail of cash deposits, international and domestic wire transfers, and inter-company transactions they suggested substantiated their claims of wrongdoing. There were red-faced denials and copious note-taking during the session, but not much was said by either Nasir or his attorney while the presentation was being made.

"Mr. Lauderbach, it is 4:00 p.m. May I suggest we call it quits for this evening in accordance with our court order, and then Mr. Nasir and I will return as requested tomorrow morning at 8:00 a.m. to continue this discussion.'

"Since that's what the court order says, that's what we'll do, Mr. Augsberger, but we expect you here at no later than 8:00 a.m. tomorrow, on the dot."

"We'll be here, and in the meantime, I would like copies of all the information that you have shown us here this afternoon so that we can put together an appropriate response."

Supercilious bastard, thought Lauderbach.

"And with that, gentlemen, let me repeat to you what I said earlier this morning. When this is all said and done, there is going to be much to be explained by the U.S. Attorney's office and the FBI for the way you have treated my client in all of this. You have interrupted his business and personal life and besmirched his reputation in an unprecedented way. There is no excuse for that. Someone is going to have to answer for this."

"That's fine with us, Mr. Augsberger," Daimler answered defiantly. "We won't quite frankly lose much sleep at this time with respect to that threat. We have much bigger problems to worry about. Just please make sure your client is back here at 8:00 a.m. sharp tomorrow morning like Mr. Lauderbach said."

CHAPTER THIRTY-SEVEN

CANTRELL BURRIS and Weber Ottman were fast buddies, but a strange-looking pair. Burris was a 6'4", 245 lb. African-American, and Ottman a 5'7", 160 lb. redheaded Caucasian. The former was a soft-spoken, polite, mountain of a man, and the latter an irascible, pugnacious little rat. The two couldn't have been any more different, either in appearance or personality, had they tried. Yet, proving that opposites can attract, they had been friends throughout high school—both barely graduating—and had lived, worked and played together since. A big night for the two was a Cubs or Bulls game and about three hours of steady beer drinking afterward. Both men were nuts about women, but that was a one-way street in almost all cases. If a young woman lacked sufficient judgment to accept a date with either one, that date almost always turned out to be the only one.

Neither Burris nor Ottman kept jobs for very long. It wasn't in their nature. They were in their early twenties, but they had done just about everything poorly educated guys with little incentive could do by way of employment. They had been construction laborers, stocked shelves in various stores, driven cabs and trucks, menial factory jobs and so forth. You name it, and they probably would have done it for a short while. They were hard workers when they were employed, but no job ever lasted very long. They were still "trying to find themselves," as they would say to anyone who questioned their inability to stay in one position or another for very long. That was something one of them had heard some guest psychiatrist say on an Oprah rerun once.

Sometime around the first part of October, both Burris and Ottman—who were unemployed once again at the time—managed to find new work together with Chicago Airport Systems, Inc., the contractor for facilities maintenance at O'Hare International Airport. It wasn't much: mopping floors; cleaning urinals; emptying wastebaskets and all; but it was work and the position came with health benefits, something not all their many jobs had. Finding work with the same employer, at the same place, and on the same shift had another little side benefit. They could share the ride to work, and that was something of a godsend. Ottman's old 2009 Nissan Altima was on its last legs.

The morning of the second Friday in December began as usual for Burris and Ottman with both men sleeping until the last minute, slapping their alarm clock numerous times before getting up around 5:30 a.m. to start their day. Most mornings were the same. First stop on their way to work at O'Hare, just a few short miles away from their cheap Schiller Park, Illinois apartment, was always the Minot Coffee Shop on Irving Park Road for a quick bite of breakfast—cold cereal was the extent of their own culinary skills. Breakfast took about thirty minutes. That usually allowed them just enough time to arrive at the airport and punch in without being late. Today, however, the situation would be tragically different.

Finishing their breakfasts, Burris and Ottman paid for their meals, leaving their typically inadequate tip, and then sprinted from the coffee shop to their car for the quick ride to the airport. Just as they reached their car, a young man asking Cantrell Burris if he had a light for his cigarette approached them. As the good-natured Burris was reaching into his pocket to remove his lighter, he could hear his uncouth buddy, Ottman, mumble something like "We're late, Cantrell, tell that raghead son-of-a-bitch to take a hike."

Burris was about to tell Ottman to "shut his filthy mouth," when the muffled sound of two well-aimed shots from a silenced 9 millimeter handgun were heard and both rounds tore through his chest, splattering blood all over the side of the car and sucking the life immediately from him. Burris died where he stood. Nearby patrons exiting the coffee shop heard Ottman yell out "Holy crap! Help, help!" but didn't hear the two additional shots from a second assailant that also dropped him in his tracks, only ten feet from where his lifelong friend lay.

The murder the two buddies and roommates might well have been overlooked as being nothing more than a couple of guys being in the wrong place at the wrong time were it not for the circumstances of the twenty-four-hour period surrounding their deaths. During that same period of time, no less than two additional janitorial employees of Chicago Airport Systems would lose their lives in a similar fashion. Several area police departments were affected and a task force was immediately formed to coordinate the investigation. The FBI was asked to assist. Initially, the investigation oriented around the possibility of recently terminated and potentially disgruntled employees of Chicago Airport Systems, but no lead was ruled out. If some nutcase was out there, he or she needed to be stopped soon to avoid more deaths. Once the police found out what they were dealing with, they felt they had only a small window of time— perhaps hours—before the media linked all of the killings and made it front page news. When that occurred, the investigation would immediately become more difficult.

◊◊◊◊

BY 8:00 A.M. of the second Friday in December, Special Agent Merritt Daimler arrived back to the office after finally getting a good night's sleep at home, and went immediately to the interrogation room where Sammy al-Dajani was still being questioned. Sammy looked up as Daimler entered the

512

room—as he did whenever the door opened or closed. It was as if he was searching for someone, anyone, who might be the person sent to rescue him from this horrendous ordeal he was undergoing. Seeing Daimler, his eyes fell. It was now going on four days of questioning. When will this end, he agonized?

Daimler motioned all of the interrogators out of the room, and they quietly and immediately complied. He then took a seat across from the now horribly tired and emotionally drained Sammy, who had once again laid his head across folded arms on the table in front of him. Other than intermittent, mandatory periods of sleep or rest, the questioning had been unrelenting for the period of time Sammy had been in federal custody. Daimler lightly touched Sammy's arm as he spoke in as calm and caring a manner as he could muster under the circumstances. The veteran FBI agent thought he would give it one last try. He wasn't sure, but he somehow had the feeling that they were running out of time if they were to have any hope of interdicting the bio-weapon attack they felt certain was in the offing.

"Mr. al-Dajani, it's been quite a few days now, and I believe you and I both know that we are running out of time for you to do the right thing for your fellow man if you are in any way inclined by now to do so. We are amassing more and more information that tells us you know a great deal more than you're telling us." Sammy didn't raise his head, but Daimler sensed he was listening. He felt Sammy's arm tense as he spoke. "I firmly feel that you are our only hope for avoiding the deaths of many thousands, perhaps millions of innocent people around the world. If this insidious weapon that we think is out there is loosed on an unsuspecting public, it could be a disaster of epic proportions. In the mobile society that we live in today, there will be many, many innocent men, women, children, sick and infirm that will no doubt succumb to the ravages of such a horrid weapon. As Colonel Ghadamsi so eloquently explained to you the other day, what would be the honor in that? The slaughter of innocents is expressly forbidden not just in your faith, but that of every religion in the world. Mr. al-Dajani, I appeal to your decency as a human being. Help us if you are able."

Sammy sat up slowly. His face and eyes held the look of a horribly tired and desperate man. Daimler sensed he might be reaching him for the first time. Sammy pushed slightly away from the table and sat with outstretched hands draped over his knees, staring down at the floor for what seemed a very long time. Sighing resignedly, he finally looked up at Daimler and simply asked, "What is it that you wish to know?"

Daimler didn't at first know quite how to react. This ordeal had been a rather long haul, and he had just about given up. "Are you, uh, ready to answer our questions, Mr. al-Dajani?"

Sammy looked away from Daimler, staring at a blank wall as if looking at something far off in the distance. "Yes, yes, I am." He replied.

"May I ask a few of our people to come back in with us?" Daimler asked cautiously.

"Sure, whatever you wish."

Daimler hurriedly motioned to whatever unseen persons were behind the large two-way mirror that nearly covered one whole side of the room, and then exited to visit with them in the hallway. He was met by a rapidly increasing group of excited agents outside the interrogation room. "I think some of you may have heard what he said. He appears ready to talk with us, ladies and gentlemen, and I want to move fast. Make sure the videotape is rolling with backup at all times. I want no more than two other people with me in the room with him at any given time—if possible only those who have had a positive rapport with the man up until now. Someone see if we can't also get Imam Ghadamsi back in here. I think al-Dajani liked him. He could be a reassuring back up to us. Additionally, someone give Deputy U.S.

Attorney Lauderbach a heads up as to what may be coming down here. It wouldn't hurt to have he and his people looking in over our shoulders." Glancing around at the assembled group, Daimler asked anxiously. "Now quickly, who are my two people?' Two agents raised their hands, and everyone else nodded as if in agreement. "Alright, Seilor and Erickson, it's you and me. Let's get back in there now, and someone make sure those cameras are rolling."

"Mr. al-Dajani, I've asked agents Jim Seilor and Lon Erickson to join me, if you don't mind," Daimler said upon reentering the room. "I want some extra ears listening to what you have to say. This is extremely important. Can I get you anything before we begin?"

"A cup of coffee only, please, Mr. Daimler."

"Coffee it is, my friend. Jim, get us a few cups of coffee if you don't mind." Daimler motioned for Agent Seilor, who left immediately to get coffee all around. "While Jim gets coffee, Mr. al-Dajani, let's get started right away. I feel we have little time."

"Fine, what do you need to know?"

"Well, to begin, tell us what you know about any terrorists that may be operating in this city or any other city in the country for that matter, and what if any attack they may be planning. We have a multitude of related questions, but they would all be but background for getting at that, anyway. In the essence of time, what if anything do you know along those lines?" Daimler was reaching with that question. Thus far all that Sammy was suspected of doing was perhaps facilitating an unregistered money transfer business, but the thinking of the JTTF was that any information they could get on that might help lead them to any impending attack with a WMD.

The agents waited patiently for Sammy to respond. That question was far-reaching and admittedly still only conjecture on their part, but they had little time to waste. The situation called for a "hail Mary." They could see he was

515

thinking it over one last time. For a moment he still looked uncertain, but then an expression of relief seemed to cross his face. Noticeably sighing, he took a sip of the hot coffee that Agent Seilor had just brought back in, hesitated for a moment and then began to speak. "Gentlemen, I am a member of an al-Qaeda offshoot organization named al-Sahaba—or as one would say in English, The Companions of the Prophet—peace be upon him."

"Al-Sa...what, Mr. al-Dajani. Can you spell that for us?" Asked a totally shocked Agent Erickson.

"Yes, al-Sahaba, S-A-H-A-B-A. As with its now parent organization, al-Qaeda, it's a group dedicated to the establishment of a worldwide, pan-Islamic state, establishing Islam as the one and only true religion. Its followers are willing to do whatever is required with whatever means is at their disposal to accomplish these ends."

"Including the use of biological weapons, Mr. al-Dajani?" Daimler asked.

"Yes, including the use of biological weapons."

"What do you know then, about any impending attack of that sort in this country? Our intelligence informs us that such an event may soon take place, and with potentially disastrous effect. We must stop such a thing from happening." Daimler had a pleading tone to his voice.

"Your sources are correct. An attack of that sort is imminent, and it is al-Sahaba that has been given the so-called divine mission of carrying it off."

"You've got to tell us all that you know, Mr. al-Dajani. An attack of the sort you describe could result in the loss of millions of lives. You must help us avoid that. What can you tell us? When and where is this attack to take place?"

"Well, it was originally planned for sometime during the twenty-four period surrounding what this country's Christian crusaders call Christmas eve—but I was to have been part of the operation, and I have been missing now for days, as you know."

"So, are you suggesting they might change the time of attack?" Daimler asked.

"I wouldn't know for sure, but I would almost be certain that al-Sahaba's leader—a man known to me as Ismail Hamadi, who is located here in Chicago—might well change the date of the attack if he thought the organization's plan stood the chance of being compromised in any way. My disappearance for this length of time has in all likelihood caused no small amount of anxiety for Mr. Hamadi and his leadership group. He and I met almost weekly—usually every Wednesday—and he knows I would never leave without notice, particularly so close to the date of such an operation. He is a very volatile, ruthless individual who will stop at nothing to complete his mission, and from what I can tell most of his leaders are as equally committed as he. Would Hamadi move the attack up if he felt al-Sahaba's plans were at all threatened? Absolutely!"

"How was the attack to take place?" Agent Seilor questioned as all three agents took copious notes.

A self-satisfied smile spread across Sammy's face for a brief second before he got serious once again. "It really is quite ingenious." He answered. "About two weeks ago, al-Sahaba took delivery of what we have been told was a shipment of an extremely virulent form of Smallpox virus pathogens. These pathogens were contained in aerosol canisters of—and this is the ingenious part of it—room deodorizer. The canisters are designed to be used in those little timed spray units you see anymore in a lot of the restrooms in commercial buildings and public places around the city. The plan specifically calls for the canisters to be deployed in the public bathrooms of major airports across the country at the height of the upcoming holiday travel period. As people pass through the restrooms, they will inhale aerosolized droplets and carry the disease with them, spreading it as they come in contact with people across the country. In a matter of days, a plague will be visited upon this

517

country such as it has never seen. This is a particularly ugly form of Smallpox. I have seen a videotape of its effect on people. From what I understand, this country is quite unprepared for such an event."

The three agents and the now very large group behind the mirror in the room adjacent to the interrogation room were speechless. No one said a thing for a painfully long moment. Daimler's mouth, throat, and lips were dry for some reason. He took a long drink of coffee before he spoke. "Did you say airports plural, Mr. al-Dajani? Do you mean this weapon is going to be unleashed in multiple locations around the country?"

"Yes, that is what I said."

"Then please, in God's name, tell us that you know about where those locations are, Mr. al-Dajani."

Sammy had a serious look on his face as he replied. He was finally in a position of power for the first time since he had been taken into custody by the FBI, but things had already gone too far with his admission. "Mr. Daimler, I am not perfectly certain. I am not part of the command-and-control structure. However, from everything I have thus far been privy to, it is my understanding that simultaneous attacks are supposed to occur at the major airports in New York, Washington, D.C., Chicago, Detroit, Miami, Dallas/Fort Worth, Los Angeles and Seattle when this all comes down. Those are the places that I believe I know, but there may be more."

"How was this to take place? How were the pathogens to be delivered?"

"It's really quite simple, actually. There are cells in all of the cities I have mentioned, and they have been planning this for some time. The idea for it all was originally the brainchild of al-Qaeda leader, Sheik bin Laden and his people long before this country's Seal team killed him. They were working on this even before 9/11, but were only recently able to find and obtain the kind of bug that would work the way they wanted. The plan is to show that there are myriad ways to reach this country and others, with potentially far greater devastation than any attack on a big city high rise might result in. All these cells have people who have, of all things, found positions as lowly janitors, both full and part-time, who regularly clean the bathrooms in the busiest areas of all of these terminals. At the prearranged, synchronized time they will deploy the aerosol containers in the deodorizing dispensers in all of the bathrooms as I have described, and the attack will commence. "

"And you were to be a part of this, Sammy?" Daimler asked.

"Yes, believe it or not, I'm a banker who has a part-time night job as a janitor. I have recently worked three nights a week for Chicago Airport Systems, the outfit that maintains the O'Hare facility." Mouths were agape at the simple ingenuity, yet ugliness, of the plan Sammy was unfolding.

"To my understanding, don't O'Hare and a lot of the major buildings around this city have air sampling systems that would detect airborne pathogens of the sort Sammy is talking about here?" Erickson asked of Daimler and Seilor.

Sammy responded before anyone could answer. "Yes, gentlemen, they do, but those systems and many others like them across the country are not real time. They take samples by way of filters that are removed about every four hours or so, holding to a fairly rigid schedule. These filters are then taken to another location and tested. If you know the schedule and have observers watching real-time, as our people do, you can time your attack in such a way that you could have perhaps better than a four hour window in which to release the weapon on the public and have them all travel to many, many destinations across the country before the alarm can be sounded."

By now, excited telephone calls were being made to multiple interested parties throughout the Department of Homeland Security. An encrypted live feed of Sammy's confession was also being televised to numerous agencies around the country. The wheels of response were rapidly being put in motion. Anti-terrorist teams were being notified and assembled as Sammy's explanation of how the attack would unfold continued.

"When did you say this was to take place, Sammy?" Daimler asked.

"By my most recent understanding, the attack was to take place in all of the locations I mentioned sometime during the hours leading up to Christmas Eve, but now I'm not sure. As I said before, they are by now no doubt worried about my absence. The contingency was always there to move in a much shorter time if the Christmas Eve plan went awry."

"How would they move in that regard? What changes would they make, Sammy?" Agent Erickson asked.

"Well, all of our people are of course Muslims. The original plan called for them to be on duty Christmas Eve, ostensibly to allow the Christian employees the opportunity to be off. If anything changed in that regard, then the fall-back plan called for designated al-Sahaba operatives to take out certain employees of the janitorial companies either the day of or before the time the alternate attack was changed to, and then al-Sahaba operatives would be conveniently available to stand in. Rather simple and ingenious, wouldn't you say?"

"Oh, my gosh!" Agent Seilor exclaimed, with a sudden look of horrified recognition crossing his face. "Please, excuse me, but Merritt, Lon, I need to talk to you both in the hallway immediately, if I could." Seilor stood and walked out of the room as he spoke, motioning for Daimler and Erickson to follow. "We'll be right back, Sammy!"

Once in the hallway, Seilor whirled around and breathlessly explained his actions to Daimler, Erickson and other agents quickly gathering. "Guys, it suddenly dawned on me. I overheard a discussion upstairs this morning about a double murder over in the O'Hare area, and there is some sort of coordinated investigation going on between the police departments in several communities out there. I guess there have been a handful of similar killings that have occurred in that area during the last several hours or so. They were contacting us for potential assistance. God help us, but I want to recollect all of those victims worked for a janitorial company or some such thing. Uh…that Chicago Systems Sammy just mentioned may be the one. I don't recollect. They were thinking it might be a disgruntled employee or something. You don't imagine…?"

"I do indeed, Jim. Sounds like this thing may be coming down right now." Daimler's voice sounded panicked. "Let's get back in there for heaven's sake. We've got to find these people and find them fast."

The agents quickly reentered the room with Sammy. "Sammy, if what you have told us is correct, we have reason to believe this attack you've described may be happening as we speak. You've got to tell us what you know and tell us fast. Where, if at all possible, might we find these cells?" Merritt Daimler asked.

"Well, I have no idea as to the whereabouts and plans of any of the cells in the other cities I mentioned, only that their attacks were to coincide with the one here in Chicago. However, the informal headquarters for operations and planning here in Chicago has always been a business called Dominion Janitorial Supply located right downtown here in a warehouse in the 1600 block of West Ontario."

"Could they be there now?"

"I don't know. That location was to be the planning and staging area, but I just don't know."

Daimler stood immediately to leave the room. "Lon, you bring in a couple of other agents and continue the questioning of Sammy here. Jim and I will leave now and try to gather a strike force to hit that warehouse on Ontario that Sammy just described to us. Maybe we'll get lucky, and these al-Sahaba will be there, but we will also need to simultaneously put together a strike force to hit O'Hare just as soon as possible. Notify everyone throughout DHS chain of command. Only God knows what they may want to do. Air traffic will no doubt have to be grounded until we contain this thing. Additionally, we'll need S.W.A.T. and HazMat teams all around, at the warehouse here in downtown and at O'Hare. Immediately notify TSA as well. They should start rounding up their janitorial crews right now. They could be installing these devices as we speak. Come on guys, let's get on this thing now. I want to be in on the raid at the warehouse, and then depending on what we find there, I'm headed to O'Hare. Let's get cracking!" Daimler turned to leave with most all of those assembled outside the interrogation room, commenting back over his shoulder as he left. "Lon, as you're grilling Sammy more, find out if he has any information about whether Nasir is involved in any of this al-Sahaba thing, either directly or indirectly. He's due back here with that obnoxious attorney of his sometime during the next hour or so, and I would bet a month's pay he is. If he doesn't show we'll know for darn sure."

CHAPTER THIRTY-EIGHT

BY THE time Merritt Daimler and his now rather large inter-agency task force arrived at the Dominion Janitorial Supply, Inc. warehouse on West Ontario, the Chicago Police Department and units of the Chicago Division of the U.S. Marshal's office were already on the scene and had cordoned off a four block area surrounding the site. Citizens within the vicinity were being evacuated as quickly as they could be located. Disaster response units of the U.S. environmental Protection agency and the Chicago offices of the CDC arrived at the same time as the FBI, complete with HazMat gear. Three S.W.A.T. units, two on the ground and one heliborne, were ready to enter the building when the word was given. Court orders were in hand, and everyone was set to move once Daimler arrived and was adequately apprised of the situation and gave the order to "go".

"What's our situation?" Daimler asked as he and his contingent exited their car and approached the on-site command-and-control team. "Anyone know how many people we have in the building?"

"Crazy thing, Merritt," answered Captain Tyler Shaughnessy, the senior man on location with the Chicago PD, "we've got infrared heat-seeking scanners taking this building in from all sides, and we're detecting absolutely no one inside that building."

"You've got to be kidding me. When in the devil are we going to have something to start going our way with this thing? I didn't figure we could be so lucky as to catch these guys with their pants down and still in possession of whatever devices they're planning to use. Damnation!" exclaimed Daimler. His men knew he had to be frustrated. He was a fairly religious man and seldom known to curse. "All right, let's move on this thing right away. I want S.W.A.T. teams accompanied by EOD specialists first, followed immediately by the teams of bio-weapons specialists on site. Make sure everyone is masked and move with as much dispatch as adequate caution will allow. We don't know that this building isn't booby-trapped, and we also don't know how contaminated the place may be."

Once all of the necessary people were in place and properly masked, and the Senior S.W.A.T. commander gave the order to move, it took exactly thirty seconds for the maneuvering elements to fully enter the building. Six members of one team hit the front entries, a similar team hit the back, and another rappelled easily to the roof of the warehouse, smashing through a door leading to the third floor of the building. One by one, each room was cleared by the tactical units, followed immediately by EPA and CDC teams utilizing hand-held air sampling units in an effort to determine whether there was any evidence of chemical or biological agents anywhere in the building's atmosphere. All over the building voices could be heard shouting, "Clear! Clear! Clear!" Someone yelled out, "I'm getting nothing here, no positive readings at all. It looks as though whoever was in here may have left and taken their dirty ditty bag with them."

After the warehouse was completely cleared, and it was determined there were no chemical, biological or explosive hazards on the premises, the entire strike force moved in. The JTTF was amazed with what it found. The building was stacked floor to ceiling with literally every type of building maintenance supply imaginable. There were floor waxes, cleaning chemicals, buckets, mops, floor buffers, paper goods and every other kind of imaginable material necessary to substantiate the terrorist front's supposed business. The place was immaculate with hardly anything out of place. Five vehicles were parked inside the large building, two step vans, two panel trucks and a complete semi-tractor trailer combo sitting in one end of the building. Everything was so well organized that it almost appeared as though little if any actual business took place there.

"Special Agent Daimler, you want to come over here and take a look at this?" An FBI agent assisted by one of the HazMat specialists had come across something they wanted him to look at. "Does this mean anything? Didn't you say that what we were looking for was air freshener?"

As Daimler and his command group headed toward the voices, the senior CDC official on location signaled everyone inside the building through the use of a bullhorn that it was now safe to remove their protective masks. The building had been cleared for the presence of any contaminants. No one needed to be told a second time. It was winter, but it was still stifling inside the masks. "What have you got for us over here?" Daimler asked the agent that had called out for him. Removing his mask, he felt a rush of fresh air hit his face.

"Does this appear to be anything like what you wanted us to be looking for, Special Agent Daimler?" The agent and the CDC technician were standing over a half empty pallet covered with what appeared to be pieces of hurriedly sliced shrink wrap that once encompassed its contents. The area around that pallet was the only place in the building where anything appeared to be in disarray. Left on the pallet were a few remaining cartons labeled on one side with an Alpine-type logo and the words MOUNTAIN AIRE Antiseptic Room Deodorizer. On the reverse side, each carton was similarly marked with what appeared to be the same wording written in the Cyrillic alphabet—a dead giveaway as to its possible Russian origin.

"I have absolutely no idea, but it certainly fits the

description of what al-Dajani described for us," Daimler responded. "Say, Doc, can you folks from the CDC take this material away and analyze what's in these canisters as quickly as possible? We need to see if these canisters contain any of the stuff we're looking for."

"We'll get right on it!" Dr. Marian Elliott, the senior CDC official on location, yelled out for some of her people that were dressed in the white HazMat suits. "Guys, get over here and get all of this stuff picked up, onto our trucks and back to lab as soon as possible. Take the pallet, the shrink-wrap lying around it and everything that has anything to do with this shipment of so-called room deodorizer. I want it all tested for evidence of any bio-hazard whatsoever, every canister, every box, every stitch of it. Then get back to me with the results ASAP and waste no time. I want this like yesterday. Oh, and whatever you do, handle everything with extreme caution. Treat it like it's covered with some of the worst stuff imaginable—because it might actually be."

"Think this is what we're after, Doc," Daimler asked.

"Well, if it isn't, then I would bet we're certainly looking for something packaged very much like it. Fits the bill, doesn't it? Room deodorizer, made in Russia from all appearances." Dr. Elliott shook her head disappointedly. "I have this feeling in my gut, however, that what we are after may already be gone. What if we just missed these guys, Merritt? What have we done to cover our butts out at O'Hare?"

"Well, let me assure you, we haven't been sitting on them. There's a huge inter-agency reaction force that hit O'Hare about the same time we hit here, and since it appears there isn't much to do here at the moment for you, me and most of our key people, what say we all head out that way as quick as we can."

"Man, that'll probably take us forever right now, Merritt. Rush hour will be starting in about twenty minutes."

"I'm aware of that, but there's a helipad on the building

just down the block, and I've got two choppers on the way there now. We can be over to O'Hare within the next half hour or so."

As task force members jumped into large dark green Chevy Suburbans marked U.S. Government for the run down the street, it was easy to pick out the building with the helipad. It was the one where an unmarked UH-60 Blackhawk helicopter was already landing on the roof, with a second hovering nearby. "What have our people done out at O'Hare thus far to get things under control there to your knowledge, Merritt?" Dr. Elliott was attempting to get the best estimate she could of the situation while on the run. Others on the team listened intently to Daimler's answer. "And what if anything are we doing in some of the other locations around the country where your guy said this same nightmare might be happening?"

"Well, hopefully, between all of our people, your people and the folks from the TSA, we'll be able to do an end run on this thing out at O'Hare. As for all the other locations around the country where al-Dajani indicated similar attacks might be taking place, well our folks, and the DHS augmented by military have similar operations also mounted in all of those places as we speak. DHS took the National Advisory alert to Imminent threat level days ago, and if they haven't done so already, are probably in the process of grounding flights all over the country. That's certainly what I would do."

"Do you think we really have a chance of interdicting so many potential attacks?"

"Well, supposedly anti-terror task forces are undertaking operations similar to ours in all of the cities mentioned by al-Dajani in an effort to find and eliminate these bad guys before they can hit with this ghastly stuff, but your guess is as good as mine. We really don't know who we're looking for at any of those locations, so we're hoping beyond hope that they're all following the same plan of attack. If that is the case, then perhaps we'll get lucky and stop all of them. We can only pray!"

◊◊◊◊

BY LATE afternoon on the second Friday evening in December, in eight separate airport locations around the U. S., now independently operating al-Sahaba terror cells were preparing to unleash attacks on unsuspecting air travelers. Innocent looking janitorial employees began arriving at their respective workplaces for shift changes, punching in, picking up their cleaning carts and seemingly going about normal workday routines of emptying trashcans, cleaning floors and scrubbing out toilets throughout the facilities in which they were assigned.

One week earlier, at a joint meeting in Chicago, national al-Sahaba commander, Ahmed Khalid, had provided each of the cell leaders with a territorial allotment of two cases, or twenty-four canisters each, of special air freshener, which were to be taken back with them to their respective areas of operation. Precisely at 5:00 pm EST on the day of attack—allowing under strict instructions from Khalid for changes in time zone—these canisters were to be inserted into room deodorizing dispensers in high-traffic restrooms situated throughout busy air terminals all over the country. Literally at exactly the same time nationwide, measured sprays of liquid droplets, heavily laden with active, powerful weaponized Smallpox virus would begin releasing into the air every sixty seconds. During the four to eight hour window the terrorists felt that they might have before the attack might be detected at any one of those locations hundreds, perhaps thousands of passengers would be exposed to the sprays within but a very short time. Those people would more than likely then in turn depart to hundreds of different destinations around the county bearing contagion to other unsuspecting infidels. The terrorists calculated that the resulting plague would wreak complete and utter devastation, causing the

9/11 attack to pale by comparison. It would be the "wake up call to all the non-believing world," had been Khalid's claim.

At precisely 3:00 p.m. CST (4:00 p.m. EST), two Blackhawk helicopters carrying the bulk of the DHS strike force that had just raided the al-Sahaba warehouse on West Ontario in downtown Chicago, touched down on the relatively clear top level of the parking deck next to terminals 1-3 at Chicago's O'Hare International Airport. Heavily armed men and women ran down the stairs and crossed the street between the parking garage and the terminal using the glassed-in overhead walkway at terminal level. By this time, the Chicago Police and the TSA were also herding hundreds of frightened and befuddled passengers out onto the street surrounding the building. The anger and complaints that would usually accompany such a situation were noticeably absent as visions of a 9/11 or other similar events since were on the minds of most.

As the situation unfolded, Ahmed Khalid watched in horror from the vantage of his waiting Yellow Cab just outside the lower level entrance to the baggage area. His heart began to race. Khalid was uncertain whether any of this situation had anything to do with the attack his operatives were currently undertaking, but he had to consider the fact that there was a strong possibility. Had the mysteriously absent Saud al-Dajani given up the operation? *If so, he's a dead man,* was Khalid's first thought.

Khalid quickly grabbed his cell phone and frantically began to hit preset phone number codes. The first number he dialed was that of operative, Abdullah Amar. The phone rang several times before a prerecorded voice came back with the message, "The cellular number you are dialing is currently not in service or the service user is out of range. Please try to place your call again at a later time." Khalid began to panic. He then dialed the phone numbers of all four of the other operatives, only to be met with the same response. Could someone be jamming cellular communications in this vicinity, he wondered.

Inside all three domestic terminals TSA security officers and federal agents now began to search the premises. Wherever Chicago Airport Systems cleaning personnel were found, they were surrounded, told to lie down on the floor to be searched and were cuffed. As officers approached, two young men on the cleaning crew were just exiting the bathrooms next to the security gates adjacent to the ticket counter of a major airline. They looked at the approaching security officers and then at each other and began to run. They nearly reached the exits, but were surrounded just inside the doors by security personnel, guns drawn and at the ready. "Halt, halt or we'll shoot! On the floor, on the floor!" An agent yelled.

One of the young men reached inside his work smock, pulling out an object that looked to all of the security officers like a gun. He whirled, pointing what appeared to be a weapon. Three officers fired at once, all hitting the young man. One shot pierced his head just above his right eye, exiting the back of his skull and ending up in the door frame directly behind. The other two rounds simultaneously punched through the man's heart and lungs. Blood splattered in a plume behind him, and as he fell, his shoulder went through the unopened door, shattering glass all around. Abdullah Amar was dead before he hit the floor.

The second young man seeing what had happened to his partner immediately dropped to the floor and onto his belly, arms outstretched with legs spread wide apart, taking the appropriate position without receiving any such instructions whatsoever from the security officers and agents that were fast surrounding him. He had no desire to experience the same demise as Amar.

"Get cuffs on this guy right now and get the HazMat teams up here right away. We need those bathrooms that these two guys just came out of, and all of the others in this area checked out right away. They may have already planted the devices. Then by heavens, I want every cleaning person in this place rounded up. Seilor, Seilor, have you got that list for me?" FBI Special Agent Daimler had arrived on the scene from downtown just in time to observe the apprehension that had just taken place. The list he was yelling for contained all the names of Chicago Airport Systems cleaning personnel that records indicated had recently punched in and were supposedly on duty. They would need to account for all of them to begin looking for al-Sahaba operatives.

By 4:15 pm, word came back to the command elements of the anti-terrorist strike force that all of the cleaning personnel who had punched in and had not punched back out, were now in custody at the O'Hare TSA command center, and were already undergoing intense questioning. Priority was being placed on young males who fit a Middle Eastern or Asian profile, with seemingly little concern for political correctness. Word had come back that at least in the bathrooms where the two young men had exited, the air had been tested and found free of any airborne hazards. Located on the cleaning carts left in those restrooms, however, were eight replacement canisters for the deodorizer dispensers, all marked with the Mountain Aire logo like those back at the warehouse on Ontario. The canisters were being sent away for immediate testing, and the carts of all the cleaning crews were being checked for more. If Sammy's information was correct, they would need to account for sixteen more canisters.

As word eventually came back to Daimler and his team that a search of the cleaning crews and carts had disclosed not only three more suspected terror operatives, but additionally resulted in the finding of thirty more canisters of Mountain Aire room deodorizer, which might or might not contain pathogens. The JTTF team was elated. If they were lucky, the labs would find all of the Smallpox-laced canisters within the bunch and a disaster would have been prevented, at least here in the City of Chicago. *God willing*, thought Daimler, *we'll have the same luck in the other cities where other similar operations are supposed to be taking place. At least we now know what we're looking for.*

As the JTTF's anti-terrorist reaction force continued their search of all the nooks and crannies within the terminals, confused passengers outside, unaware of the situation that had just unfolded around them, clamored to learn when flights might resume and they could get on with their travels. Lost in a sea of public and private transportation jockeying for position to carry away the throngs of passengers who had decided to give up on the day, was one yellow cab driven by a highly distraught and thoroughly disillusioned Ahmed Khalid. He could only pray that at least some of the other cells around the country had fared better than it appeared his men in Chicago had done that day. He would be leaving this city and perhaps the country at his earliest opportunity.

◊◊◊◊

AHMED KHALID was certain that the undoing of al-Sahaba's well-planned, but hurriedly executed attack was in great part the result of some major breach in security, and that Saud al-Dajani's unexplained absence was at the root of the situation. There was little, however, that he could do about it now. He was instead on the run, leaving Chicago for Dearborn, MI within hours after the botched attack at O'Hare. It would be much easier to disappear into the large Muslim community there until he could determine the extent of the damage to his organization and decide upon his next move.

Counter terrorism operations similar to those which the DHS mounted at Chicago's O'Hare International to successfully interdict the biological attack that was attempted there by al-Sahaba, were concurrently undertaken by like teams in all of the seven major U.S. cities mentioned by

532

Sammy al-Dajani in his warning. The results in all of those places were equivalent to that of the Chicago task force, with groups of four to six terror supects being apprehended at each of the major airport terminals in those cities. Arrests were, by and large, made without major incident, in New York, Detroit, Washington, D.C., Dallas, Los Angeles and Seattle, and the same would have been the case in Miami had not two operatives chosen to resist there as they had in Chicago. When asked to surrender by anti-terrorist forces, they opted instead to attempt an escape under cover of gunfire. It was a futile, suicidal attempt that led to the death of both at the hands of government agents.

What was particularly gratifying to the DHS units in each of the cities where al-Sahaba cells were apprehended, however, was the fact that they felt reasonably certain they had in all likelihood recovered all of the bio-weapons canisters assigned for use by each cell. According to what Sammy had indicated, all eight cells had each been consigned two cases of twelve aerosol canisters each containing the Smallpox pathogens, and that is exactly what was recovered in each of the cities where raids were conducted. An even more amazing fact was that, except for Miami, none of the canisters had been deployed. Even there only four canisters had been inserted into the dispensing units before DHS authorities interrupted the operatives in the act. Those were the two terrorists who tried to fight it out with government agents. A major containment operation was undertaken to mitigate the effects of any pathogens that might have reached any passengers or first responders.

DHS units remained on full alert under a continuing Threat Advisory at the highest level of Imminent, inasmuch as it was suspected that not all al-Sahaba operatives may have been apprehended. Others might yet be loose elsewhere who could still be in possession of viable Smallpox pathogens. CDC units in all major cities around the country were working around the clock, looking for any epidemiological signs that might indicate an outbreak of the disease.

CHAPTER THIRTY-NINE

ONCE THE circumstances of Tariq Nasir's situation became apparent to Global United's Board of Directors, a special meeting of the board was hurriedly convened on the Monday following the al-Sahaba attack. Leading the agenda was a discussion of the recent findings by the Office of the U.S. Comptroller of the Currency of numerous, significant regulatory violations, and a determination of what actions needed to be taken to protect both the customers and shareholders of the bank. In attendance to ensure decisions made were in accordance with expectations of regulators were Cass Price and Latisha Caldwell.of the OCC.

At this meeting, a resolution was passed requesting that Nasir take a leave of absence from his position as Chairman of the Board, stepping away from active involvement with the bank, its Board of Directors, or any of its committees, until the results of the government's investigation into his bank and other business involvements were more fully known.

Further, Global United's President and CEO, Scott Kruse, was asked to do the same. This action was based upon criticisms expressed of him by the OCC in its initial report of examination regarding his overall administration of the bank and inability to adequately explain away the source of numerous, troubling regulatory violations. Particularly troubling to the directors was the fact that many of the violations held the portent of pecuniary action against the bank—and perhaps its Board of Directors personally—for their failure to ensure proper administration of BSA and AML regulations as required by law. Logan Hart, Executive Vice President, was asked to assume the responsibilities of Chief Executive Officer at Global United on a temporary basis until full disposition of both Tariq Nasir's and Scott Kruse's situations was determined and appropriate action taken by the bank's board.

Both Nasir and Scott were absent from the meeting where these actions were taken, Nasir because of his ongoing joust with the U.S. Attorney, DHS and FBI, and Scott by request of the board. One of the longer-term board members, attorney Taylor Parriott, chaired the meeting at which regulators were in attendance.

"From what you say, Ms. Price, it would appear that Global United can expect a significant number of violations in the final report the OCC will soon issue on its examination of this bank. Is that correct?" Parriott was a no-nonsense veteran of a multitude of legal battles spanning nearly forty years of practice as an attorney, and thirty years on the bank's board of directors. Specializing in civil law, with a long list of small to medium-sized commercial clients throughout the Chicago area, Parriott had always been a good resource for management and the board in troublesome matters involving bank customers of that type. The situation currently unfolding between the bank and the OCC, however, was something new and different for both he and the rest of the board. One could tell by the looks on their faces that they were concerned about what might come from the highly critical report of examination that was about to be issued by Cass Price and her team.

"Regrettably, that's quite correct, Mr. Parriott. I am afraid there will be numerous violations cited in our final report of examination regarding Global United's handling of regulatory requirements of the Bank Secrecy Act and various Anti-Money Laundering regulations that have been strengthened by the Freedom Act. Further, since many of those violations had to do with the bank's relationship with Mr. Nasir, it looks like we will also be citing a number of violations of Regulation 'O', the rules covering the handling of business relationships between the bank and its Insiders."

"What might this result in for the bank?" Parriott asked.

"We have yet to decide the severity of the administrative action the OCC will be taking with regard to the bank," said Cass, "but at a minimum Global United will no doubt be required to enter into a Memorandum of Understanding relative to corrective actions that will be required to address the bank's lack of compliance in these areas. And we may very well determine it necessary to issue a Cease and Desist Order relative to certain situations and people within the organization. If the latter were to be our decision with Mr. Nasir's legal problems being a contributing factor, regulatory required divestiture of his holdings might not be wholly outside the realm of possibility."

"Those things being said, Ms. Price, can you give us any insight at this time relative to the insider problems you have encountered, and what criticisms the OCC may be considering leveling at members of bank management?" Parriott continued. "As I think you can well appreciate, when it comes to Mr. Nasir, the rest of us here on the bank's board do feel we are in a bit of an awkward position. We all clearly know what our responsibilities are to depositors of the bank as directors, and we are prepared to take whatever action is required of us to do what is right by them. We also, however, have a responsibility to shareholders, and Mr. Nasir represents a controlling seventy-five percent interest in the ownership of the bank. So, until we know the status of his situation overall, it would seem we might still need to be cautious in our actions relative to him. Wouldn't you think? What additional insight can you give us regarding his situation?"

"Latisha, do you want to pass those out?" At Cass' direction, OCC examiner Latisha Caldwell got up from the table and once again began to circulate a sheaf of papers to each director and officer present at the meeting. "Gentlemen, at this point in time I am not really able to tell you much regarding the investigation by outside, non-banking legal authorities into Mr. Nasir's business and banking activities, but I can certainly give you some details as to what we at the OCC will be citing in our list of violations and exceptions. Latisha is right now passing out to each of you a report that summarizes the various regulations where we have found violations or irregularities worthy of citing. This report also contains a detailed listing with full description of all the transactions that are prompting our criticisms. Mr. Hart and his people were provided with this late Friday, and I believe are already investigating those transactions to provide explanations as to their purpose, if that can be determined. Obviously, since as you can see Mr. Nasir and his companies play a prominent role therein, this will no doubt require a great deal of cooperation on their part in researching each of those transactions."

"Well, can you at least give us some idea as to what concerns the OCC most about these transactions?"

"All I can tell you now is that in our opinion, the bank was inappropriately exempting Mr. Nasir and certain of his business interests from proper reporting of transactional activities that in every respect should have been reported to FinCEN on a regular basis. This would be bad were it for any customer, but for an insider who is supposed to have a clear understanding of laws and regulations associated with such activities, the situation is particularly egregious. We think your actions today, asking Mr. Nasir to take a leave of absence from active involvement in the bank until a full understanding is obtained regarding these matters, is exactly in keeping with what we would expect you to do under the circumstances, regardless his percentage of ownership. The same is true with respect Mr. Kruse. His working relationship was extremely close with Mr. Nasir. We too want to know how much he knew about Mr. Nasir's situation and how much he was involved in these activities before we can express comfort regarding his continued involvement with Global United."

"Might I interrupt to ask a question that has been on my mind, folks?" asked Kenneth Townsend, President and CEO of Quantum Pharmaceuticals, another of the more outspoken members of the bank's board of directors. "Does any of this also have anything to do with the absence of Mr. al-Dajani, our Senior Vice President of Operations here at Global United? Because if it does, I think we should be taking some similar action with him until the board has some answers to all of this. Nobody has said anything about him yet, but word gets around. Most of these violations you folks from the OCC and these other investigative agencies are looking into fall within his areas of responsibility, and to my understanding, he has been absent from the bank since a short time before all of this information was brought out. Can your people offer the board any insight on that, Ms. Price, or if you can't, what about you Logan? What can either of you tell us about that?"

Logan and Cass caught each other's eye. Logan could tell Cass preferred that he respond to this question, and Logan knew that he needed to take great care with how he answered. Townsend had hit on the one thing that neither he nor Cass felt much at liberty to say anything about. No one was yet privy to Sammy's apprehension and detention, and the DHS still wanted to keep it that way for a while until they had finished more of their investigation and were ready to release more details about the foiled al-Sahaba operation. "Gentlemen," Logan injected, "let me respond to Ken's question if Ms. Price and the board do not mind."

"No, Mr. Hart, please do go ahead with what you have to say," Cass answered.

"Certainly, thank you, Ms. Price. Well, to answer that question, gentlemen, Sammy al-Dajani is still absent from the bank trying to take care of some important personal matters, and we are yet uncertain as to when he will be returning. However, Ken has definitely hit on something. Most of these problems and criticisms have occurred in Sammy's area of responsibility, and I think we need to know more about his involvement and any explanations he might offer before we decide if he should continue here at the bank as well. I think it is definitely in order for him to be included in your resolution requiring that he take a similar leave of absence when and if he does return."

"The OCC would concur with Mr. Hart's recommendation gentlemen," Cass added. "From what we understand, Mr. al-Dajani also had a fairly close relationship here at the bank with Mr. Nasir and many of his associates, and it was his oversight and decision-making that led to many of the criticisms we have in these areas of concern. The OCC would be tremendously uncomfortable with Mr. al-Dajani's continued involvement here at the bank until we have satisfactory answers to a great many questions about how a number of things were handled in his areas of responsibility. We think it most appropriate that he at minimum take a similar leave of absence until we have those answers."

"That says enough for me I would say, Ms. Price. What about the rest of you gentlemen? Does someone want to make a motion to that effect?" Taylor Parriott queried the remainder of the board.

"Taylor, I will make such a motion to amend our previous resolution, adding Mr. Saud al-Dajani to the list of those required to take mandatory leave of absence when he returns from his trip, until the extent of these problems with our regulators and his part in them can be realized." Kenneth Townsend emphasized his motion with a slap of his open hand on the table.

"And I will second that!" Jonas Latham, President of Triton College, hurriedly added.

"We have a motion and a second to add Saud al-Dajani to the list of those required to take leave of absence until these matters can be cleared up. Is there any further discussion?" Parriott glanced around the table for a brief moment in an effort to allow time for concerns to be voiced. "Hearing none, gentlemen, let's have a show of hands on this. All of those in favor of the amended motion, please signify by the uplifted hand." The hands of all directors went up slowly and deliberately. "It looks unanimous. The motion passes!"

"If we are done with that, Taylor, may I please ask Ms. Price a couple of additional questions?"" asked Terrance Paul, one of the directors and second generation owner and operator of Paul's Rathskellers, a very successful chain of German-themed restaurants located around the metropolitan area,

"You may indeed if she has the time. Ms. Price?"

"Ask away, Mr. Paul, and for that matter, let me encourage everyone else on the board to do the same," Cass answered. "These are all very serious matters, gentlemen, and you as board members have the responsibility to see that any and all problems are rectified. It also isn't unfathomable that both legal and monetary penalties might individually face each of you as board members should our examination prove gross negligence on the part of any or all of you as board members. So, by all means, I'll take whatever time is necessary to answer your questions."

"Well, the question I have, quite frankly along the lines of what you just said, Ms. Price, is what will be the outcome for Tariq Nasir as it relates to his ownership and involvement here at the bank if it turns out he is in any way culpable relative to these violations you are listing in your report?"

"Well, Mr. Paul, depending on how the overall

investigation goes that is surrounding him at this time, our action could perhaps go as far as to require that he resign from the board, and as I alluded to before, divest himself of all ownership in the bank and bar him from any future ownership or management involvement in any other federally-insured banking institution. Now, I would hasten to add that all of that remains to be seen, but we do take such matters as these quite seriously, and as regulators, we will take whatever steps are necessary to ensure that financial institutions within our jurisdiction are run in a safe and sound manner. In a nutshell, we will be looking very closely at the manner in which this board responds to these violations and the corrective actions that are taken. We will remain closely involved with your board throughout this entire situation."

"You know, as I think of all that is being said here, Ms. Price," interjected Taylor Parriott once again, "it dawns on me to ask whether you and the OCC are aware that a great deal of the Global United stock that is owned by Mr. Nasir's family is held in irrevocable trusts where beneficial interest is in favor of Mr. Nasir's two young sons, Faoud and Hassan. What about such action by the OCC and other regulators under those circumstances? Does that situation muddy the waters any for you?"

"Yes, Mr. Parriott, we were indeed quite well aware of that situation, and there may well be some legal issues there that we will need to contend with. One important question there will no doubt be how much discretion or authority Mr. Nasir is able to exercise over the way those shares are voted. It is my understanding that his sons are still but young men, and that he has full proxy on all those shares as trustee. Depending on what the situation is relative to his continued involvement here at Global United, that may well be an issue for us to contend with. I thank you for bringing the matter up to us, but we were indeed fully aware that situation existed. I guess nothing is ever simple. Is it?"

◊◊◊◊

AT 8:00 A.M. on the Monday following the al-Sahaba attacks, Tariq Nasir arrived at the Dirksen Building on N. Dearborn to continue his interrogation by FBI officials regarding his possible involvement in illegal financial and recent terrorist activities. Previously planned for the Friday before, Nasir's second day of questioning had been preempted by all the activities surrounding the al-Sahaba attacks at O'Hare International and elsewhere around the country.

Having had three extra days to plan and organize a suitable response, Nasir was not only accompanied by a full contingent of attorneys from the prestigious law firm of Carrier, Augsberger and Kafir, but was additionally bolstered by a rather raucous crowd of Muslim supporters demonstrating outside the FBI's building. The news about Nasir's situation was out now, and the crowd was convinced he was being made a scapegoat by the DHS and FBI in a knee-jerk reaction to the foiled al-Sahaba terrorist attack at O'Hare International the day before. Additionally aware that several Muslim clerics and community leaders had been brought in for questioning along with Nasir, the nearly out-of-control demonstrators were marching, carrying signs and chanting in protest.

Carrier, Augsberger, and Kafir had been on retainer with the Nasir organization since the mid-1990's. So, it was no surprise that senior partner Steven Augsberger was at Nasir's elbow from the start in this situation with the FBI. Augsberger enjoyed the limelight, reveling in seeing his face on camera and being at the center of highly publicized, controversial cases. "High profile cases are good for business," the cocky, tall, blond, fifty-something attorney constantly reminded his younger associates. Case in point was the current situation regarding Tariq Nasir. Augsberger's thumbprint was all over its immediate notoriety.

Anyone who knew Augsberger could have predicted

his use of the media to garner public support for his client. As an example, in order to help Nasir avoid too much publicity coming and going from the Dirksen Building, the FBI had offered to allow him and his entourage access through a covered rear entrance, but Augsberger declined the gesture. He chose instead to march his client directly through the gauntlet of demonstrators and waiting media purposely to allow him access to the press. The ploy was working. The little forays through the press line had already generated several prominent articles in both local and national newspapers, questioning whether Nasir might not be a high-profile victim of the DHS's effort to shift public scrutiny from its having supposedly allowed the al-Sahaba attacks to progress as far as they did without detection.

Due to his local prominence, Nasir's situation was hot, front-page news from the moment he was brought in for questioning by the U.S. Attorney and FBI. After the attempted terrorist attacks at O'Hare and other locations around the country, the investigation into his situation was beginning to receive national attention. News teams from all of the major networks were quick to set up direct satellite feed operations outside the Dirksen Building, AmeriPAK headquarters, and Nasir's various residences. Additionally, once Nasir's involvement with Global United Bank of Chicago was fully known, teams of reporters sniffing a possible major story there as well were also camped outside the bank's offices. Gaggles of news people shoved microphones into the faces of bank staff and customers as they entered and exited the bank. The increasing notoriety of the Nasir investigation not only frustrated the investigators involved in looking into the matter, but it was fast becoming both an embarrassment and aggravation to the staff, management, and board of directors of Global United. The situation was having a disquieting effect on bank clients as a whole and had even resulted in a mini "run" on the bank by many of its less sophisticated depositors, some of whom

544

hailed from the bank's ever-increasing book of business with Chicago's Muslim community.

Monday turned out to be the first full day of questioning that Tariq Nasir was actually subjected to. When he had been picked up the previous Thursday, not much by way of interrogation took place, thanks to the roadblocks thrown up by attorney Augsberger and his associates. The same was true for the days intervening when the FBI, DHS and other supporting agencies were all working feverishly to interdict the al-Sahaba attacks in Chicago and various other cities around the country. Such was not the case for the days following the attack, however. By then, additional agents had been brought in to assist investigating teams in all of the cities where attacks had occurred, and the DHS was making every effort to get to the bottom of how another terrorist organization like al-Sahaba had come so close to wreaking havoc once again on an unsuspecting American public. Every aspect of the planning, financing, organization, and execution of the attack was being looked at, and it was felt that Nasir might well hold some answers to many of their questions if the money trail could be pieced together.

"Good morning, ladies and gentlemen, let's get started. Shall we?" Special Agent Merritt Daimler, had purposely kept Nasir and his bevy of attorneys waiting until the very last minute before he, his associates and representatives of the Chicago-based U.S. Attorney's office walked into the FBI conference room on the fifth floor of the Dirksen Federal Building. "Mr. Nasir, Mr. Augsberger, we appreciate your timely arrival here this morning. We have much to accomplish. It helps to be able to start on time."

"Can you tell us how long this will take today, Mr. Daimler?" Augsberger glanced at his watch with a look of impatience. "My client, Mr. Nasir, has some very important meetings later today that he needs to make if we can finish in time."

"Well, Mr. Augsberger, I hate to be a bucket of cold

water, but I'm not sure I can guarantee your client will be able to make those meetings. As I indicated a moment ago, we have a lot to cover. It may well take days more than hours to accomplish what we need to do here."

"I hope you realize how much damage this whole affair is causing my client and his companies, Mr. Daimler. We really must protest."

"Protest away, Mr. Augsberger. We're looking into matters of great importance to national security, and we still think your client may be in possession of information that could be extremely helpful in our investigation. As inconvenient as it may be for Mr. Nasir, I am afraid we're going to need enough of his time that he could end up missing many meetings over the next few days."

"Well, may I suggest we get started then?" Augsberger preferred to at least think he had the upper hand, and he didn't very much feel as though that was the case at the moment. He knew that the authorities suspected Nasir of somehow being either directly or indirectly involved in the recently foiled terrorist attacks around the country, and that they were hot on the trail of any person or piece of information that could lead them to any remaining perpetrators. He would need to take great care in how he handled himself and his client's situation. "The sooner you get started with your questions, the sooner my client can clear himself of any suspicions, which I can assure you he will do."

"That's fine with us, and we indeed hope that will be the case, Mr. Augsberger. We too want to move this investigation along. It is imperative for a number of reasons that we do so. I can assure you that there will be no delay on our account." Daimler had little time or patience for self-important attorneys like Augsberger at a time like this. There was too much at stake for the country. "I would like to get started by introducing special agents Jim Seilor, Lon Erickson and Harry Cutter of the FBI, and I think you know

Tom Lauderbach and Mike Benson from the U.S. Attorney's office. These gentlemen will be the individuals handling most of the questions we have for you today, Mr. Nasir."

"You're not going to be part of these meetings, Mr. Daimler?" Augsberger seemed concerned that Daimler was not going to be part of the interrogation.

"No, not at this time, there are a number of other aspects to this case that currently require my personal attention. I may sit in from time-to-time to see how we are progressing and to keep things moving along, but these gentlemen will handle most of our questioning of Mr. Nasir. They're the people within our organization who are most familiar with the particulars of the case we're pursuing, at least as such relates to Mr. Nasir anyway. So, with that, I'll turn this over to Special Agent Seilor, and take my leave for the moment." Daimler immediately exited the room without further explanation, leaving Agent Seilor in charge.

"Thanks, Merritt!" Seilor muttered at the retreating Daimler as he left the room. "Mr. Nasir, I believe all of us have numerous questions we need to ask. So, if no one has any problems with me doing so, I will be the one to start out." Seilor shuffled a stack of papers in front of him as he glanced around the table for a response. Augsberger noticed that all of the agents and Assistant U.S. Attorneys had similar looking stacks of information in front of them. "We also plan to record these sessions with Mr. Nasir in their entirety for future reference, Mr. Augsberger. Do you have any problem with that?"

"No, we have no problem with that, as long as I am also provided an exact duplicate of the video for my use."

"Fine, we have every intention of eventually providing you with a copy of any recordings made of our interrogations of your client, but you should know in advance that there may be a slight delay in our doing so. Providing you or anyone else with video copies of any of these proceedings before a federal judge agrees with the efficacy of such a release, could prove most counterproductive to our investigation. The last thing we need is for videos of any of our questioning of your client to make their way into the press' hands until the timing is appropriate for doing so," said Seilor.

"That's totally unacceptable," said Augsberger, "and I very much resent your implications as to us releasing anything to the press. We demand immediate copies of any and all videos of Mr. Nasir's sessions with you people."

"Well, demand away and be offended all you want, Mr. Augsberger but we have no intention of seeing these sessions with your client being played out on local and national news. That sideshow we're fairly certain you orchestrated out in front of our building this morning with you and your client wading through press and paparazzi, is a prime example of why we would feel the need for such a delay. That promenade and accompanying long-winded diatribe could all have been totally avoided by using the private entrance to our building as we offered, but you chose not to do so, and we think we know why," said Seilor. "Now what say we get started here before days of questioning turn into weeks?"

"Fine, let's get started," snapped a chagrined Augsberger.

"Now that we're past that, Mr. Nasir, let me first begin this morning by asking you some questions regarding the unregistered hawala business you seem to be running by way of most of your AmeriPAK company subsidiaries, and then..."

"Now see here, Mr. Seilor," objected Nasir, "I fully intend to be as cooperative as I can relative to this entire affair, but I think we are going to be wasting a great deal of your time and mine if you think hawala has anything to do with any of my companies. I told all of you gentlemen this last week. I was raised by a hawaladar, and I have been around the business all of my life. My family has been in that business for many generations. However, my involvement in any of that ceased when I moved to the United States many years ago. Neither I nor any of my businesses have anything to do with hawala."

'Well, we think we can show otherwise, Mr. Nasir, but I'll get to that in a moment," continued Seilor. "First we would like to ask you a number of questions regarding the organization and makeup of your companies. We'll be making inquiries about the people you have involved and then try to get a handle on the kind of businesses in which each of those companies is involved. Further, I and my colleagues here want to discuss at length the relationships you and your companies have with Global United and its staff as that bank's Chairman of the Board and majority shareholder. Of particular interest to us are the many international financial transactions the bank handles for you, and the tremendous amount of offshore banking it appears you and your companies are involved in as a result of those transactions."

Nasir shook his head and sighed. "Ask away, gentlemen! I have nothing to hide regarding any of these things, but there is much you've mentioned that I and/or my people may need to research to respond sufficiently to your questions. There are a great deal of transactions that take place on a daily basis between both my companies and the bank that I have neither the time nor inclination to personally follow in great detail. As you are well aware, I have multiple companies run by a slew of capable managers who oversee operations on a day-to-day basis. I will do whatever I can to answer any and all questions you may ask, but you have to understand that I may in many cases need to rely on research done by those managers in order to answer you fully and accurately."

"We're fully understanding of that and glad you're so cooperative, Mr. Nasir," Agent Seilor tried to look Nasir directly in the eyes as they spoke, but found it difficult to do so. When Nasir carried on a conversation with anyone of authority, he had a tendency to look away from that person's face as they spoke, acting as though the whole conversation was beneath him. Seilor really didn't care much for the supercilious businessman. "I know you're painfully aware our investigators acquired a voluminous amount of business and accounting information from your people some days ago when we executed several search warrants at your various offices and banks. We since have had numerous members of our staff poring over that documentation for hours on end, and suffice it to say, there is much about which we have questions."

"Let's hope your questions bear fruit in your investigation, Agent Seilor," Augsberger interjected. "The damage caused to my client and his companies by these intrusions are significant, and we think unwarranted. Someone will have to account for that."

"We've heard you say that a number of times now, Mr. Augsberger. I think we have gotten your message," Seilor said disgustedly. "We think everything we've done to date and plan to ask you about is indeed warranted, and believe very strongly our investigation will prove that out." Seilor stood and retrieved from a credenza behind him what appeared to be several copies of an approximate two-inch thick set of documents, held together by three-ring binders. Turning back to Augsberger, he dropped two sets loudly in front of the cocky attorney.

"What's all this?" Augsberger asked.

"Well, Mr. Augsberger, that's two copies of background information for the questions we plan to ask your client about this morning. You may keep them for both your reference this morning and later use in pursuing any related responses. At the top of our list of questions we would like to pursue is an inquiry into the myriad financial transactions Mr. Nasir's various companies enter into on a regular basis for both their own accounts and between the various companies. You will find listed there by company, those transactions over the last three years about which we are most curious. In that regard, it seems strange to us and worthy we think of investigation that all of the AmeriPAK companies are heavy users of cash in a manner atypical to similar companies within their same industrial sector. We would like to discuss that, and for that purpose have once again provided related accounting information by company. Nearly all of your AmeriPAK subsidiaries, Mr. Nasir, have large cash positions on their balance sheets, and they have numerous inter-company accounts receivable that appear to very likely relate to transfers of such cash between themselves. We want to know about that. Further, all of your companies maintain deposit accounts in banks located in offshore havens where business transacted is often of a questionable nature. We are interested in having you and your people provide explanations as to the need and purpose of these many, many transfers."

"Now see here, Agent Seilor, there is nothing illegal about having offshore accounts." Attorney Augsberger appeared thoroughly frustrated with the FBI's line of questioning. "My client..."

"No, wait a minute, Steven, let me respond to that," Nasir interjected. "I have nothing to hide here."

Augsberger shrugged his shoulders, sighed and leaned back in his chair gesturing submissively. "Fine, Tariq, have at it if you wish, but I won't be silent if I think you're heading down a path of conversation that will hurt our cause here. Please, understand that's my job. If you won't let me do it, then I am of no use to you here."

"I understand, Steven, and I thank you. Feel free to jump in at any time, but I am sorry, I want to respond to the baseless, scurrilous accusations these people are attempting to lodge here against me and my companies." Nasir turned and for once stared directly at his government accusers as he leaned forward and pointed his finger to emphasize his response. "An extremely large portion of my business is international, ladies and gentlemen, and if you have investigated all of my companies enough as you say you have, then you must certainly realize that. Hence, the basis for the many international transfers and offshore accounts to which you refer. As for the cash and the inter-company liabilities that many of my companies often carry on their books, well, I am sorry people. That is the way that I choose to run my company. There is nothing whatsoever insidious about that, and I defy you to prove that there is. We deal with a great deal of people who prefer to use cash. Therefore, we keep a lot of it on hand. I know where you're headed with this, and I categorically deny it. I am not in the business of hawala!"

"Well, if that's the case, Mr. Nasir, there should be a satisfactory audit trail that our accountants ought to be able to follow," Seilor responded with an equally determined look to his face. "And something that we're going to ultimately have to discuss before all is said and done here is the fact that your father, Mahmoud, owns twenty-five percent of your holding company, AmeriPAK, Inc., when by your own admission, he indeed is in the business of hawala. So, we're going to need a thorough discussion of that before too long."

Nasir was silent.

"As for the hawala thing, we think the fact one of our country's intelligence operatives was able to execute a rather large transfer of money originating from a hawala-type money transfer organization seemingly run by your father in Pakistan, and culminating in delivery through an officer in your jewelry store operation would seem to suggest some major, potential problems for you in denying your involvement and that of your various companies in the money transfer business. We believe we've found all of the trappings of a very large hawala operation within your organization, and we think we will eventually prove that. As the saying goes, 'If it walks like a duck, and quacks like a duck, it's probably a duck', Mr. Nasir. We are fairly certain you and your people are operating an unregistered money transfer business that is significant in scope, and if that indeed proves to be the case, sir, it is a felony under current federal law for all of those involved, including you."

"I am sorry, Tariq, but I must insist that you make no further comments at this time until we have an opportunity to look all of this information over and respond." Augsberger was insistent.

"No, Steven, I am sorry, but what these gentlemen are saying is absolutely untrue, and I believe we can adequately prove that to them if given the opportunity. I want to continue here if we could. I want to know all of their questions." Nasir glanced around the table at all of the government representatives present at the meeting. He appeared defiant, confident and unruffled. "Mr. Seilor, ladies and gentlemen, I was only recently made aware about this supposed instance where Yussef Ibrahim, the head of my jewelry company, may have been involved in the transaction to which you refer. Mr. Ibrahim was a former associate of my father's in Pakistan before he came to this country and started working for me. So, it could be possible that he may have been assisting someone in my father's organization in such a matter, but if so, he was doing it entirely on his own and without my knowledge or authorization."

"And if he did so with monies from your jewelry stores, Mr. Nasir, what then?"

"Well, then he did so without my knowledge or permission."

"The amount transferred and delivered to our agent, Mr. Nasir, was in excess of $100,000. Just how is it that you would be so ignorant about the fact that large transactions of that sort were taking place using your money, without your knowing it? We find that hard to believe." Seilor looked intently at Nasir. "We have already checked all of Mr. Ibrahim's accounts at your bank and any other institutions where we suspected he might hold accounts, and he certainly has not shown the personal wherewithal to deliver up such an amount of money to someone unless he had access to a substantial amount of cash, the kind of cash your companies must keep on hand most of the time, Mr. Nasir.

"Once again, I have never denied the fact that my companies utilize a great deal more cash than many other companies of their type or size, Mr. Seilor. However, we also account for all of that cash on our books. I am certain you will not find an entry there for such an amount or for such a purpose; and if you do, then perhaps Mr. Ibrahim may additionally be guilty of the crime of embezzlement in that regard. I will have my accountants look closely at the books of Crescent Jewelry. "

"Books can be manipulated and cash accumulated in such a way over time, Mr. Nasir, that activities of the sort we are describing can easily be hidden. It may take us some time, sir, but we are confident we can and will eventually determine if what you say is or is not correct." Seilor's tone was as determined as Nasir's. "For the last several days, and continuing over the next few weeks, we will have an army of government investigators poring over the books of your various companies, looking for answers of our own to all of our questions. How cooperative you and your people are in that investigation and in answering all of the specific questions we have already come up with and will be presenting to you over the next little while, will go a long way toward proving what you say is true or not."

"I am sorry, Tariq, but I really must again insist that you make no further comments at this time until we have an opportunity to look all of this information over and respond."

Nasir continued to ignore Augsberger's admonitions, and calmly and confidently looked around the table at all of the government interrogators. "I and all of my people will cooperate in every way we can, ladies and gentlemen. Ask all of the questions you wish. I will attempt to answer whatever I can, but there may be much about which I will need to defer until my people can obtain the necessary information. Give us adequate time on any questions of that sort, and we will attempt to answer everything as quickly as we can. As I said before, I am confident that when this is over, you will find neither me nor any of my companies to be involved in any wrongdoing."

"As I said before, Mr. Nasir, we sincerely hope that turns out to be the case, but there is much thus far that is frustrating and delaying our investigation, not the least of which is the fact that Mr. Ibrahim appears to be missing and unavailable for questioning. Our sources tell us that Yussef Ibrahim is now in Pakistan and has been for a few days now. What do you know about that, and what assistance can you give in helping us convince Mr. Ibrahim to return to the United States right away so that we can question him about all this?

"Yes, I understand Yussef is in Islamabad visiting family. Apparently, someone in his immediate family is ill, and he was called home. I can certainly try to get in touch with him and see if I can convince him to return, but I can make no assurances in that regard."

"Well, you are his employer, aren't you? Surely, he would listen to you." Seilor was having a difficult time hiding the sarcasm in his voice.

"It is possible, but I cannot guarantee that."

"That's kind of what we thought you might say, Mr. Nasir. We have already been in touch with Mr. Ibrahim. He repeated the story that someone in his family had a health issue that required his presence there, but we consider it a complete ruse. He is doing everything he can to avoid returning here for questioning. We have started applying pressure on the Pakistan government, but they seem reluctant thus far to assist in Ibrahim's return to the States for questioning. Looks like they're heading down the same path they did in the A.Q. Kahn debacle some years ago, when we determined he was behind a long-running clandestine program to sell nuclear weapons technology to people around the world who hardly have the best interests of this and other democratic countries at heart. Kahn proved to have fairly good friends in high places, and it appears as though your Mr. Ibrahim does as well. We are getting little to no cooperation in an effort to extradite him back to this country for questioning."

"Well, as I said, I can contact him and ask, but beyond that, I can guarantee you nothing either.

"Yeah, right!" Seilor remarked sarcastically. "This is your way of cooperating?"

He and all of the government investigators around the room looked at each other in exasperation. It seemed as if they were being thwarted at every hand, but they were determined. They might have let Yussef Ibrahim irreversibly slip through their fingers, but if at all possible, they would not let the same thing happen with Tariq Nasir. They were sure he was the hawaladar to whom all answered in the AmeriPAK organization, and they would dig through company records and question him and his people until they proved that was the case.

CHAPTER FORTY

TARIQ NASIR had put nearly twenty-five years into building the AmeriPAK business empire when his problems with the DHS and regulatory situation at Global United Bank of Chicago arose, and if he now wasn't careful all of his hard work might well end up amounting to nothing. Since the recent terrorist attacks at O'Hare and around the country, the noose around Nasir's neck was feeling tighter by the day. Investigators from several branches of government were diligently working together to build a case portraying him as one of the country's preeminent, unregistered purveyors of alternative money transfer services—or as some were putting it, "the hawaladar of choice to terrorism." If they proved their case—and it increasingly looked as though they stood a good chance of doing just that—he could easily be facing criminal charges serious enough in nature to make him the last in a very long line of Nasir family hawaladars.

Working diligently for years to obscure the existence of the underlying family business of hawala beneath the cloak of legitimacy provided by the AmeriPAK, Inc. group of companies, Nasir had hoped and prayed that this day would never come. He had come to enjoy the life of wealth, prestige, and power he had carefully built for himself in this "land of opportunity." Heeding his father's advice, however, Nasir nevertheless prepared carefully for the potentiality of a day like this from the time he became an American citizen and went into business for himself. Large amounts of money, representing years of profit from the activities of both the AmeriPAK companies and his family's burgeoning international hawala operation were secreted in offshore bank accounts scattered around the globe in countries where numbered and/or nominee accounts are the rule of the day. These now large sums of money had mostly also been transferred to these havens via the Nasir hawala network, making it extremely difficult for the U.S. Departments of Homeland Security, Justice, and Treasury to perhaps ever trace and find the money. The same was true relative to reaching through to the assets of AmeriPAK, whose ownership was largely shielded by its incorporation under the laws of the country of Luxembourg, and the added veil of trust ownership of the stock, with related beneficial interest resting in the names of Nasir's young sons, Faoud and Hassan. With power of direction over the trusts retained by Nasir himself, it could conceivably take years of legal wrangling before law enforcement agencies of the U.S.—or any other country for that matter—would be able to understand who owned what and seize any assets. By the time they did, steps both could and would be taken to ensure that little was left upon which to attach.

Further, for nearly three years now, Nasir's computer hardware and software marketing company, Aurora Tech, Inc., had been "mining" the now internationally popular crypto-currency, Bitcoin, in a large way at a clandestine facility in south Chicago. Working through a growing team of highly technical hawaladars, Nasir had for some time now not only been successfully sheltering illicit profits and assets via large purchases of Bitcoin stored in exchanges around the world, but had also used the ever-popular medium of Internet-based exchange as an added alternative method of transfer for his family's hawala business. With family Bitcoin deposits held in various exchanges around the world already approaching a current market valuation of the mid-eight figures in U.S. dollars, Nasir considered the mining, buying and selling of crypto-currencies like Bitcoin to be a new field of endeavor that held great promise for the Nasir family operation.

By New Year's Eve, however, it was becoming increasingly evident to Nasir that perhaps the time had come for him to put into play a long-standing plan for emergency departure. The FBI, DHS, and other investigators were asking more and more well-documented questions that were increasingly difficult to answer, and Nasir's usually upbeat, pugnacious attorney, Steven Augsberger, was beginning to sound more defeatist and conciliatory by the day. Augsberger's parting suggestion to Nasir àfter a shortened day of questioning on New Year's Eve had been, "We may want to discuss some sort of plea bargain, Tariq. I hate to say it, but barring any proof we can offer to the contrary, I'm beginning to worry the government's case is looking stronger by the moment. You may want to take the holiday to think this situation over. Discuss it with your wife, and then let's get together in my office first thing next week, before we head back over to the Dirksen Building. Our inquisitors are interested in a few days off. So, we don't have to meet with the FBI again until then. Let's use the holidays to decide what we want to do."

"Alright, Steven, I will do as you say, but I am unsure as to what good that will do. I still contend I have done nothing wrong, and that I am being falsely accused," Nasir adamantly responded. "I will think about what you said, but as of now, there is no way I plan to admit to something I did not do. I have paid you and your firm a lot of money through the years, and I still expect you to vigorously defend me in this matter. I suggest instead that it is you who should take these next few days to think about how you are going to help me through to a satisfactory conclusion of this whole horrible ordeal. So far, I don't think they've documented a leg to stand on, my friend. Why then should I capitulate." Nasir turned on his heel and stomped away, knowing as he did how disturbingly correct Augsberger no doubt was. This would probably be the last time he might be dealing with the cocky attorney in person. Nasir had a plan, and it was no doubt the time when he needed to put it into motion.

◊◊◊◊

TARIQ NASIR had for many weeks—even prior to his apprehension by government authorities—been under around-the-clock government surveillance by rotating shifts of agents parked in the front of his River Forest home and elsewhere. Amazingly, no added security measures—such as an ankle monitoring device, etc—were instituted. The increasingly embarrassing ordeal had, however, prompted him to suggest to his wife that she and their two sons move into the family's downtown condominium until, as he put it, "the temporary inconvenience of this affair can be put to rest." It took little urging. The situation was taking its toll on Melissa and the boys, and there was little current love loss between her and her husband. The more distance she could put between her sons and their father's current situation, the better she liked it.

Nasir had a plan for departure though, and it was ingenious in its simplicity. It began early on New Year's Eve, with Nasir uncharacteristically walking his wife and sons to the car for the government agents parked in the front of their residence to clearly see. He embraced and kissed his sons, and then went back into the house, had a leisurely meal and spent the evening reading in front of the fire, rising from time-to-time to visibly appear at the window and stare out at the agents. After doing this most of the evening, he went to the window one last time around 10:30 p.m., stared out at the agents again for a protracted moment, and then closed all of the curtains across the front of the house in a contrived display of consternation.

At around 11:00 p.m., Nasir exited a side door to the house, crossed the drive and threw two large bags of trash in an outside dumpster, activating for the agents' benefit numerous security lights around the perimeter of the home. The primary purpose of this little exercise was to clearly show the agents that there was a battery of exterior lights tied to motion sensors for security purposes. Upon reentering the house, Nasir waited for the exterior lights to time themselves out, and then he threw a hidden switch deactivating them all. Fully dressed, Nasir sat down once again in front of the fire and waited for various lights on timers and strategically located around the house to sequentially turn themselves off, beginning in the living room and working their way upstairs to the master bath and bedroom, simulating someone readying themselves for the night.

Both of the agents parked in front of Nasir's house watched as the last light in the master bedroom went out, and then the agent on the passenger's side slid down in his seat, closed his eyes and commented to his partner. "Ah, finally! It looks like our guy's calling it a night. Report in that Nasir's hit the sack, and then you take the first watch. Wake me at 3:00 a.m., and I'll take the second. It's been a long night, and I need some shuteye."

Once the lights were out, Nasir seated himself near an upstairs window and watched the car in front of his house through a crack in the curtain until 1:00 a.m. When that time arrived, he bundled himself up and went to the rear of the house, where he carefully exited through a pair of double doors leading to the patio. Fortune was with him. It was a dark, overcast winter night. Trudging quickly but quietly through the knee deep snow blanketing the heavily wooded several acres to the back of his estate, Nasir made his way to the adjoining property, climbed the fence separating his property from that of his neighbor's, and made his way through the neighbor's yard, exiting on a quiet, tree-shrouded cul-de-sac. Once he reached the street, Nasir then hurriedly walked ten blocks to a large commercial storage facility, owned and operated by Aurora Development, his real estate development and construction company. There he punched in a security code that automatically operated the front gate. When it opened, he immediately made his way through the maze of buildings to a garage-sized unit where he undid the lock. Inside was a dark green 2014 Subaru Outback.

The Outback was licensed and registered in the name of a Mr. Michael Robert Perricone, an alias used quite frequently by Nasir when traveling, in anticipation of just this sort of situation. Masquerading as a supposed Italian-American immigrant had proved successful in the past as a way of masking Nasir's true ethnic identity. His physical appearance was reminiscent of many men of southern Italian extraction, and if the occasion ever arose where it was necessary to embellish the pretense, Nasir spoke fluent Italian. At other times, unlike most Pakistani Americans, Nasir also spoke English without even the slightest hint of an accent.

In the back of the Subaru were all the necessities for a quick, clandestine departure: luggage loaded with clothing and personal necessities; credit cards; and forged documents of travel such as a drivers license, an Italian passport and a U.S. work visa, all bearing the Perricone alias with Nasir's picture. As an added touch, there were also several packages in the car that were nicely gift-wrapped for the holiday. Nasir was headed for Canada, and his story at the border was to be that he was going there to celebrate the New Year with friends.

Nasir's plan for leaving the country also entailed a very strict schedule. To meet its requirements he had to make good travel time, but he would also need to drive carefully. He would have only one chance at leaving the country in this fashion. The last thing he could afford was to be stopped for some minor traffic violation, and by some fluke be recognized.

Nasir's plan called for him to reach the Canadian city of Toronto by midday of January 1st, giving him plenty of leeway to catch an Air Canada flight to Paris, France that had a departure time of 10:30 p.m. Leaving the River Forest storage facility at 2:00 a.m., he would take I-94 south around the Lake and head directly to Detroit, Michigan, where approximately five hours later he would cross the border into Canada by way of the Ambassador Bridge to Windsor, Ontario. From there, it would by his estimate take another five hours or so driving time to Toronto International Airport, where using tickets obtained for him through a Canadian associate, his flight itinerary called for him to take Air Canada flight 882 from Toronto to Paris with an arrival time of just under eight hours. After a short layover in Paris on January 2nd, it would then be another seven to eight hours to Islamabad by way of Pakistan International Airlines flight 734.

Everything worked surprisingly well. In spite of pervasive concerns with border security between the U.S. and its neighbors both north and south, the crossing at Windsor was quite easy to negotiate. Border security with Mexico was a great deal more discerning at checkpoints, but many Canadian border guards still had an extremely cavalier attitude about the whole situation. Nasir had no problems whatsoever. Using a fake birth certificate and passport bearing the Perricone alias when asked for identification by the border guards, he managed to enter Canada with little questioning. By the time Nasir was crossing the Canadian border, the FBI agents parked in front of his house back in River Forest, IL were just being relieved from their all-night stake out.

"Been pretty quiet, guys." Agent Harry Cutter wearily commented to the two young agents relieving he and his stakeout partner of the previous night. "Our friend, Mr. Nasir, sure isn't much for celebrating. He didn't even make it until the New Year. Went to bed before midnight, and there are no signs of any activity yet. Since it's the holiday, he's probably sleeping in. We think he's home alone too. Wife and kids left yesterday. Maybe you guys will get lucky and he'll stay put today. You can listen to one of the games on the radio or something." It would literally be near evening of January 1st. before the FBI would realize Nasir was missing.

◊◊◊◊

TARIQ NASIR'S father, Mahmud, and lifelong friend and business associate, Yussef Ibrahim, met Nasir at Islamabad International Airport when his plane arrived from Paris on the morning of January 3rd. Both men greeted him with traditional embrace and fervent, repeated kisses to both cheeks, Ibrahim repeatedly laying his hand over his heart and bowing his head to Nasir by way of obeisance.

"Assalamu alaikum my father. How wonderful it is to be home and with you again. I have looked forward to this moment for some time." Tariq Nasir held his father's hand and spoke softly as he looked endearingly into the eyes of the older man.

"Wa alaikum as-salaam to you also, my son. It is good to have you home. I too have longed for some time to have you back with us. The circumstances surrounding your return are most unfortunate, but we are nonetheless pleased to have you here where we can be in control of your destiny as a family." The elder Nasir slid his arm around his son's shoulder, motioning toward the airport's entrance. "Come, let us leave this place as quickly as possible. Islamabad has too many eyes. You might be recognized—what with today's technology, you maybe already have. I've made arrangements for you to pass immediately through customs, and we have a police escort to our home. The quicker we get to the safety of our compound, where we can discuss what our next steps may need to be, the better." The three men quickly exited the terminal to a waiting limousine. "No one has amazingly contacted us yet to inquire as to your possible whereabouts, Tariq. Could it be possible that the U.S. authorities may not have detected your absence yet?"

"I can't really believe that would be the case, Father. I've imagined them grabbing me by the arm at any moment. Yet, I suppose it is possible." Nasir chuckled and shook his head, seemingly pleased with himself. "Things have admittedly gone far smoother than I thought they would thus far. I have been traveling under an assumed name and by a covert route, looking over my shoulder at every turn. U.S. authorities have no doubt detected my absence, and I have every confidence they will have their agents looking for me here quite soon if they haven't already. I imagine Pakistan would be one of the first places they will look when they find I am gone. Have we coordinated the situation with our sources in the government here? Once it is determined that I am here, I am certain unbelievable pressure will be brought to bear on the Pakistani government to cooperate with my return. U.S. investigators are insistent that I am somehow directly involved in a recently foiled terrorist plot that blew up in the face of some al-Qaeda splinter group operating over there. They will want my return."

"What do you know of those attacks, son? They have been all over the news. Were we involved in any way?"

"You know, I'm really unsure, Father, I have no concrete knowledge that we had any involvement with them. In accordance with your instructions, we have always tried to avoid facilitating any extremist elements whenever we were aware of what the situation was." Nasir turned and gestured toward Yussef Ibrahim. "What if anything might you know about the situation, Yussef? Do you think there is any way we might have been involved?"

"No, Tariq, I do not believe it to be so," answered Ibrahim, "but as you say, we really can't be sure. During the past few months, there were a series of fairly large transactions emanating from different locations and directed to the same young man, a fellow who introduced himself as a Mr. Hamadi—Ismail Hamadi if I remember properly—but I doubt that was his real name. The amounts were substantial and really didn't fit the profile of the recipient, but he was very cordial and paid all of the necessary fees. He offered no information about himself beyond that, and of course, I asked no questions. That is the way I have always been instructed to operate. I hope you do not feel I erred in that regard."

"No, no Yussef, you did as you have always been instructed," answered the elder Nasir, "but I would have to say that none of what you have said is particularly reassuring. Considering Tariq's detainment and questioning by U.S. authorities, and the fact that it appears the international Financial Action Task Force is searching diligently for you, Yussef, it would appear we could use a little more discernment in our choice of who we do business with. That is now neither here nor there. I would say they must certainly suspect we are involved."

"I would agree, Father. The U.S. Departments of Justice and Homeland Security seem intent on finding out as much as they can about our hawala business. They seem to already know a great deal about you and our family. They are currently investigating every aspect of AmeriPAK operations worldwide; and they with the U.S. Office of the Comptroller of the Currency are looking closely into our family's ownership at Global United Bank of Chicago. To that end, they have also enlisted the assistance of numerous key people within the bank for their investigation. Things do not look good at this time with respect to our investment there."

"Well, we have friends in very high places of responsibility within the Pakistan government who owe us a great deal. Many of them are the same people who came to the aid of our old friend, Dr. Abdul Qadeer Kahn when the U.S. government tried to obtain his extradition some years back for supposedly trafficking in nuclear weapons technology. I have called in some very old obligations, and they are prepared to do the same for you or anyone connected to our family if the need arises, my son. All we need do is ensure that we all are here in this country and under Pakistani control."

"Let's hope things work well in that regard, father. We have much at stake financially if the U.S. Government is able to prove up their case and attach our holdings both in that country and worldwide. When I left, they admittedly seemed to be piecing together a formidable case against me. Some time ago, I took steps to shelter as much in cash and other assets from attachment should anything untoward such as this recent turn of events take place. Much has for example been transferred to numerous offshore account havens, and a tremendous amount of cash has even been converted to a number of the new crypto-currencies like Bitcoin. So, a goodly amount of our assets are protected. Yet, should they decide to do so, the U.S. government could bring a great deal of pressure to bear on this country's president and his people."

"Well, let's not worry about that today, my son. As I said, we have many powerful friends working on our behalf as we speak. Such things can wait until tomorrow. As for now, you have a mother, sisters, family, and friends waiting at home to celebrate your return. It will be a wondrous homecoming." Mahmoud and Tariq Nasir looked quietly at each other for an uncomfortable period, with the elder Nasir finally breaking the silence. "I am sure, however, that you are thinking what I am, Tariq. The only people missing, who would make this all complete, are my grandsons. If that is indeed what you are thinking, I couldn't agree with you more. I too ache to have them close to me in my old age. Allah willing, they will be with us one of these days. Plans are currently in the offing to make that happen, and we can discuss that tomorrow. There is much that Faoud and Hassan must learn, and a great deal that you and I need to pass on to them. By the time you and I depart this earth, there will be a tremendous mantel of responsibility for them to assume."

CHAPTER FORTY-ONE

AFTER A seven year hiatus, Myrna Brock was pleased to once again be the administrative assistant to Global United Bank's chief executive officer, even if it was only an interim situation, and by default. She was finally planning to retire, but if her boss, Logan Hart, had any chance of being appointed permanent CEO of the bank coming out of all this Nasir mess, then she wanted to at least stay around long enough to see that he was settled in properly. Logan was the kind of hardworking, knowledgeable, considerate banker she felt ought to be running an institution of this sort. The way Global United was growing, and what with all the regulatory and other problems the bank had been experiencing—such as the OCC's prolonged involvement, and the quick exit of people like principal shareholder, Tariq Nasir, former president, Scott Kruse, and others—Logan Hart was in her opinion just what the doctor ordered.

Myrna had her whole working career invested in the bank, and she had assisted some awfully good bankers in her day, such as former owners, the Flannery family. Yet, "Mister" Hart—as she still unwaveringly referred to him or any other officers of the bank, regardless of age—was perhaps in her opinion one of the best she had worked for thus far. If the board of directors was to decide to turn the current CEO, Scott Kruse's, leave-of-absence into a formal dismissal, and Logan Hart was to take over the reins permanently, she felt she could finally retire with a clear conscience, knowing the bank was in good hands.

"Mr. Hart, you know it's been a while since we've heard from her, but I have Ms. Price from the OCC on the phone again for you. Do you want to take it?" It had indeed almost been a week since Cass Price had for any reason called to talk with Logan, and Myrna had almost arrived at the conclusion that the relationship she figured was developing between the two might just be a figment of her imagination. She was relieved the lady regulator was calling again. Myrna noted a little age difference between the two— Cass being several years younger than Logan—but she still thought they would make a great couple. "Should I put her through, sir?"

"Certainly, Myrna, thank you!"

"I can connect you now, Ms. Price. I'm sure Mr. Hart will be pleased to speak with you. How are you, by the way? It has been a while since we've heard from you."

"I'm just fine, Myrna. I hope it's the same with you. Before you put me through though, how's our guy doing? How do you think he's holding up under the pressure of all his added responsibilities and what's been going on?"

"Well, if you ask me Ms. Price—and you can quote me on this if you like—I think he's the best CEO we've had around here in quite some time. Spirits are up amongst the staff in spite of all the troubles the bank is experiencing, and things seem to be more organized and under control better than they have been for quite a while. By the time Mr. Kruse returns—if he does—I'm confident things will be running pretty smoothly around here. Just the way you regulators would like them if you get my drift. A number of people around the bank, me included, are rather hoping the board of directors might see fit to make Mr. Hart's appointment a permanent arrangement."

"That's nice to hear, Myrna, and I'm not really surprised. He has impressed all of us here at the OCC. I'll keep your comments in strictest confidence."

At the height of the OCC's recent, prolonged examination of Global United, conversations between Logan and Cass had sometimes taken place on multiple occasions during any given day, and it wasn't rare for them to communicate via Internet videoconferencing and e-mail during off hours and evenings. After the recently thwarted terrorist attacks at O'Hare and other locations around the country, and the subsequent meeting between the OCC and Global United's Board of Directors where Logan was appointed interim CEO, however, conversations between the two had taken a hiatus. The OCC was in possession of its requested Memorandum of Understanding from Global United's Board of Directors, and necessary staff and other changes were quickly being made in accordance with that agreement. So, regular communications between the two hadn't been as necessary as they had before, at least not for business reasons.

"How goes the war, Logan?"

"Great, Cass! You might say there's no shortage of dimension around here since you and your team dropped the results of your examination on us and finally left us to clean up all of Global United's dirty laundry, but we're making progress." Logan was actually excited to hear Cass' voice. He found himself visualizing her as he spoke. He had wanted to call her but had been reluctant to do so for a multitude of reasons. Myrna Brock hadn't really been all that far off the mark in her assessment regarding their relationship. Something more than a professional acquaintance had developed between the two, but both were obviously reticent to acknowledge it.

Concerned first and foremost with the conflicts inherent in a relationship between he as a banker, and Cass as a regulator with direct oversight of the troubled institution it was currently his to manage, Logan had convinced himself for more than a week to leave well enough alone by avoiding calling Cass, when it was heavy on his mind to do so.

Hearing from Myrna that Cass instead had chosen to break the ice by calling him first, he knew as he picked up the phone that he wouldn't be able to pass up the opportunity to see her again. "It's great to hear from you, Cass. I've missed our visits. I was hoping you might have a reason to get in touch. Is this a personal or business call?"

"Well, it's mostly business, and quite frankly, rather serious business at that, but I too have missed our frequent conversations. Perhaps we can make it a little of both before we hang up."

"Great, I'm in agreement with that. So, let's get rid of whatever 'serious business' you have to discuss as quickly as we can. How can we help you?" Logan could tell Cass was hesitating a bit. He hoped it had nothing to do with what he had just said.

"Well, I really have nothing immediate that I need from you, Logan, beyond that which you and your crew are already working on relative to your responses to our examination and the other interrogatories I know you're also involved in for the DHS, Department of Justice, and so on— at least not for now that is. I was really calling to more or less give you a heads-up regarding a very serious situation that has arisen with regard to your Mr. Nasir."

"I hope you're being facetious when referring to Tariq Nasir as somehow being someone I might still lay claim to." He chuckled, but it was becoming hard for Logan to hide increasing disdain. "The more I know about Mr. Nasir, the more uncomfortable I am with him being involved in any way at Global United, in spite of the fact that he is the bank's principal shareholder. I really wish I would have known more about him before I made my decision to join this organization. I rather think I would have decided otherwise."

"Let me assure you, we here at the OCC are beginning to have a greater appreciation by the day for what you say, as we delve more and more into Mr. Nasir's activities. Let's just say we feel fortunate to have you at the helm right now, Logan."

"Well, it's early yet in all of this, but thanks anyway. You said you had something you wanted to tell me about Nasir, however?"

"Yes, yes I did. About half an hour ago, I received a call from Merritt Daimler over at the FBI, and even though I have the sneaking suspicion he'll probably call you regarding this as well, I felt I ought to call and let you know what he had to say. From what Merritt tells us, the authorities spent most of last week grilling Mr. Nasir and a number of his key AmeriPAK people regarding the makeup and operation of their businesses, their relationship with Global United and other banks, and their possible involvement in certain other nefarious activities of concern to the DHS and others. All of this was supposedly going on under the watchful eye of a bevy of Nasir's attorneys. Well, I guess last week before the holiday, the situation was getting rather testy. Merritt and his people were confronting Nasir and his attorneys with more and more sensitive and potentially embarrassing questions that needed answering. By the time New Year's Eve arrived, I guess things were ready to blow up, with the prosecutors and FBI taking Mr. Nasir into custody. Then over the holiday things took an unexpected turn."

"We all figured that something rather involved was going on, Cass. FBI agents and assistant U.S. attorneys were in and out of here most of last week, asking for more and more information. We could tell things were probably getting pretty serious. I guess that is what I was referring to a moment ago with my inferences regarding Tariq Nasir. What happened over the holiday though? What do you mean when you suggest things are ready to blow?"

"Well, I mean just that. As I think you may be aware, since this whole affair began with Mr. Nasir, he has apparently been free on his own recognizance by court order. He's been required to be available for questioning and remain in the City until all of this was finished one way or the other, but beyond that, he's been free to run his companies to the extent he still could, and spend his nights and weekends at home. In keeping with that agreement, I guess Nasir had supposedly gone home for the New Year holiday with the understanding that he was supposed to show up again this morning with his attorneys for further interrogation. Agents had regularly been posted at his residence, and I guess late New Year's day they became a little uneasy and decided to check out the situation. The FBI entered his residence, and he is nowhere to be found. He was last seen at the house late New Year's eve, but it appears he must have sneaked out sometime during the night. They apparently have a nationwide, all-points bulletin of some sort out on him. Interpol is also involved. They actually plan to put him on their Most Wanted List, I guess."

"Oh, that's just great! At this point, I really don't care if Nasir ever returns as far as the bank is concerned, but the media will again have a field day with this if he doesn't show up. There'll be a renewed round of public scrutiny and news stories about the bank, and that will no doubt precipitate another spate of customer discomfort to deal with."

"Look, Logan, we will do everything we can to set customers minds at rest if that happens. If need be, we'll put some people at the bank to help field questions and complaints. Global United may have been a conduit for a great deal of questionable transactions and handling of Mr. Nasir's various relationships with the bank under previous management, but you and the board are working to correct all that. Aside from the OCC assessing some punitive regulatory actions that won't really be all that horribly debilitating in the long run, the bank is still reasonably sound to our best estimate. We will be alongside you to attest to that publicly."

"Oh, we all know that to be the case, Cass, but none of this certainly makes all that we have ahead of us any easier." Logan leaned back in his chair and uttered a sigh of exasperation before continuing. "I think there were many here at the bank who were hoping that things might work out for Mr. Nasir and company. I guess this sort of shoots that in the fanny. Doesn't it?"

"Yes, I would say if he doesn't show up soon, it certainly does."

"What about Sammy al-Dajani and Scott Kruse?" asked Logan. "What does their situation look like right now?"

"You know, I asked Merritt that same thing. He wouldn't say much about Mr. al-Dajani other than to say he was 'still in custody, and will no doubt remain that way.' He indicated that they would 'have an announcement about his disposition forthcoming.' I don't know what that all meant, but it doesn't sound all that good for Mr. al-Dajani. As for Scott Kruse, I guess they haven't found too much on him yet that would seem to suggest that he was directly involved in any illegal activities with Mr. Nasir or any of his people, but according to Merritt, 'he is still under investigation.' Whatever may come of that investigation, however, I guess I would have to say the OCC may have some problems of its own in having Mr. Kruse return to the bank. Global United was under his management when all of this took place, and at best, it seems to us that Mr. Kruse deferred far too much to Mr. Nasir in many areas where he should have held his ground. This all resulted in violations that were sufficiently egregious to make his return to the position of CEO at Global United probably unacceptable to us. I don't know if you and your board of directors are so inclined, Logan, but I would say your situation as CEO has the potential of being much more permanent than anyone may have figured to begin with."

"At this point, Cass, that's one I'll have to think about some before giving a decision if the situation arises. I would never leave the bank in the lurch and have made it a personal commitment to see that things are back up and running well before I would ever leave. There is a lot of work ahead for whoever takes this job permanently. Besides, after all of this, I've received another offer that I must admit is a bit enticing."

"Oh, really, and what might that be, if I could be so bold as to ask." There was now a tone of insecurity in Cass' voice.

"Well, if you can believe it or not, were I to take the position, I would be back working for the government again after all these years."

"Really, can you tell me exactly what it might be, and all?" Cass asked with bated breath.

"Yes, yes, since its you, I think I can. About three days ago, I received a visit here from a representative of the U.S. Treasury Department's Office of Foreign Assets Control, and apparently they had been referenced my name relative to a new position they had opening up in their Office of Terrorist Financing and Financial Crimes. It's a new investigative unit that has the need for a few people with, shall we say, special background and capabilities that they feel I possess. I'm not sure, but I have the sneaking suspicion that Merrit Daimler may have been involved in them approaching me."

"You know, my conversation with him contained no mention of this, but I can believe that might be the case. He went on and on about how talented and specially capable you were."

"That's kind of him to say. As you know, he and I go back a long ways. Feelings like those are mutual."

"Well, that's a real bombshell, Logan, but please know that I wish you well whatever it is you end up doing. You would, I am certain, be fantastic were you to decide you might want to go over to OFAC, but I—or should I say we—here at the OCC have a great deal of confidence you would do an equally great job if the opportunity arises for you to stay with Global United. I hope you think long and hard about it before you pass on a Global United offer. They need someone like you."

"Oh, I can assure you that I would at least do that. I owe the bank that much if such an offer happens." *Also wouldn't mind staying here if it meant I might be able to continue dealing with you*, thought Logan. "Let's forget about that for now, however. Any other 'bombs' like the Nasir thing you want to drop on me today, Cass? Because if not, like I started to say before, I have something a little personal I would like to discuss."

"No, I guess I have ruined your day enough. There may be more later, but that is all the business for now. Why, what else do you want to visit about?"

"Well, quite frankly—and don't shoot me when I ask this—just how verboten might it be for you and I to perhaps get together for dinner sometime in the next few days, and this time someplace different than Rosario's? After all we've been through over the last several weeks, I would really like to have you join me for a relaxing repast and conversation, without having to say a word about banking, hawala or anything else like it. Do you think that might be possible?"

"Logan, are you asking me, the dragon lady of the OCC—as I know some around here call me—out on a date? There are those in both your shop and mine that would think you were out of your mind." Cass was embarrassed to admit to herself she had been hoping something like this might come from her conversation with Logan. She could tell from the warm feeling on her face that she was blushing.

"Yeah, I guess I am doing just that. How about it? Any chance you could join me some night this week?"

Cass and Logan were both well aware they would be stepping into murky waters if she accepted his offer. Bank regulators meeting socially with bankers whom they oversaw, really wasn't something that was looked upon with favor by the OCC. There was a painful moment of silence.

"Tell you what, Mr. Hart. I think you know by now how much of a stiff shirt I am about rules and regulations, but I tell you what I might be willing to do. I'll meet with my boss and tell him about your offer so that things are completely above board. If he has no great problems with me meeting you for dinner, I am willing to do so if we go Dutch, so to speak."

"Are you kidding me? I didn't invite you to dinner to have you pay your own way."

"I know, and I appreciate that, but it is the only way I will do it at this time. Furthermore, I wouldn't be surprised if this dinner between the two of us doesn't signal an end to our professional interaction. If my director gives me any okay, I suspect that will be a caveat"

"Good grief, you're making me feel like a criminal here." Logan laughed nervously. "I wouldn't want to get you in trouble or hurt your career in any way."

There was a brief pause. "Look, Logan, I think I would like to do this. You let me take care of things on my end. I'm really the one with the restrictions. I am serious that it might mean an end to my direct official oversight of Global United Bank of Chicago if we do this, but you let me worry about that. How does tomorrow night sound? With the holidays over we shouldn't have any trouble getting a reservation at just about any restaurant we want."

"Sounds great to me, Cass. It's been years since I've said this one, but if that works for you, then 'it's a date.' I'll find us a place and time and let you know before the day is out. Okay?"

"Great! I'll look forward to hearing from you!" There was a slight hesitation. "You know, the thought just occurred to me. None of what I just said would be of the slightest bit of concern were you to take that position at OFAC. Not really wanting that to happen when looking at it from the OCC's point of view, but I'm just saying."

"Yeah, you're probably right about that. Another thing to really ponder when making any decision along those lines."

"Well, enough of that," said a now fully embarrassed

Cass Price. "Let me know the where and when of things real soon regarding dinner. I'll make no other plans and be looking forward to your call. And who knows, maybe one of us will have more news on our Mr. Nasir by the time we talk."

"Yeah, well, one of us might well have some information to talk about along those lines, but if you'll remember, that subject was supposed to be off the table on this occasion. So, let's temporarily forget about the hawaladars of this world when we get together. I'd just like to know a bit more about Cass Price this time, if you don't mind."

"Ok, understood! You've got it, Mr. Hart. Can't wait to hear from you."

MAKING A CONNECTION

THANK YOU FOR READING

DEAR READER: To everyone kind enough to have read their way to this point in my publishing debut, please, accept my heartfelt appreciation. It is indeed a pleasure to make your acquaintance; and it's my sincere hope we are embarking on a lasting relationship that will provide you much in the way of enjoyable, future reading.

The HAWALADAR is the first book in a trilogy—with the second installment targeted for the fall of 2020. Logan Hart, Cassandra Price, and Tariq Nasir, principal characters in the first book of The Money Trail Series, will once again provide partial back-drop to the storyline of the second offering that is chock full of excitement and international intrigue.

After overseeing the turn-around of a major troubled financial institution, Logan Hart has left the staid world of commercial banking and accepted a new position as an operative within a special investigative division of the U.S. Treasury Department's Office of Foreign Asset Control. OFAC is the federal agency responsible for detecting and interdicting financial-related threats to the safety and soundness of the United States and its allies. The job description for the position has a prosaic ring. Yet, it is anything but.

As was the case with The HAWALADAR, the second book of The Money Trail series will deal with international threats that are eerily existential in nature, a palpable leap from the headlines of today to the pages of your book. If you found the first book in this series to your liking and would be interested in reading the next installment, send an e-mail to my address that follows below, and I'll ensure you receive advance notice of its release. I promise it to be a page-turner.

BOOK REVIEW

IF YOU have indeed found your reading of The HAWALADAR to be both enjoyable and enlightening, I would thoroughly appreciate your being so kind as to LEAVE A REVIEW of the book. It really would mean a great deal to me as a writer.

SOCIAL PLATFORM

WEBSITE: http://davidastearns.com

EMAIL: daiuydav@davidastearns.com

SOCIAL MEDIA SITES: Facebook Twitter
                      Instagram